WINTER'S
ORBIT

EVERINA MAXWELL

WINTER'S
ORBIT

TOR

A TOM DOHERTY ASSOCIATES BOOK
NEW YORK

WINTER'S ORBIT

Copyright © 2021 by Everina Maxwell

All rights reserved.

A Tor Book
Published by Tom Doherty Associates
120 Broadway
New York, NY 10271

www.tor-forge.com

Tor® is a registered trademark of Macmillan Publishing Group, LLC.

The Library of Congress Cataloging-in-Publication Data is
available upon request.

ISBN 978-1-250-75883-5 (hardcover)
ISBN 978-1-250-75885-9 (ebook)

Our books may be purchased in bulk for promotional, educational, or busi-
ness use. Please contact your local bookseller or the Macmillan Corporate and
Premium Sales Department at 1-800-221-7945, extension 5442, or by email at
MacmillanSpecialMarkets@macmillan.com.

First Edition: February 2021

Printed in the United States of America

0 9 8 7 6 5 4 3 2 1

TO EM
THIS BOOK WOULDN'T EXIST WITHOUT YOU

WINTER'S
ORBIT

CHAPTER 1

"Well, *someone* has to marry the man," the Emperor said.

She sat, severe and forbidding in a high-collared tunic, in her reception room at the heart of the warren-like sprawl of the Imperial Palace. The arching windows of the tower were heavily optimized to amplify the weak autumn sunlight from Iskan V; the warm rays that lit the wrinkled Imperial countenance should have softened it, but even the sunlight had given that up as a bad job.

Across from her, in a formal uniform that was only slightly crumpled, Kiem—Prince Royal of Iskat and the Emperor's least favorite grandchild—had been stunned into silence. He was rarely summoned to an Imperial audience unless he'd done something spectacularly lacking in common sense, so when the Emperor's aide had called him, he'd racked his brain for a cause but had come up empty-handed. He'd half wondered if it was about the Galactic delegation that had arrived yesterday and stirred up the palace. Kiem wasn't a natural when it came to politics; maybe the Emperor wanted to warn him to stay out of the way.

This was the opposite of staying out of the way. Kiem had braced for a dressing-down, not to walk out of the room engaged to a vassal diplomat he'd never even met.

He opened his mouth to say, *I don't see why anyone has to marry him,* then thought better of contradicting the Emperor and shut it again. This was how he got himself in trouble. He rephrased. "Your Majesty, Prince Taam has only been dead a month."

It sounded awful the moment it left his mouth. Taam had been Kiem's cousin, after all, and the Imperial family was technically still in mourning. Kiem had naturally been shocked when he heard of the flybug accident, but at the last count he'd had just over forty relatives ahead of him in the succession, mostly cousins, and he hadn't known Taam particularly well.

The Emperor gave him a withering look. "Do you think I am unaware?" She tapped her fingertips on the lacquered surface of the low table beside her, probably giving him a second chance to remember his manners. Kiem was too disturbed to really appreciate it. "The Thean treaty must be pinned down," she said. "We are under significant time pressure."

"But—" Kiem said. He scrabbled for an argument as his gaze followed the movement of her fingers. The low table was crowded with official gifts, mainly from vassal planets: crystal plates, a bowl of significant mosses, a horrible gold clock from Iskat's Parliament. Among them, under a bell jar, a small Galactic remnant glowed softly. It was a color Kiem's eyes couldn't process, like a shard of glass that had been spat out of another dimension. Even its presence in the room made Kiem's brain uncomfortable. He made himself look away from it, but unfortunately that meant looking at the Emperor.

He tried again. "But, Your Majesty—marrying Taam's *partner*—" He was vaguely aware of who it was. Prince Taam and Count Jainan, the Thean representative, had been one of the royal family's more intimidatingly polished couples, like the Emperor had ordered them built in a synthesizer. Iskat bound treaties with marriages—always had, right from when the first colonists settled on the planet—and one of the unspoken reasons that Iskat had so many minor royals was to have representatives on hand when they were needed. Kiem had nothing to disqualify him: he wasn't a parent, overly religious, opposed to monogamy, gender-exclusive, or embarrassingly hung up on someone else. That didn't mean he could stand in for Taam, Jainan's partner of five years. "Ma'am, surely you need someone more"—*dignified*—"suitable. Prince Vaile, maybe. Or no one? Forgive me, but I don't see why we have to find him another partner."

The Emperor regarded Kiem as if painfully reminded of the differences between him and Prince Taam. "You have not paid any attention to the political situation, then."

Kiem rubbed a hand across his forehead unconsciously. The air in the Emperor's rooms always felt dry and slightly too hot. "Sorry."

"Of course not. I see you were drinking last night. At the carnival?"

"No, I—" Kiem heard himself sound defensive and stopped. He hadn't been falling-down drunk for a long time now, but the script between him and the Emperor was apparently carved in stone from back in his student days, when every summons turned out to be an Imperial reprimand for his latest minor scandal. "I only went for the afternoon."

The Emperor glanced at the shifting pictures in the press folder on the table. "Press Office informs me that you put on a troll costume, joined a carnival procession group, and fell in a canal in the middle of the parade."

"It was a kids' group," Kiem said. He would have panicked about trying to explain the newslog photos, but he didn't have any panic left over from being summarily engaged to a stranger. "Their troll dropped out at the last minute. The canal was an accident. Your Majesty, I—I'm"—he cast about desperately—"too young to get married."

"You are in your mid-twenties," the Emperor said. "Do not be ridiculous." She rose from her seat with the careful smoothness of someone who received regular longevity treatments and crossed to the tower window. Kiem rose automatically when she did but had nothing to do, so he clasped his hands behind his back. "What do you know about Thea?"

Kiem's spinning brain tried to latch on to some relevant facts. Iskat ruled seven planets. It was a loose, federated empire; Iskat didn't intervene in the internal affairs of its vassals, and the vassals in return kept their trade routes running smoothly and paid taxes. Thea was the newest and smallest member. It had been assimilated peacefully—the same couldn't be said of all the Empire's planets—but that had been a generation ago. It didn't usually make the headlines, and Kiem didn't pay much attention to politics.

"It has . . . some nice coastland?" Kiem said. All he could come up with were some tourist shots of green and sunny hills falling down to a cobalt-blue ocean, dredged up from some long-forgotten documentary, and a catchy snippet from a Thean music group. "I, uh, know some of its"—the Emperor didn't listen to music groups—"popular culture?" Even he winced at hearing how that sounded. That wasn't a basis for a relationship.

The Emperor examined him like she was trying to figure out how his parents' genes had produced something so much less than the sum of their parts. She looked away, back to the view outside. "Come here."

Kiem obediently crossed to the window. Below, the city of Ar-lusk sprawled under a snow-heavy sky, pale even through the light-optimizing glass. The grand state buildings jutted up through the city like veins of marble emerging from rock, two hundred years older than anything else in the sector, with a jumble of newer housing blocks nestled around them. The first real snow of the long winter had fallen yesterday. It was already turning to slush in the streets.

The Emperor ignored all of that. Her gaze was fixed on the far side of the city, where the spaceport spilled down the side of a mountain like an anthill. Silver flashes of shuttles came and went above it, while berthed ships were nestled in huge bays dug into the mountainside. Kiem had known the bustle of local space traffic all his life. Like most Iskaners, he'd never made the year-long journey to the far-off galactic link—the gateway to the wider galaxy—but the Empire's vassal planets were much closer, and ships hopped between them and Iskat all the time.

One ship, hovering unsupported next to a servicing tower, gave Kiem an immediate headache. Its matte-black surface sucked in all reflection and gave off rippling shimmers that had nothing to do with the angle of the sunlight. Kiem squinted at the size of it. Nothing that big should be able to float in planetary gravity. It was nothing like the shard on the Emperor's display table, but it was definitely weird shit that didn't come under the normal rules of physics. He took a stab. "The Galactics?"

"Do you read nothing but tabloid logs?" the Emperor said. It seemed to be rhetorical. "That ship belongs to the Resolution. Despite its frankly absurd size, it contains one Auditor and three administration staff. It can apparently jump through links under its own power and is impervious to mass scanners. The Auditor—whom I will admit to finding deeply unsettling on a personal level—is here to legally renew the treaty between the Empire and the Resolution. Even you cannot have missed this. Tell me you know what the Resolution is."

Kiem stopped himself from saying he didn't actually live under a rock, even if Iskat was a year's travel from any other sector. "Yes, ma'am. It runs the rest of the galaxies."

"It does not," the Emperor said sharply. "The Resolution is just that: an agreement between ruling powers. It runs the link network. Iskat and our vassals have signed our own set of Resolution terms, as have other empires and Galactic powers. As long as those are in place, we can trade through our link, keep our internal affairs to ourselves, and be certain no invading force will use the link to attack us. We are due to sign the treaty on Unification Day in just over a month. The Auditor, if all goes well, will look through our paperwork, sweep up those remnants the Resolution is so obsessed with, witness the treaty, and *leave*."

Kiem blinked away from the eye-watering Resolution ship and looked at her instead. Her gnarled hand briefly touched the flint pendant at her throat in a gesture that might have been stress. Kiem couldn't remember a time when her hair hadn't been pure white, but she never seemed to age. She only got thinner and tougher. She was afraid, Kiem realized. He felt a sudden chill; he'd never seen her afraid.

"Got it," he said. "Play nice with the Resolution. Give the Auditor the VIP treatment, show him what he wants, send him away again." He made a last-ditch attempt. "But what's that got to do with me and the Theans? Surely marriages are the last thing you want to worry about now."

That was the wrong thing to say. The Emperor gave him a sharp, unsparing look, turned away from the window, and made her way stiffly back to her chair. She smoothed out her old-fashioned tunic as she sat. "It is inevitable," she said, "that in a family as large as ours, there are some who are more capable of handling their responsibilities than others. Given your mother's achievements, I had higher hopes for you."

Kiem winced. He recognized this lecture; he'd last heard it after his incident at university, just before he'd been exiled to a monastery for a month. "I apologize, ma'am." He managed to keep quiet for all of a split second before he said, "But I still don't understand. I know the treaties are important. But the man Thea sent—Jainan—already married Prince Taam. Just because Taam's dead doesn't mean the marriage didn't happen."

"Our vassal treaties underpin our treaty with the Resolution," the Emperor said. "They formalize our right to speak for the Empire. The Auditor will check that all the legalities are in order. If he finds out one of our marriage links is broken, he will decree there is no *treaty*."

Kiem had been too young to remember the last Galactic treaty renewal and had never bothered to learn much about the Resolution, but even he felt a vague sense of horror at the prospect of an Auditor scrutinizing something he was responsible for. The Auditors were supposed to be meticulous at finding mistakes and unnervingly detached from human concerns. He swallowed. "Yes, ma'am."

"You do not need to be astute or political," the Emperor said, her tone returning to normal. "You merely need to stand in the right place, mouth some words, and not offend the entire Thean press corps. Thea has recently had some internal difficulties with protests and student radicals; our political links are not as strong as we would like. A new marriage will help smooth matters over."

"What does that mean?" Kiem said.

The Emperor's lips thinned. "The Theans are dragging their feet on everything we ask. Our mining operation in Thean space provides valuable minerals; the Theans keep finding new ways to complain about it. At the moment I have one councilor advising me to give up and make Thea a special territory."

"You wouldn't," Kiem said, shocked. Iskat only installed a special governing body if the planet was too lawless to have one of its own. Sefala was the sole special territory in the Empire, and only because it was controlled by raider gangs. "Thea has its own government."

"I have no desire to," the Emperor said testily. "I have very little appetite for another war, and this would be the worst possible time. Hence you will be signing a marriage contract with Count Jainan tomorrow."

For the first time he could remember, Kiem was utterly lost for words.

"There are no legal complications," the Emperor continued. "You are of age and acceptably close to the throne. He will—"

"*Tomorrow?*" Kiem blurted out. He sat down hard on the uncomfortable gilded chair. "I thought you meant in a few months! The man lost his life partner!"

"Don't be absurd," the Emperor said. "We have precious little time before the treaty is signed on Unification Day. Everything must be watertight by then. On top of everything else, we agreed to rotate the planet that hosts the ceremony, and twenty years ago we held it on Eisafan, so this time it will be Thea's turn. The Thean radicals have no concept of stability. If they perceive any weakness, we can expect them to use the occasion as a focal point for discontent. The Auditor may conclude Iskat does not have sufficient control over the rest of the Empire to keep our Resolution treaty valid. There must be a representative couple in place to disprove this, with no visible concerns, smiling at the cameras. You are good at appearing confident in pictures. This should not strain your capabilities."

Kiem clenched his fists, looking down at the floor. "Surely in a couple of months," he said. The creases around the Emperor's eyes started to deepen; she never reacted well to pleading. However much effort Kiem had put into sobering up, he'd never been able to hold his ground against her. He tried one last time. "Tell the Auditor we're engaged. We can't just force Count Jainan into this."

"You will cease this quibbling," the Emperor said. She came back to her desk, propped her hands on it, and leaned across. She might be elderly and slow but her gaze reached into the squishy parts of Kiem's fear receptors like a fishhook. "You would have me break the treaty," she said. "You would destroy our tie to the Resolution and leave us cut off from the rest of the universe. Because *you* do not care for duty."

"No," Kiem said, but the Emperor hadn't finished.

"Jainan has already agreed. That I will say for Thea: their nobles know how to do their duty. Will you dishonor us in front of them?"

Kiem didn't even try to hold her gaze. If she chose to make it an Imperial command, he could be imprisoned for disobeying. "Of course not," he said. "Very happy to—to—" He stuttered to a halt. *To forcibly marry someone whose life partner just died. What a great idea. Long live the Empire.*

The Emperor was watching him closely. "To ensure Thea knows it is still tied to us," she said.

"Of course," Kiem said.

A thin plume of smoke rose from the dome of the palace shrine. The air outside was cold and smelled faintly of ceremonial resin. Jainan nav Adessari of Feria—recently bereaved, newly betrothed—stood atop a sweep of stone stairs, looking out over the frost-touched gardens of the Imperial Palace of Iskat and forcing himself to focus. He still had duties to carry out.

The gardens' bare, elegant lines were starker now that the snows had begun and all the living plants had been cut back or buried for spring. The pale stone paths and winding marble walls lay like the quiet remains of a prehistoric creature around him, like a scattering of bleached bones merging with the hill below. Every path started and ended with the carved crest of Iskat embossed in a flagstone: the single curved line of the Hill Enduring.

Jainan couldn't appreciate the gardens as he should, or even really see them. Ever since Taam's death his head had been full of fog. He methodically paced from one side of the staircase to the other to keep warm.

He felt hollowed out. The responsibility of binding the treaty between Iskat and Thea had always felt heavy on his shoulders, but now it was a solid weight on his back and in the pit of his stomach. He and Taam were symbols of the relationship between the two powers. Jainan had been honored to be picked for the role, even if it had turned out to be largely ceremonial: he wasn't an ambassador or a negotiator and wasn't supposed to involve himself in the politics. But he had known for five years that he would eventually stand in front of a Resolution Auditor to renew Thea's treaty and do his part to keep the galactic link open and the sector protected. Now that was all in doubt.

It had become increasingly difficult to concentrate in the last week as the Emperor's Private Office stepped up preparations to replace Taam. Jainan had put his stamp on the permission forms—it was unthinkable to leave Thea without a treaty pair—but they hadn't yet confirmed his Iskat partner. It could be any one of dozens of minor royals. Jainan wasn't familiar enough with Taam's cousins to even judge the possibilities. The uncertainty was like a cobweb across his face; he constantly had to brush it aside to think about anything else.

He had to focus. A stream of palace residents started to appear at the other side of the gardens, hurrying to the shrine for Taam's last memorial service, hunched against the cold. Jainan scanned their faces but none of them were familiar. Jainan was due at the ceremony as well, albeit he'd only been given the invitation yesterday. It was understandable that he'd been informed late; all the Iskaners he spoke to were busy with the Resolution visit and had more important matters to deal with. Jainan himself hadn't seen the Auditor yet. He'd been told to avoid the Resolution visitors until the new marriage was formalized and he and his Iskat partner could speak for the treaty. Jainan knew the importance of putting up a united front.

At last Jainan's wait paid off: a figure in a general's uniform appeared on the long, gravel path that led to the military headquarters and the barracks, trailed by two other officers. Jainan took a sharp breath and set off at a brisk walk to intercept him.

Taam was—had been—a colonel in the Iskat military. In the aftermath of the flybug accident, Taam's old commanding officers had swept in to take control and direct Jainan through all the funeral preparations: stand here, go to this ceremony, don't talk to the press. Jainan had complied like a man in a trance. It wasn't his role to contradict senior officers in the Empire's military.

"General Fenrik," Jainan said, stopping in the middle of the path. "Could I—" He had to catch himself. *Have a moment of your time* sounded presumptuous. "May I ask you something?"

General Fenrik was a broad-shouldered, austere man with clipped white hair, a cane, and the no-nonsense air of someone who had led the Empire's military forces for forty years. A polished wooden button pinned to his breast pocket was emblazoned with an old version of the Imperial crest. His gaze bore into Jainan without recognition. "Yes? What? Be quick."

One of the lower-ranking officers behind him prompted him with Jainan's name in a murmur. Jainan knew the officers Taam had worked with: this one, with a flint brooch neatly pinned to her collar and a severe, scraped-back ponytail, was Colonel Lunver, who had taken over Taam's military duties. She had little patience for civilians and less for vassal planets.

The prompt seemed to spark Fenrik's memory. "Ah. Taam's partner. What do you want?"

"About the ceremony," Jainan said. His mouth was dry. He couldn't afford to cause trouble, but he had duties other than his Iskat ones. "Prince Taam has had Iskat rites. There are also some Thean clan rituals—"

"Thean rituals?" General Fenrik's eyebrows rose. He didn't have to say, *Taam was an Iskaner,* or *the Imperial family has to follow Imperial custom*; both of them knew that.

"I can promise it will not be disruptive," Jainan said, trying to make up lost ground. He should have found a more tactful approach, but there hadn't been time. "The new Thean ambassador will be in attendance, and the Thean press will take note of what happens at the ceremony."

"What do you need?" the third officer asked, slipping the question in deftly as Fenrik frowned. Jainan knew him as well: Aren Saffer, Taam's old deputy, breezy and nonchalant. Aren's tone was almost sympathetic, which made the back of Jainan's neck prickle with embarrassment. But Jainan was too numb to let that stop him.

Jainan rapidly calculated the minimum level of ritual observance that might avert hostility in the Thean media. "If I could just have five minutes for a recitation during the ceremony. It would be most appropriate when the funeral images are dedicated."

"Why didn't you take this to the stewards?" Fenrik said.

"They were . . . unhelpful," Jainan said. The shrine's stewards had flat-out refused to change the ceremony, which Jainan understood, since the request came at the last minute. General Fenrik was Jainan's last avenue of appeal.

The general examined him, as if he suspected Jainan was trying some sort of political trick. Jainan endured the scrutiny. Five minutes wasn't really enough for a clan recitation, but he could see even that was pushing the boundaries.

But Fenrik apparently decided five minutes was a small price to pay to end Jainan's petitioning. "Take care of it," Fenrik said to Colonel Lunver, who snapped her mouth shut on what she had been about to say and saluted. Fenrik gave Jainan the briefest of nods and moved on, clearly intending to spend no more time on it. His two officers sketched a bow to Jainan and followed.

Jainan stepped back to let the three of them pass. He ought to feel relief, but he only felt the cold prickle at his back and a distant dread of the ceremony itself. He had no room to indulge those sentiments.

He waited a moment to pace after them, keeping his distance from the gathering crowd of attendees. He couldn't face condolences. As he drew nearer to the front gates, he could see a view down the hill toward the city of Arlusk and a queue of flyers approaching the palace, waiting to disgorge their guests. The low dome of the palace shrine rose up to his right. The press had been allowed up to the doors: half a dozen aerial cameras circled around the marble dome, snapping pictures of the attendees. There was no way to avoid them. Jainan made sure his expression was neutral.

Inside the shrine, the smell of resin hung starkly in the air under the high stone rotunda. The space under the dome was at least free of aerial cameras. The spectators milled around to fill up the seats that circled the edge of the shrine; a uniform gleam came from the rows of decorated military officers, broken up by civilians in sober, light-colored clothes.

A line of seats was reserved for the twelve treaty representatives. The Eisafan representative was expansive as usual in a flurry of extravagant bronze-and-cream capes, with her royal partner beside her and a gaggle of staff standing behind. Her hair was woven through two heavy flint rings—an ostentatiously Galactic way of showing her gender. The delegates from Rtul and Tan-Sashn had chosen to dress in Iskat mourning grays like Jainan; they looked grave and impassive. Sefala's seats were both occupied by Iskaners. The Kaani representative had not even made an appearance. Jainan felt a distant admiration for their ability to find a different niche Kaani malaise every time they were disinclined to attend something.

Someone tapped his elbow. "Your Grace?"

Jainan pulled his arm away and stepped back. It was a young man, tall and skeletal, dressed in a Thean-style tunic. Jainan took a moment to realize the white and navy was a set of colors he knew: the clan style of the Esvereni. This must be the new Thean Ambassador.

"Count Jainan of Feria," the Ambassador said, and waited for Jainan's nod of confirmation. "My name is Suleri nal Ittana of the Esvereni. I was hoping to catch you here."

Jainan bowed. He and Taam were supposed to be above politics, but surely nobody could complain if he greeted the ambassador from his own home planet. "Your Excellency. Congratulations on your appointment."

The Ambassador gave him a dispassionate smile and said, "Thank you. To tell the truth, Your Grace, I was beginning to worry about you. I've invited you to the embassy several times over the last few days. You haven't responded."

Jainan took a short breath. It had taken a long time for Iskat to accept the appointment of a new ambassador, precisely because the last one had tried to interfere excessively in palace affairs. Inviting Jainan to the embassy before he even married his next Iskat partner made it look like Thea intended to start that all over again. This Esvereni should have been briefed, but then, the Esvereni had never been known for their tact and political restraint—Jainan caught the old pattern of thought and squashed it. Thean clan biases had no relevance on Iskat. "I apologize. I have been busy with religious duties."

The smile thinned. "I'm sorry to hear you're so busy, Your Grace. Unfortunately, since the Resolution is here for the treaty ceremonies, I have more to ask of you. I need to know you'll at least take part in the remnants handover. No one on my staff is authorized to interact with the Auditor."

Jainan hesitated, feeling the horribly familiar loss of a thread that had slipped out of his grip. There were several Resolution ceremonies before the treaty was renewed, he knew. One of them saw each planet hand over all the xeno remnants they had found over the last twenty years, uncovered from space junk nets and dig sites and terraforming refuse. Thea had found some minor shards that must be given up to the Resolution. Jainan would play his part, of course, but his new partner had to agree. He stepped aside to let a party of civil servants take their seats. "Yes, though I'm still awaiting the schedule—"

"Of course," Ambassador Suleri said. "I couldn't ask you to do anything without Iskat's approval."

Jainan shut his eyes for a brief moment and felt a flare of something uncharitable. A new, inexperienced ambassador from a rival clan was yet another problem to navigate, another chaotic factor in the equation. Suleri did not know how easy it would be to ruin the balance of relations. "I will send you my schedule as soon as humanly possible," Jainan said. "I promise. The wedding is tomorrow. I will know by then."

He saw something taken aback about Suleri's expression at

tomorrow, but Jainan was too tired to read it. Suleri cleared his expression and bowed. "Tomorrow, then. I'll expect a message."

Jainan turned away feeling like he had just crossed a floor rigged with explosives. He took his seat with moments to spare before the ceremony started.

As a row of priests filed in, the Eisafan representative leaned over. "Your new ambassador seems to have had some difficulty getting an invitation," she murmured under the next set of chanting. "My staff had to help him. Are you having any trouble?"

Jainan stared straight ahead. "The invitations were sent out late," he said. Taam had generally handled the other treaty representatives. Jainan could feel it even now, in the way the Eisafan representative looked at the empty chair beside him before she addressed him. "Thank you for your assistance."

"Our pleasure," she said, and sat back. Eisafan was the model planet of the Empire: richer and more populous every year, integrated with Iskat at every level. Eisafan would not have had a problem getting its ambassador invited to any event.

Jainan forced himself to pay attention to the rest of the ritual. The one-month Mourning was a formal Iskat ceremony, the style of it dictated by Taam's sect. He had technically followed a different sect from Jainan, but in truth Taam had only joined one because the army expected it, and neither he nor Jainan had paid much attention to ceremony outside of the high holidays.

Jainan breathed out as the chants curled upward. This was the sixth funeral ceremony in a month. He barely remembered the details of the previous ones—they blurred into one long row of priests and grave-faced soldiers, watching while Jainan struggled to remember his part in rituals he'd never attended before.

He was at least used to that by now. He stood when one of the priests beckoned him and walked steadily up to the circle of offering tables, which were crowded with gray-framed pictures of Taam. The rotunda was quiet. The press wasn't allowed in until the end.

Jainan lit a coil of waxed rope set into a resin pot, and a thin plume of smoke rose, adding to the haze in the dome. He should feel something, but instead he was numb; the numbness had a chill and a weight like a pool of icy water. He stood with the burning taper in his hand and watched the wisp of woodsmoke spiral upward. In front of him, a priest whispered a formula Jainan was not properly allowed to hear. Taam's face looked back at him from every angle—flat, lifeless, nothing like Jainan had known him—but the soaring space above was empty and calm.

This was when he should start the recitation. Jainan realized with a jolt that he hadn't made sure that Lunver had warned the priests. She'd be seated in the front row with General Fenrik, but he couldn't turn around now to look at her, and if the priests weren't expecting it, he would make this very awkward. But Taam had married into the Feria clan, however little that meant to Iskaners, and Jainan felt deep in his bones that it would be wrong to say nothing. He closed his eyes and spoke.

It was an old chant and a simple one: it listed the names of Feria's core clan for the last few generations, spooling out one by one like a thread pulled from a tapestry. The first names dropped into dead silence. Jainan had to clear his throat several times as he recited. Even after that, his voice was still irritatingly quiet and hoarse. He had not spoken in public in a long time. He caught sight of a priest who had frozen while she collected Taam's pictures—had she been told about this? Was Jainan ruining the ceremony? He felt prickles of mortification on his temples, but he couldn't stop halfway through.

At last he came to the end of it. The final names—Jainan's parents—fell into the hush. Jainan listened to the echoes die away. His mind had gone blank with relief; he couldn't remember what he was supposed to do next. There was an awkward pause. The priest in front of him coughed.

Pressure wrapped Jainan's chest like an iron band. Iskat religious ceremonies ran on smooth rails with no pauses. The spectators would think he was going to pieces. He hurriedly looked down and remembered what he was supposed to do; he picked up the stick of charcoal that lay beside the incense burner and smudged a line on the table in front of each of the white-framed photos. Taam's image stared calmly at him, oblivious to Jainan's mistakes.

"Thank you, Your Grace," the priest said. Jainan tried not to hear the censure in it. "Please be seated."

Jainan turned away from the central table. He had to get himself together. He couldn't afford to let the palace think he was falling apart.

Before he could say the final blessing and move, there was a muted disturbance at the doors to the shrine. They opened halfway, letting in a sliver of pale light and a handful of people. Jainan felt cold; the press weren't supposed to be let in yet. He had spoiled the timing of the ceremony.

But these weren't reporters. Two of them had the oddly cut clothes and broad, folded collars of people from the wider galaxy. Each had a shimmer in front of their left eye, as if the light was diverting itself around an obstacle.

The last one must be the Auditor.

The Auditor was dressed unassumingly like his two staffers—Jainan couldn't see any ornaments from here but knew his gender from reports—but the most startling thing was the shell of soft illumination that cut off his eyes and most of his face. It wrapped around his forehead and eyes like armor, a color that Jainan's visual receptors refused to parse. Jainan thought he saw human features through it but couldn't quite make them out; he felt nauseous when he looked at it.

Jainan couldn't imagine why the Auditor had come to a religious ceremony that had nothing to do with politics. But the Auditor didn't seem to be there to make a scene; he sat in the back, nonchalantly, with the air of an anthropologist making observations. As he sat down, he moved like a person, and his head turned on his neck like a person, though his face was an unsettling blank. It took Jainan a second to realize the Auditor was looking at him.

Jainan was used to spikes of panic. He knew nothing showed on his face. It was unfortunate that the Auditor had walked in to see one of the treaty representatives standing frozen, having just disrupted an Iskat ceremony by insisting on Thean customs, but it wasn't a disaster. They would have a chance to show a better picture of unity later, when Jainan's new partner was chosen. Jainan tried not to think of how his partner would view this morning's events.

He brought himself back to the duties in front of him. He turned back to the offering tables, consciously keeping every movement under control, spoke the final blessing of Taam's Iskat sect, and bowed his head correctly before he turned. He couldn't think of the future; it was a terrifying void; but if he could only control the present, he would at least do that to the best of his ability. Thea could not afford for him to falter. Whoever his partner was, they would understand the need to keep the treaty stable must override everything else.

CHAPTER 2

Oh hell. Oh, *hell*. Kiem managed to reach his rooms before he collapsed facedown onto the sofa. Summoned out of the blue today, married—*married!*—by the end of tomorrow. He wondered if they'd told his unfortunate partner the schedule yet.

He'd always known he would marry at some point and probably not for love, though he'd had a vague notion that eloping might be fun. It was just that even in Kiem's most realistic moments, he'd thought at least he and his partner would have a few months to get to know each other. But to convince a grieving stranger not to resent everything about the situation after being forced into a rushed marriage—that would take more than being persuasive. You'd need to be a bloody miracle worker.

Which meant he would end up shackled to someone who resented everything about him, and Kiem was going to be the *lucky* one in the arrangement. It would be worse on Count Jainan. This wasn't an equal partnership: as Thea was the junior partner in the alliance, Jainan was the one who'd be expected to fit his life around Kiem's. And he was probably reading through Kiem's press record right now and wishing it had been Kiem instead of Taam in the flybug accident.

Kiem let his head sink into the cushions and groaned.

"Your Highness," his aide said from the entrance, faintly disapproving. "The couch is for sitting, the bed is for lying, and the shuttleport bars are for whatever unholy combination of both you're doing there."

Kiem rolled over and half sat up. As usual, Bel looked like the model of a royal aide, with a freshly laundered coat and her hair in a mass of impeccable braids. When Bel had taken up her post she had told Kiem she would adapt to Iskat custom, and she didn't do things by halves; she indicated her gender with flint-and-silver earrings, and had even switched from her Sefalan accent to an Iskat one.

The open door behind Bel let in the clatter of footsteps and background noise. Kiem had been given overflow rooms in Courtyard West, among two floors of residences in a refurbished palace wing that used to be a stable. It wasn't strictly an Imperial residence, but at times like this Kiem would have gone mad in the hushed solemnity of the Emperor's Wing. This was at least better than moping in silence. "What about sprawls of despair?" he said. "Do we have special furniture for that? Put that on the list: source despair furniture for living room. Did I tell you I'm getting married?"

"I am aware," Bel said. She shut the door behind her, reactivating the silencing seal, and gestured with one hand above her opposite wrist. Her silver wristband picked up the gesture and projected a small, glowing screen in the air by her elbow. "I heard twenty minutes ago."

Kiem caught the real disapproval in her voice this time. "Hey, *I* only heard ten minutes ago!" He made a face. "I can't believe you knew I was getting married and didn't tell me."

"You were literally in a private audience with the Supreme Emperor when I heard," Bel said. She tucked an escaped braid back into her strict hairdo, a sign she was mollified. "Your betrothed is Count Jainan nav Adessari of Thea, twenty-seven years of age, Feria clan. I have pulled all the files on him I can find, and you will find the folder first in the queue when you open your screen."

"You are a miracle worker without peer," Kiem said. He pulled his hand out from under a cushion and tapped his wristband to activate it. His earpiece gave a soft ping and a light-screen popped up in front of him: a glowing square that hovered at chest height. Text began to spill over it. "What am I supposed to know about Thea? What did *you* know about Thea before all this?"

Bel paused for a fraction of a second. "Not a lot," she said. "I'm still reading up. Terraforming success, lots of farmland and stable seas—must be a nice place to grow up, I suppose? It used to be quiet, but I see it in the newslogs more frequently now. Clan-based culture."

"What do the clans do?" Kiem said. "Keep track of your great-aunt's birthday?"

"They *govern*," Bel said. "Clans are vastly extended family groups linked to Thean prefectures. Members don't even have to be from the same family. Feria would be one example."

"Oh shit, right, I should have known that. I don't know the first thing about this, Bel." Kiem dragged a hand through his hair distractedly. "What am I going to do?"

"Oh, I'm glad you asked," Bel said, in the voice that meant Kiem was about to do paperwork. "You're going to go through your schedule, like I've been trying to pin you down to do all morning."

Kiem threw up his hands in surrender. "Okay! Schedule."

Kiem's main room had picture windows opening out onto the courtyard gardens; he didn't usually keep filters on the glass, so the diffuse light from the clouds outside was pale and clear. With a gesture, Bel turned one of the windows into an opaque display wall. She made his calendar appear on it with a swift flick of her fingers. "You'll need to free up some time to read the contract papers before you sign them tomorrow," she said. "You'll need another block of time for the congratulatory calls, and the Emperor's office has suggested you receive Jainan in the half hour before the ceremony."

"Yes. Absolutely. Do we have drinks? Make sure we have drinks. Wait, we only get half an hour?"

"Can I cancel the lunch with the school outreach group that you have right before?"

"Cancel it, in the name of Heaven, cancel *everything*," Kiem said. "What's everyone going to think if I'm off having lunch when I'm about to get married? The Emperor will skin me."

"You have Imperial immunity," Bel said dryly.

"*Count Jainan* will skin me," Kiem said. "And he'd be right. Don't suppose we could get him to come in the morning as well—or tonight?"

"Do you want me to ask?"

Kiem angled his personal screen and stared down at it. "No," he said. "No, actually, let's not make any demands."

Bel gave him a look that wasn't quite sympathy and then went into the study to make the calls away from him, always a stickler for etiquette. Kiem waved his hand at the screen hovering in front of him. His wristband read the motion and opened Jainan's file.

The man in the photo at the top was half-familiar, a face in the distance at Imperial engagements. He was solemn, his features fine, his brown skin a shade paler than Kiem's. Something in his grave, dark eyes made the picture not unfriendly but intense, as if he were caught in the middle of a serious conversation. He wore a formal Thean uniform, which seemed to involve a lot of green and gold, and his long black hair was bound back. A wooden pendant was tucked discreetly into the cord that tied his hair, carved with some kind of Thean pattern that Kiem didn't recognize.

Kiem stared. It was the first time he'd really looked at that face. *You lucky devil, Taam,* he nearly said out loud—but somewhere between his brain and his tongue he managed to censor it because *what the hell was wrong with him*, Jainan was in mourning. Kiem tore his eyes away from the picture and looked down at the history file. Jainan's marriage to Taam had lasted five years. He was highly educated—

"He has a *doctorate* in deep-space engineering!" Kiem called to Bel in the study. "At twenty-seven! How the hell am I going to talk to someone with brains like that?"

"You have practice with me." Bel's voice came floating back, amused.

"You don't count! You get paid to dumb things down for me!" Kiem scrolled farther down the page. "This says he got a planetary award for a new fuel-injection method when he was eighteen. Do you think he could marry you instead?"

"Depends. Are you going to be able to stop talking long enough to sign the contract?" Bel said, with a trace of exasperation that meant she was trying to get work done. Kiem took the hint and flopped back to lie on the couch and read. The light-screen floated over his head.

There was a short list of Jainan's published work. He didn't seem to have done much in the past few years, so perhaps after he'd married Taam he'd taken up something else. Maybe it was something Kiem could talk more easily about. Like dartcar racing.

It didn't seem likely, somehow.

Kiem scrolled farther down. There wasn't a hobbies section. Why wasn't there a *hobbies* section? Who compiled these files and left out the important bits, like what the hell they could talk about? Kiem ran a quick historical search on Jainan, which turned out to be a mistake: everything public on Jainan showed his golden marriage with Taam, from wedding footage to a depressingly perfect article about their winter holiday cabin. Jainan looked young and happy in the engagement vids, starkly different from the recent picture, which Kiem now realized must have been taken after his bereavement. He and Taam had been perfect figureheads for the alliance with Thea. No wonder the Emperor was sore about losing that marriage.

Kiem let the screen disappear and stared up at the sky through the windows, watching the clouds move above the skeletal trees outside. Jainan wouldn't hold automatic rights to accommodation, so he'd be moving in with Kiem, at least until Palace Estates found them larger quarters. But that could take months. They'd have to split Kiem's living quarters for now. Jainan would probably want to have his own space as much as he could, to get away from Kiem. They'd have to figure out what to do with the bedroom. "Bel, can we put up a wall in here?" he called. "I can just make another room, right?"

The door chimed. Kiem waved it open, then saw who it was and slightly wished he hadn't.

The chief press officer was a stout, short man with a bald head that reflected the light and a presence like a bear in a room full of nanotech. He wore a thick wooden bracelet on each wrist and gave the distinct impression he would have preferred brass knuckles. "'Morning, Kiem."

"'Morning, Hren," Kiem said, somewhat warily. Hren was the Emperor's direct appointee, and he and Kiem didn't have the best of working relationships. "Everything all right?"

"Yep," Hren said. "Congratulations on getting hitched."

At that moment, Bel came out from the study and said, "Another room? Oh—Hren Halesar. Good morning."

"Let's try that again," Hren said, ignoring her. "Congrats on your marriage."

"Thanks?" Kiem said.

Hren sat down on the chair opposite the couch and pushed up his shirtsleeves. "So you haven't memorized your press statement."

"I have a press statement?"

"I'm afraid we've only just received it from your department," Bel said coolly. "I was coming now to inform his highness."

"Get it on his damned wristband, then," Hren said. "Five minutes ago. We've talked about this. *First thing* you do in any event is—"

"I know, get the lines to take, I know." Kiem hated being given press statements. You weren't only supposed to use them with the press but with everyone who asked you a related question, and it made him feel like a robot. But crossing Hren never went well. "Go on, Bel, what are they?"

"There are two pages of various statements," Bel said. "Here it would be that you accept congratulations and are proud to continue the alliance in memory of your revered cousin Prince Taam."

"What about Jainan? Shouldn't it mention Jainan?" said Kiem. "Some kind of compliment, maybe?"

"Kiem," Hren said patiently. "He's a diplomatic representative, not one of your groupies."

"I just thought—"

"Listen, Jainan knows this is a political arrangement and isn't going to expect flattery. I've talked to him."

Kiem winced at *political arrangement*. He probably shouldn't be visualizing his oncoming marriage as a hostile council meeting, but once he had the image, it was hard to get it out of his head. "Right."

"Your persona needs to change now that you're married, you understand?"

"I'm reformed," Kiem protested. "It's not a persona thing."

"Yeah, I've heard that before," Hren said. "Heard it when you and your friends flooded your school with the ice machine."

"I was fifteen," Kiem said defensively.

"Then again when you lost six months' allowance betting you could climb the dome on the shrine, and your friend told the press."

"I was *seventeen*," Kiem said, but realized it wasn't helping his case. "I didn't really understand money yet." That sounded even worse. He'd been properly hauled over the coals for that one, both by the media and by the Emperor, which had been somehow more painful than his fractured ankle. "Look, I know I've screwed up, but those were all years ago."

"Then you auditioned for that game show while you were at

the College, and we had to force the media house to wipe the footage."

Kiem didn't have a defense for that. Hren jabbed his thumb in Kiem's direction to emphasize his point. "No more tell-alls. No more blow-by-blows of your latest hangover. You've got just under a month to sell the public on this marriage before Unification Day. The bloody Resolution takes public sentiment into account when they audit the treaty. And on the same topic, you're going to have to start taking more care over the charity groups you work with, understand? No politics."

"That's charity fundraising. Not politics."

"I'll tell you what it's not, it's not *smiling at the bloody camera*," Hren said. "Even if the Thean logs felt warm and fuzzy about us—which they don't—a death and a quick remarriage would still be a tough sell. I need something that doesn't give the fringe outlets any traction. What's this about another room?"

It took Kiem a moment to recall what he and Bel had been talking about. "Nothing important," he said. "Jainan's going to need his own room, but I know it'll look bad if we don't live together. We'll just do some remodeling in here, add a bedroom—" He broke off at the look on Hren's face.

"Add a *bedroom?*" Hren said. "Did you agree to this marriage or not? You want the Thean press to run stories about it falling apart before it's a week old? They can get some nice mileage out of that, link it to the weaknesses in the Thean alliance, find some of those fucking teenagers who've decided unification protests are the new big thing. No construction work."

"I—what? You can't expect him to sleep with me."

"Don't like the look of him? Too bad. Suck it up."

"That's not it!" Kiem said. "He's just *lost his partner*, I'm pretty damn sure he's not going to want to! Marriage, fine, but not sleeping together."

"You start putting in new bedrooms, some contractor's going

to tell the newslogs," Hren said. "That's out. Thanks to you, your friends, your old housemates, and everyone down to your College halls cleaner, I have detailed cuttings about every starstruck airhead you've ever jumped into bed with—"

"*Hey,*" Kiem said, "none of them were like that."

"—which is the only part of my work-based knowledge I want to carve out of my head with an industrial laser, but you set yourself up for this. The newslogs expect to know about your sex life. You're fair game. Do what you want once the bedroom door shuts, but you're going to pretend to everyone else that you and the Thean are happily married."

"Everything in my rooms is private," Kiem said stubbornly. "Nothing's going to leak. And this isn't your business anyway."

"This palace has more leaks than a sewer pipe on a junk ship." Hren looked at Bel, just a glance.

Kiem's eyes narrowed. "Bel's more discreet than any of your press office staff."

"I can always find you someone more reliable," Hren said, and Kiem realized he was being blackmailed. Hren had enough of the Emperor's ear to have some pull over hiring decisions and Bel was technically paid by the palace. Prince or not, Kiem didn't have the leverage. He didn't have to look at Bel to know that she knew it too. Hren had never gone this far before. Kiem hadn't been worth blackmailing. Kiem felt, with some uneasiness, that he had stepped over an invisible line into a different political world from the one he'd occupied yesterday.

"No construction work," Kiem echoed. "Right."

"Right. I'll release your press statement to the journalists." Kiem considered protesting that he hadn't even read it yet, but he could recognize when he didn't have a leg to stand on. Hren got to his feet. "Have it memorized by tomorrow. I'll see you at the signing ceremony."

Kiem saw him out. It wasn't until the door had shut that he

turned to Bel, threw up his hands, and said, "How is everything somehow *worse*?"

It continued to get worse. The head steward came early the next morning with a program for the ceremony and a mind-numbing list of details for Kiem to sign off on. No sooner had Kiem dragged himself through that than the congratulatory calls started coming in.

Most of them were from people he barely knew. The people who cared about the Thean alliance were a world away from his life up until now: nobles outside the palace called, as did foreign parliament officials and high-ranking bureaucrats. The Thean president called. The secretary of Imperial Affairs called. Kiem took the calls in the formal vidchair in the study, where sensors would project a freestanding image of him, and prickled with discomfort when each new person's projection appeared in front of him. The Advisory Council called from one of their meetings, his cousin Prince Vaile sitting demurely among them, and took turns congratulating him with depressing sincerity. Vaile just gave him a wry smile. Kiem tried deviating from his press statement, but midway through the call with the Eisafan consul he realized that *I'm very happy* wasn't appropriate either, since Jainan almost certainly wasn't.

By the twelfth call, he was desperate enough that he declined the next person, jabbed the dispenser into life and coaxed it into disgorging a comfort-food sandwich that wasn't on its menu. He got Bel a coffee and shoved it her way as she came into the room with a light-screen floating beside her. "I'm out," he said. "No more calls. I've gone collecting for the Friends of Educationally Disadvantaged Puppies."

"You didn't really need to be on that last one anyway," Bel said, shutting off her screen and taking the coffee. "Count Jainan is due in ten minutes. What is in that sandwich?"

"Chocolate," Kiem said, just as Bel's wristband beeped. He groaned. "Tell me that's not another one," he said, but Bel was already raising a finger to activate her earpiece.

She slipped back into the other room and held a short conversation. When she leaned out again, Kiem had gestured another sandwich out of the dispenser and was feeling mutinous. "I'm supposed to be getting ready to meet Jainan, I can't spend the whole day—"

"Count Jainan's sister," Bel said. "Lady Ressid. Are you going to take it?"

Kiem swallowed, the food suddenly feeling like a solid lump in his throat. This was the first contact from anyone who actually knew Jainan. "Put it on the vid." He sat on the edge of the vidchair, back straight, and tried to look like someone who was thoroughly in charge of all the political sensitivities of a rushed marriage. It would help if he had any idea how that sort of person looked.

A projection flickered into life: a Thean noble in rich cream silks and pearls, standing, her long hair swept up in an elaborate, feather-like confection anchored with a wooden comb. Kiem blinked and adjusted his perceptions just in time. Gender on Iskat was easy: anyone wearing flint ornaments was a woman, wooden ornaments signified a man, and glass—or nothing—meant nonbinary. It was a straightforward system that even Galactics used. But Bel had said *sister*, so Ressid must be female despite the comb. Jainan might have humored Iskat customs in his photo, but apparently that didn't mean the rest of Thea adhered to them.

"Lady Ressid," Kiem said, with a seated bow.

Lady Ressid's eyes were almost the image of Jainan's in the photo, but there was something harder in them. "Prince Kiem," she said stiffly, and curtsied.

"An honor to hear from you," Kiem said. He kept a wary eye on the projected caption to the side of Ressid's image where Bel was pointedly displaying *proud to continue the alliance in memory of my revered cousin*. But Ressid didn't immediately congratulate him. There was a split-second pause, and Kiem suddenly realized that the crease at the corner of her mouth was a sign of strain.

"I am calling to formally request access to my brother," she said. The words came out clipped and hard, like a hail of small stones. "If Your Highness is pleased to grant it."

That was a weird way of announcing a visit. "Well, of course," Kiem said. "Glad to have you to stay. When?" The call was coming from Thea: the flight took a few days each way. "I thought we usually got these requests through your Foreign Affairs Bureau—wait, we're going to be in Thean space next month for Unification Day. I think it's on your orbital station. Aren't you going to be there?"

"I didn't mean that," Ressid said. "I meant access to call Jainan." The line of strain hadn't moved.

Kiem stared at her, nonplussed. He was completely at sea with Thean formalities. "That's got nothing to do with me." Wait, it must be a ceremonial thing. Only ingrained training in royal manners stopped him from casting an agonized look at Bel off-screen, but she was apparently just as confused, because the screen caption flickered and changed to *???* instead of a script. "Um, forgive me. Is there some kind of formal response?"

The line at the corner of Ressid's mouth creased, deepened, and then disappeared as she forcibly smoothed out her expression. "It is a practical matter."

"Oh. Then—wait, is this about him moving living quarters?" The realization was a relief, because now he had some clue about what was going on. "That won't be a problem. He's only moving within the palace, his ID should work fine. The palace systems will route his calls here." Jainan should know that; Kiem had no idea why Ressid was asking *him*. But maybe Jainan hadn't paid much attention to the palace systems. "And he'd have his wristband anyway."

Ressid drew a short, sharp breath, and Kiem couldn't figure out why. He looked hopefully at the caption, but Bel didn't have any helpful background information for him. "Your Highness," Ressid said. "I would like an undertaking that I will receive a call from Jainan within the next two weeks."

Alarm bells started ringing in Kiem's head. So Jainan wasn't in contact with her. Apparently he was bringing his own family problems to the marriage. Kiem could imagine how he would take it if he turned up and Kiem had already sided with his sister in their family feud—that would be a *great* start to a life partnership. "I can't give you that."

Ressid recoiled, only fractionally, but Kiem could sense her anger even through the projection. There was a silence. Kiem, probably because he was what Bel called an inveterate people pleaser, tried to fill it. "I'll tell him you called, though," he said. No—shit—that would just be pressuring Jainan if he really had cut off contact. Jainan must have a reason for not wanting to hear from his sister. "Uh, if he asks."

For a moment he thought Ressid was going to shout at him. He sat up straight and set his shoulders; he didn't like shouting, but the quickest way out was usually to let people get it off their chests. But even the slight movement seemed to give Ressid pause. She gave him a look that was barely short of a glare, then wiped all expression from her face and said, "Allow me to offer you my congratulations, Your Highness."

"Thank—" Kiem said automatically, but before he'd even finished, Ressid's projection disappeared. She'd cut the call.

He got up uneasily from the vidchair. "What was that about?" he said. There was something there that he'd accidentally put his foot in. He'd have to see if Jainan raised it. Kiem wasn't the poster boy for great family relations, however hard he tried, but he'd never been involved in an actual family feud.

"Your guess is as good as mine," Bel said, finally picking up her coffee. "You really have to stop now. Jainan's due in three minutes." Even as she spoke, the chime sounded at the door. Bel checked the feed. "That's him."

"Oh, shit," Kiem said, tugging at the jacket of his ceremonial uniform frantically. "Is this thing creased? Do I have time to change? Have we got drinks?"

"No, no, and drinks are in the cabinet as usual," Bel said. "Just let him get the occasional word in edgewise and you'll be fine." She took her coffee into the study and hit the door release on the way past, leaving Kiem to hurry over and receive Jainan.

CHAPTER 3

Jainan nav Adessari was standing by himself outside the door. Kiem had expected a small crowd of aides and assistants, not a single, preternaturally calm person with the assurance of a negotiator in a war zone.

Kiem had the photo in his head, but it was still a shock to see that grave stare right in front of him. Jainan's dark eyes gave a hidden spark of electricity to an expression that was otherwise entirely proper and neutral. His clothes were Thean, a half-sleeved tunic with a blunter, looser cut than Iskat styles, in a muted blue that split the difference between a formal outfit and mourning grays.

Jainan cut his eyes away and bowed. It was a formal bow, a shade more correct than what was required from a count to a prince. Kiem realized with a spike of embarrassment that it was probably a polite way of telling him he was staring.

He snapped himself out of his frozen moment and stepped back, bowing formally himself. "Welcome! Glad you could make it, my name's Kiem, nice to meet you. I mean, properly. I know we've sort of seen each other in the distance at functions. Thanks for, um, agreeing to all this. Come in, come in."

Jainan rose from his bow and looked at Kiem thoughtfully. Kiem wasn't given to blushing, but he almost felt his face heat as he heard his own voice sounding even more inane than usual. *My name's Kiem,* like Jainan wasn't aware whose room he had visited. And *thanks for agreeing to all this*? Jainan knew as well as Kiem that it wasn't as if either of them had a choice.

But all Jainan said was, "Jainan. A pleasure, Your Highness. It is more than an honor to be invited." As he stepped over the threshold, he took in the tall windows and the gardens outside with a quick dart of his eyes. He moved gracefully, almost soundlessly, and Kiem suddenly felt clumsy and awkward in comparison. Even more so as he lumbered back out of Jainan's way and Jainan's eyes went to him briefly, then cut away again.

"Sit down, please," Kiem said hastily, when he realized Jainan was politely hovering. He waved to one of the chairs clustered around his coffee service, a samovar with an old collection of cups that he had always ignored in favor of the dispenser, but it was traditional to have it for guests. Jainan sat on the edge of a chair, highly composed. The blue-gray of his uniform drew the color out of his face but didn't take away from the smart shape it cut around his shoulders—Kiem stopped staring. "I, uh. I hope you didn't have to interrupt anything to come?"

"No," Jainan said, soft and measured. "My last appointment was the one-month Mourning for Prince Taam, which finished yesterday."

Wrong question, *wrong question*. "Ah. I didn't realize that had already happened."

"I apologize," Jainan said. "I should have sent you a reminder."

Kiem winced. He'd gone to the public first-day and ten-day Mournings, but protocol said he wasn't close enough to Taam to still be going to memorials a month later—he couldn't remember speaking to him in years. That was before he was engaged to marry Taam's ex-partner, though. He should probably have badgered someone for an invitation after yesterday's bombshell. "Right. Yes. Um. Would you like a drink?"

"If you're having one," Jainan said politely.

Kiem was very much planning to have one, more so with every word this conversation progressed. He got to his feet. It seemed wrong to have anything ordinary, so he poured a glass of pale spirits from an ornate bottle half-full of preserved berries. "Silverberry wine? Coffee? What would you like?"

Jainan glanced at the second glass Kiem was holding. "Water . . . ?"

Kiem decided he was imagining the disapproval there and brought a chilled bottle of water to the table with a glass. There was an awkward moment when Jainan attempted to rise to take the drink and Kiem wasn't expecting it, but they got through it with no more than a minor splash on the table. Jainan stared at the spill like it was a tragedy. Kiem winced again. He was apparently going to have to be much neater from now on. "Don't worry, I'll get something for it later."

"I'm sorry," Jainan said.

"Uh, no, don't be sorry." Kiem said. He felt the stifling layer of politeness lying over them like velvet. He sat down and put his head in his hands. "All right," he said. "Can we speak plainly? Sorry. I'm not great at tiptoeing around things."

What went across Jainan's face wasn't exactly a change of expression. It was more like looking at the surface of the water down at the harbor and sensing that something had just moved underneath. His back straightened and he placed his hands on his knees. "Please," he said. "Go ahead."

Kiem took a deep breath. Right. They were going to clear the air. "I think we'll have a better chance of making this work if we're open with each other," he said. "I know you're not going to be over the moon about this. To be honest, I don't know what the Emperor was thinking." It was probably a measure of the stress they were under that neither of them even bothered to look over their shoulder.

"The treaty," Jainan said. His expression was entirely neutral again.

"The treaty," Kiem agreed. "But look, this wasn't your first choice. I wasn't expecting it either, but we're stuck with it. Can we at least agree we'll try and make it work? I know you'll need space to—to grieve. We can just act the bare minimum to sell the marriage to the palace, and drop it when we're in private."

Jainan smiled. It was an odd, distant smile and didn't seem to be particularly happy, but it was a smile. "It's funny," he said.

"What is?" That didn't sound good.

"Prince Taam—we had this conversation. One very much like it."

Taam and Jainan had started off their marriage like this? Kiem felt obscurely heartened, although the circumstances weren't exactly the same. "So . . . we're okay? I promise I'm not an axe murderer."

"That part he didn't say," Jainan said.

It took a moment for Kiem to realize that was a deadpan joke, and he grinned. "Maybe he was. I mean, you have to be explicit."

Jainan's expression shuttered completely, and he put the water down.

"No—I—oh, shit, sorry. I didn't mean—" The door chime rang again. Kiem only just stopped himself throwing up his hands in frustration. There should be some kind of law against him opening his stupid mouth. "Well, it wasn't as if we were doing anything important. Come in!" he added, raising a hand to gesture the door open.

It was the head steward with two attendants. He bowed punctiliously. "Your Highness, the contract is prepared for signing in the West Solarium. Are you and Count Jainan ready?"

Kiem felt mutinous. "Are we?" he said, casting a glance at Jainan, who was probably about as unwilling as he was. But Jainan was already standing, which shamed Kiem into pushing himself to his feet. He offered Jainan his arm.

The moment he'd done it, he froze and wished he could take it back. He hadn't meant to put Jainan on the spot. But before he could turn the movement into anything else, Jainan was moving over to him and slipping a hand through the crook of his arm.

His touch rested lightly and securely. Was he forcing himself? Kiem couldn't tell. The skin beneath Kiem's uniform jacket felt hotter than it should.

"Your Highness," the steward said again.

"We should go," Jainan said, quietly enough to reach only Kiem's ears. He was looking ahead.

Kiem forced his eyes away from Jainan. "Yes, right," he said. "Look at us, punctual from the start. Oh, hey, Hren."

The chief press officer nodded at him. "Memorized your press statement yet?"

"I thought I'd just improvise," Kiem said cheerfully, to make Hren twitch. But Hren only glared at him, and for some reason Jainan's grip shifted on his arm. "I mean, yes," Kiem said. "Know it back to front." He stopped trying to make conversation.

The walk up to the solarium was enveloped in a silence that felt almost funereal. Kiem would usually have tried joking with the attendants, but it would be rude to start talking to anyone who wasn't Jainan. But whenever he thought of something to say to Jainan, he remembered that Jainan was being walked into a forced marriage with the only person in the palace who could possibly be tactless enough to call his late partner an axe murderer, and Kiem bit his tongue. He experimented silently with several phrases but couldn't find one that might fix things. At the top of the sweeping marble stairs, just before the last corner, he gave up and muttered, "Sorry."

"For what?" Jainan said. The door slid open, and Kiem lost the chance to reply in the flash of lenses.

He squinted through the first couple before automatically raising his free hand. "Hi, good morning—" There was a barely noticeable increase of pressure on his arm. Jainan had stopped. Surprised, Kiem tried to pause as well, but now Jainan was moving again, and Kiem wondered if he'd imagined it.

The initial flurry of flashes died down. When Kiem moved his arm a fraction, Jainan removed his hand immediately and stepped a little away. Apparently he'd been steeling himself to be near Kiem. Kiem tried not to show he'd noticed.

"Your Highness! How's it feel to be married?"

Journalists. Kiem relaxed—journalists seemed like the least difficult thing to deal with right now. He grinned and shook a couple of hands. "'Morning. I'm not, yet. Hi, Hani—any tips? You got married last year, didn't you? Your partner took that shot of me falling in the canal a couple of days ago."

"Yes, which is why she didn't get credentials for this, isn't it?" The polished woman with silver eye implants tilted her head. "How long have you known Count Jainan?"

Kiem spread his hands disarmingly. "I don't make the press lists. And we've met a few times—we're, uh, getting to know each other."

"How does he feel about your lifestyle?"

"Hey, aren't you guys supposed to be the *sympathetic* part of the press corps?" Kiem protested. "I don't do that anymore. I'm responsible now." He was almost starting to enjoy himself by the time he glanced over at Jainan.

Jainan was holding himself stiffly; a reporter stood in front of him about half a pace too close. Jainan shook his head and said something. He wasn't moving away, though, so Kiem was about to turn back to the others when he heard the reporter say, "—Prince Taam—"

All right, that was enough. "Oi, Dak, who let you in here?" Kiem said, cutting across Jainan. "Weren't you behind that piece on the Emperor's brother needing plastic surgery?"

"What?" Dak said, turning without batting an eyelid. He was a solidly built, middle-aged journalist who worked for one of the larger aggregators. "That's quite an accusation there, Your Highness. I had nothing to do with that."

"Yeah, well, it was your phrasing," Kiem said, by no means sure about that. "So you're on thin ice. Show some bloody respect for the deceased. Taam's off the record, as is this conversation. Jainan, I think we're starting?"

Jainan gave him a look that was no less blank than the one he'd directed at the reporter. "Of course," he said. "Excuse me." He gave Dak a polite bow of his head and bypassed him. Kiem put himself on the side next to the reporters and blocked any more questions with a friendly wave, strolling up to the antique desk they'd dug out for the signing.

The West Solarium was a large, hexagonal room, filled with pale light from the windows set into its dome-like ceiling. The metal ribs of the dome were brushed with pale, butter-yellow highlights, so it was one of the more cheerful rooms in the palace. Kiem took that as a good omen.

The ceremony was sparsely attended. Guests stood around in loose groups; not many of Kiem's relatives were there, given the short notice, but he saw a couple of his cousins and waved. Many of the guests were minor Iskat dignitaries in high-collared, richly colored tunics. There was a scattering of people in formal Thean tunics or robes, with jewels embroidered into the fabric rather than set into Iskat-style belts. There were fewer Theans than Kiem would have expected; fewer, in fact, than the military officers in dress uniforms, who stood talking in their own groups without so much as glancing at the other guests. They must have come for Jainan's sake, since he and Taam would have moved in military circles. Kiem felt a moment's guilt that he didn't recognize any of them. Bel was sitting at the side next to a minor steward, wearing a pristine formal tunic and a poker face; Kiem caught her eye and felt fractionally better about the whole thing.

The head steward was in top form. "Ah, good. Your Highness, over here, please—and Count Jainan, this side . . ."

"Was that all right?" Kiem muttered to Jainan, just before they parted. "You looked like you didn't want to be in that conversation. I—uh—there'll be a chance to talk to the press after, if you want."

"No," Jainan said. "Thank you." An aide bobbed up like a tug-boat and piloted him to a pile of documents.

Kiem reluctantly turned to his own separate pile. There was a goose-feather quill beside it and a pot of red ink. Kiem eyed them with misgivings. Handscribing was bad enough at the best of times, and adding pots of ink into the equation wasn't going to make it any better.

A small knot of people at the back parted for a purple-robed judge and the Thean Ambassador beside her. The Ambassador bowed to Jainan. Jainan gave him a startled glance and then looked down at the documents, not responding.

Kiem squinted at the Ambassador, a tall and bony man in a patterned Thean tunic whom Kiem didn't think he'd met. What was wrong there? Kiem tried a friendly smile. The Ambassador took a moment to adjust the wooden bracelet on his wrist before he acknowledged Kiem with a shallow bow, his expression cool. "Your Highness."

"Good to see you here, Your Excellency," Kiem said, half an eye on Jainan. Jainan didn't seem to have many friends, did he? Come to think of it, there really weren't many Theans here. Kiem was sure when Prince Helvi had married her Eisafan partner the room had been half Eisafs, though of course Eisafan was a much more populous planet and a much more important relationship. The Iskat minister for Eisafan had been in the front row of that ceremony. Kiem said without thinking, "Have you seen our Minister for Thea?"

"Ah," the Ambassador said. His expression wasn't exactly a smile. "You're a little late there, Your Highness. Your Minister for Thea retired last year. Your side hasn't been able to agree on a replacement yet."

"Your Worship, may we begin?" the head steward said to the judge.

Kiem wanted to ask who was dealing with Thean affairs if Iskat hadn't appointed anyone, but before he could say anything, the Ambassador gave him a brisk, impersonal nod and stepped back to join the other spectators. Jainan was still looking intently at his contract, as if wanting to get the whole thing over with. The judge made a careful gesture over her wristband.

The sound of a gong rang through the room. All thoughts of Thean politics fled Kiem's brain as the judge started a rolling declamation of the standard wedding spiel. Kiem swallowed hard.

He'd never been the focus of a ceremony before. The sound of a gong heralded things like the arrival of someone important, or a marriage, or an official appointment. Kiem had screwed up enough exams and had a bad enough reputation with the Emperor—not even counting the nightclub scandal—that nobody had ever considered giving him an important post. He'd always thought that had been for the best, but here he was, and there weren't only his own concerns at stake. He heard the Emperor's voice in his head: *I have very little appetite for another war.*

Half the press corps had cameras up. Kiem tried to look appropriately solemn but felt it came out as something of a grimace, so he settled for normal. He sneaked a look at Jainan to see how he was managing it. Jainan's face was still pleasantly blank. Kiem wondered how he did that.

In spite of the clear solarium roof, no sunlight made it through the muted gray of the clouds. The judge's voice was a sonorous rumble. *Traditions from the foundation of the Empire, valued alliance with Thea* and so on, until finally she reached the end and wound up with some nondenominational blessings that wouldn't offend anyone's sect. She solemnly folded her hands on the table in front of her and said, "Your Highness, Your Grace, you may now agree to the terms and seal the contracts."

Kiem grabbed his quill and leaned over to dip it in the inkpot, offering Jainan a quick smile. Jainan wasn't looking at him. Instead he reached for the inkpot himself—nervous and too fast—accidentally nudged Kiem's hand, and knocked the pot over.

A flood of red splattered over the table, pooling on both the documents. "Shit!" Kiem said, blocking a rivulet with the side of his hand in a helpful gesture that on second thought was no help at all. The pot itself rolled, smearing a dark crescent of red over wood and paper. Jainan lunged after it. It hit the carpeted floor with a faint *thud*.

That broke up the frozen moment among the onlookers. "Careful!" the steward said, bustling up with even less idea of how to be helpful than Kiem. Two junior stewards came up to do more practical damage reduction with handkerchiefs and pieces of paper. Kiem extracted his hand with only a moderate amount of red ink smeared on his sleeve. The judge, annoyed, waved at the press corps to stop the suddenly frantic photo-taking, and Kiem abruptly had to bite the inside of his cheek to stop himself from laughing. He looked around for Jainan.

Jainan had knelt to pick up the inkpot. He was still crouched on the floor, the pot clutched tight in one hand, frantically dabbing at the carpet with his handkerchief. He glanced up at Kiem. "S-sorry," he said. "I don't—I don't know what happened."

Kiem crouched down, sobering up. "Don't worry about that, they'll get it cleaned up later. Here, I'll take the pot—it's going all over your hand." He nearly had to pry it out of Jainan's grip. "Are you all right? Get much of it on you?" He stood and offered Jainan a hand.

"I'm fine," Jainan said. He took the hand. "I'm sorry for the disruption." His grip was warm, with callouses on the fingers, and for a moment Kiem was distracted. But when Jainan was on his feet, he tried to pull his hand away as soon as politely possible. Kiem let go hurriedly. A steward offered Jainan a wipe for his hands.

Kiem jumped as Bel tapped him on the shoulder. She passed him a handkerchief. "Don't say anything," Kiem muttered.

"Just try not to get it on your face; the press will think you broke your nose again," Bel murmured. She gestured to two of the stewards, who had magically produced a tablecloth to hide the stains. A third laid out a fresh set of contracts, which Bel straightened then stepped back with a meaningful look at Kiem that said, *Try not to have any more disasters.*

"We resume the ceremony," the judge said.

"Right," Kiem said. He tried to ignore the after-impression of Jainan's hand on his, like a ghost touch. Before there could be any more accidents, he grabbed the quill and signed his name with only a minor blot. Beside him Jainan dipped his own quill in the remaining pot of ink, taking great care. His hands were shaking. That must be adrenaline; it hadn't been *that* embarrassing.

There was a round of polite applause. Jainan set the quill back and straightened, turning to Kiem.

Oh shit. Kiem had managed not to think about the fact he was going to have to kiss him, whether Jainan wanted it or not. *All right*, he told himself, taking a wary step away from the table. *Just keep it impersonal.* Jainan stepped in, and Kiem's gaze was caught by the unconscious elegance of the movement, by his dark eyes and the slight natural crookedness of his mouth.

No, Kiem told himself. Just because Jainan was his type didn't mean Kiem couldn't act poised in front of the cameras.

Jainan took another step and closed the distance, his hand coming up to rest on Kiem's chest. Desire sparked across Kiem's skin like a current. His breath stopped under the touch, and before he could think about it, his hands came up to clasp Jainan's waist—but *no, what was he doing?* Jainan was in mourning. Kiem managed to stop himself from instinctively pulling their bodies in closer. Jainan froze in response, staring at him from a couple of inches away as if wondering what had gone wrong. Jainan clearly decided after a moment that Kiem wasn't going to take the initiative; he tilted his head and leaned in dutifully. Kiem gave the whole thing up as a bad deal, leaned forward, and had the most excruciatingly awkward kiss he'd ever had with a person he was extremely attracted to. They both tried to draw back at the first contact then realized their mistake, and Jainan's nose bumped against Kiem's clumsily, and they both drew back again. And despite all that, even the light pressure of Jainan's lips had Kiem's heart beating off-rhythm in his chest.

Jainan stepped back. Kiem dropped his hands back down as if he'd been burned. He managed to catch Jainan's eye with a grimace of apology. Jainan only looked blank.

"Gentlemen! To the front, please," the steward said. Belatedly, Kiem held out his hand, and they both turned toward the reporters. Hren flashed him a hand signal that meant Kiem was booked for interviews afterward.

"Your Highness? Count Jainan?" a reporter called out. "What does it feel like to be married?"

"Wonderful," Jainan said. Kiem felt a tremor go through Jainan's hand.

That question had been directed at Kiem. He pulled up a smile from somewhere. He didn't want to know what it looked like. "Great!" he said. "It's great."

CHAPTER 4

The empty hoverchest bobbed in the middle of Taam's rooms, but Jainan didn't start packing straightaway when he returned. Instead he sank into a chair and held his head tightly, tightly, as if he could squeeze his skull into a better shape and relieve the pressure.

In the few words he and Prince Kiem had exchanged after the ruined ceremony—the ceremony Jainan had ruined—Jainan had tried to find an opportunity to apologize but hadn't been able to get the words out. Stupid. Useless. All he'd managed to do was turn down Prince Kiem's offer to help with the packing and retreat, like a coward, to Taam's rooms. Leaving Prince Kiem to think him ungrateful as well as unfit. He had turned down the post-ceremony interview requests, as well, and hadn't realized until it was too late that Prince Kiem seemed to have accepted them and had gone off to give the interviews on his own.

Jainan's head gave another stab of pain. There was always some negotiation around the terms of the vassals' treaties before the Resolution agreement set everything in stone for the next twenty years. Thea was not a significant political force and did not have the leverage to negotiate more favorable terms. It was the smallest of the Empire's seven planets; it clung to its allied province status and the independence it brought. Jainan needed Prince Kiem on his side. He had made an appalling start today.

It wasn't really a surprise that Jainan had made a poor impression. Prince Kiem was confident, charismatic, and as good-looking as Taam had been. Like Taam—like any Iskat royal—Kiem would expect his public and personal life to go smoothly. He had clearly been doing his best to conceal his disappointment in his marriage that morning. Prince Kiem was at least less naive than Jainan had been.

Enough. Jainan rose to his feet. This was self-pity. He had only one duty now—to keep up appearances in his new marriage—and even if he could never be liked, he could at least be agreeable. He wouldn't cause inconvenience by delaying his packing.

He moved mechanically around the familiar rooms, gathering his possessions and fitting them into the chest. He'd always been neat and he'd tried to keep it that way. It surprised him, though, how little space everything packed down into. His devices, toiletries, and shoes filled only a fraction of the chest. The clothes took longer, as he pulled them out of the wardrobe one by one, trying not to touch Taam's uniforms that still hung there. He'd meant to send someone a memo about them. His head was all over the place these days.

He had run a superficial search on Prince Kiem when he'd first been given his name. The results seemed hopeless: Prince Kiem at parties, Prince Kiem with a string of partners, and one report where he was apparently tipsy and balancing on a statue in Arlusk's main square. Jainan knew there was nothing he could do to appeal to someone like that. The only glimmer of hope had been something buried in a long profile by a gossip log: *Prince Kiem says he's easygoing,* it said. *He likes to enjoy life. Ask him about his career, and he'll only tell you he didn't join the army because it sounded like too much hard work. You certainly won't catch him advising the Emperor.*

Jainan hadn't read further. If Kiem liked things to be easy, Jainan could at least manage that.

The rooms' storage units were concealed cunningly in the Iskat style, slotted gracefully into the curved white pillars and walls, their handles invisible until you touched the right spot.

Jainan opened them all, checking he had missed nothing of his among Taam's possessions. He didn't touch any of the contents. But in the lowest unit in the corner, which only opened halfway because of Taam's desk, he found a box at the back with Thean scribing on it.

His hands slowed as he slid the lid away. He hadn't seen these in years. A Thean ceremonial knife he'd once thought he would wear at his wedding. A clan flag from his aunt. A slim paper volume of classical poems Ressid had given him, insisting they wouldn't be available in the Empire—Jainan was not a poetry reader, but he had never been able to convince Ressid of that. He cut off the memory swiftly before it made him unnecessarily maudlin.

These things didn't really have a place here. Perhaps it was finally time to clear them out. But even as he thought that, he found himself taking the box and packing it in the bottom of the hoverchest. There would be another corner for it, maybe. He'd probably lose it again; he seemed to have been getting steadily less organized over the past few years. Taam would have laughed.

As Jainan turned back from the hoverchest, his wristband gave a chirp that meant it had hit another error. It had been be-having erratically for weeks. Jainan tried to clear the error, but as he did, he saw it was pinging Taam's account to refresh a backup file. Taam had always stored some of his backup accounts on Jainan's device. Jainan had forgotten.

His headache sent up another flare of pain at this unexpected responsibility. He tried to convince himself it wasn't important. The investigators looking into the flybug crash already had all the data from Taam's devices. Jainan could be forgiven for just ignoring this.

He had never ignored something that had to be done, though. He shut his eyes for a brief instant, breathed out, and brought up a small screen from his wristband to call Internal Security.

The call didn't go through to the agent working on the case, of course. They had stopped answering him some time ago, when the investigation wound down. The person who appeared on the screen was a low-level Human Intelligence processor.

They recognized Jainan immediately, smoothing out their expression and resigning themself to wasting their time in a way that made Jainan's skin crawl. He knew they did not consider him credible.

"Yes, Your Grace?"

"I wanted to inform you that I found some more of Taam's files," Jainan said. He could hear himself sound even more stiff and formal than usual. "I believe it to be a backup. It is protected by a passphrase."

Taam's various messaging and storage accounts had been a tangle of different encryption layers, all of which were compulsory for military officers. Jainan knew Internal Security had managed to get most of the relevant keys and passphrases from Taam's superiors, but it seemed nobody had known Taam well enough to have a full overview of his life. That person should have been Jainan.

"The investigation isn't currently active, sir," the agent said.

"I know."

The agent paused. "Please pass us a copy and then delete it. Someone may visit to ensure it's been completely wiped."

"I will have moved quarters."

"Yes," the agent said. It wasn't as if they didn't know where Jainan was going. "Thank you for your information."

Jainan watched the screen in front of him die. He felt exhausted; maybe that was relief. He sent a copy to Internal Security, but discovered the file wouldn't delete without a passphrase. Never mind. He couldn't read it anyway, and the investigation was inactive.

He shouldn't even be thinking about this anymore. He had a new partner, a new duty that required all his attention. He couldn't be distracted by stray thoughts of Taam. He and Taam had spent five years together—five years that ended suddenly, brutally, like the punch of a demolition claw through a wall—and that was it. That marriage was over.

A white indicator light glowed on the wall. Jainan turned and opened the door in the split second before the chime had a chance to sound.

A smartly dressed staffer stood outside. Jainan consciously ran through the Iskat social cues: her wristband was emblazoned with a crest, thus she must work for the palace, and her earrings were obviously flint, so at least she could be clearly read as female. Iskaners thought their gender presentation was very simple—wooden decorations for men, flint for women—but it was sometimes impossible to spot a bead or stone if it was displayed discreetly, and some people wore neither. The staffer wasn't wearing a uniform tunic. She must be someone's aide.

"Count Jainan?" The aide bowed. "My name is Bel Siara, Private Secretary to Prince Kiem. His highness has sent me to assist you."

Jainan automatically bowed back. She looked vaguely familiar—Jainan must have seen her around the palace at some point, but he was bad at remembering people and worse at making connections. This transition might have been easier if he'd known people outside Taam's immediate circle, but just moving out of Taam's rooms was like moving into a city full of strangers.

"Honored to make your acquaintance," he said. The formal phrase came out easily, polished by use, but then he had to think of what to say next. He had to stop his breathing from speeding up. Bel Siara was in a position to do him a lot of damage if she decided she didn't like him. "I've packed. I'm ready to go." He turned before she could reply and keyed the chest closed.

The lid slid shut, and the chest unmoored itself, bobbing toward the door as he touched the handle.

"Allow me," Bel said and moved in to take a pull cord instead. Jainan backed off and let her.

Prince Kiem lived in an entirely different part of the palace. Taam had been given rooms in the Emperor's Wing, the high-security heart of the palace, though of course he was several floors away from the Emperor. Prince Kiem seemed to have missed out on those; the Courtyard Residence was a long, echoing building of white stone that housed lesser relatives and high officials. Like all the grand buildings of the palace, they were linked with a snakelike maze of glass-covered walkways. Iskaners had a compulsion for glass roofs and windows that showed the sky, which had always baffled Jainan, as for most of the year there was nothing there except a blanket of clouds. Iskaners called it a *fine autumn day* if it stopped snowing for an afternoon.

Jainan used the walk to go over his half-formed apologies for the ceremony. He never got the chance to use them: when they arrived, Prince Kiem's rooms were empty.

The suite was a smaller version of Taam's, built according to the same model. Jainan had been there before, on his brief, panicked visit before the ceremony, but he still stopped in the doorway, disoriented again by how much difference the furnishings made to the atmosphere. Bright lighting picked out the edges of the mismatched coffee service and a cheap, cheerful rug, chosen by someone with more enthusiasm than talent for interior design. The main room was tidier than it had been earlier. Iskaners liked their surroundings to be largely a pristine white, he knew, but Jainan felt there had been more color then, just because more things had been strewn around.

Bel waved him in ahead of her. "He's gone out. Make yourself comfortable. I can get you a drink, unless you'd like to direct the unpacking?"

"I can unpack myself," Jainan said. She must be busy with her own duties.

Bel gave him a swift, calculating look, as if trying to sum him up and not making much headway. "Of course," she said after a moment. "Let me show you the rooms."

The bedroom was spotless as well. A sudden rattle against the window made Jainan turn his head, and he caught the shadow of a raptorial bird as it bounced off in a flurry of pinions and claws. Jainan had learned to be wary of Iskat's birds. Even the ones Iskaners called *sparrows* would attack a human; anything much larger had to be exterminated.

"Oh yes, keep the window shut or the doves will get in," Bel said. "And don't feed them, that's what started the problem in the first place. Here." She opened an entirely separate wardrobe. Two columns of drawers also stood open.

"I don't need this much space," Jainan said.

"We can clear more, if—excuse me?"

Jainan silently keyed open the lid of the hoverchest. It was only half filled.

Bel looked at the contents. "I see," she said. Jainan tried not to read any disapproval into it. "But we've cleared it now, so you might as well claim it. His highness will just fill it with his rubbish if you don't."

Jainan felt his entire back knot up. "I don't—I don't need it," he said. "I don't want to argue with his highness."

Bel gave him an odd look. Jainan couldn't meet her eyes and instead focused on pulling his belongings out of the chest.

"Let me know if you need anything," Bel said at last. "I'll be in the study. Prince Kiem says don't hesitate to ask for anything."

"Thank you," Jainan said.

"To be clear, that means ask *me* for anything," Bel said. "Kiem doesn't know how to work the requisition system and will just call up twenty people until someone gives him something to make him stop."

"Thank you," Jainan said again. He had the excuse of turning to the wardrobe, so he didn't have to hide his expression as she left.

If Prince Kiem had said that, Jainan could guess why. Guilt about the rushed marriage and Jainan's bereavement. That explained some of the things Kiem had said at the ceremony as well. Guilt about Jainan, which led to Kiem extending favors. And if Jainan took advantage of that, it would poison the well that much sooner. Jainan was familiar with how guilt turned into resentment. The only thing to do was to try and make Kiem happy, and Jainan was uniquely incapable of that.

His clothes fit into half the space in the wardrobe. The box from Thea went into the back of a drawer. He emptied the chest slowly, and when it was empty, he shut it down until it was a thin flat block floating at chest height. He pulled it out of the air and faltered. Jainan would have taken it to Taam's aide normally, but he didn't want to disturb Bel.

He felt a sudden, crushing desire to be back in familiar territory. At least he'd known the *rules* there. His head gave another stab of pain.

Bel put her head around the door. "Message from Prince Kiem," she said. "He's apparently made dinner arrangements. Would you go to the Room of Birds in twenty minutes? It's in the Southern Tower by the Emperor's Wing. I can show you the way."

Jainan hesitated. Bel was intimidatingly brisk and efficient, and he had no desire to take up more of her time. "I know where it is," he said. It wasn't a dining room. He had a recollection of it from a palace tour when he'd first arrived, formal and empty, sometimes used for receptions. The palace had more reception rooms than it knew what to do with.

"I suggest formal wear," Bel said. "Do you need anything else? No? I'll be off for the evening, then. I'm on call—here, I'll send you my contact data for your short list." She spun her finger, and an image of a navigation wheel appeared just below her hand.

"No, I—I need mine recalibrated." Jainan touched his own wristband, which had not worked properly since they'd shut off Taam's account. Now it would need to be linked to Prince Kiem's. But Bel was going off duty, and he didn't want to keep her. "I'll ask

Prince Kiem tomorrow." That didn't in any way lessen the cold tension at the back of his neck.

When he reached the upper floor of the Southern Tower, he couldn't remember exactly which of the gold-swirled doors he should open, but it didn't matter: an attendant bowed to him and ushered him to the right one.

It opened onto a forbiddingly large reception room that looked out over a panorama of the city of Arlusk and the snow-covered mountains beyond. The smooth whiteness of the walls was broken up by circular tapestries depicting various Iskat birds, predatory and alien. The rest of the furniture was carefully crafted to fit in with these antique treasures: the chairs and side tables were made of polished wood, only lightly brushed with gilt. There was a table set for two by the window.

Prince Kiem was rising swiftly from it, so swiftly that he knocked the chair backward. Jainan stiffened. "Ah—oh, damn—excuse me—" Kiem somehow hooked his foot under the chair before it hit the floor and awkwardly flipped it up again. He turned back to Jainan and offered him a bow. "Sorry about that. Do you, er, want to sit down?"

Jainan was still frozen. The table was spread with snowy linen and glittered with twelve types of cutlery. Tiny dishes had been set out with geometric position, each holding a delicate morsel of food. There was a candlestick clawing its way up from the middle of the table. It was meant to be *romantic*.

Jainan couldn't do this.

"I, er, I mean—maybe you don't—" Kiem spread his hands helplessly. "I didn't mean to ambush you. If you're not feeling well, that's fine. You can order in food to our rooms. I can go somewhere else. Or, or something."

Whatever happened regarding dinner, they were going to be sleeping in the same bed tonight. Jainan forced himself not to step back. Running away now wouldn't help anything. It was only a formal dinner; he had sat through hundreds of formal dinners.

"No, it's fine," he said. He took three steps forward and sat, stiffly, and remembered to add, "It's lovely. I'm honored."

Kiem gave an exaggerated sigh of relief. *A joke,* Jainan thought numbly as Kiem sat down. "Sorry it's not exactly a big wedding banquet. Official mourning and all that. I did get us one of the bottles of Gireshian champagne from the cellars, though." Kiem grabbed for the bottle by the candlestick and waved it hopefully. His bracelet, a square wooden bead threaded with a cord, clinked too loudly against Jainan's empty glass. "Thirty years old and spent three years on the ship here. Can I—oh, wait." He pulled the bottle away, looking stricken. "You don't drink, do you?"

Giresh wasn't in-system. Systems outside the Empire could only be accessed through a link, and Iskat's nearest link was a year's travel away, so trade and interchange with the wider universe was slow. Out-system goods were luxuries; Kiem was offering him something that would have cost him a chunk of his allowance to acquire from the cellars. Jainan pushed his glass an inch toward the bottle. "Please do."

"Er, right," Kiem said. He filled his own glass as well then held it up. "To Thea."

Jainan blinked. Something in his chest ached. But it was just politeness—reputation in the press aside, Prince Kiem was a diplomat in a family of diplomats. Jainan held up his glass. "To the Empire." The taste of alcohol burned at the back of his throat.

Iskat meals followed a rigid progression. They always started with the salt course: a collection of small, sharp-flavored bites of fish and meat and pickled vegetables. Then a tiny ceramic cup of tea, drunk piping hot to clear the palette—no Iskaner drank tea outside meals, and they looked askance at you for suggesting it—then the sweet course, with fish or seafood in sweet sauces and crisp wafer cakes on the side. The bulk of the food would come in the mild course, where at last rice and bread would appear on the table. Kiem made appreciative noises at the spread. Jainan was not hungry.

The last plate of the salt course appeared at his elbow from a hovering waiter, holding two silvery wafers of fish and a scattering of seagrass. Jainan automatically inclined his head and picked up the correct cutlery. He gripped it a little in preparation for speaking.

"Blizzards coming early this year," Kiem said from across the table, at exactly the same time as Jainan said, "I would like leave to apologize."

There was a dreadful silence. Jainan dropped his gaze to his food, his shoulders knotting up with the effort of keeping his back still and straight, and then Kiem said, "What for?"

Jainan paused. "The ceremony."

Kiem put a hand across his face and groaned. "Oh hell, I'm sorry too. That was awful, wasn't it, let's never speak about it again."

The relief sat in Jainan's stomach like acid. "Yes."

"They could have waited a *week*," Kiem said, immediately disregarding his own request. "Would a week have killed them? Hundreds of civil servants in this palace and not one of them could figure out how to suspend a treaty for a week?"

Jainan looked down at his meal and carefully separated the fish from the seagrass with the tip of his knife. A faint citrus tang rose from it. "Mm."

"Hey, so, a whole meter of snow this month. That's a *lot*, huh? This is the time of year when my mother always started swearing about the weather and got herself posted spaceside."

Jainan blinked. But before he had the time to respond, Kiem launched into a stream of consciousness that was apparently every thought he had ever had about early winter weather. Jainan scrambled to pull himself together enough to reply. When Kiem finished on the weather, there wasn't even a break before he switched to the food ("Apparently hazelnuts are making a comeback—ever tried hazelnuts?"), the latest news on Sefalan raiders ("Bel's from Sefala, you know, she gets her news from the Sefalan Guard over there.") and the orbital shuttle gridlock the Resolution ship had caused ("Won't be cleared within the week, I've got a bet on it with the deputy station controller.").

The stream of chatter started to become soothing. Jainan fell thankfully into autopilot, dredging up opinions so bland they might as well have been written by the press office. Kiem was good at feigning interest: he managed to look like he was hanging on every dull word. Jainan knew it was a diplomatic front, but it made the conversation easier. Kiem took up more space than Taam had; he was constantly gesturing to make a point or nearly putting his elbow in the butter. Jainan tried not to look at his body, his deep brown skin and the smooth curve of his forearm. It felt wrong to let himself be distracted.

The sweet course came and went, with a rich savory soup leavened with honey and a cluster of sugared fancies on the side. Then more of the scalding tea. The sky through the windows had turned a deep, dusky blue, and Jainan's eyes kept going back to the encroaching dark above and the way the palace lights flickered and glinted from a few errant snowflakes. Year after year, the heartland of the Empire seemed eager to tilt its orbit away from Iskat's star; winter came on swiftly in this part of the planet, always.

Try as he might, Jainan was losing the thread of Kiem's conversation. It had been a long day. In the lull between crises, tiredness crept up on him like paralyzing serum, making his spine ache and his mind slip. The clink of cutlery and the candlelight reflected on the dark window was too familiar; it could have been any of the hundreds of banquets he had attended with Taam since he came to Iskat. Kiem was a stranger on the other side of the table. His features didn't really resemble Taam's, but right now the two of them looked more similar than they should.

And then it wasn't just resemblance. The room blurred, and

Taam was sitting in Kiem's place, handsome and charming, speaking to an indistinct dignitary on his right. The lump of soft bread in Jainan's mouth turned to ash; he couldn't swallow. Taam laughed at a joke and turned back. The moment he did, the smile was gone, wiped cleanly from his face.

Let's go home, Jainan thought. Taam's mood would only get worse if they stayed. As if he'd heard, Taam leaned toward him and reached out. Jainan kept his hand still on the table.

"Jainan?" A brisk tap on the back of his wrist made him jump. It was Kiem, leaning over with an anxious expression. "Are you all right?"

"Yes," Jainan said, pulling his hand away. Grief worked in strange ways. He was supposed to make a fresh start with Kiem; he could not let him know why he'd spaced out. "Fine. Just tired."

Kiem pulled his hand back immediately. "Yeah, it's been a long day. We can skip the rest of the course—"

"No," Jainan said desperately. He forced Taam entirely out of his mind. He couldn't ruin this as well. "It won't be a problem. Everything is fine."

Kiem paused. "Right," he said. He nodded to the footman who cleared away their teacups. "So, um. The little crest on your jacket—it's some kind of Thean family crest, right?"

"This?" Jainan said, thrown by the change of direction. He touched the emblem sewn on the collar of his tunic.

"Heraldry and stuff is a bit of, uh, a hobby of mine," Kiem said. "What's the border mean?" He seemed to mistake Jainan's hesitation for reluctance. "Or is it private?"

Jainan was so off-balance that he nearly said, *Yes, that's why my clan displays it on everything.* But even if Kiem could come up with a witty remark every second sentence when he was on a roll, as he'd proved for the last hour, Jainan himself wasn't socially adept enough to joke without causing offense. "It's not private," he said. "This is Feria's emblem. The border alters depending on your position in the clan." Kiem tilted his head, radiating interest. Jainan might have suspected him of flirting, except Jainan had watched him at the wedding, and Kiem had been like this with everyone from the journalists to the judge. Jainan kept close tabs on Kiem's body language, waiting for signs of boredom—if Jainan had known heraldry was a hobby of his, he could have led with it.

At some point Jainan looked down at the remains of the mild course and realized he had been doing most of the talking for the last ten minutes.

Kiem followed his gaze. "Huh. We seem to have run out of food." He propped an elbow on the table and raised his eyes back to Jainan's. "Coffee? We could go somewhere and get coffee. Or you could come back to my rooms—uh—I mean, our rooms?" Jainan had the distinct sense that Kiem's script hadn't gone as planned. "I guess technically you could invite me. I mean, or we could go back and not have coffee!" He waved his hands in front of his face. "Or I could go somewhere else and you could go back—or you could, uh—"

A flicker of amusement leapt up in Jainan. "Would you like to come back to my rooms for coffee, Prince Kiem?" he said gravely.

It came out before he could think too much about it. He stopped, almost wanting to take it back, but then Kiem gave a surprised, delighted smile. Jainan hadn't seen *that* smile before. He dropped his gaze back down to the table, but someone with a personality as intense as a laser cannon was focusing it all blindingly on him, and he wasn't *immune*.

"Can't think of anything I'd like better," Kiem said, abandoning the last scraps on his plate. "Shall we?"

The euphoria from their brief accord couldn't last. On the walk back to Kiem's rooms, it drained away even as Kiem kept up his stream of chatter, leaving Jainan with only low-level dread.

Even Kiem seemed more subdued and lost the thread of what he was saying as he opened the door, which was probably for the best, since Jainan hadn't heard a word he'd said in the last five minutes.

The problem was hope. Against all the evidence, some part of Jainan wondered if there was a chance that he could be good enough for Kiem tonight, if they could lay the foundations for a happy, stable marriage that would hold the treaty together. It wasn't even as if there was a logical reason for hope. Jainan knew from his grim foray into the gossip logs that Kiem had at least half a dozen previous lovers. More women than men, and every one of them beautiful, confident, looking like an effortless match for Kiem even in passing paparazzi shots. People Kiem had picked, not had forced on him. Jainan couldn't compete.

He let go of Kiem's arm once they were inside. Every movement he made felt awkward. He sat on the edge of a couch to stop himself from hovering and then realized that he was making things even more awkward—what was this, a wedding night or a polite visit? He couldn't work out what to do with his hands.

The images and vids accompanying the gossip log articles hadn't captured Kiem well: in person he had a compelling vivacity, as if he contained fractionally too much energy for the confines of his body. He turned a wall screen off, made the lights brighter and then dimmer, flashed a distracted smile at Jainan, and ended up making a beeline for the samovar. "Right! What would you like? Bel hooked up the dispenser so you can mix any flavor—"

"Just coffee," Jainan said abruptly. His tongue felt thick in his mouth. He hadn't meant to interrupt.

He swallowed in the silence that followed and listened to the mechanical clicks of hot water pouring. Kiem turned with a coffee cup in either hand. They didn't match, as if he'd inherited bits and pieces from different people; one was heavy and deep brown, the other was army issue from a division Jainan didn't recognize. He glanced up, attempting to read Kiem's face, then wished he hadn't. The easy smile wasn't there anymore.

Kiem put the larger cup down in front of Jainan. "Okay," he said. "I think something needs to be said."

Jainan didn't touch the coffee. He stared at the table beside it. "Yes?"

"There's only so far we need to go with this wedding night thing," Kiem said. He sat down heavily beside Jainan. "I mean, we can't get you separate rooms. Press Office has pretty effectively vetoed that, since they say it will get out to the newslogs. But we're in private here."

"You don't want to sleep together," Jainan said. His lips felt numb.

Kiem's arm jerked, spilling his coffee on the table. "No! I didn't say—damn." He put the cup back gingerly, his elbow brushing Jainan's. "It's not that I don't *want* to. But it's—you're—this is obviously not the best situation, and I can't imagine you, uh. We don't have to do anything, is what I mean. I can sleep on the couch."

Realization hit Jainan like a fist to the gut. He had failed so badly to communicate that Kiem assumed he was rejecting him, assumed Jainan was not even going to try to make the marriage work. Jainan was going to doom this from the start by being too cold, too stiff, too uptight.

He turned to Kiem beside him and put his hand on the back of Kiem's neck, trying to remember how to do this properly, and kissed him.

After a heart-stopping moment, Kiem responded. Jainan's heart was hammering so hard it sent a wave of dizziness to his head: he couldn't tell if it was the relief or the kiss. *Concentrate.* He didn't have to be terrible at this. He was focusing so hard that he almost missed the little pleased noise Kiem made when they broke apart, and Jainan stopped in shock when he realized what it was.

Luckily, it didn't seem to matter. Kiem took a breath and

bent his head, kissing Jainan's neck. It was good—of course it was good, Kiem knew what he was doing—and for a peculiar moment, the constant tension in Jainan's head disappeared. It was replaced by an odd sense of openness, like light flooding in through a window. Was that the alcohol? Jainan didn't care. He opened the first few buttons of Kiem's shirt, shaky with relief. It was working.

Kiem's hands closed over his. Jainan stopped.

"Is everything all right?" Kiem said. Jainan looked up at his face. Kiem was frowning.

The shaking. Jainan took a deep breath, made himself still. He could do this. This had worked before. "Yes?" He made his voice softer, persuasive. "Do we have to stop?"

Kiem broke into a smile, though it was only an echo of the one earlier. He tried to kiss Jainan again, but Jainan was already on his feet, tugging Kiem up and toward the bedroom. Kiem was suggestible, which made it both easier and harder than Jainan was expecting, but they reached the bed soon enough. Jainan slid Kiem's shirt off, and Kiem obligingly shrugged his arms out of it and reached for the clasps of Jainan's jacket.

Kiem's fingertips were warm. That, of all things, was the most destabilizing sensation. Jainan caught himself on his elbows as he lay back on the bed. He had no time to dissect this sudden strange feeling that had nothing to do with the marriage or the treaty and everything to do with Kiem's fingers on his chest. The pounding of his heart started to change cadence. He pushed himself up on his elbows. He had to concentrate, he had to control himself, Kiem would notice if he wasn't concentrating—

Kiem pushed away. The air that had been too hot around Jainan was suddenly too cold. Jainan opened his eyes, a flash of panic rising, and then he saw Kiem's disconcerted expression. The panic crystallized into dismay, a dismay that ran through him like mercury, no less unpleasant because he knew it had been inevitable. Jainan had failed.

He should have sat up immediately and reached out. He should have acted surprised that Kiem might want to stop. But instead he just lay there as a wave of numbness swept over him. And in that moment, he saw Kiem's expression harden.

"I'm sorry," Kiem said. His voice was quiet. Jainan apparently wasn't the only one who could change his voice to hide his feelings. "I'll go."

Jainan opened his mouth to say, *Don't,* and then he shut it again. He couldn't dictate who Kiem wanted to sleep with. He'd thought he could hurry them both into it and hide the sliver of ice inside himself that made him disappointing, but he'd been wrong. *The problem isn't someone's type. The problem is you.* He couldn't force Kiem to be attracted to him.

"I'll go," Jainan said, instead.

"*No,*" Kiem said, almost violently. Jainan held very still, but Kiem wasn't looking at him. He was on his feet, opening drawers at random until he found some sort of cloth—a bedsheet. "Never mind. We'll sort something out. I don't—make yourself at home. I'm sorry." The door slid open, and while Jainan was still pushing himself up, protests on the tip of his tongue, Kiem had left.

The door slid shut before Jainan could reach it. He stood frozen in front of it, his hand just outside the reach of the sensor trigger, the blank, white surface only inches from his face. He could go through. It wasn't locked.

But what would he say? There was no way to fix this.

He turned away. Kiem had made his intentions clear: Jainan had the whole room to himself, and Kiem would make his own arrangements. Jainan looked at the bed. Everything in him recoiled. He briefly entertained the thought of sleeping on a chair, or on the floor, but dismissed the idea as ridiculous. He was not someone who made dramatic gestures. He was practical, and discreet, and a dependable partner. He didn't have to be liked.

He lay back on the bed and stared at the white ceiling. Sleep would come. It always did.

CHAPTER 5

"I'm going to geo-tag you," Bel informed Kiem when he came through the door the next morning. "I checked all your usual breakfast spots and couldn't find you. I even checked the janitors' canteen. Answer your *messages*."

"Sorry," Kiem said, swallowing the last of his breakfast roll. Morning light streamed through the window, highlighting the folded bedsheet on the back of the sofa more clearly than he would have liked. The bedroom door was still shut. He assumed Jainan was asleep. "I went for a walk."

Bel gave him a disbelieving look. "By yourself?"

"Yeah," Kiem said. Bel didn't lose the skeptical look. He added, "I met a security guard when I was in the Ash Garden. We had a nice chat. Told me about tree borers or something."

"Well, that's a relief," Bel said. "I was starting to think you were coming down with something." She flicked her fingers and sent his calendar to the wall screen. "You're down to meet the Auditor this afternoon. The Resolution calls it *instation*, but I understand it's just an official confirmation of you two as the Thean representatives."

"Great, great," Kiem said. He supposed it couldn't go worse than last night. "I'm ready to be instated. I'm so official and responsible it makes elderly monks weep. What else?"

"You're still scheduled for a College event this morning. Are you planning to go to it, or has the Emperor given you a new schedule now that you're married?"

Kiem hadn't even thought of that. "She didn't say anything like that." He looked at the rest of the calendar, which showed the usual roster of events and charity bashes. "We need to show up for the Resolution ceremonies—and Unification Day, of course—but she didn't give me anything else official. Hren said she wants to keep the whole marriage low-key. Only necessary press."

Bel gave a quiet *hah*. Her opinion of Hren Halesar wasn't high. "I hope Press Office is really enjoying today's coverage, then. Want to see the reports? They made me laugh," she added, which was never a good sign.

"Let's see the damage." Kiem threw himself onto the couch. It was going to be a far cry from the glowing coverage of Jainan's first wedding. "Shit, Jainan's schedule. I should have asked him—" He broke off, glancing at the closed door of the bedroom.

"He's awake," Bel said. "He went out to exercise in the garden."

"He did?" Kiem crossed over to the big windows and looked out into the courtyard gardens, where slender trees rose from between the paths in the shadow of the palace towers. The sun glowed white behind a haze of freezing mist.

Jainan was a whirl of movement in the space between the trees. He held a stick in his hands and went through some kind of martial arts drill like it was a dance, so fast that the stick was almost blurred as he spun and thrust. His undershirt left his arms bare to the shoulder even in the morning cold. His feet crunched into the frosted grass. Kiem stared.

"Quarterstaff," Bel said. "It's a Thean thing. I'll send you a primer."

Kiem made himself turn away from the window, rubbing a hand across his forehead. He had no right to be staring, not after he had screwed up so spectacularly last night. "Right. Yeah. Thanks." He should at least know what it was, if Jainan was that good at it.

"Headache?" Bel said. She was giving him her neutral private secretary look.

"Sort of," Kiem said. He saw her glance at the folded sheet

and groaned. "Oh, look, *fine*. I might need another pillow for the couch. Don't leak it to the newslogs."

Bel, uncharacteristically, hesitated. "I can get you another bed."

"Not worth the risk," Kiem said.

"A folding bed, then," Bel said.

"The couch is fine."

"The couch is *not* fine. Nobody will see a folding bed."

Kiem found he was leaning back against the wall. He drummed his fingers on it. He wasn't used to feeling defensive. "Yeah, all right. Whatever."

"Kiem," Bel said bluntly. "Are you okay?"

Kiem opened his mouth, then shut it again. How did you *say* that? How did you say, *My partner thinks it's his duty to sleep with me, even though he isn't into it in the slightest?* Kiem hadn't ever been in bed with someone who wasn't fully on board with the idea, and he'd now discovered he didn't like it one bit. He couldn't remember what he'd done to give Jainan the wrong impression. He'd thought Jainan had been flirting. He'd been badly wrong.

But none of those were things he could air out of the bedroom, even to Bel. "Yeah. It's not *me* you should be feeling sorry for." He gave his best nonchalant shrug. "Could have been worse. I know a whole bunch about heraldry now. Ask me about clan patterns. Now let's see those cuttings."

He reached over to the table for the red press folder, a collection of text filmies between discreet blank covers. It updated itself every day but he usually dipped into it once a week or so, just to check that there wasn't anything awful. As he sat down and opened it, a fan of images reshuffled themselves above their accompanying articles. Most of them showed the post-wedding kiss or the official final photo—Jainan's smile was sweet and dignified, Kiem's looked inane, but that was normal—but a couple of the newslogs had gone with shots of them signing the contracts. Kiem's hand still had red ink on it.

Kiem looked morbidly over the headlines that went with

them. *Restrained but romantic: Prince Kiem marries Thean count in discreet ceremony.* The Resolution and the treaty renewal had been discreetly relegated to the second paragraph. And another one: *Prince K's royal wedding—it's the perfect match.* They'd put in the quotes from his press statement, which he'd virtuously stuck to during all the interviews afterward. Kiem was usually not that bothered about press coverage, unless it actually got him exiled, but he could imagine what Jainan would think when he saw those articles. Most of them had raked up Taam as well, in a "tragically grieving Jainan finds love again" way that made Kiem feel ill. It would almost have been better if they'd gone all-out on the Galactic politics.

"Turn over," Bel said.

"I don't think I want to." Kiem turned to the back, where the press office usually put the negatives. Two images appeared of them all trying to rescue the documents from a pool of spilled ink and Kiem looking perilously close to laughing. Luckily they hadn't gotten Jainan in those shots. Then the third came up.

The kiss itself was fine. There were only so many ways a kiss could photograph badly. But one of the aggregators had managed to get Kiem approaching Jainan just a few seconds before it, and it was easy to read the panic on Kiem's face. *Forced for the Galactics?* the headline blared. *Playboy prince hitched to Thean after last partner's death.*

Kiem slammed the folder shut and put his head in his hands. He bet that had been Dak. They'd have blacklisted whoever sold the photo, but that didn't help *now.* "Don't show Jainan that," he said. "Do you think he reads the news? Shit, of course he reads the news."

"How much context do you want?" Bel said. She held out another folder.

Kiem looked up at her. It was the same press-office red, but it had a different serial number on the front. "Where did you get this?" He opened it to find the folder packed with headlines and tiny newslog articles, so dense that he had to touch an individual article to enlarge it. The one he'd picked turned out to be something incomprehensible about trade tariffs. The newslog it came from was unfamiliar.

"Press Office. It's a copy of the Thean Affairs folder," Bel said. "Thean sources. I thought you might want to stay up to date, but I'll send it back if you don't."

Kiem nodded slowly. The mass of text made his brain hurt, but it usually paid to listen to Bel. "I guess we should have it for Jainan, anyway."

"Jainan—that was another thing," Bel said. She turned to the desk and picked up a pearly, bubble-like diagnostic shell wrapped around a wristband that wasn't hers. She threw the diagnostic display up on the wall. It blinked up an error and a passphrase request. "Jainan and Prince Taam seemed to have shared accounts. Prince Taam's has been deactivated, so the system keeps trying to wipe Jainan's."

"Wait, wait, wait," Kiem said, holding up his hands. "Shared *personal* accounts? Maybe Jainan and Taam shared an official account."

"Jainan said he didn't have an official one," Bel said. "This is the only one the wristband has access to." She clasped her fingers together, and the warning disappeared. "His account was a subsidiary. If he gave his passphrase I could tie it to yours instead, but then you'd be able to see his messages."

Kiem pressed his knuckles against his forehead. Every time he turned around he seemed to see the shadow of Jainan and Taam's marriage. It seemed pretty unlikely that he and Jainan would ever be close enough to read each other's messages. It didn't even sound that romantic to Kiem, which was probably further proof they were badly matched.

"We're not really that close," he said. He remembered last night and winced. "We're definitely not that close. What if we—"

The garden doors slid open. Kiem and Bel both turned as

Jainan paused in the doorway. He was slightly flushed from the exercise but not breathing heavily. He held something that Kiem realized was the stick, telescoped down to carry. "I'm sorry," he said, "I was just outside."

Kiem stared at the stick—the quarterstaff—which had folded down to something bronze-sheened and no larger than Jainan's hand. It kept Kiem's eyes away from Jainan's face and disordered hair, which were reminding him of last night in a distracting way. "Uh, good morning," he said. "Nice morning for . . . martial art things. Right?"

There was a short pause. "Yes," Jainan said. He sounded wary, which was understandable, because Kiem was making no sense at all. "Did you want me? I was late getting up and couldn't see you anywhere."

"No, no, not at all, I mean, yes, I mean—wristband! Right!" Kiem turned to the screen, trying to dispel last night's memories. The screen was still showing the passphrase request. "Bel says your wristband—"

Jainan was already looking up at the display. "Oh," he said. "I'm sorry." He crossed to the table and picked up the diagnostic bubble. The pearly gel yielded when he pressed a finger into it to activate the wristband's print sensor. "I didn't realize it needed another pass." He whispered a passphrase.

The error screen cleared and the wall filled with messages. Kiem blinked, not sure what he was seeing, and then realized they were Jainan's and looked away.

Jainan was watching him. "Was that all?"

Kiem cleared his throat. "Press Office sent over the cuttings from the wedding." He turned to the folders on the low table. "Do you want to have a look? It's not pretty."

Jainan placed his quarterstaff on a side table, neatly aligning it with the edge. When he turned back, he seemed a shade more sallow, but his expression hadn't changed. Kiem might have imagined the reaction. "I would like to see."

Kiem handed him the folders. He hadn't been careful; his fingers nearly brushed Jainan's arm, and Jainan all but dropped the folder trying not to touch him. Kiem hastily stepped back, wondering how he'd gotten it so wrong last night as to think Jainan actually wanted physical contact. But there wasn't anything he could do about that, so he turned away to give Jainan some space and poked at the diagnostic shell. It looked like Jainan's passphrase had automatically bound their accounts together. Surely there was a way to fix that.

"These are the interviews you did after the ceremony," Jainan said, without looking up. He had turned to the other folder. "I apologize that I didn't stay."

"You had to pack," Kiem said. "No need to apologize. Anyway, some of the articles came out pretty rubbish, sorry about that, did my best. Anything about us in the Thean folder?"

"There are a number of articles," Jainan said, skimming the thick blocks of text. He couldn't possibly have had time to read all of that. "Most of them are neutral; the tone is fairly standard for our—I mean, for Thea's mainstream outlets." He paused, glanced at Kiem, and then said, "I am afraid the fringe newslogs are much more volatile. Many of them are less than complimentary about Iskat. Four of them name me as a traitor to the planet."

"What?" Kiem said, nearly fumbling the diagnostic shell. "That's ridiculous. That's *offensive*." Jainan gave a miniscule shrug, his eyes still skimming over the folder. Kiem strode a couple of abortive paces across the room and turned back. "Can we blacklist them? Bel?"

"They were never on the list in the first place," Bel said. "They're Thean outlets. You might as well invite the Sefalan gossip logs."

"But they can't just *make up*—" Kiem started, then broke off when he saw Jainan try to say something. Jainan shut his mouth. "Go on."

It took Jainan a moment to apparently reformulate his sentence. "There is a great deal of detail here."

He'd gone back to Kiem's post-wedding interviews. Kiem frowned, distracted from his indignation, and tried to remember what he'd said. "Is there?" He thought he'd been pretty impersonal, but he was used to the press. "Which bit?"

"The—" Jainan paused, and his finger skated over several articles as if he didn't want to touch them. "No, it's not important." He looked back at Kiem. "I was just going to shower."

"Right," Kiem said. "We'll—Bel will fix your wristband. We're meeting the Auditor this afternoon, and I have to go to a reception at the College first. How do you feel about university visits?"

"I can be ready in ten minutes," Jainan said.

That was heartening news and distracted Kiem from the whole press debacle. At least there was *something* they could do together that didn't involve romantic dinners that bored Jainan to sleep. "Take your time; it doesn't start until eleven. Is there anything you need?"

"No," Jainan said. It would have been abrupt, but he had an odd habit of leaving a pause afterward, as if it was open to negotiation. He waited for a moment, then disappeared into the bathroom. Bel pulled the messages off the wall and took Jainan's wristband into the study, leaving Kiem by himself with the newslog articles.

"Minor problems," Kiem said to the accusing spread of press folders. The Thean one was currently showing a newslog image of a Thean politician who looked very much like Lady Ressid. "A few articles, one bad night, so what? Don't look at me like that. I can fix this." He shut the folder and stared at the wall.

Arlusk wasn't even the biggest city on the planet—there were industrial settlements on other continents and a data-sink sprawl farther toward the ice-covered south—but it was the oldest. The Imperial College, Iskat's principal state-affiliated university, was in the part of town built in the first flush of enthusiasm after the colony started to thrive. The grand granite facades and shabby modulus builds were as familiar to Kiem as his own living room.

This was an official visit, though, so he and Jainan sat in the back of one of the palace's official flyers as it crawled slowly downhill. Bel had booked a palace chauffeur and sent them off with a briefing pack in a folder, since Jainan's wristband still wasn't working, and an injunction to Kiem not to promise any-one funding under any circumstances.

Now the briefing folder glowed gently on Jainan's lap as he sat facing Kiem. Jainan seemed deeply immersed in the mundane de-tails of the Imperial College, so with an enormous effort, Kiem had managed not to say anything for the last five minutes. The back seats had always seemed like more space than you really needed, but right now Kiem was acutely aware of where his feet were and had moved them several times to avoid touching Jainan's.

Kiem's wristband pinged. "Oh, right," he said, forgetting he was trying to be quiet. Jainan looked up, and since Kiem had al-ready disturbed him, he decided to read the message off anyway. "Bel's warning us that there'll be a couple of photographers. I suppose there's interest because of the wedding."

"Is that a problem?" Jainan said.

"Not really," Kiem said. "They'll probably just want shots of us and the chancellor—or me and the chancellor, if you don't want to be in it. You probably did all that with Taam."

"Taam didn't do many charity events," Jainan said. He paused to pick his words, which seemed to be a habit of his. "His position made a lot of demands on his time."

"Right, of course," Kiem said. "He was a—a colonel, right? Not much time for fundraisers." Taam had done something more useful with his life than Kiem and entered the military as an officer. Kiem didn't think Taam had commanded a ship, but he'd been fairly high up the chain. Kiem had a vague idea that his unit was involved in mining operations.

Jainan didn't answer the question. He was looking out the window as they went through the Imperial College's sweeping, spired gates, which were gray against the shower of snow they'd had that morning and in need of recoating. "I've been here before," he said. "I came to a public lecture a few years ago."

"Wow, and you understood it?" Kiem said. "I studied here. Dropped out before exams came around." It had been the climax of an inglorious school career and hadn't come as a huge surprise to anyone, least of all his mother or the Emperor, but telling the newslogs had been uncomfortable. "Turns out being royal can only take you so far if you don't have the brains."

"I'm sure you do," Jainan said, then stopped. "You must—well."

Kiem realized that sounded like he was fishing for compliments and hastily tried to fix it. "No, honestly, thick as a brick. Ask any of my ex-professors. I got on with them all right, though, so last year they asked me to be one of the patrons anyway. Don't need to be a good student for that."

Jainan had his finger on his place in one of Kiem's ex-professors' biographies. "I'm sorry," Jainan said, "I don't think I can remember everything in this. Is there anything you want me to say to anyone in particular?"

"You don't have to *remember* the briefing," Kiem said, somewhat appalled. "You'd go mad if you tried to remember it. It's just there in case you wanted to look something up. You'll want to talk to the professors in your doctorate subject, won't you? Sorry, I'm no good at science; you'll have to remind me what it was in."

"Nothing important," Jainan said as the flyer came to a halt and settled to the ground. He closed the folder.

"Uh," Kiem said. "Right." He surreptitiously checked his wristband for his own briefing.

The reception was in a vast central hall, which had peeling paint on the walls and an echo that magnified the conversations of the hundred or so donors and staff members mingling there. The chairs were the same cheap ones Kiem remembered sitting on in lectures. The excuse for the reception was the artwork from graduating students temporarily lining the walls, and Kiem made vague appreciative noises at it as their student escort towed them toward the Imperial College chancellor.

"Ah! Your Highness! Glad you could make it!" the Chancellor boomed. She was a statuesque figure in tweed and pearls and smart braids, and she turned away from her conversation to bow to them. An ornate flint buckle winked from her belt. "And this must be Count Jainan. Honored by your presence, Your Grace. I do apologize for the journalists. We have to let them in, you know." She waved a hand at a short, round girl in flowing fabrics that Kiem recognized as Hani Sereson's partner, whom he'd last seen behind a cam lens just after he'd fallen into the central canal. She gave them a brilliant smile and started taking rapid-fire photos. Jainan, in the corner of Kiem's vision, seemed to shift very subtly into the background. Kiem moved forward to cover him and gave the camera a wave.

"And congratulations, may I say?" the Chancellor continued, turning to Jainan. "Let me shake your hand." Jainan's eyebrows rose slightly as she crushed his hand in her grip. Kiem grinned at him and also accepted a bone-bruising handshake. "Always a delight to have palace support. A delight."

"No, no, pleasure's all mine," Kiem said, extracting his hand, somewhat the worse for wear. "Especially since I know several professors are thinking something about bad pennies turning up. Have you met Jainan, by the way?" The photographer finished a last set of shots and moved on. "He came to one of your lectures a while ago. Has a doctorate in deep-space engineering—extraction of something I can't pronounce from asteroids. I can now come to this sort of thing on his coattails."

Jainan looked embarrassed. "It was a long time ago," he said. "And it was nothing groundbreaking."

"Oh come on, it's still a *doctorate*," Kiem said. This just succeeded in making Jainan freeze up.

"Can't have been that long ago," the Chancellor said. "*Long ago* is for us decrepit wrecks to use." She caught the arm of a professor going past them in a black official gown. "Isn't that right, Professor Audel?"

"Eh?" Professor Audel said, turning around. Her long, graying hair straggled down her back, held out of her face with clips. "Decrepit wrecks? You or me?"

"I think the Chancellor's implying some of us are young and irresponsible," Kiem said, holding out his hand again. "Pleased to meet you, Professor. What field do you work in?"

"Professor Audel is one of our foremost engineering experts," the Chancellor said. "Audel, Count Jainan is an academic engineer from Thea. You three must have a lot to talk about." She clapped both Jainan and Professor Audel on the shoulder and shook Kiem's hand again, pulverizing the few bones that she'd left intact on the last round. "Do excuse me, sire. Must get to the old meeting-and-greeting. Look forward to talking to you later. I'm sure you'll be asking all your normal questions about our outreach programs."

Kiem had been deputized by two separate charities to do just that, and he shrugged good-humoredly. "You know me too well, Chancellor."

"Regolith extraction, eh?" Professor Audel was saying. "Interesting, *very* interesting. We have four people on regolith rigs and solar shielding right now. There's a lot of crossover with the military, who as usual have ninety-nine percent of all the available funding. And of course, the question is huge on Thea."

"Yes," Jainan said. "I think we have a good half of the Iskat military's mining capability in our sector. I'm afraid I haven't paid much attention to it in the last few years."

"Of course," Professor Audel said. "Politically *fraught*, though, isn't it, with the revenue sharing agreement and the close-planet debris issue. Now, the equipment problem on the larger asteroids is the cracking issue in places like the Alethena Basin—"

"I don't believe that's actually the issue there," Jainan said. It was diffident, but it was an actual interruption—the first real one Kiem had ever heard him make. Kiem paid closer attention. "I think it was shown that the stabilizer seeding there in fact failed owing to fluctuations in the environmental radiation."

"Well that's—hm. Jainan." Professor Audel peered at him, her eyes sharp in her wrinkled face. "You're not J. Erenlith who published that thesis on regoliths, are you?"

"I—" Jainan said, then stopped, flustered. Kiem suppressed his I-told-you-so grin. "I—that was a long time ago."

"Excellent!" Professor Audel said. "I suspected it was a nobility pseudonym. That explains why I never found the author. We must get you in for a consultation."

For some reason Jainan glanced sideways at Kiem. "I don't know if I can commit to that."

"Have you moved into another field?" Professor Audel asked. "Surely you can still do a consultation."

"That—depends," Jainan said. He looked at Kiem again. "Am I likely to have time?"

"Time?" Kiem said, bemused. As far as he knew, Jainan's schedule wasn't packed, or surely they'd have had people chasing Bel already. On the other hand, if Jainan didn't want to do it, the time excuse was a good one, but why ask him? "Well, depends what else you're planning to pick up. Up to you, of course." He couldn't help adding, "For what it's worth, I think it's a good idea."

Jainan inclined his head. "I would be glad to consult, Professor," he said. "Though I can't promise I remember anything useful."

"You never forget how to calculate," she said. "And fresh eyes will be invaluable. Now, about the solar radiation. Did you consider the knock-on impact of the inner system adjustment—"

Kiem didn't understand one sentence in three of the conversation that followed, but he watched, absorbed, as Jainan quietly but fluently rose to the professor's challenges with answers Kiem couldn't even begin to grasp. It was like watching a musician transform when they picked up a violin. After a few minutes, though, Kiem realized from Jainan's sideways glances and de-railing attempts that Jainan was concerned he was bored. As it would be completely inappropriate for Kiem to say, *No, I could watch you do this all day,* he murmured something instead about leaving them to it and went to find the Chancellor and badger her about outreach programs.

That led to ten conversations with other people. Kiem en-joyed these events; he did have to accept several compliments on his marriage, but somehow that didn't feel as awkward now as it might have been. "I see Audel's cornered your partner," one ad-junct remarked, as they both stood in front of an artwork doing something thematic with coat hangers. "Does he want rescuing?"

"He's fine," Kiem said. He considered name-dropping Jainan's thesis but refrained because he wasn't entirely sure how to pro-nounce some of the words in the title.

"Audel must be over the moon," the adjunct said knowingly. Kiem thought he might be in engineering as well. "She's been waiting to get her hands on someone who worked on Kingfisher."

"Kingfisher?" Kiem said blankly.

"The mining operation," the adjunct said. He turned away from the coat hangers and tilted his head. "You know? Prince Taam ran Operation Kingfisher. The Thean mining venture—you *must* know, it was in the news when the extraction probe exploded. Two people died."

Kiem didn't remember. He didn't usually pay attention to news that didn't involve him. "I don't think Jainan's working on that. He's not military." Surely if Jainan was working on an operation he'd have meetings in his schedule, deadlines, that sort of thing. Kiem honestly had no idea what a normal job involved. "Two people *died*?"

"Deep-space mining is no joke, Your Highness," the adjunct said. "That's why the military runs it."

When Kiem went to find Jainan again, Professor Audel had roped in some of her graduate students to the discussion. Whatever it was that had brought Jainan's dark eyes to life had intensified, and when he raised one slim hand to make a point, Kiem had to stop himself from staring *again*. Kiem slowed his steps, reluctant to interrupt. But when Jainan caught sight of him, he politely extracted himself from the conversation of his own accord and was by Kiem's arm a few moments later. "Sorry. I got caught up."

"Me too," Kiem said. "Lots of well-wishes to pass on to you. Consider them passed on. Someone mentioned Operation Kingfisher?"

"Taam's operation," Jainan said at once. He frowned, puzzled. "Did they want to talk to me about it? Someone else is in charge now."

Kiem wasn't going to bad-mouth Taam in front of his bereaved partner. "Just a mention," he said hastily. "Complimentary!"

"I wasn't involved in it, really," Jainan said, sounding almost regretful. "There was an obvious conflict of interest for a Thean. I'm sorry, I'm holding us up—did you want to leave?"

"Well, unless Professor Audel wants to adopt you," Kiem said. "She looked well on the way to it."

Jainan paused. "Does that cause any problems for you?"

"Me?" Kiem said. "Oh, you mean with the charity links and stuff? No, no, it's great for me, the more we do for the Chancellor, the more I can push her to put resources into outreach. And *that* gets three separate education execs off my back."

"I'm glad," Jainan said, and he did actually—for the first time since Kiem had met him—sound pleased.

Kiem grinned. "Roaring success," he said. "Let's get lunch. We both need a break. Ready for the Auditor?" He didn't realize he'd offered Jainan his arm until Jainan took it. Then it was too late, but Jainan seemed as relaxed as Kiem had ever seen him.

"Of course," Jainan said. As they emerged from the hall into the courtyard, a light dusting of snow started to fall.

CHAPTER 6

The Auditor's temporary office, deep in the palace, had once been an innocent reception chamber before the Galactic delegation turned it into a cave for Resolution business. The walls were now covered with screens, though the screens didn't act the way Kiem was used to; they unrolled like tapestries and had a solidity that a light-screen lacked. They showed lists of data and images, seemingly unconnected to each other, and the junior staff moving around the covered walls somehow manipulated the images without obviously gesturing at them.

Some of the displays Kiem expected, like the prominent web of faces and names that showed the treaty representatives. The Emperor was at the top. Connected to her by a web of lines were a handful of faces Kiem didn't know, but their clothing styles suggested they were the vassal representatives. Next to each one was an Iskaner prince. CONFIRMED glowed in pale letters beside each face. There were two gaps: he and Jainan must be the last two to be instated.

It wasn't only the screens that were weird. Parts of the room were sectioned off by curtain-like shimmers. Some of them were slate gray, hiding whatever was beyond them, but some were transparent: two staffers stood behind one in a corner, obviously talking, but no sound made it through the shimmer.

Another slate-gray curtain fuzzed and parted like water as the Auditor stepped through it. Kiem took a sharp breath. He was never going to get used to the Auditor's face, like a cloud of luminous gas had swallowed half of it. He didn't know where to look.

"Count Jainan," the Auditor said. His voice sounded jarringly like a normal human's. "Prince Kiem. Please be seated, and we'll run you through the process."

"Sounds painful," Kiem said, then exchanged a glance with Jainan—who didn't smile—and regretted joking. They followed the Auditor through the curtain. There was a table set up with a gel hand-sensor in the middle and a few chairs that were mercifully free of Resolution weirdness.

The Resolution weirdness was supplied in full measure by the Auditor, who summoned a junior staffer to the table with no apparent signal then took a seat across from Kiem and Jainan and stared at them. Kiem assumed he was staring. It was hard to tell.

"I am role four-seven-five," the Auditor said, apparently as a polite introduction. "My committees are Renewal—sub-chair; Low-Population Sectors—member; Artifact Nonproliferation—member. I have 0.0052 voting shares, currently suspended for duties." He gestured to the staffer next to him. "My colleagues on this assignment are un-roled."

The staffer who sat next to the Auditor was more normal: a young, official person with a checklist and an intricately bordered collar that probably had some meaning for Galactics. "I am about to ask you some personal questions," the staffer said politely, without offering a name. "I apologize for any offense caused."

"I can't imagine what offense you'd cause," Kiem said, nonplussed. "Er. Jainan?"

"I have nothing to hide," Jainan said, looking straight at the Auditor's nauseating lack of a face.

It turned out neither of them did. As the staffer worked their way down the list, Kiem and Jainan answered with their full, official titles, their birthplaces and dates, their precise position in the governing hierarchies of their respective planets. The staffer wanted to know about Taam, and Jainan gave his details in a careful, emotionless voice. The checklist dwelled on their right to speak for their planets: Kiem described his meeting with the Emperor, and Jainan gave them a copy of some document from the Thean president. They gave their biometrics—the handprint scanner felt odd and clung to Kiem's palm in a way he wasn't entirely comfortable with. The Auditor watched them, unmoving, but the swirling shell clinging to his face moved whenever either of them spoke.

"And your genetic parentage?" the staffer asked.

"This is going to take a while," Kiem said cheerfully. "Prince Alkie and Sarvi Tegnar were my principals—there's a statutory minimum from the royal side for inheritance—but I've got ten gifters, and you'll need my genome record for who gave what. My mother even got General Fenrik to donate some pairs," he said as an aside to Jainan, "*that* obviously didn't take. I think he's still embarrassed about it."

The staffer entered that on a screen. "And Your Grace . . . ?"

The Auditor spoke, his head angled toward Jainan. "I believe Thea has a cultural taboo against discussing genetic inheritance—you should have the background downloaded."

"Ah," the staffer said, after a pause. Their eye-screen flickered. "You can pass us a redacted version."

Kiem finally looked at Jainan, who was showing some emotion for the first time in this whole meeting: he was visibly mortified. It was starting to dawn on Kiem how much he didn't know about Thean etiquette. "No," Jainan said, after clearing his throat. "My parents are core Feria. You may have my full genetic record, but you will have to request it from my clan."

The staffer nodded and entered something on their checklist. They gestured to the Auditor, who leaned forward.

"Have you ever been involved in the study of remnants?"

"What?" Kiem said. He remembered the glowing shard on the Emperor's display table. "No. I'm not an archaeologist."

Jainan shook his head. "My field is deep-space engineering.

I believe Thea has given you a list of every remnant discovered since the last renewal."

Kiem was starting to get a handle on the Auditor's body language, he found. At least, he could tell when that cosmically unpleasant attention was landing on him rather than Jainan.

"Iskat has found a relative abundance of them this time around," the Auditor said. "Some remnants were inexplicably missed on the last few contacts you had with the Resolution, but fortunately they have come to light in recent years. Including a notable major remnant, which you seem to have used to construct a therapeutic machine."

"Have we?" Kiem said.

"The list refers to it as powering a 'Tau field.'"

"That's not for therapy," Kiem said blankly. That was a nasty part of Iskat's history in the previous century, now something from low-budget war dramas. "It's—I don't know, some sort of interrogation field? I thought it had been dismantled. I didn't know it had a remnant in it."

The Auditor's lips flattened in what Kiem realized was a smile, as if Kiem had sidestepped some sort of difficult question. The assistant noted something down.

"Taam—Prince Taam—was your cousin?" the Auditor said, with a slight, almost undetectable emphasis on *cousin*.

"Yes. Through the Emperor. My grandmother."

"And you were put in the chain of responsibility via your wedding," the Auditor said. "Which was when . . . ?"

"Yesterday," Kiem said. As he said it, it sounded uncomfortably thin. He realized he was tapping his foot and stopped himself. This couldn't be pleasant for Jainan either.

The junior staffer looked at the Auditor at some signal Kiem didn't catch. "Thank you," they said formally. "That concludes the interview." It did? Kiem felt he should have added more detail, but the staffer was already dismissing them. "If you could wait outside the privacy screen?"

Jainan was on his feet before they'd finished speaking. Kiem didn't blame him. The *privacy screen* parted around them again—Kiem couldn't help shutting his eyes as he stepped through it—and left them in the main room, with a sea of moving visualizations on the walls around them.

"That was fun," Kiem said. "Sorry about the genetics part. Do you think they're grading us?"

"I don't know," Jainan said. He glanced around the walls with a tense, hunted look. Kiem couldn't make head or tail of the displays. The Auditor seemed to be collecting data like a magpie—one section had extracts from modern history articles; another, population estimates; this one, some paragraphs from the Foundation laws. Another one was about electromagnetic space fluctuations in the Outer Belt—Jainan's attention lingered there—and another seemed to be about stage magicians and hypnotists. There was no pattern.

Kiem was diverted by a flicker of movement. "Hey, it's us," he said. "Finally." The web of treaty representatives on one wall shifted to make room for pictures of Kiem and Jainan's faces, filling the last two gaps.

The tag that flashed up beneath them said UNCONFIRMED.

"Looks like they didn't like us," Kiem said. It was meant as a joke—this was probably just a paperwork delay—but Jainan didn't seem to take it as a joke at all. He had gone still in a way that reminded Kiem of someone standing on the edge of a cliff.

The privacy screen dissolved once more as the Auditor stepped through, trailed by his staffer. "Thank you for your time," the staffer said serenely. "You may go."

"Excuse me," Jainan said. "What does our status mean?"

"Your Emperor will—" the staffer began.

"Wait," Kiem said. The Auditor, standing coolly separate from his own staff as if he were another species, was starting to get on his nerves. Kiem gave a polite nod to the staffer and stepped past them, putting himself in front of the Auditor. "I think you owe us an explanation. The treaty renewal is in three weeks. How long does it take to confirm us?"

Kiem was now standing disturbingly close to the swirling shell across the Auditor's face. Kiem's eyes suggested urgently that staring at it was bad for him, so Kiem tried looking at the embroidery on the Auditor's shirt designs, at his ear, and finally at the wall beyond. The Auditor focused on him.

"One purpose of the audit is to ensure the parties are authorized to speak for their planets," the Auditor said, his voice as calm and rational as a textbook readout. "The Resolution cannot confirm Iskat and Thea are entering into the treaty voluntarily when the designated Iskat representative was murdered last month."

The silence was like sudden pressure on Kiem's hearing.

"Murdered?" he said. "No. Wait. That's not—that's not what happened." He glanced over at Jainan, who had a strange, calm look in his eyes, as if his whole world had just cracked and there was nothing he could do about it.

"The aggregated data suggests otherwise," the Auditor said, as precisely and unemotionally as if he were talking about the weather. His face shell was moving constantly now—Kiem had the feeling it would be changing color, if he could recognize any of the colors in it. "Thean news sources show discontent from multiple angles. Official communications have broken down. When the Thean representative requests sight of the investigation into the death of a politically bonded partner, and is denied . . ." He shrugged, an oddly human motion. "I cannot instate either of you at this point."

"Denied what?" Kiem said. He'd missed something.

"No," Jainan said, as if he understood.

The Auditor turned away. His shell had stopped moving, as if he had lost interest in further conversation, and the staffer smoothly stepped in front of him to prevent Kiem from following the Auditor behind the privacy screen.

"The instation process is not up for debate," the staffer said. They sounded perfectly reasonable. Kiem might have felt less off-balance if they'd shouted.

"There must be an appeal," Jainan said, something desperately controlled in his voice. "Or a process for—for replacement. We must have a treaty."

He wasn't wrong. Kiem started to realize how serious this was. The Resolution treated each comma of its interplanetary agreements like a law of nature. If Iskat and Thea couldn't provide representatives that satisfied them, there wouldn't be a treaty. And if there wasn't a treaty, Iskat's peace terms with the rest of the universe would have all the formal weight of something scrawled on the back of a napkin. Surely this was some sort of temporary setback, though. Everyone *wanted* a treaty.

"The Auditor is still processing the political context," the staffer said. In the first flash of personality they'd shown, they glanced at Kiem and said, "Your partner has apparently not been entirely honest with you."

"Jainan?" Kiem said, nonplussed. Jainan just shook his head. Kiem filed that away as *ask later*. "Look," he said to the staffer, "you have to do something. The Emperor isn't going to be happy."

"The Auditor will discuss it with your Emperor," the staffer said politely. "You are, of course, free to do the same."

Kiem would have paid money to see the Emperor and the Auditor trying to out-stonewall each other under less important circumstances. "All right!" he said. "All right. You talk to the Emperor. We'll ask the palace about Taam's accident. And then we can fill in your form Thirty-Four B or whatever and get this sorted."

"We appreciate your cooperation," the staffer said. The data on the walls moved around, patternless and chaotic. The UNCON-FIRMED tags beside Jainan's and Kiem's pictures didn't change.

The door shut behind them as they left. There were officials passing in the corridor, but a sharp right turn took them to a landing on a quiet staircase, where an arched window looked out on the dome of the palace shrine and the grand entrance hall behind it.

Jainan stopped as soon as they had some privacy and immediately turned to Kiem. There were lines of tension around his eyes. The shrine dome framed his head and shoulders, making his figure seem smaller. "I have not held back anything of significance."

"What are we talking about?" Kiem said plaintively. "Jainan, I have zero idea what the Auditor meant. Surely someone would have told us if Taam was murdered. And what did he mean about you and the investigation?"

Jainan ran a hand across his face, the first visible sign Kiem had seen of his control cracking. "It was nothing. Nothing important. I asked Internal Security for the crash data after the accident—Taam's flyer was army-issue, but I know the military gave them the flight logs. I was told only the investigators had a need to know. They were right. This is irrelevant. There is no way Taam could have been murdered."

Kiem leaned against the bannister next to him and frowned, trying to make sense of this. "Internal Security said you didn't have a right to know about the investigation?"

"It was an accident," Jainan said, though more as if he was trying to convince himself. "This is a mistake. The Auditor must confirm us."

"Internal Security refused to give you the *crash data*?" Kiem said. "The crash your partner died in? You're an engineer, aren't you? You could have helped them read it."

There was a pause that Kiem couldn't parse at all. Then Jainan touched his newly fixed wristband and said abruptly, "I am not making this up."

"I didn't say—" Kiem broke off as Jainan, suddenly intense, brought up a light-screen in front of him and started spinning through his messages.

The stairwell had no display screen. Jainan turned to the wall instead, which was inlaid with the brushed-steel crest of the Hill Enduring, and projected his messages on top of it. Kiem wished he would stop doing that. He was prepared for Thea to have different notions of privacy, but it felt wrong to see *all* of Jainan's correspondence. He tried to glance away surreptitiously until Jainan found the one he wanted to display.

"Here," Jainan said. Kiem looked back. Jainan had put up a conversation with several officials: Internal Security, palace civil servants, some military bureaucrats. "I would not bother you with this," Jainan said, his voice sounding as if his control was fraying, "except you should know what he was talking about. I don't know how the Auditor brought this into his data set. I thought it was private."

Kiem scanned the messages with a growing sense of indignation. Jainan was right, he had asked for information, and he'd been refused. "This is ridiculous," Kiem said. "You could have genuinely helped—even if this murder stuff is rubbish, it could have given you some *closure*—" He fumbled in his pocket for his seal, which, for a miracle, he hadn't lost. The lump of gold, engraved with Iskat's crest, hummed as he brought up a small screen on his wristband and tapped the seal against it. The seal bled a golden patch onto the screen, forming a miniature version of the royal crest. Kiem signed some text across it—a quick demand Internal Security find the data and hand it to Jainan—and sent it to Jainan to add to the message chain. "There. See if that helps."

"Oh," Jainan said. He sounded startled, as if Kiem had broken some sort of rule. Kiem admittedly didn't pay a lot of attention to palace legislation, but he was fairly sure asking Internal Security for some information wasn't against the law.

"The Auditor can't be right about Taam," Kiem said, dropping the seal back in his pocket. "Someone would have told us."

"I would just like to know," Jainan said. The lines around his eyes hadn't disappeared. He glanced out the window toward the shining dome of the shrine where Taam's Mournings had all been held, shook his head slightly, and pulled his messages off the wall in the manner of someone determined to be business-like about things. "Perhaps we should get back."

"Yes—we should brief Bel," Kiem said, galvanized into action. He fell in beside Jainan as they started down the stairs. "She might have some ideas. Honestly, this is absolute nonsense. A Galactic from the other side of the universe telling us we can't speak for our own planets." At the foot of the stairs, a glass door led outside. Kiem waved it aside and gestured Jainan ahead. "Maybe Bel will find it funny. Taam might have found it funny."

Jainan gave him an odd look as they passed through the door and into the cold sunlight outside. "No," he said. "Taam would not have found this funny at all."

CHAPTER 7

A week passed. Jainan felt suspended, like a fragment caught in the force between two fields. The idea that Taam's death might have been murder was farcical, absurd, but the memory of the Auditor saying it circled around his head until he was banishing the thought dozens of times a day. He could do nothing about it. No Iskaner was obliged to tell him anything. Internal Security failed to reply to Kiem's nudge; even Taam's old colleagues were quiet. Nobody had a duty to interact with Jainan except Kiem.

Kiem was—in public and in private—friendly, considerate, and good-humored. This had nothing to do with Jainan: Kiem was friendly and good-humored to everyone Jainan ever saw him with. Kiem was the person everyone knew, and it showed wherever he went. He walked into a crowded room and three people would immediately greet him like an old friend. Jainan had trouble remembering people's names; Kiem remembered their children's names. Every time Jainan thought about how he must look to Kiem—with his awkwardness, his stiff speech, his painful inability to say the right thing in the right situation—he felt a part of him try and spiral into self-pity again. He didn't let that happen.

His first appointment with Professor Audel was at the Imperial College, on a clear and sharply cold day that dawned free of snow. Even taking a flyer to the College felt more intimidating without Kiem there. Not only had Kiem known where to go, but his easy confidence also attracted people's attention. By himself,

Jainan had to shake the feeling that everyone was staring at him instead. He couldn't remember the last time he'd had a reason to leave the palace grounds alone.

Jainan got lost twice in the College's twisty buildings, a couple of which were unheated and already below freezing. Professor Audel's office, when he reached it, was in a corridor as stuffy as a sauna. There was a better-kept section adjoining it—Jainan passed three lab entrances, and glanced in with curiosity, and away with regret. The professor's room had a nameplate and a doorbell. He gave it his thumbprint.

The door opened. The person behind it wasn't Professor Audel, but one of her students.

The student stared as if Jainan had just landed there on an incoming meteor. "Sweet God, you came."

Jainan knew that accent. The student was *Thean*. Jainan fought the urge to step back. "Is Professor Audel in?"

"Professor!" the student yelled behind him—no, *her*. The way she'd tied her clan neckscarf was definitely female. Jainan had spent so long on Iskat that he was looking for the wrong signals. An unwelcome memory rose from his first few weeks: *How do you not understand what a woman is, Jainan? Do they not have them on Thea?* At the time, Jainan had laughed. Now he blinked as the student called, "You were right, he's here!"

"Yes, dear," Professor Audel said, emerging from an inner part of the rooms. "Would you do me a favor and make the coffee. Count Jainan—do you go by 'Count'?"

"No," Jainan said. The Thean student had mercifully stopped staring at him and gone to unearth a battered samovar from under a pile of old lab equipment. Disconcertingly, the pattern on her twisted scarf was one of Feria's. "Just Jainan, please."

"Jainan, then—why don't you sit down." Professor Audel started sorting through more junk behind her desk. "I'm sure I had—where's it gone?"

Jainan looked around the room. There were only two obvious

chairs. One of them was behind the professor's desk, and the other was occupied by a glass aquarium. The water it held was so dark it must have had a photoagent in it, and it was probably contributing to the faintly chemical smell that permeated the room. A flipper broke the surface and disappeared again.

"Oh, that's just our goldfish," Professor Audel said. "Move her."

"She's in three hundred liters of water, and the hover assist broke," the student pointed out. She kicked what looked like an old porcelain samovar, beautiful but chipped, and it emitted a faint chime. "Sit here, Count Jainan." She met Jainan's eyes and shoved out a crate. There was a challenge in there that Jainan didn't understand. "Sorry it's not the style you're used to."

Taam would have intimidated her into politeness by now. Kiem would have already extracted her name and exactly what was bothering her. Jainan could only look away. "It's fine," he said. He sat on the edge.

"Can't find the abacus," Professor Audel said, emerging with her hair clips askew. "I have your conclusions from the net, though. Oh dear, look at me jumping into work. One of my bad habits. Gairad, is that the coffee?"

"Coming," the student said, pouring from the samovar. She passed Jainan and Professor Audel cups of extraordinarily strong coffee then pulled up a beanbag and took the third cup for herself. Something about her profile was naggingly familiar.

An illustration of the Iskat sector hung on the wall behind the professor's desk. Unusually, it was drawn so Thea dominated the foreground, distinctive with its glittering ring and the cobalt-blue tint of its seas. The artist had delineated a network of ship journeys in gold. Thea had never been easy to reach: the asteroid fields were extensive and difficult to navigate, but there were lines to Rtul and the majestic bulk of Eisafan, and one desultory route to Kaan. But all of those were dwarfed by the gleaming web of trade routes that looped around Iskat and spiraled out to the sector's one remaining galactic link. The threads were so dense that they came together in a golden river pouring through the known clear paths to Thea: in the picture, it looked like you could take a rowboat from Thea to Iskat's shores.

"Now then, dear," Professor Audel said, "didn't someone say you just got married? How are you finding it?"

Jainan choked. "We're very happy," he said. "Thank you."

"Well, to each their own," the professor said. "I tried it twice, and the second time was no better than the first. Don't let me spoil your optimism, though."

"It's his second marriage, Professor," said Gairad, with the long-suffering tone of an eighteen-year-old who is more intelligent than everyone around them. "I told you. He's our treaty representative."

"I'm afraid I'm not up to date on politics," the professor said to Jainan. "It's been very helpful to have Gairad around. So much of this seems to be politics. Maybe you two know the same people?"

Gairad was looking at him. Jainan could tell. He was tense even before she opened her mouth and said, "Know the same people? Professor, we're *related*."

Cold dread went through Jainan. "Are we?" he said, trying to make it as neutral as possible.

"My aunt's cousin is Lady Ressid's oath-sister," Gairad said. Now the accusation in her voice was unconcealed. "I started at Bita Point University four years after you left. Lady Ressid came to my farewell ceremony on Thea when I switched to study here."

And that meant—though the connection was distant—Jainan had clan duties to her he hadn't fulfilled. Another name on the list of people he had let down. "I," he said, then stopped. He couldn't explain to her why he hadn't been in contact. He'd had issues with his security clearance; his current Iskat obligations and his old Thean ties had proved difficult to balance. He didn't like to think about it. Those were the sacrifices you had to make as a diplomat.

"Aha," said Professor Audel, who had been rummaging in her desk drawer and clearly not paying attention. "Here's our own model. Is that enough small talk? I think it is. Jainan, take a look at this."

Jainan turned away from Gairad with relief that felt like a breath of air. Professor Audel placed an abacus cube on the desk, each side about the length of her thumb. It lit up with a soft glow and started projecting its built-in programs: models and lines glowed in three dimensions in the air above it. Jainan recognized the outlines with a pang. He no longer remembered all the details of his own field.

"How much of the current thinking have you followed since your thesis?" Professor Audel asked. "None at all? Oh. Well then, you may not be following Operation Kingfisher and how it's been going. Or not going, I should say."

"He should know," Gairad said. "He was married to the man who ran it! Prince Taam, Professor, I *told* you."

"Oh, you're that one," the professor said. She regarded him for a second longer than was comfortable. "I did wonder how they got a new representative in so quickly. So you do know about Kingfisher, then."

Jainan shook his head, his throat suddenly tight. "Prince Taam didn't discuss his work," he said. "I wasn't following it." His related field had been part of the reason he'd been put forward for the marriage, but that had led nowhere. Taam had never taken interference well, especially early on, when Jainan hadn't realized his own academic explanations came across as patronizing. "I only had an idea it wasn't going as well as it could."

"Beset with problems," the professor said. "One might say riddled with them. Equipment failures, poor planning, workforce problems, supplies going missing—and two rogue solar flare incidents, which were the only things nobody can be blamed for. Heaven knows how the military organizes its operations; it's a miracle they managed to conquer *anywhere*."

The two Theans in the room winced. Jainan saw Gairad scowl

and suddenly wished he hadn't shown any reaction himself; he was supposed to be a diplomat. He distracted himself by staring at the colorful projection. If he was honest, he felt a vague prickle of disloyalty to Taam at even listening to criticism of his operation. "Deep-space mining has always had disasters."

"Oh, I'm not casting aspersions," Professor Audel said, without batting an eyelid at this blatant lie. "I did a stint as a military engineer myself; it's not a walk in the park. But this points to some spectacular incompetence."

"And you've developed . . . a new extraction method?" Jainan said, pulling the conversation into a safer channel. "To mine trace elements?"

"Yes," Professor Audel said. "You see, planning failures aside, we—my students and I—think all the Thean sector extraction could be done at half the cost. We've started to reach out to the military, but you know what they're like. The only way to get them to listen is to beat them over the head with something. So we need a regolith expert, and then here you came—ah!" She pushed herself up from her desk. "I just remembered where your thesis abacus might be."

She disappeared into the inner room. Jainan opened his mouth to disclaim any expertise, but she was gone before he could get it out. He was suddenly very aware of Gairad's eyes on him.

"So," Gairad said conversationally. "Are you going to skip out on this like you've apparently skipped out on everything else?"

Jainan placed his hands very carefully on his knees and said nothing.

"I only ask," Gairad said, "because I should probably warn Professor Audel. I told her you've flaked out on everything you started since you came here, but you saw her. She doesn't listen to anything that doesn't involve pressure equations or reptiles."

Jainan only realized then how much the nausea in his stomach had faded in the last few days, because it was coming back now.

Limit the damage. Kiem had trusted him with this and wouldn't be pleased if he fell at the first hurdle. "Where did you get that from?"

"It's common knowledge in the expat circle," Gairad said. "Which you'd know if you didn't treat all Theans like we were *radioactive.*"

Jainan swallowed. "It's not that."

"Isn't it? What is it, then? You're too good for us since you became an Iskaner?" Gairad crossed her arms. "I thought you just didn't have time for clan ties to a student, but *everyone* says you cut them off. Even Lady Ressid. She's been pissed with you for three years now, by the way."

Jainan fought the urge to flinch. "I'm sorry," he said. "There have been diplomatic considerations."

"The Ambassador didn't believe you'd see Professor Audel either," Gairad said. "He'll be shocked."

"I'm sorry," Jainan said again.

Miraculously, that seemed to take some wind out of her sails. "You should tell Lady Ressid that."

Jainan just shook his head. He felt his hands were perilously close to shaking; he gripped the edge of the crate to stop them.

"I don't see why you're so attached to the Iskaners," Gairad said. "They're technically our enemies. Were our enemies."

"We've been unified for decades now," Jainan said. He knew the lines. He'd had this conversation before, mainly with friends of Taam who didn't seem to understand the difference between *unify* and *assimilate* and why that might matter to Thea. "It was peaceful."

"Maybe it shouldn't have been," Gairad said. She'd picked up her cup again and was pretending to fiddle with it, but Jainan could see her glance at him. "Maybe we should have fought them off."

Jainan found himself at a loss. He'd thought it was common knowledge that they'd unified when the Resolution recognized Iskat's control of the link, the gateway to the rest of civilized space. There had been no shots fired, but Iskat's tariffs for foreign ships were prohibitive. Iskat was a generous trading partner with its vassals, its royalty was mainly pageantry, there was a parliamentary check on the Emperor—the clans had agreed unification was the best option. Nothing was ever perfect.

"Would that have made things better?" he said.

"If we'd taken over the link."

"That's absurd," Jainan said sharply. The sector had once boasted two links, but the nearby one had collapsed in on itself last century, as they sometimes did, leaving only the inconveniently far-flung one past the Outer Belt, and the resulting skirmishes for control of the remaining link had formed the Empire in the first place. Thea had stayed out of the conflict. It had little military capability; Theans were latecomers to the sector and had focused mainly on agriculture. Jainan could easily imagine the outcome of Thea pitted against the rest of the Empire. They would be blown off the face of their own planet. "Who are you getting these lines from?"

"They're not *lines*," Gairad said, sounding offended. "I've got friends back in Bita. We have a right to our opinions. Did you know the Ambassador tried to make me attend Unification Day? He was trying to say it's a *condition of my scholarship*. Hah."

Jainan had his share of younger relatives, and there were always pockets of radicalism at universities, but he hadn't heard any of them talk like this before. It gave him a nebulous feeling of unease. Unification Day was barely a month away. "Unification Day is necessary. The Resolution won't deal with us separately now that we've signed up to Iskat's treaty. We need to maintain goodwill."

"Goodwill," Gairad said derisively. "Iskat runs a Tau field for interrogating noncitizens."

"They don't," Jainan said. He could see he wasn't getting through to her; his spike of frustration surprised him. *You live on Iskat,* he wanted to say. *You can see they're not all monsters.*

"The Tau field was never used on a Thean. It's being surrendered to the Resolution with the rest of the remnants. War dramas are not documentaries." This was the kind of misunderstanding his marriage had been meant to solve. He had done nothing to help, had he?

"Why wasn't it surrendered before?" Gairad said. "They renew that treaty every twenty years. The Iskaners have had the Tau field for way longer. Have you got a clever answer for that?" When Jainan said nothing—he was disturbed to find he didn't know—she grimaced. "Whatever. You still abandoned your planet." She got up and paced back over to the samovar to refill her coffee. "Now you're going to get me in trouble for this."

Jainan let out a breath that was almost a laugh. "That isn't something I'm in a position to do."

There were long seconds of silence. They could both hear Professor Audel clattering in the inner room. Gairad seemed to remember she was getting coffee, pressed the wrong hidden button, and cursed as a spray of hot water splashed her hand. At length, she said, "Why do you look over your shoulder when you laugh?"

It took Jainan a moment to find any sort of answer to that. "I don't," he said. Did he?

"Both times," Gairad said. She dabbed her hand dry with a corner of the curtain. "Ugh. At least I can tell the Ambassador I've seen you."

"Don't—" Jainan started, alarmed, but at that moment Professor Audel came back in, holding up a cube-shaped abacus.

"Found it!" she said. "Good thing I never clear out, eh? Let's have a look." She shut down the first abacus and put the new one next to it. "Now, Jainan, why don't you talk Gairad through the basics of this? And then we can discuss the consultation work you'll be doing on the project."

Jainan pried his fingers away from their death grip on the edge of the crate. This, at least, was something he could do. He found himself more grateful for that than he would have thought possible. "Of course," he said. "Happy to help."

When Jainan returned Kiem was in, for once, frowning over a tablet with the expression he got whenever anyone made him do extended reading. It was midmorning on a bright, cold day, and the pale dawn sky had deepened to a porcelain blue. On Thea, birds might have been chirping outside the window, but this was Iskat, so instead there was the occasional sharp tapping as the skeletal predators Kiem and Bel called *doves* made another attempt on the glass. They made a rattling noise with their beaks whenever they were thwarted. It was starting to become familiar.

Kiem looked up hopefully when the door opened. "Jainan!" he said, brightening up and casting the tablet aside. "You went to the College? How was it?"

That was the helplessly compelling thing about Kiem, Jainan had found: he was always glad to have company, whoever you were. Jainan had to remind himself that it wasn't him specifically Kiem was happy to see; Kiem still went out of his way to avoid touching Jainan when they were anywhere near each other. Kiem just preferred company over solitude. "It went . . . well," Jainan said. It had, on balance. "Yes. Well."

"Do you like it? Are you going to do the project?"

"Professor Audel has asked for further help. Yes." Jainan knew this would help Kiem's leverage in the College, so Jainan expected him to be pleased about that and he was; Kiem was almost transparent when he was pleased about something.

"Let me know if you need anything, okay?" Kiem grabbed his tablet again, though he'd thrown it far enough that this involved an undignified lunge on the couch. "Also! I wanted to tell you. I was researching Thea."

It was oddly restful, the way Kiem would fill all the awkward spaces just by talking if you let him. Jainan let it wash over him as he sat down, momentarily banishing the ever-present doubts about Taam and Thea. "Mm."

Kiem waved a hand. "Well, all right, I got Bel to research Thea and send me the important bits. But listen, I was reading up about clans. Your system is really complicated, you know that?"

"Whereas the Imperial family system is very straightforward," Jainan said.

Kiem's face cracked into that smile again. "Right! Right. Nothing complicated *here*. I heard someone once assassinated an Emperor by dropping a full printout of *Who's Who* on her." The corner of Jainan's mouth quirked with amusement. Kiem was already away again. "But listen, I read in this thing that it's traditional to have a clan flag on the wall at home. Is that something people actually do?"

"Most people," Jainan said. He wasn't sure where this was going. "It's not a requirement."

"I thought maybe . . . there?" Kiem gestured at the blank wall opposite the desk. "I was going to message your ambassador to get one, but I wanted to check with you. This is Feria's design, right?" He turned his tablet around to show Jainan.

Emblazoned gold on green filled the screen, bordered with white. Jainan reached out without thinking and took the tablet out of Kiem's grip. The flag in the image was a standard replica from a big Thean chain, not one you could just buy here. They probably weren't even exported to Iskat: of all the Empire's vassal systems, Thea was the least integrated and had the smallest expat community, and besides, most people would bring their clan flags with them in their luggage.

"It's wrong, isn't it," Kiem said, breaking the silence that Jainan didn't realize had fallen. "Argh. Sorry."

"No, that's not—" He was aware he probably owed Kiem some sort of reaction, but it was hard to focus on anything outside the deep, disconcerting lurch he felt, like a foundation pile had cracked and was threatening to shift. "You don't need to buy one. I have one." He rose and went into the bedroom.

Kiem followed him. "You do?" He hesitated on the threshold. Kiem always paused when he came into the bedroom to get something. Every time he did it, Jainan was sharply reminded that no matter how impersonally neat he kept the bed, he had driven Kiem out of his own bedroom.

This time, though, Jainan was focused enough on pulling the box out of the drawer that he just looked over his shoulder and said briskly, "Come *in*. Don't hover."

The moment he said it he wished he could take it back—that was appropriate for other students back in his lab on Thea, not the palace where he was a diplomat. But Kiem didn't take offense, only grinned sheepishly. "Sorry."

As Kiem came in, stopping a careful two paces away, Jainan lifted the lid of the box and took out a folded cloth. His fingers were oddly clumsy; it took two tries before he could get a proper grip. He held it up, and it tumbled open in a waterfall of stiff green silk.

Now that he looked at the flag, it would take up most of the wall. Whatever had propelled him to pull it out curdled into embarrassment. He had to say the obvious. "It's too big."

"It's *incredible*," Kiem said.

The embarrassment was slow to drain away, as if it took time for it to notice it was no longer needed. "Oh."

"Isn't it valuable, though? It should probably go under glass. It looks antique."

"It doesn't go under glass," Jainan said. "But—are you sure? This will alter the look of your rooms significantly."

He had said something wrong. Kiem was staring at him. "They're your rooms too."

"I know," Jainan said. "But this might be a little much."

"Jainan, there's hardly any of your stuff here."

Now he had upset Kiem, and Jainan hadn't even seen it coming.

He closed his eyes briefly and started folding up the flag. "I didn't mean—I'm sorry."

"For *what*?" Kiem said. Jainan couldn't answer.

In the silence, Bel appeared at the door and saved him from having to come up with something. "Your Highness," she said, "you are not only terrible at checking your messages, but you're infecting Count Jainan with your bad habits."

Jainan jumped and gestured his wristband awake, but Kiem just gave a disarming wave of his hand. "Was it important?"

"That depends," Bel said. "It's about the delicate political balance between your two planets, but you can carry on arguing about wall decorations if you like."

Jainan tensed, but perversely that seemed to puncture all the tension in Kiem like a balloon, and he laughed. "No sense of aesthetics. Go on, Bel."

"Colonel Lunver and her deputy, Major Saffer, want to see you," Bel said. "I've been chasing the crash data you asked for. The colonel says they have it, but she wants to talk to you about your problem with the Auditor first. She's the one who took over Taam's role."

"She's got the flight logs from Taam's crash?" Kiem said.

"She seems to think so," Bel said. "You have to go in person, though."

"Well, finally," Kiem said. "My only other plan was walking into the Emperor's office and throwing a tantrum."

"That might have worked," Bel said. "Either that or got you arrested. I'll tell them you're on your way."

"Her aides would have shot me," Kiem said. He grinned at Jainan, and for a moment Jainan was almost taken in by Kiem's unfounded optimism. It made everything that had happened—the Auditor, Taam's accident—seem like solvable problems, like Kiem thought he could make the world swing onto an easier path by sheer force of expecting that it would. Jainan knew this was absurd. And yet here Kiem was. "Let's go and see what Colonel Lunver has for us."

CHAPTER 8

The palace sprawled like a coral reef on a seabed, sprouting wings and structures that housed enough officials and advisors and soldiers and royals to populate a small town. One of the branches was Central One HQ, an imposing military building where Operation Kingfisher had its headquarters. It was on the opposite side of the palace from Kiem's rooms, but he knew the way. He'd worn a path from the residential wing to General Tegnar's office every time she was back on-planet, since she all but slept at her desk—though that had been years and years ago.

"So, Colonel Lunver took over Operation Kingfisher from Taam, huh?" Kiem said, as they walked through the gardens laid out between the inner and outer buildings of the palace. "Is she a friend of yours?"

Jainan hesitated. Kiem was getting used to Jainan's hesitations. Not much came out of his mouth that hadn't been thoroughly weighed and considered beforehand. "I knew her. She's worked with Taam before. I don't believe she would consider me a friend." He ran one gloved hand along the edge of a low wall as they walked, clearing the snow in front of a flower bed full of bare woody stems. "Major Saffer is a different matter. Taam had a close friendship with him. He would frequently come over for dinner."

Kiem's gaze snagged on a tangle of stems in the flower bed and he forgot the conversation. He lunged to catch Jainan's wrist. "Watch out—"

A small bird erupted from the thicket with a screech of fury, rocketing up into the sky and narrowly missing taking a slice out of Kiem's ear with its razor-sharp wing pinions. Jainan had jerked back, away from Kiem's lunge, and now looked up at it in incredulity.

"Ground nesting," Kiem said apologetically. "They don't like being disturbed."

"I will never get used to your wildlife," Jainan said.

"They don't generally mean any harm," Kiem said. He poked a careful finger into the nest it had left behind. "I think they use the creeper flowers to line their nests. There's not a lot of greenery around at this time of year."

"Ah," Jainan said, sounding faintly startled. Kiem saw him examine the climbing creepers at the back of the flower bed and notice the pale, nearly transparent flowers unfolding under the few dark leaves that hung on through winter. "I didn't realize anything was flowering." He glanced up at the sky as if the bird might come back, but it had probably found somewhere else to shelter for the day. "It might be charming if that creature hadn't just tried to kill you."

Kiem brushed a stray twig off his elbow as they emerged from the gardens and into the front yard of Central One HQ. "It was just being . . . you know. Enthusiastic. Which entrance do we take for the Kingfisher offices?"

Kingfisher was in a different part of the building to his mother's old stomping grounds, and Kiem didn't know the labyrinth of alabaster corridors very well. Jainan silently indicated the way to the right office, though even he had to guess at the last few turnings. "I've forgotten," Jainan said apologetically. "I wasn't here all that much."

The junior of the two officers met them at the door. Major Aren Saffer turned out to be a sandy-haired, energetic officer with pale freckled skin and one hand stuck permanently in the pocket of his uniform. A casual wooden pendant on a chain around his neck marked his gender. Kiem liked him immediately. He'd expected Aren to be some medaled stick-in-the-mud like most of his mother's military friends, but he was much younger than that crowd, and he seemed genuinely pleased when he saw Jainan.

"Oh, don't stand on ceremony," Aren said when Kiem shook his hand. The office was a high-ceilinged room with a polished wooden floor and a silver bird emblem mounted on the far wall. Apart from that, it barely looked like the headquarters of a major operation: only a handful of soldiers occupied the rows of empty desks. "We're still recovering. Losing Taam was a body blow, if I'm honest. Really knocked us off course. But he would have wanted us to keep going—right, Jainan?"

Jainan didn't respond. He hadn't come fully into the room, but had stopped to stare at a picture on the wall adjacent to the door: a memorial image, surrounded by gray flowers, showing Taam in full military dress. Taam had the right kind of jawline for that photo. He looked like something out of a war documentary.

Aren tilted his head to one side, smiling quizzically. The small movement made Jainan start, and his attention came swiftly back to the other two. "Of course," Jainan said. "I'm glad to see your memorial."

"Hell with the memorial. I'm glad to see *you*," Aren said. He'd been smiling—he had an easy, constant smile—but now he sobered up, and his gaze on Jainan was intent. "You must be finding it hard; I thought you'd dropped off the face of the planet. You should have been in touch sooner."

Even with his very limited experience of Jainan, Kiem suspected that wasn't the best approach. Jainan closed up visibly and said, "Your concern is appreciated."

"Is your boss around?" Kiem said cheerfully. "Understand this is top secret stuff, this crash data. My aide said you had to hand it over in person."

This worked to smooth over the awkward moment. Aren

showed them into an office where an officer with a colonel's insignia was waiting, her hands clasped behind her back. Kiem had never met her before either: she was maybe in her late thirties, with an air of deliberateness and unusually straight hair scraped back into a severe plait.

The object of her attention was the screens covering one wall of the office. A string of text said OPERATION KINGFISHER—HVAREN BASE. They showed a bustling remote office with the same silver bird emblems mounted around the walls. From the view out the window, it looked to be somewhere out in the mountains; it seemed like a big on-planet office for a spaceside operation, but Kiem supposed the military had to find something to keep itself occupied.

She turned as they came in. "Your Highness," she said. She waved a hand and the screens on the wall went dark. "Thank you for coming. Please take a seat. Saffer, you too."

Kiem warily sat on one of the uncomfortable chairs. The office was austere and chilly; he should have brought a jacket. Next to him Jainan turned his head to keep both of the officers in view. "You wanted to see us, Colonel?" Kiem said cheerfully.

Colonel Lunver put her hands formally on her knees and said, "I understand the Resolution has absolutely refused to instate you."

Kiem felt a bit like he'd opened a door and found an unexpected pit of spikes. "Er," he said. "I wouldn't say *absolutely refused,* as such. It's more like a delay."

"A delay," Colonel Lunver said, her skepticism obvious. Kiem wasn't sure why she was allowed to interrogate him—he would have expected that question to come from the Thean embassy—then he remembered that Kingfisher operated in Thean space. Jainan clearly thought she had the right to an opinion.

"They must do it eventually," Jainan said, quiet and intense. "We both have the correct chain of authority. There is no legal reason to deny us."

Beside him, Aren tipped his head and made a noise through his teeth. "That's assuming the Resolution thinks like humans," he said, with an apologetic look at his senior officer. "Not sure that's the case. Who knows what they're actually looking for?"

Jainan gave a single nod and folded his hands in his lap. Kiem felt a moment of dismay. He'd been working under the assumption that this was a temporary hiccup. But Jainan was the one with diplomatic experience; if even he agreed they might not get instated, they could really be in trouble.

"We've been working on the Auditor from our side," Lunver said. "I hardly need to explain military affairs to the son of General Tegnar—"

"You really do," Kiem said apologetically. "I haven't spoken to her in months."

"—but we care about keeping the Thean treaty stable just as much as Jainan's embassy," Lunver said. "Just as much as the late Colonel Taam, in fact. We're not the only ones who've been nagging the Auditor: Internal Security and the Emperor's Private Office have also been in on the act. But we haven't gotten far. Given that, I have a suggestion for you."

"Go on," Kiem said. At this point he'd take any advice.

Lunver said briskly, "Step down."

"I'm sorry?"

"Step down," Lunver repeated. There was a thin window in the corner of the office; the light coming through it glinted off the flint brooch at her collar. "The Auditor doesn't seem to like how rushed your appointment was. We can convince him to accept Jainan: he's Thean, and he was appointed according to due process. The problem seems to be you."

"Oh," Kiem said. He felt like a hole had opened up in his stomach, which was ridiculous, because this hadn't been his idea in the first place. He said the first thing that came to mind: "I honestly don't know how they appointed me. The Auditor said the problem was Taam."

"The problem is Taam's replacement. The paperwork must have been rushed," Lunver said. She sounded mildly aggrieved, as if intergalactic politics was just another obstacle in the way of her operation. "The investigation into Prince Taam's death is unlikely to find anything new—even Internal Security can't make up evidence where there isn't any. However. If you resigned your position, the wedding was annulled, and Jainan remarried, we could make certain the Auditor is happier with the next representative."

Kiem tried to get his thoughts straight. "I'll step down if it will help," he said. "If that's what the Emperor wants—"

"Do you have an alternative?" Jainan interrupted. Kiem stopped talking. Jainan was sitting very upright in his seat, staring at Lunver. "Who would you replace him with?"

"Apologies, Your Highness," Lunver said to Kiem, "but it should be someone less connected to Taam. The representative doesn't *have* to be a prince. Upper nobility, or a general, perhaps. With the cooperation of the Theans, of course," she added, with a nod to Jainan.

"I fail to see how that will solve the problem," Jainan said.

Kiem, who had been about to open his mouth to say he didn't mind, stopped and rethought. This was how he screwed things up: he went along with what other people wanted and he didn't think. "I'm with Jainan here," he said. "Not sure that's going to fix anything. The Auditor *said* the problem was Taam—speaking of, how about that crash data?"

He looked around hopefully, as if they were having a friendly meeting rather than hearing a senior military official ask for his resignation.

"Your refusal has been noted," Colonel Lunver said. She sighed. "Your Highness, I don't want to have to take it up to the Emperor."

"She'll be so pleased. I think she misses me when I'm not in her inbox," Kiem said. He changed his tone to plaintive. "The crash data? I thought that was why you agreed to see us."

Lunver glanced at Jainan as if she'd expected something more from him, then grimaced and rubbed a hand across her face. "Saffer."

"I'll get you that," Aren said, hastily getting to his feet. "This way."

As they followed him out, Aren frowned over a mini-screen hovering over his wrist. "I have all the personnel records for the unit," he said as an aside to Kiem, "so the colonel got me to track it down, but I'm not really senior officer material. Too much management rubbish." He leaned against an empty desk, spinning through some options, and then entered a command sign. "It has to go through Internal Security. There." He finished the command with a flourish and grinned at Jainan. Even talking quietly, their voices echoed in the old room. Jainan kept glancing at the handful of soldiers within hearing. "That's a fairly ghoulish souvenir you want, but it should be with you within a week or so."

Kiem refrained from saying that apparently the officers hadn't needed to see them in person to transfer the data after all, which was not making him feel any more well disposed toward Lunver. Jainan's eyes went back to Aren's face. "A week."

Aren's mouth took on a rueful twist. "'Fraid it's an Internal Security issue," he said. "They put a block on all the investigation materials, so we have to go up the chain of command to get them released."

"But you have the crash data," Kiem said. "Come on. Jainan's been trying to get it for weeks. I gave it a royal seal. I don't want to start getting official about it—do us a favor."

"I—" Aren looked between them, but Kiem thought he'd got his measure, and he was right. Aren gave a fluid shrug, shot a mildly guilty look at Lunver's office door, and gave another command. Jainan's wristband buzzed. "All right, then. Jainan's got a copy." His voice lowered, semi-comically, as if he was letting them in on a secret. "Please don't hand it to your friends back home."

The line of tension hadn't left Jainan's face. "I wouldn't."

"Why shouldn't he?" Kiem said.

For a brief moment Jainan and Aren both looked as if Kiem had grown a second head. "Oof," Aren said. He traded glances with Jainan. "How to put this, eh? Kingfisher isn't *hugely* popular on Thea."

"Mm," Jainan said.

"Sort of dead-cat-in-the-river levels of popular, in fact. Look." Aren gestured another command and a screen sprang up vertically above the desk. After a moment's browsing, he threw up a fringe-press article with the headline *Iskat's Mining Smash-and-Grab*. And another, with a university logo: *Activist Drones Sabotage Refinery*. A third just said *Sorry, Were You Using Those Minerals?* over a smiling picture of Taam.

Jainan had gone a shade sallower. "I hadn't seen those."

"Idiots," Aren said cheerfully. "Students and fringe obsessives, mainly. But to answer your question, Prince Kiem, that's why we're running a lot of Kingfisher at high classification. I was assigned to the op as the strategic comms officer to try and fight this sort of bad press, but the positive spin just didn't take. Hey, *there's* a thought." He threw himself back into a sprawl in the desk chair and eyed Kiem speculatively. "We've got a strategic comms post going spare. Spinning Kingfisher to the Thean newslogs. You'd be a natural."

"Uh," Kiem said blankly.

"Oh, come on," Aren said, half laughing. "Don't pretend you don't know what I'm talking about."

Kiem took a stab. "Because I look great in a uniform?"

"You use that well, sure," Aren said, grinning. "It's more how you were the royal family's biggest embarrassment a few years ago, and now you get asked to charity galas and interviewed for homemaker magazines and handed a diplomatic marriage." He folded his arms and leaned back. "Half the planet seems to have bought this 'turned over a new leaf' story. I'm serious—if you can pass the physical, I'll swing you a major's commission on Kingfisher. We need someone who can work the press."

"I don't—what—" Kiem scrabbled for what to say. He felt faintly sleazy, though it wasn't as if it was a lie: he and Bel *had* positioned some stuff based on how the newslogs would take it. "I don't do that on purpose." He glanced at Jainan, who had linked his hands in his lap and was staring down at them. "I'm not the military type."

"Skies above, now I've put my foot in it," Aren said. "Didn't mean to make you uncomfortable, believe it or not. I'm sorry." He sat back in his chair, stretching his legs out in front of him, and looked between them, now completely sober. "I get why you asked for the data, Jainan, but I hope you're wrong. I know you won't mind me saying that."

Aren had a point. Jainan hadn't voiced any suspicions out loud, but if the crash hadn't been a chance failure, then the Auditor was right: Taam's death wasn't an accident. And if Internal Security hadn't caught it, they were either incompetent or had decided to cover it up. Kiem felt slightly queasy at the thought. They didn't have any proof. Yet. "Will you be in trouble for skipping the approvals, Aren?"

Aren waved a hand. "I'm a forgiveness-over-permission sort. Really, though, don't send these to the Thean embassy. The new ambassador seems like a good old boy, but every time we've told him something, it's gone straight to those fringe logs I showed you."

"No," Jainan said. "Of course."

"Then go ahead," Aren said. "Knock yourself out. I hope to hell you don't find anything, but"—he crooked his head to one side, his face wryly sympathetic—"I get it. Forget the politics. No one can fault you for being sensitive about this."

Kiem wouldn't have pinned Jainan as overly sensitive, but Jainan didn't react to that either, apart from a movement of his throat as he swallowed. "You've been . . . very helpful," Jainan said. He glanced at Kiem, and Kiem realized this was probably a signal that he didn't want to talk about Taam anymore.

"We'll leave you to the important military stuff," Kiem said, getting to his feet. "Can't have civilians underfoot all the time, right?" He leaned over the desk and pumped Aren's hand.

Aren grinned. "Believe me, you're not half as bad as the civil servants. And honestly, I've been worried about Jainan. Anything I can do—you only have to ask." He held out his hand to Jainan, who took it gingerly. "You only ever had to ask."

Kiem held himself back until they were outside and in the shadow of the Emperor's Wing. "So," he said. "That went . . . well?"

Jainan paused. "Taam found Colonel Lunver valuable," he said abruptly. "Taam did not suffer fools. I think it would be a good idea if you got on well with her and Taam's unit."

"Right," Kiem said, gathering certainty. "We're liaising with the military. I'm a model liaison. Should we invite them to dinner? I cook a mean pancake. Only pancakes, though. I suppose we need to make sure we get on with everyone involved in the investigation."

Jainan had half smiled, but it faded almost as soon as it appeared. Kiem still couldn't quite read him. It sometimes felt like a song playing just out of earshot, or a step on a staircase in the dark. "Yes," Jainan said. "We do."

CHAPTER 9

As the winter deepened, the Resolution and the Empire paced toward Unification Day with the heavy, unswerving tread of two automatons converging. Jainan had listed the ceremonies that led up to the treaty signing; he checked them off as they passed. Most of them took place behind closed doors with the Emperor and her increasingly harried-looking team of aides, but one couldn't be completed without the vassals: the formal handover of what the Resolution called *proscribed material*. The remnants. Jainan hadn't paid much attention to them, but the ceremony must be crossed off the list. Kiem and Jainan were required to attend as the Thean representatives: they would surrender everything found on Thea since the last treaty.

Jainan spent the four days leading up to that ceremony obsessing over Taam's crash data. He used to feel his time in the palace drag, but now it slipped through his hands like water. Fortunately Kiem seemed to get invited to every dinner and charity gala in Arlusk, so it wasn't hard to keep Jainan's preoccupation away from him. Things had always turned awkward with Taam whenever Jainan became obsessed with something like this; Taam had joked that Jainan should just join a monastery where they'd let him retreat into his own world for years on end.

Jainan knew on some level that this was displacement. His duty was to attend the ceremonies and represent Thea, not to fool around with log forensics for an investigation that Internal Security already had in hand. But the Auditor's refusal to instate him and Kiem had shaken him—it must sort itself out, he told himself, nobody could genuinely want to break the treaty—and he needed something to focus on.

He found nothing in the crash data. Every line of the logs supported Internal Security's conclusion of a natural compressor failure causing a catastrophic leak of fuel into an adjoining thermal chamber. Any attempt to artificially induce that failure would have stood out like a sore thumb. Jainan wasn't an expert in landside craft, but he knew the basics; a badly maintained compressor was a common failure point. The data was almost textbook.

When the remnants ceremony came around, it should have been a relief to give up on the crash logs. Instead, Jainan stared into the mirror as he changed his outfit and felt like a ghost hovering outside his own body. He must look respectable. He and Kiem were to act like a happy couple. The Thean embassy had tried to invite them to a reception afterward; Jainan knew Bel would turn it down as not commensurate with Kiem's status. Imperial Princes were expected to put the palace first.

Kiem was late—Kiem was often late; he seemed incapable of looking at the time—and he turned up in a flurry of apologies. Jainan smiled mechanically, the ghostlike feeling floating around him like a layer of film, and accompanied him to the event.

The remnants ceremony took place in the palace's largest stateroom, the Chamber of the Hill Enduring. The Hill Enduring was Iskat's crest, a sparse, instantly recognizable curve, but Jainan had never been told the history. The day before, he had absently asked Kiem about the original hill. "I don't . . . know," Kiem had said, as if just realizing this himself. "It must be on one of the planets the first terraformers came from, but we've been here for four hundred years. Probably eroded by now, wherever it is."

The shape of the Iskaners' long-abandoned horizon was emblazoned on two walls of the stateroom. Several hundred beads of light hung from the roof like the dense hearts of galaxies, shedding a soft light on the endless gold braid that adorned the military officers and royals in attendance. The stateroom was set up around a wide ceremonial dais at one end, which currently held an assembly of stands, glass cases, and incongruously heavy lockboxes. Remnants.

The remnants came in sizes from an obsidian-like stone that could fit on a coin up to an opaque lump of metal the size of a small dog, with compressed strata that seemed to bleed further into each other as you watched. Jainan had seen remnants before, of course. His university had a minor shard on loan in the xenotechnology department, but he had been deep in his own research and uninterested in something with no practical use and so many Resolution interdictions around working on it.

He was unprepared for the feeling of dozens of remnants clustered together, which was like walking into a garden thick with swarming bees.

The Auditor stood to the side of the dais, quietly conferring with the Emperor's aides. His staff moved among the remnants, which Jainan realized were grouped by planet: the cases with the Thean remnants had clan insignia showing who was involved in the digs that found them.

The rest of the room was set up more informally. This was Iskat, so of course there was a meal: the salt course was set out but as yet untouched. Dozens of guests were milling around the tables. Jainan saw a couple of the other treaty representatives. Kiem was in his Imperial family uniform, which was not quite military but showy enough that he could hold his own, while Bel wore a flowing, gold-accented coat with her usual self-assurance. Jainan faded into the background in his blue-gray Thean ceremonials. They weren't technically correct, but his green-and-gold clan formals were aggressively Thean and would have stuck out.

"How's it going?" Kiem murmured as they entered side by side. "With the crash data, I mean."

Jainan started. He hadn't thought he'd been bothering Kiem. But of course Kiem was expecting a result after the fuss Jainan had made over the crash data, and of course Jainan had nothing. He didn't want to admit he had wasted Kiem's time. Jainan didn't know if it was because of the persistent feeling he'd somehow made a mistake in his own analysis, or just an unwillingness to admit defeat. "I would like to do one more check."

"Sure," Kiem said. He looked behind him—Jainan understood the impulse, the remnants felt like a buzzing presence just behind your shoulder, wherever you turned—and shook himself. "I'd offer to help, but you know, I add up two and two and get fried fish."

"Fried whitebait," Bel said absentmindedly. Jainan followed her gaze to the pristine display of food: white seafood with carefully arranged splashes of color from herbs and vegetables in glittering tiered trays. Iskat haute cuisine had an almost forensic air. "Salmon. Is that Eisafan saltfish?"

"Leave some for us," Kiem said.

"If you're quick." She flashed both of them a sideways smile. "Oh, and don't forget you have to leave early. You have the Thean embassy reception straight afterward."

The Thean reception. Jainan swallowed on a suddenly dry throat. "I assumed we weren't going."

"Oh," Kiem said. He stopped in his tracks, his expression suddenly guilty. "Ah. Shit. Sorry. I may have assumed we were. They phrased the invite like you knew about it already. I'll tell them we had a change of plan."

"You've accepted," Jainan said blankly. "Oh. I didn't mean— I'll go. Naturally." He was rattled; he would usually have phrased that more smoothly.

A gong sounded to signal the start of the ceremony. Jainan shoved everything out of his mind to deal with later. Ambassador Suleri met them at the front of the room; he gave Jainan a crisp, polite greeting and a set of keys. The embassy had arranged everything. Jainan was only required to take the keys to the Auditor.

The formal part of the ceremony was over quickly. The Auditor dealt with all the representatives exactly the same, from Eisafan's twenty-person entourage to Jainan and Kiem, unaccompanied, and didn't show a flicker of recognition. The presence of the remnants was much worse when you were close; all of the representatives kept giving little starts at nothing and glancing at thin air as if they'd just seen someone they knew. The Auditor's staff took the keys, opening boxes and running handheld scanners across the remnants inside.

"Now what?" Kiem said under his breath. "What does he do with them? They make my skin crawl."

"It was in the briefing," Jainan said, then realized his mistake when Kiem took on the embarrassed, sidelong look of someone who hadn't read it. "Ah. The tests take several days. When they've finished, they'll be put in cold storage on the Resolution ship. The Resolution apparently uses an ice planet to store them—it's a strategy for long-term neutralization."

Kiem looked doubtful, but at that moment Bel muttered something under her breath and tapped Kiem's elbow. "Look over there," she said. "That's quite a special guest."

"Who?" Kiem said. He scanned the far end of the stateroom, which was crowded with knots of commercial moguls and their guests. Bel indicated a heavyset man in spacer fashion of a style that wasn't Iskat or Thean.

"That man is Evn Afkeli." Bel turned so her back was to the knot of people. "He runs one of the big raider congloms—the Blue Star. He's the one who spaces merchants whose companies don't pay ransoms."

Raiders. Jainan had to think for a moment before he recognized what Bel was talking about: the organized crime gangs that hopped among the asteroid belts and outer worlds, hijacking ships on minor routes and running their tendrils into planetside businesses. He remembered reading that they found an open harbor in Sefala, where the Empire struggled to keep order.

"Someone invited a Sefalan pirate to lunch?" Kiem said in a murmur no louder than Bel's. "How does that work?"

"Evn Afkeli's a legitimate businessman," Bel said. "The Guard doesn't have anything on him."

"What a chance," Kiem said. He was starting to grin. "Think I'll go over and say hi."

"Don't," Jainan said. He didn't realize how sharply it had come out until he saw Kiem's sideways look. Jainan was on edge: the buzzing of the remnants behind his shoulder seemed to be trying to materialize into some kind of presence. "Sorry," he said, making an effort to cover it up. Kiem would do what he liked. "Of course. Would you like me to come?" He couldn't even put words to the flood of repulsion that welled up in him.

"You know what," Kiem said, "I changed my mind."

The raider's face was set in deep, serious lines and barely moved at all as he spoke to a military officer. The lack of expression sent an unpleasant prickle down Jainan's back. "How do you know his name?"

Bel shook her head. "She's being modest," Kiem said. "She used to work for the Sefalan Guard."

"I'm not being modest," Bel said, "I'm reminding you that raiders are bad news, since you seem to have missed that from all the Iskat children's animations about them."

"Modest *and* has a full range of helpful tips," Kiem said cheerfully. "Hey, they're seating people. Care to accompany me to dinner, Your Grace?" He gave a mock bow and offered his arm.

Jainan smiled mechanically and took it. Bel slipped off toward the drinks table as Jainan followed Kiem to the other side of the hall from the Sefalan, and steeled himself for the long and awkward meal that was to follow.

He hadn't factored in how it would feel to be accompanied by a different partner. Kiem seemed to recover quickly from the eerie aura of the remnants that made all the guests constantly cast nervous glances at empty air, and he promptly made fast friends with the person on the other side of him. He introduced them to Jainan as Master Sergeant Vignar, who ran logistics at

Central One HQ. Ten minutes later Vignar and Kiem appeared to have bonded for life over old dartcar races. Jainan concentrated on his food, made small talk with the Kaani treaty representative opposite him, and monitored Kiem with half an ear. At first he split his attention, but as he made his way through the sweet course, he realized he wasn't going to have to jump in, or run two conversations simultaneously, or field Kiem's bad mood. He could feel his own state of mind improving as the meal went on.

The Kaani representative, a tall, elegant person with a habitual air of finding amusement at someone else's expense, picked at the remains of their sweet course while watching Jainan.

"It's good to see you at events again," they said.

"Thank you," Jainan said warily, as if it wasn't compulsory. Kaan's representative had come to the palace after him and Jainan hadn't seen them around much. Kaan scoffed at the concept of gender, but their representative had capitulated to Iskat custom far enough to have a glass bead braided into the hair by their ear. Jainan was so out of touch he couldn't even remember their name.

"I was starting to think," the representative continued, "that our hosts had just decided to abandon your treaty."

Jainan's hand tightened around his fork. His first panicked thought was whether Kiem had heard, but Kiem was still embroiled in his dartcar conversation. Jainan kept his voice level with an effort. "Excuse me?"

"I keep hearing Thea is being stubborn about its resources." The Kaanan delicately speared a last piece of fruit from the sweet course. "Naturally, in Iskaner terms, that means your negotiators said *maybe* when Iskat expected them to say *yes*. You did get allied province status because you were amicable, after all. Do try the passion fruit, it's very good," they added. "The hothouses over here so seldom get it right."

Kaan liked to stir up trouble. It was how they did politics; Jainan knew this and yet still felt a twinge of disquiet. The stateroom around them was full of Iskaners. "Thea shares its resources generously," Jainan said. "We've been an allied province for decades. We've renewed the Resolution treaty several times already. Nothing has changed."

"Except the factions on Iskat," the representative said mildly. "Are we dealing with a commercial empire, a parliamentary system, a dictatorship, a military oligarchy? You can't say, can you, because Iskat throws all of them at us at different times. I wonder how much of a grip the Emperor really has on everything that's going on. Of course, Thea's little gripe about your mining resources takes the heat off Kaan, where we really *are* stubborn. I am grateful."

There were flippant responses and political responses; Jainan discarded all of them. Instead he watched the representative's eyes, which weren't part of their affable expression, and said, "Why did you bring up my treaty?"

"Oh," the Kaanan said, casually straightening the cuff of their robe, "you're our test case, if you like. How much do you have to annoy Iskat before you end up as a special territory?"

Treaties changed, for better or worse, but even in the wrangling that led up to the Resolution renewal, no allied or satellite province in the Empire had ever dropped to special territory status. Jainan could feel his heartbeat speed up. It was the kind of absurd, troublemaking thing that Kaani politicians threw out to set hares running. He clenched his hands under the table and said nothing.

In the face of Jainan's silence, the representative gave him a charming, impersonal smile. They could have been discussing the weather. "My embassy's conversations with our Iskat counterparts have been . . . unproductive, this time around."

"Have you mentioned this to the Thean embassy?" Jainan asked quietly. He couldn't seem to slow his heart rate. "Do you have any evidence?"

"Evidence? This is *politics*," the Kaanan said. "I have talked to your embassy, as a matter of fact. Everyone has rather cut you out of the loop, haven't they? And this is honestly just gossip." They rose to their feet in a rustle of bright formal robes. "Speaking of, I must circulate. Lovely talking to you."

"What was that about?" Kiem murmured in his ear.

All of Jainan's thoughts fled in a rush of cold alarm. He was supposed to be a goodwill representative. He was not supposed to get involved in politics, and he was especially not supposed to embroil his partner in it. That entire conversation should have been left to the embassy and their Iskat counterparts. He felt his breath shorten. "Nothing of importance."

"Thea's an allied province," Kiem said. He was frowning, as if this reminded him of something. "The Empire shouldn't just be able to change that."

Jainan could not think straight. His heart would not slow down. It felt like someone was whispering in his ear. "I couldn't comment."

"I suppose not." Kiem gave him a faint echo of his normal grin. "I was never great at politics. Oh, hey, Vaile," he added, as someone tapped him on the shoulder. "Haven't seen you in months. Thought they sent you to Rtul. How's it going?"

"Swimmingly! But, Kiem, *three* kinds of cake?"

The ornately dressed Prince Vaile gave Jainan a pretty nod. Jainan almost didn't see her. There was a presence behind her shoulder. For one moment, Taam stood there, much more real than he'd been even during the wedding night dinner. Jainan's breath stopped.

This was a remnant-induced hallucination. It wasn't real. Jainan rubbed a hand swiftly across his eyes, and the image disappeared.

Vaile and Kiem were talking. Jainan rose. "I must go and, and talk to . . . excuse me." He bowed to her, keeping a semblance of control over his ragged breathing, and struck out blindly into the crowd in the stateroom.

Enough people were starting to rise and circulate that he didn't stand out. He saw nobody he recognized. He was too on edge to even pretend to be sociable; faces loomed vividly as he strode through the crowd, and he found himself pushing through a glass door to the gardens outside.

The sudden cold air on his skin was a relief, as was the way the buzzing from the remnants faded out. The geometric hedges of the inner palace garden radiated out from where he stood, snow-covered and monochrome. Jainan picked a direction at random and plunged into the small paths, walking fast, forcing his heart rate to level out. It had been a hallucination. Resolution technology was associated with unpleasant mental phenomena.

He needed something to focus on. A couple of minutes later, he found himself sitting on a stone bench, breathing the astringent scent of Iskat's winter-blooming flowers as he opened Taam's fly-bug logs to go over them again. The noise of the party had faded into the distance. He knew combing through Taam's crash data was obsessive and pointless, but it was the only thing he could entirely control.

Events and visualizations scrolled through his hands in a river of color. He stared at them, forcing himself to concentrate. He could imagine the flybug jolting in the air, failing to respond to Taam's increasingly desperate commands, slipping nose-down into a death spiral. The compressor had been giving out maintenance warnings for months. It was all in the data.

The cold stone of the bench pressed into the back of Jainan's legs. Taam's perfect, textbook crash data.

Like a free-spinning gear clicking its teeth into alignment, something in Jainan's mind started to tick. He gestured a command sequence over his wristband. More screens came up, floating in the cold air, requesting data from various research libraries Jainan had once been a member of. He searched for his old university access keys, slowly at first, and then with more impatience. When he found them the screens changed into lists and lists of materials.

He found it in a second-year undergraduate textbook under *failure analysis*. A textbook example of a gradual compressor malfunction.

He arranged the textbook and Taam's data side by side. It wasn't a one-to-one correlation. The component IDs were different. The time stamps on the compressor events also looked different, but when he examined them, they were all offset by exactly the same amount, as if someone had just shifted them forward by the appropriate interval. His skin prickled.

He would expect a compressor failure to take place the same way every time. It was mathematically possible that the similarities were a coincidence.

He stared at the time stamps and tried to shake the persistent feeling that he was going mad.

"Jainan? Count Jainan!"

Jainan's head snapped up. He had lost track of time. Through the trees, he could see the conservatory had emptied out, leaving only staff clearing away the meal. The figure hurrying out of a walkway in the opposite direction, huddled into a greatcoat against the Iskat cold, was a Thean embassy staffer.

Jainan glanced behind him automatically, clenching his fist to kill the screens. But though there were open paths behind him, he was socially trapped. It would be unforgivably rude to ignore her. Jainan rose to his feet instead and bowed stiffly. "A good afternoon to you."

"And to you, Your Grace." Jainan knew the staffer by sight— Lady Fadith of the Nasi clan. The Nasi clan was a close ally of Feria. "Are you leaving for the reception? I just had a meeting that overran, but we shouldn't miss more than the first ten minutes. May I offer you a lift?"

A cold wash of dread slid down Jainan's back. He realized he had automatically suppressed his wristband alerts as if he were still a university student with no responsibilities. There was a stream of messages from Kiem and Bel. He had been out here for—sweet God, half an hour—and they should have left for the reception twenty minutes ago. Kiem must be there already. "You received our acceptances?" he asked pointlessly, to stall.

Fadith took it in stride. "Prince Kiem accepted for both of you, Your Grace. Have your plans changed?"

He had effectively run off and hidden himself before a public appointment. His nonappearance would cause Kiem considerable embarrassment, all because Jainan couldn't control himself or keep track of time. This would test the limits of even Kiem's patience. It was not a pleasant prospect.

Lateness would also be embarrassing, but perhaps it could be smoothed over. He pulled himself together. Kiem would already have left in the official flyer, so this would be quicker than asking Bel for a backup vehicle. "No," he said. "Our plans haven't changed, but Prince Kiem is going straight there from another appointment." The next words were hard to force out: he had been proud as a teenager, and a dislike of asking for things had been the one aspect of it that he had never managed to shake. "I would appreciate a lift."

He caught a moment's surprise from Fadith, but Jainan was detached, now, and any embarrassment was far away. "Of course, Your Grace. My flyer is at the gates. Do you . . . need a coat?"

His coat. It would be odd to go out without a coat, but they were already late. "No."

Fadith paused, then shrugged it off with a smile. "You're a fully adapted Iskaner, Your Grace. I freeze even in this." She put her hands farther in the pockets of her greatcoat and strolled toward the palace entrance. Jainan said the right things in response to her small talk, mechanically, and shivered.

It wasn't until they were in the flyer, the city spread out on the hill below them, that Fadith said, "So, I was meeting the Iskaners about the mining operation—"

Jainan held up a hand, the motion jerky. Fadith broke off. Jainan had to struggle for what to say, after being that rude, but he managed it. "Please," he said. "I can't talk about politics."

"This is hardly politics, Your Grace," Fadith said, a note of wariness in her voice. "And you have an interest."

"I *don't*," Jainan said. There was a long, tense pause. "I have no interest."

"I apologize," Fadith said. She sounded more distant with every exchange, as if everything Jainan said was the wrong answer. "I didn't mean any offense."

They passed the rest of the journey in an awkward silence. Jainan messaged Bel with a stilted apology. Fadith offered up the occasional comment on the weather, but Jainan was too busy wrestling with his growing sense of nausea to give any more than short replies. A Thean reception. Dozens of Theans, including those he had defaulted on clan obligations to. And Kiem—who would not only be watching how he acted, but would be embarrassed and angry on top of it. It made Jainan's dilemma over the crash data seem almost unimportant.

By the time they reached the reception, the wind had got up into what Iskaners called a needlepiercer: a relentless, icy wind that went straight through your clothes. The warmth of the embassy was a shock. The other shock was how *Thean* the hallway of the embassy felt, after such a long time on Iskat, with its tiled floor and walls covered with brightly colored flags. A square archway led into a crowded room where Jainan could see the colors of several other clans.

"Jainan! Hey!" Kiem emerged from the crowd the next moment as if he'd been watching for Jainan. Behind him was the person he'd been talking to, who looked taken aback. Kiem's forehead was creased and he was more intent than Jainan had ever seen him. Jainan slammed down on the unhelpful instincts telling him to move and instead stayed motionless.

Kiem reached out to take his arm then seemed to think better of it and turned toward the cloakroom, now empty of latecomers. "Um, can we have a moment in private?"

In private. Of course. Jainan turned numbly to follow him and, as he did, the textbook logs faded into the back of his mind.

Kiem led them behind a rack of coats and cast a harried look at the back of the cloakroom to check for any attendants. "I couldn't find you after lunch. Bel got your message—you didn't have to come, you know. Are you feeling okay? You didn't look well, and then you just disappeared."

They were in for an argument. There was no point in spinning it out and increasing the risk that an outsider would overhear, so Jainan cut straight to the end. "I understand I have embarrassed both of us," he said. If he could even manage to sound apologetic it might help, but his voice was its normal frustrating monotone. "I was extraordinarily rude. I apologize."

Kiem grimaced. "Ouch, okay, I guess I deserved th—wait." He broke off and looked more closely at Jainan. "You're serious? You're serious." He looked almost lost. "You're really serious," he said again.

Jainan realized he'd pressed a finger to his temple. He took it away. "I don't know what you want me to say."

"I don't want you to say anything!" Kiem said. He was pressed against an incongruous row of fur coats behind him. It felt faintly absurd, like they were having an argument in a closet. Taam had never shown this much emotion outside their rooms. "Did I say something wrong at lunch, before you left? If it was anything I said about Thea, and if there's any way I can fix it—"

"Will you please be clear," Jainan said, his frustration making it come out louder than he meant it to. "I don't. I can't. I can't read your mind. Will you please be clear what it is you want from me."

There was a silence. Kiem said, "What?"

Kiem had hundreds of expressions. When he was focused on someone—the way he was focused on Jainan now—the tiny shifts around his eyes formed a new one every moment, handling dozens of inputs from his guesses and knowledge about the other person like a suite of algorithms executing, except he somehow ran it on pure instinct. It was obvious how he had no difficulty understanding most people. It was equally obvious he wasn't coming up with any answers appropriate for Jainan.

It made Jainan feel even more unmoored from reality. He hesitated to even mention his amateur conclusions from the crash data. It was entirely possible he had imagined everything he had read in the last hour.

"Count Jainan? Your Highness?" Light flooded into the space as someone pushed the rack of coats aside. "Is there a problem?"

It was Ambassador Suleri, resplendent in his formal clan robes and a gold chain. An aide pulled the rack further aside. Kiem spun around, looking guilty. "Um—Your Excellency—no, no problem, we were just, um."

But the Ambassador wasn't even looking at him. He was looking at Jainan. And though Kiem had nothing to feel guilty for, Jainan had a litany of dropped clan obligations and snubs he tried not to let show on his face. "Good afternoon, Ambassador. I apologize for my tardiness to the reception."

"Prince Kiem told us you were unwell," the Ambassador said. His voice was neutral, but the look he directed at Kiem had something else in it. "We were not expecting you to come at all."

Jainan took a sharp breath, trapped between Kiem's cover story and his own ill-considered actions. "I was unwell," he said. "I felt . . . better, unexpectedly."

"How convenient," the Ambassador said. "I'm glad."

Jainan wasn't looking at Kiem, but his skin crawled at how Kiem must be reacting. He reached at random for something that would get them out of this. "Are there refreshments?"

The Ambassador's gaze didn't break from his. "Indeed," he said. "In the main room. I will be honored to present you both. This way, Prince Kiem."

"Right!" Kiem said. "Right. Honor to be here."

Jainan was going to have to face other Theans at some point, whatever he did. He arranged his face into blankness and caught up with Kiem. "After you."

CHAPTER 10

Jainan's stomach churned as they passed through the square archway and into the large reception room. Two fountains provided a faint mist to break up the dryness of the Iskat winter. The walls held a complete array of clan flags, all of which were as familiar to Jainan as basic velocity equations, and the room was full of expat Theans. Most of them wore Thean fashions with a clan emblem; many had gone as far as full formals. Jainan's blue-gray ceremonials were technically too subdued for the occasion. He was out of place.

A few of the small groups near the door broke up to stare at them as the Ambassador personally announced their titles.

"Offer your arm," Jainan murmured to Kiem. They were expected to be a couple. Kiem started, then obligingly held it out. Jainan took it, leaned over and kissed him lightly on the cheek. He was steeled against the inappropriate change in his heartbeat at being so close—a physical reaction, it couldn't be helped—but he wasn't expecting to actually feel the tremor as Kiem recoiled from him. Kiem was too well-mannered to step away, though, and Jainan pulled back quickly enough that nobody noticed the reaction.

"That boy over there is glaring at us," Kiem said under his breath.

"Girl," Jainan said. "That's . . . a clan member of mine. Gairad." He *shouldn't* have come. His head was hurting enough that pleading illness wouldn't even have been a lie. "We might have to avoid her."

He expected to have to come up with an explanation. But all Kiem said was, "Right, can do," and steered them into a conversation with a mix of Theans and Iskaners on the other side of the room.

It didn't go well. Every third Thean they met had some query for Jainan on where he'd been, and how he'd been doing, and why he hadn't been in contact. At Jainan's silences, Kiem deflected most of the questions, but ten minutes of that apparently put Kiem on edge enough that he started to stress that Jainan was in mourning. It was going badly. Jainan knew it was his fault, and desperately started to plan how he might excuse himself and unshackle Kiem so he had a better time. He could plead a headache and find a quiet corner to check the crash data again.

He went off to fetch them drinks, leaving Kiem to talk to an intense young staffer about the Resolution. When he returned, he realized with some horror that the man had veered off into a historical description of exactly what the Thean public had thought of each of Iskat's Ministers for Thea. Kiem was wearing one of his listening expressions.

Jainan acknowledged the staffer and subtly cut him out of the conversation. "I like him," Kiem said as Jainan steered them away. "Vivid grasp of metaphor."

"Mm," Jainan said, and handed him his drink before they joined the next set of people.

Even Kiem's energy couldn't last forever. Sometime in the second hour he murmured to Jainan, between conversations, "They're really not fond of me, are they?"

Jainan felt cold. "It's not you," he said. They had stopped in a niche away from the hubbub of conversation. Above them, a sandstone statue reached out its arms and poured water into a square stone trough beside Jainan's hand.

"Well, you know them better than me," Kiem said dubiously. "But I'm getting the feeling it really is."

Before Jainan could reply, Lady Fadith interrupted them. "Your Highness," she said, "Could the Ambassador have a quick word? With Count Jainan as well?"

Kiem met Jainan's eyes. Jainan said, "I'll go."

"The Ambassador requests Prince Kiem's presence too," Fadith said firmly. "It will only take a moment of your time."

There was no way to politely refuse, although the back of Jainan's neck was prickling. He almost wished it was about his conversation with the Kaani representative, but of course the embassy would barely see that as significant. This would be about Thean social obligations. He didn't want to drag Kiem into it. But Kiem just said, "Of course, I've been wanting to speak to him anyway," and followed Fadith into the private part of the embassy, to a large, well-appointed office that was obviously the new Ambassador's.

It needed to be large. There were several people there already, not even counting the tall, skeletal presence of the Ambassador behind his desk. Jainan was finding it harder to breathe. He recognized all of them: a scattering of important senior diplomats and three or four people wearing his own clan colors. Gairad was in the corner. If he was going to be hauled over the coals for defaulting on his social duties, it seemed unfair to do it in public like this.

There were barely enough chairs. They had made up the numbers by dragging in a rickety plastic one obviously from a canteen. Fadith ushered Jainan to the free space at the end of the couch, and before Jainan could intervene, the Ambassador had nodded Kiem to the spare plastic chair.

Jainan recoiled from the thought of how Taam would have reacted, but Kiem sat without batting an eyelid.

"Nice to see you all here," Kiem said. "I'm afraid I don't have many names—Your Excellency, of course . . . Lady Fadith . . . and that must be Gairad in the corner." He looked around hopefully, as if for more introductions. Gairad had looked up at the mention of her name, focusing a suspicious look on Kiem. Kiem gave her one of his disarming smiles.

It didn't do much for the tension in the room. Lady Fadith, still standing, didn't offer introductions. She rested her hand on the desk beside her and said, "I'm sorry to have to bring you up here, but you know the issue we're going to raise."

"Uh," Kiem said. "Not a clue, actually."

Ambassador Suleri watched them sardonically. Jainan said, through a dry throat, "I do."

"Mm," Suleri said. "Your Highness and Your Grace understand, I assume, that though Thea is small, our relationship as an allied province requires a delicate touch and significant attention from both sides. You will also be aware"—and now he looked from Jainan to Kiem and back again—"that the current arrangements have not been ideal, from our point of view, for quite some time."

Kiem frowned. This conversation must seem very odd from where he sat, Jainan thought. "You mean, you're getting pushback?" he said. "Look, I don't know what you're expecting from me, but to be honest with you, I'm not very deeply involved in politics."

Lady Fadith inclined her head to Kiem in a half bow. She was rubbing her finger and thumb together in a nervous tic down by her side, where she probably thought nobody would notice. She *should* be nervous, Jainan thought distantly. She and the Ambassador were bordering on rudeness to an Imperial Prince.

"It is difficult," Fadith said, "when we don't have any communication at all with our treaty principal."

Jainan thought of trying to explain, felt sick, and looked at the floor.

"Um," Kiem said. "If he doesn't want to talk to you, then I'm sorry." There was an odd note in his voice. When Jainan looked up, Kiem was sitting up straighter, almost bristling. He looked ridiculous in his plastic canteen chair. "But if he doesn't, he probably has a good reason."

"Does he?" Suleri said. "Your Highness?"

"What?"

The Esvereni had never scrupled to point out what was wrong with other prominent clans, but Jainan had no idea why Suleri would do something as rash as needling Kiem. The last

ambassador had been a *diplomat*. "I hesitate to imply it," Suleri
said, "but some would say it might be quite convenient for your
side for Thea to have no representative in the palace."

"Wait," Kiem said. "What are you saying? That I've stopped
Jainan from talking to you? That's ludicrous. How would I do
that? I've only known him a week."

The Ambassador merely lifted his shoulders. Everyone in the
room was now looking at Kiem. "All I can say is that my staff
tell me Count Jainan has disengaged with everyone in this room
over the last—"

"No." Jainan forced himself to unclench his jaw, which felt
like it was locked in place. If he didn't explain this now, it would
poison the entire bilateral relationship, when in fact this was
Jainan's personal problem. "It has nothing to do with Prince
Kiem. Your staff *know* it doesn't. It's the security clearance issue."

"Ah," Ambassador Suleri said. He didn't sound greatly convinced, though his staff must have told him. "Yes."

"What security clearance issue?" Kiem asked.

"My security clearance was revoked a while ago," Jainan said.
His voice was level and only a little hoarse. He could get through
this.

"*What?* Why?"

One of the other diplomats leaned forward: the cultural attaché. She was one of Ressid's friends. "And your security clearance stopped you from speaking to us about anything?" she asked.
"Even a message about the weather? You spoke to Lady Ressid for
a while after the issue was raised."

Jainan shut his eyes briefly. There was no easy way to put this.
"I was encouraged not to." That was true, but it wasn't the whole
story. He'd become tired of being cross-examined over what he'd
said; he'd become tired of the arguments; he'd taken the easy
way out.

Kiem pushed back his chair. "*Encouraged not to?* Who by?"

"Your Highness, please sit down," Lady Fadith said.

Jainan hadn't even bothered to look up; he recognized Kiem's I-can't-sit-still jitters. "Security," Jainan said. "Internal Security. It was a routine matter." He took a breath and stopped himself before he said anything else.

"So," Ambassador Suleri said, before Kiem could say anything. "Can I take it this will be easily resolved?"

"No," Jainan said.

"Yes!" Kiem said at the same time, then looked at Jainan and amended it to, "Somehow. Maybe not *easily* resolved, but—what the hell, they told you not to talk to your *family*?"

Jainan had pressed a finger to his temple again. This time he didn't take it away. "Prince Kiem—" he said. He didn't even know what he was going to say to him, but dragging everyone through his dirty laundry in public—*excruciatingly* in public—was more than Jainan could stand.

But even the name seemed to have an effect. Kiem raised both his hands in front of him and said, "Sorry. We'll talk about it." He turned back to the Ambassador. "Thank you for raising it. No, really. We'll look into it." There was still an odd note to his voice.

"Please do," Suleri said, his voice sardonic. "I look forward to our closer collaboration."

Lady Fadith murmured, "Jainan, if you would like to have a word in private . . . ?" Her gaze on him felt uncomfortable.

"No," Jainan said for the third time, more desperately. "I am feeling slightly unwell, still. Excuse me." He stood. "Thank you for the invitation."

"Yes, very much!" Kiem said, shaking the Ambassador's hand heartily. "Hope to see you at many more!"

Jainan wouldn't have believed it was possible to extract themselves from the room and the reception in less than five minutes. But somehow Kiem did it by clapping shoulders and grabbing hands and making loud comments about the next reception, and they made it out before the pain in Jainan's head had time to grow any more. Jainan led them down a back staircase to the foyer. Kiem was unusually quiet until they reached the entrance. Then he took a breath, but he was interrupted by Gairad barreling out of the main room and nearly crashing into him.

"Count Jainan!" she said. "Sweet God, I thought you'd gone and I'd have to trek to the palace. Here." She passed him the thumb-sized silver circle of a secure data coin. "Professor Audel asked me to give you this. It's got the files the military let us have from Operation Kingfisher. She says to go through it and see if you can work out what extraction methods they're using. I'm trying to make a refinery plan."

Jainan stared down at the data coin. His mind was so far from Audel's project that it took him a moment to even process what Gairad had said. "Thank you," he said eventually, and slipped it into his pocket.

Gairad didn't move. "I wanted to say," she said, "I didn't know about the security clearance thing."

"No," Jainan said. He tried to think of something else to say, and couldn't.

"So, I'm sorry," she said.

Jainan blinked. "What?"

Gairad drew back uncomfortably. "I'm not saying it again," she said. She half turned, looked back over her shoulder, and said, "I'll tell Lady Ressid."

"*Wait—*" Jainan said reflexively, but she was already lost in the crowd.

"The Ambassador will tell Lady Ressid anyway," Kiem said from behind him. "As will at least a dozen other people by the end of the day, if I'm reading them right. The attendants can't find your coat."

Jainan turned, distracted. "I came without one."

"Why did you—okay, you know what, never mind." As an attendant opened the door, Jainan felt warmth enveloping his shoulders and realized it was Kiem's coat. Kiem was still talking as he settled it around Jainan. "I told Bel I was going to walk back. I thought I was going to want to clear my head. Do you mind? The other alternative is that I call her now and we wait, but it'll take ten minutes."

Jainan thought of staying in here where the Ambassador could pull him aside for a word. "No," he said. "Let's walk." He started to shrug out of the coat.

"No. Yes. I kind of thought that—wait, what are you doing? Please wear the coat."

"It's your coat."

"I'm the one who didn't plan ahead for a lift! Look, I don't get cold. And I'm wearing a jacket." Jainan almost glanced at him, but stopped himself before he made eye contact, and didn't argue further.

Outside the embassy, the wind hit them with a flurry of snow-flakes. The embassy was on the edge of the old part of town; it was a short walk back to the palace along streets covered with powdery drifts of snow and packed ice, all uphill. Kiem started off at a brisk, determined pace quite unlike his usual stroll. Jainan quickened his stride to fall in beside him. He was glad of the coat, even if he wished Kiem hadn't given it to him: his back was already tight with tension, and the cold would have made it worse.

After the first exchange, Kiem said nothing for long minutes. Part of Jainan wanted to bring up Taam's crash data, but this would be precisely the wrong time, when Kiem was already an-noyed and Jainan doubted his own memory. All he could think of was Kiem sitting up straight on that ridiculous chair while the Ambassador and the senior staff of the Thean embassy took turns to reprimand him over something completely outside his control. Jainan couldn't even think of what Taam would have done in that situation; his skin prickled trying to imagine it.

He threw a glance at Kiem, who was walking beside him with his hands shoved deep in his pockets against the cold. His face was set in a slight frown. After a while Jainan couldn't bear the waiting any more. "What are you going to do?" he said. Too direct. Much more direct than he would have been with Taam.

Kiem had started in the middle of a step when Jainan spoke, and now he turned his head. "Huh? What am I going to do?" he said. There was still something off about his voice, and without knowing what it was, just the oddness was enough to flip all of Jainan's danger switches. "I'm going to find Internal Security and yell at them until they fix this. Sorry, I sort of thought that was obvious. Do you want to come?"

It took Jainan a couple of steps to even begin to process this, but when he had, he forced the next words out because they needed to be said. "I don't think the clearance issue can be fixed."

Kiem didn't seem to notice that Jainan had directly contradicted him. "There must be a way," he said. "What kind of information did you actually pass on to Thea? It can't have been that bad, I can't believe—I mean, you don't seem the careless type. And Thea is our *ally*."

Jainan scrabbled for an answer. "Nothing," he said finally. It sounded just as thin and insubstantial as he'd expected; perhaps he should have made something up. He pulled the coat more tightly around him with stiff fingers. "I—I suppose there must have been something, but I have very little idea what it could have been. I sometimes discussed politics with Ressid, but only what had already appeared in the newslogs, and I never discussed Taam's work. I didn't know enough to talk about it." The artificially dry surface of the path rose into a bridge that led from the city to the palace with a clear glass windbreak on each side. The city traffic veins weren't allowed over the palace; tunnels of light arced down from the sky over Arlusk, filled with jostling flyers, and dived into a canyon below the bridge. "I know that sounds implausible."

"That should make it easier," Kiem said. The wind snaked around the sides of the windbreak and threw up goose bumps on his wrists, where the shirtsleeves met his gloves. "Don't feel you have to come if you don't want to."

Jainan had missed a step in Kiem's thought process. It was possible that Kiem just hoped Internal Security would take the whole mess off his hands.

But then again, if that was true, Jainan had information that Kiem needed to know or he would be walking in unprepared. "Kiem," Jainan said. "About the data."

Kiem threw him a nonplussed look. "What data?"

"The flybug logs from Taam's crash," Jainan said. Suddenly they were on the bridge, sheltered from the snow-laden wind by the barrier, and his voice seemed too loud in the stillness. "I—I found a similar example in a textbook." He swallowed. "In fact, identical."

"Oh, just what we needed," Kiem said. "Great. That's just great. So, what, fake logs? Or whoever collected them made a mistake—was that Internal Security or Colonel Lunver's lot? Hell, I really *hope* it's a mistake."

"It could be a mistake," Jainan said. "I could have analyzed them badly." With every word he said, the possibility he had made it all up seemed to solidify. He wished he had kept his mouth shut. "I'm sorry. I don't want to cause trouble."

"Cause trouble?" Kiem halted in midstride. Jainan nearly missed the cue, but managed to stop before he overtook him. Kiem turned to him, and what was on his face was close enough to anger to make Jainan go still.

"Okay, so let me check if I've got this straight," Kiem said. "The palace revoked your clearance and you don't even know why. On top of that, your partner dies—might have been *killed*—and Internal Security can't even get themselves together long enough to give you the right data about it. And you can't complain to your family because the palace says that you need clearance to do even that—Jainan, that's appalling. Cause trouble? You must hate us!"

For some reason that hurt, like scratching at a scab. "No," Jainan said. "I don't."

"I don't understand," Kiem said, his voice changing to bewilderment. "Why didn't you tell someone they revoked your clearance? Why didn't you tell me—Taam—*anyone*? Or did you?"

"There was nothing to be done," Jainan said shortly, because that hurt even more, and he wanted to head it off. "I agreed to marry Taam and live here. That means I agreed to be bound by palace procedures. I have no quarrel with Internal Security."

"I don't get it." They had come to a stop just before the central rise of the bridge. Behind Kiem, the palace was spread out in all its crystalline glory, the towers blurring with the white-gray snow clouds. "You got cut off from everyone. Just because the palace told you it was a matter of *security* doesn't mean that's okay!"

Jainan felt a surge of something shockingly like anger. "That's exactly what it means!" His hands had formed white-knuckled fists in the pockets of the coat. For a moment he felt almost warm, though it was a prickly, unpleasant heat. "I am here to maintain the treaty. I am a diplomat."

"What's that got to do with it?"

Now this was near mockery. "I know what it is to do my duty by my people," Jainan said sharply. "I have never shirked that."

Kiem looked strange. It seemed to take him a while to form words, while Jainan waited and tasted metal in his mouth.

"I didn't mean that," Kiem said. "I'm sorry, I would never imply— I know you always do your duty." He broke off. "Obviously." He took a step forward, closing some of the distance. Jainan felt a strange anger course through his body. "But doing your duty doesn't have to make you this unhappy, does it?" Kiem said. If Jainan hadn't known better, it would have sounded like Kiem was pleading. He stopped half a pace away and lifted his hand in an empty gesture. "Come on. Not—pointlessly. Not like this."

Jainan's rock-solid certainty started to drain away. He could be intractably stubborn, when the issue was important—it was one of the things that made him a bad choice for a goodwill representative. But this wasn't anger. He didn't know what it was, but in the face of it, his conviction was falling apart.

"It's how it is," he said instead. "You know that."

"I *don't*," Kiem said. He shut his mouth deliberately, as if challenging Jainan to fill the gap.

Jainan was silent. Kiem stared at him, still waiting for an answer, and rubbed his arms against the cold. Jainan belatedly realized they'd been standing still for too long. The tension around Kiem's arms and shoulders was turning into shivers. "Okay," Kiem said. "I think we might be talking about different things here—what are you doing?"

Jainan had pulled off the coat and held it out. "You're cold," he said before he could stop himself. Too direct: that would hit an Iskaner's pride. "It's my fault." Not much better.

Kiem stared at him and at the coat between them. He didn't move to take it. His eyes went back to Jainan's face, and that odd almost-anger furrowed his forehead again. "This is the same bloody thing."

"Excuse me?" Jainan said.

"Now it's your fault I can't survive without a coat?" Kiem said. "Am I the only one seeing something weird about this? Why didn't you tell me about the clearance issue before? Why don't I understand anything that's going on?"

Jainan's hands tightened around the fur bundle. He had brought it closer to his chest without realizing; he forced himself to hold it casually down by his side.

Kiem shoved his hands into his pockets again: a solid, unhappy shape against the landscape. "I get what you're saying about the duty thing," he said. "No, really. I'm shit at it and not exactly the pride of the family, but I get it. We're born into this, and we have to do something to be worthy of it. But everything you do is about *you* needing to be unhappy."

The cold ate into him like acid. *You're wrong,* Jainan wanted to say, but he couldn't say that to an Imperial Prince. He said distantly, "I apologize, Your Highness." He saw Kiem flinch at the title and hated himself for using formality as a weapon, but did it anyway. "I would rather not talk about this. I request." These were underhanded measures. He was an underhanded person.

Kiem recoiled, his hunched, unhappy posture giving way like a loosened spring. "I'm sorry," he said. "Oh hell, I'm sorry, I didn't mean to pry. I don't have any right. Forgive me."

He had every right. But Jainan stood there for a short eternity with his reply caught between his teeth, grateful for that small mercy even as he knew he shouldn't take advantage of it.

Movement caught his eye: a pair of fur-wrapped figures climbing up from the other end of the bridge. Every sense of danger he had flared, like someone laying their finger on an exposed nerve—he and Kiem were confronting each other, both as tense as unhappy cats. It looked like a public argument.

"Jainan?" Kiem said.

The last of Jainan's anger drained away into distant dread. "People." He didn't need to say anything else.

Kiem gave him a look of bafflement, then turned and realization dawned. Jainan had already closed the gap, and he slipped his hand into the crook of Kiem's elbow. The unwieldy bundle of coat sat incongruously under his other arm. He couldn't speak in case they were overheard, but he tried to convey by the careful lightness of his touch that he knew he had crossed a line. He kept his expressionless gaze to the front as they passed the other walkers.

Kiem glanced over at the pair. "What do you think," he asked under his breath, "can we sell it as performance art?"

It took a split second for Jainan to realize he was joking. Something terrifyingly like laughter welled up in him, in spite of the situation, in spite of everything. His hand tightened on Kiem's arm. That was a mistake, because it apparently encouraged him.

"Dammit," Kiem said, "we shouldn't have stopped, we could have charged them for tickets."

They'd been recognized. One of the figures raised a hand, changing their path so they cut across to Kiem and Jainan. "Kiem!" Their companion followed. "I thought you were at the embassy."

"Vaile!" Kiem said, with jollity that must be forced. "We left a bit early. We're just taking a walk. Seeing the city. That sort of thing. Who's your friend?"

Prince Vaile gave them both a graceful bow of acknowledgment and introduced the man beside her as a colleague from Rtul, but Jainan was struggling so hard to think of some sort of explanation other than *arguing in public* that he didn't catch the name. Kiem was doing the honors anyway, since apparently nothing would throw him off enough that he couldn't find some small talk.

". . . both look perishing cold, though," Vaile said on the back of something else. She gave their thin indoor clothes and the coat under Jainan's arm a quizzical look.

Jainan tensed, but Kiem was already talking. "It was a . . . dare," he said. There was a pause. Kiem carried on to fill it. "You see, we didn't get a honeymoon, so we have to make up for the excitement somehow." Jainan choked. "You know, dares, bets, extreme sports . . . We're going skydiving tomorrow."

Jainan fought against the rising tide of inappropriate laughter. This must be what they meant by hysteria. His squeezed Kiem's arm silently.

"Skydiving," Vaile said, in the tone of one who doesn't believe what she's just heard.

Jainan interrupted before Kiem could commit them irrevocably. "It's still under discussion," he said firmly. "Skydiving is very unfashionable on Thea at the moment."

That was an impulse he should probably have quelled. "Oh?" Vaile said.

This had apparently caught the interest of her Rtulian colleague, who leaned in. "I didn't realize you had fashions in extreme sports. How fascinating. So what *is* fashionable on Thea right now?"

Jainan had never been able to sense Kiem's stress or anger as he had Taam's and had put that down to the newness of their marriage. But now, all of a sudden, he could feel Kiem's huge, expectant glee beside him, and he blamed that for what he said next. "Bull wrestling."

"Wrestling . . . bulls?" The man's brow wrinkled. Kiem was overcome by a sudden fit of coughing, but Jainan kept his blandest expression on his face. "That sounds . . . Your Highness, are you all right?"

"Oh, yes," Kiem said. "Getting a cold. Too many dares. Do excuse us, lots of planning to do." He clapped Vaile on the shoulder, shook her companion's hand vigorously, and made a swift escape with Jainan's hand still clamped on his arm. By unspoken consensus they quickened their stride until they were over the bridge.

They neared the courtyard of the main palace entrance, where there was a scattering of people, and slowed down when they were definitely out of sight of the bridge. Jainan's rapid heartbeats slowed as well, and with it the brief warmth, and they both remembered at the same time that they were in something like an argument.

They didn't stop walking this time. The drone of traffic faded behind them as the sound-screens that protected the palace kicked in. "So," Kiem said. "I'm going around the side entrance. If I remember right, then it's closer to the staff buildings and Internal Security. Do you want to come?"

Jainan wavered. He thought about going back to their rooms and waiting dutifully while his future was decided for him. He thought about the crash data. He took a breath. "Yes," he said. "I would like to come."

CHAPTER 11

"You're *where*?" Bel said through Kiem's ear implant.

"Outside Internal Security's offices, trying to get in," Kiem said. He kicked his heels against the desk he was sitting on, caught Jainan's involuntary glance, and stopped. They were deep in the palace's staff buildings among a bustle of administrators and desks. Across a corridor, the guard they'd just talked to kept casting them uncomfortable looks. "They won't even let me in without a meeting. How quickly can you set me up a meeting? I need the head person."

"With the head of Internal Security? Not fast, their contact details aren't even published internally."

"Okay, give me their name and I'll try and bluff it."

"When I said *contact details*, that included their name," Bel said. "Searching for it probably puts you on a watch list. I'll do some digging."

"Thanks. Message me if you get it," Kiem said. He cut the call. Jainan had perched himself on the edge of a spare chair and was watching Kiem with the blank look that seemed to mean wariness. Kiem gave him what was meant to be a reassuring smile—there was no sign that it worked—and made another call. "Hey, uh, Roal. Yeah, it's Kiem. Long time no see. Hey, quick question—you know when you moved jobs, was that to Internal Security? Great, I thought so." He glanced around. The noise of the office probably covered him, but he lowered his voice anyway.

"I need a favor. I need the name of your boss and the contact pin to their office."

Jainan could definitely overhear the conversation. There was now a slight frown on his face. As Kiem finished the call, Jainan said, "Will that get them in trouble?"

"No," Kiem said, "because I won't say who I got it from."

Jainan gave him a long, scrutinizing look, and Kiem started to wonder if he'd done something wrong, but all Jainan said was, "How do you know all these people?"

"Just . . . normally," Kiem said. "Everyone does, right?"

"No," Jainan said. He fell in beside Kiem as they went back to Internal Security's receptionist.

Kiem gave the receptionist his best smile. The security guard hovered by his shoulder. "Sorry, just got the details through from my aide. Chief Agent Rakal, please, and here's the pin for their office." He made a gesture that threw a tiny display from his wristband onto the desk. "I know we're not on the list, but let them know I'm here, would you?"

"Your Highness—" the receptionist said, after exchanging uneasy glances with the security guard.

"Just—try the call, please," Kiem said. "Tell them I was really obnoxious. Tell them I'm going to rearrange through General Tegnar if Agent Rakal won't see me, and then I'll bring the general to the meeting." He didn't like bringing her name into it, but he remembered Jainan's resigned acceptance about having his communications cut off, and it was enough to stifle that faint concern. "This isn't your problem, I know. Put me through to Agent Rakal and it won't be."

"I'll just—I'll just contact their office," the receptionist said, after trading another glance with the guard. Kiem nodded thanks and wandered away a couple of steps to join Jainan.

"General Tegnar?" Jainan murmured. "Is that your mother?"

"The one and only," Kiem said. Jainan gave him a sideways look, evidently trying to square the picture of a successful general with the observed reality of Kiem. "*Really* let's try not to get her involved, she's based off-planet anyway. I don't think she knew Taam. It will take her at least a month to find out I used her name." The receptionist was holding out a speaker. Kiem strode over and took it. "Hi!" he said. "Prince Kiem here to see you. It will only take a few minutes. I hope you've got a few minutes, because I'm going to be camping out here until you do."

The voice at the other end was professionally noncommittal, but that seemed to do the trick. In a very short amount of time, a nervous-looking junior agent came out to usher them inside.

It wasn't as exciting as Kiem had thought. Internal Security's offices were like the administration areas outside, except slightly grayer and older-looking. Kiem's wristband buzzed against his skin and went dead. He glanced sideways to check how Jainan was doing but he needn't have worried: however agitated Jainan might have been on the walk back, now his face was clean of all expression and he was a model of grace and poise.

Then Kiem caught sight of an agent turning a corner ahead of them, and stopped dead.

"Your Highness?" the junior agent said.

"I know her," Kiem said. "I met her in the gardens outside our rooms last week. I thought she was a security guard."

"I can't comment on personnel, Your Highness," the junior agent said apologetically. "This way, if you please?" While Kiem was still trying to work out how to ask Internal Security if they were spying on him, she brought them to a door at the end of the corridor, scanned her bios—retina and hand movement—and gestured them through into Agent Rakal's office.

The office was aggressively nondescript, as shabby as the rest of the quarters. The only splash of color was the gold-framed portrait of the Emperor above the agent waiting behind the desk. They rose as Kiem and Jainan entered. "Your Highness."

Chief Agent Rakal—that was who it must be—barely came up to Kiem's shoulder. They were slightly built and trim in

Internal Security's black uniform, and their hair was half-braided and pulled back in a neat clip. Their neck and wrists were bare of any ornament marking gender.

They didn't come out from behind the desk, which was probably a point of some kind; Kiem ignored it and leaned over to shake hands.

"Kiem," he said. "You knew that, nice to meet you, this is Count Jainan, you may know him." *Your people definitely do,* he nearly said, but for once managed to stop himself. He needed Rakal on their side to sort this all out.

"Your Highness," Rakal said, short and sharp. "Your Grace. You gave the impression this was an emergency. What is it that needs my attention at two minutes' notice?"

"Oh, yes, sorry. Thanks for seeing us," Kiem said, in a disarming tone that notably failed to disarm Rakal. "A couple of things, actually. Can we sit down?" He nodded to the couple of chairs grouped informally around a low table for guests. It was an automatic move: things always went better if everyone felt more casual.

Rakal stared back at him impassively and said, "If you like." They didn't move.

Kiem scrambled for a response. "Right."

Rakal waited, palms resting on the desk, and raised their eyebrows at the short silence.

Kiem only hit this sort of person occasionally, and it was abysmal luck that Rakal was one of them. Some people, he'd found, just *didn't like him.* Most people he met for the first time were either friendly or they were wary and would warm up to him when they felt they had his measure. Every now and then, though, he came up against someone who looked straight into him and had nothing but contempt for what they saw. He was getting that feeling with Rakal. Usually Kiem could mark those people down and avoid them. Avoiding this conversation was not an option.

Jainan was still as a statue beside him. Kiem took a deep breath and said, "For a start, you could have told us the Auditor thinks Taam's death was murder."

"Who told you that?" Rakal said evenly.

"The Auditor, actually," Kiem said, "at about the same time as he refused to instate both of us. Was it?"

"The matter is being dealt with," Rakal said. "We have it in hand and the Emperor has been briefed. There is no current need for you to know the status of the investigation."

Kiem paused. He had never been allowed near Internal Security before, let alone had the authority to press them for case details. "Fine," he said. "All right. I'll drop it—on one condition: you get your people to fix Jainan's security clearance. There's been some kind of error."

"What kind of error?" Rakal asked.

Kiem felt the sudden onset of doubt. If this had been a mistake by some administrator deep in Internal Security's hierarchy, they could probably have solved it in ten minutes with a quick message. "Your people revoked his clearance, *months* ago—Jainan, how long?"

"Two years," Jainan said quietly.

"See, two y—what?"

Rakal gave Jainan a measuring look. "Naturally I am aware."

Kiem looked at Jainan as well, still trying to process the thought of *two years*. Jainan was standing a step back, as if he'd resigned himself to having no influence in whatever was decided. Kiem felt a sick lurch of something—guilt, anger—and didn't even try to suppress it. He leaned forward and put his own hands on the desk. "Fix this," he said, hearing an unexpected edge in his own voice. "He can't talk to his family. *Fix it.*"

"Prince Kiem," Rakal said levelly. "Let me make one thing very clear: I won't be drawn into melodramatics on security issues." They stopped Kiem's incredulous protest with a raised hand. "I am aware that Count Jainan has a level two flag on his communications. This means he was considered a potential risk for leaking classified material. As you must also know, a level two flag does not stop him from contacting whomever he wants to outside the palace. It only means we ask him to clear it with us in advance so we can monitor it."

"That's not true," Kiem said. "He hasn't had any contact at all."

Jainan shifted beside him, but didn't have time to say anything before Rakal raised their eyebrows and said, "Indeed? Then someone is lying to you."

"I am not lying," Jainan said, low and colorless. "I was discouraged from contact—I am sorry if I gave a false impression." Jainan's eyes flicked between Rakal and Kiem, and then went back to the desk. "I accept the security measures the palace sees fit to apply. I apologize for bothering you."

It would not help to shout. Kiem forced himself to breathe out and keep his voice under control. "It's really not you who needs to apologize," he said. "Agent Rakal. Your monitoring system isn't bloody working, since your people have obviously just used it to hassle Jainan into cutting off contact. Which I'm sure made things much easier for them. Jainan is unhappy. The Thean Ambassador is unhappy. *I* am *pissed off*, and very few things piss me off. I want you to take that flag off his account."

If Rakal hadn't liked him before, now the hostility over the desk between them and Kiem was like something physical. "Your Highness," Rakal said. "You cannot have a decision you don't like changed just because you want it to change. I answer to the Emperor, not to every royal who wants to throw their weight around."

Kiem recognized the sinking feeling of being backed into terrain where he couldn't win. He switched tactics. "If you'd bothered to *talk* to Jainan, you might have realized you were barking up the wrong tree," he said. "But you didn't, did you? You just cut him out because he's a foreigner. You didn't even listen to him about the crash data."

"What data?" Rakal said sharply.

"We got hold of the data you have on Taam's crash," Kiem said. "We think that log transcript came from a reference book. So either you have the wrong logs, or—"

Rakal turned straight to Jainan, clearly aware that Kiem wouldn't understand an engineering log even if someone explained it to him in short words with a cheerful science animation for children. "Who gave you that data?" they said. "It should have been under a confidentiality seal."

There was a horrible pause before Jainan said softly, "I'm not sure that's relevant."

"Someone a damn sight more helpful than *you*," Kiem said. "Where are the real logs?"

"I don't know what you're talking about." Rakal inputted something on their wristband. "This is a serious breach of security. Count Jainan, I will need you to delete the material you have obtained and to allow us access to review your account."

"What?" Kiem said in astonishment. "He doesn't have to do that. How is it Jainan's fault that there's something wrong with your evidence?"

"If permission is necessary," Jainan said, then stopped.

"You copied them to my account as well, and *I* don't give permission," Kiem said. "What gives you the right to poke around in our personal lives?"

Rakal's look gave Kiem pause, even as his indignation picked up steam, because he had come across several of Iskat's more murderous fauna while on hikes and Rakal reminded him strongly of something with too many teeth. "*Because,* Your Highness," Rakal said, as if this was something painfully obvious Kiem had failed to get, "your partner is a subject of interest in the investigation."

Kiem stopped.

He saw the slightest of movements in the corner of his eye; Jainan had gripped the edge of the table, as if he was having difficulty standing up. Even as Kiem started to turn, though, Jainan straightened, looking unsteady and ill. Rakal was watching Kiem closely. "That's nonsense," Kiem said blankly. It was more than nonsense. "That's the most ridiculous thing I've heard this year, and considering my last audience with the Emperor, that's a high bar. What do you think he did to Taam, murdered him?" Jainan shook his head urgently beside him.

There was another, even more horrible silence.

"Are you asking to be involved in the case, Prince Kiem?" Rakal said.

"I *am* involved in it," Kiem said. "He's my partner! Tell me what you're investigating!"

Rakal seemed to weigh their words before they spoke. Their voice came out cool, as if Kiem were a hostile media outlet. "Prince Taam's death was suspicious," they said. "We are investigating a number of options. There have been attempts to break into Operation Kingfisher's systems even after Prince Taam passed away. Operation Kingfisher, which, I shouldn't need to remind you, is not popular on Thea."

"That's your evidence?" Kiem said incredulously.

"Of course not," Rakal said impatiently. "That is context. I am not going to litigate the case evidence with anyone but the Emperor."

"I didn't," Jainan said, swallowing audibly. "I know there is very little use in me saying that, but I did nothing. Your people told me I wasn't needed for questioning."

"He's a *diplomat*," Kiem said. "He has no motive, you have no proof, and he's a *goodwill ambassador*. You're treating him like he came in on a raider ship! He's just lost his partner, and now you're going to drag him through an investigation? What do you think that's going to do to our relationship with Thea?"

"This is why I think we would all prefer to do this informally," Rakal said. "Either you and Count Jainan can give us access to your accounts voluntarily, or I will apply for a sealed Imperial

Justice Order. Either way, this can be done without causing further tensions with the Resolution."

"I'll take it to the Emperor," Kiem said, but he felt the negotiation slipping away.

"Do," Rakal said, and Kiem heard in the word the truth they both knew: Kiem didn't have an ounce of influence with the Emperor. Internal Security was in the Emperor's pocket.

Could he pull rank any further? He felt something like despair at the thought of it. It would be obvious he had no idea what he was doing. Rakal would just laugh, and they'd be right to.

And then, all of a sudden, Kiem realized he was going about it the wrong way. He met Rakal's eyes. "You've got to admit," he said, "our whole track record with Jainan looks bad. Jainan gives up his family and his life on Thea to come over here, and then we revoke his security clearance and isolate him. We treat him as an enemy. Cut him off from his family. People will sympathize, don't you think?"

"I couldn't say," Rakal said expressionlessly. "But I would say that most people in the palace understand security threats."

Kiem leaned in. "I have a couple of friends who might see it a different way," he said. "Journalists. You know journalists—always obsessed with the human angle. Like I said, it could get out. Could look very bad."

Beside him, he heard Jainan's soft intake of air. Kiem didn't look around; he couldn't afford to look away from Rakal.

"You would not," Rakal said.

"Oh, I'm not suggesting anyone blows the whole thing open," Kiem said. "Your half-baked *investigation* would really screw things up if it got out. But mistreatment of the Thean representative? Forbidding him to talk to his relatives? That's something we could give the press."

"You would not *invite* a scandal across half the royal family," Rakal said. They looked like they had bitten something sour. "The Emperor would—"

"Exile me to a monastery again?" Kiem said. "Already went, three years ago. I'm a world-class meditator. I don't mind being in the newslogs."

They stared at each other.

"Denying us access to evidence will not stop Internal Security's investigation," Rakal said eventually.

"I don't want to stop it," Kiem said. "I want you to find out what happened; all I'm asking is that you don't take our lives apart. And you can reinstate Jainan's security clearance while you're at it," he added. Jainan was looking at him with something like disbelief. "I want you to tell me he can call anyone he likes, please."

Rakal stared at him further, now not bothering to hide the flat dislike. "I will remove the flag."

"If you harass him, expect a bunch of newslog articles to show up on Hren Halesar's desk with your name all over them," Kiem said. "Let me put this diplomatically: you have done an absolutely shit job of being balanced and proportionate in how you treat *Thea's formal representative in the palace,* and I don't trust you."

"So you have made clear," Rakal said. "Were there any other points you wished to raise?"

"No," Kiem said. "Thanks for reinstating his clearance, though. I really am grateful. Jainan, anything you want to add?"

He looked at Jainan properly. He didn't know what reaction he'd hoped for, but Jainan barely ever reacted in public, and his poker face was intact. "No, thank you."

Kiem offered his arm—which Jainan took—gave Rakal a courtly nod, and said, "Thank you for your time." He steered them out.

The righteous anger was fading, all the more so as Jainan's grip stiffened on his arm. Kiem managed to confine himself to "You okay to head back?"

"Yes," Jainan said.

Kiem recognized that tone: it was the one where *yes* only covered ten percent of what Jainan might have said. Kiem didn't know what to do about that. When they were in a completely empty corridor, Jainan looked over his shoulder and to either side, and said, "May I ask you something?"

Kiem wasn't sure he had any answers. "Go ahead."

"I will, of course, back you up in anything," Jainan said. There was a meticulous air to his words, as if he were laying them out very carefully on a tray. "I am at your disposal. But—I do not mean to cast any aspersions on your judgment—if there is any way to avoid a public scandal in the newslogs before the treaty renewal, I would . . ." He stopped, and for the first time Kiem realized the strain it was taking him to keep his voice even. "I would rather do anything else," he finished, losing the edges of his calm. "Anything. Please."

Kiem's foot caught on a low stone step and he stumbled. "Jainan, that was a bluff," he said in dismay. "I thought you knew. What did you think I'd do, just throw you to the press? You're my partner!"

Jainan looked relieved, which made Kiem frantically try and think of what *else* he'd done wrong to provoke that reaction. But of course, he thought of Jainan: grave and dignified, his every public action totally correct, holding duty around him like a shield—of *course* public scandal would be his worst nightmare. "We'll keep everything private," Kiem said. "I can promise that."

Jainan nodded. His expression hadn't changed at all, and Kiem wondered if he even believed what Kiem was saying. If he were Jainan he wouldn't have trusted anyone from the palace as far as he could throw them. Now Kiem thought about it, he realized Internal Security hadn't even given them an excuse for the fake crash data. They'd just tried to threaten Jainan into deleting it, and there wasn't a damn thing either of them could do about it.

Kiem tried to take stock. "We can ask Aren's people about the crash data," he said. "Someone must have swapped it out before it reached us. I'll get in touch with him."

"Yes," Jainan said. They were nearly outside their rooms now. "So," he said tentatively, "I only need to clear my contacts with you?"

"What?" Kiem said. What had he missed now? "Why would you need my opinion on who you call?"

"Because . . . I thought that was the agreement we came to?" Jainan's inflection turned it into a question.

"No! What? No! I'm not going to track who you talk to!"

"Sounds wise," said Bel's voice, as she came in from the study. "Everything okay? After that call I was half expecting to have to go and bail you out of a Security cell."

"Everything's fine," Kiem said. "I mean, it's *not*—Internal Security is being cagey with us, and Taam's crash might not have been an accident—but neither of us have been arrested yet. Am I late for something?"

"You'd better fill me in," Bel said. "You're not late if you go and change now. Terraforming Assistance donor gala, remember?"

"Right, right," Kiem said. "I'll change. Jainan, do you need the bedroom?"

"I'm going to call Ressid," Jainan said. It sounded like a tentative challenge.

"*Please,*" Kiem said. "Study's all yours if you want the vidchair. Or the bedroom's yours, of course. Or here—I don't need to change, I can just go out. I'll go out."

"No," Jainan said, stopping him in midflow. "Thank you." Before Kiem realized what was happening, Jainan stepped in and pressed a kiss to his cheek, light and swift.

Jainan turned away to the study, which was a good thing, as he didn't see Kiem raise his hand to his cheek like an idiot before he caught himself.

Kiem turned away too. "Bel, he's not to be disturbed unless the palace is on fire."

"Noted," Bel said. Her eyes followed Jainan curiously.

Jainan hadn't remembered to close the door. As Kiem moved

to fix that, he could see the screen inside already lighting up with a connection. A face flickered into view: the Thean noblewoman who had upbraided Kiem the morning of his wedding. Now her expression was softer, more shocked than anything else. "I didn't believe the ID," she said. "Jainan, why are you calling *now*? Is everything all right?"

"It's. Yes," Jainan said. What Kiem heard in his voice made him reach more hastily for the switch: it felt like more of a violation of Jainan's privacy for Kiem to overhear that raw, unguarded note than anything Internal Security had done. "Yes," Jainan said again, and swallowed audibly as the door started to slide shut and hide him from view. "I've missed you."

CHAPTER 12

It took Kiem all ten days of the next week to nail down Vaile. In the meantime, he sent a series of increasingly exasperated messages to Internal Security and to the military's Signals HQ, which was supposed to be in charge of log transmission for fly-bugs like the one Taam had flown. It was like sending messages into a black hole.

Jainan worked on his Imperial College project and accompanied Kiem to events with the same detachment as before. He didn't volunteer any information about his first conversation with his sister, and Kiem would rather have set his own hair on fire than ask. Jainan didn't seem to blame him for failing to get an answer about the crash data. Occasionally Kiem caught Jainan watching him with a slight frown, as if Kiem was an unpredictable cog in an otherwise orderly machine.

Some things coaxed Jainan out of his shell. Professor Audel or one of her students seemed to call him every day for animated discussions about their deep-space mining project. And on the day that Vaile returned from orbit again, Kiem found Jainan in the gardens outside with that Thean student, Gairad, who was also part of the Feria clan. Kiem had been trying to figure out clan etiquette from talking to Jainan and the few Theans at the embassy who seemed approachable, as well as reading the occasional memo from Bel, but the whole system of clan relationships took some effort to get your head around.

It looked like some kind of lesson: Gairad held a quarterstaff above her head while Jainan stood in front of her and corrected her grip. His own quarterstaff leaned against a tree a little way away.

"—can't *get* it," Kiem heard her say.

"You will. Try again." Jainan took up his own staff and turned it crosswise in front of him. "Ten!"

It seemed to be a code word. Gairad spun in the melting snow, brought her hands together on the staff, and swung it at Jainan's stomach. She obviously had grounding in the techniques, but the strike was slow, and Jainan blocked it easily. "That was better. The farther down you can get your grip, the more momentum you'll have." He finally caught sight of Kiem standing in the doorway and broke off.

Kiem waved and came forward, seeing as he'd interrupted them anyway. "Looks like fun. Can I join?" he asked, half-jokingly.

"Oh." Jainan seemed surprised, but instantly recovered. "Of course. Please." He handed Kiem his own bronze quarterstaff. Kiem took it gingerly. It was much heavier than he'd expected but couldn't be traditional metal, since it wasn't cold. "Ah, not quite." Jainan put his hands over Kiem's—for once without diffidence—and shifted his grip. "You want to hold it here."

His touch was warm. Kiem tried not to think about that as he settled his hands around the staff. "Didn't mean to hijack your lesson," he said. "Just show me one move."

"Jainan, the pair forms," Gairad said. She seemed refreshingly unbothered by the fact Kiem was a prince. "Can we try form five?"

"Yes. Kiem, would you mind?" Jainan picked up a white handle from the ground, which folded out into something like the quarterstaff Gairad was using, cheaper and flimsier-looking than his own. "Traditional quarterstaff has twenty basic moves, and one to six are for fighting with an ally. Since we have three people, Gairad's form five could do with work."

"I haven't had anyone to practice with," Gairad said defensively. Kiem spun his staff experimentally beside her, fumbled it, and lost his grip. It clattered to the ground around Gairad's ankles. Gairad picked it up and handed it back to him with a martyred air. "At least I can be better than you. That's motivating."

Kiem grinned at her. "My form five's perfect. Legendary, even. Angels weep."

The corner of Jainan's mouth twitched. "Of course," he said. "But Gairad needs to practice." Had that been a smile? Kiem wasn't sure.

Once Kiem had his grip sorted out, the basics of quarterstaff turned out to be fairly easy to grasp. Form five meant Gairad doing a sort of crouching spin and taking her imaginary opponent out at the knees, while Kiem's part was simpler—he stepped forward next to her with what Jainan called a disarming strike, which meant hitting out with his staff at wrist height. They tried it a few times against thin air. Eventually, Jainan seemed satisfied with that, and readied his own staff. "All right. Kiem to hit, please." He stepped in front of them and held up a block.

"Uh." Kiem said. Gairad nodded and crouched, but Kiem didn't move. "You want me to . . . attack you?"

There was a pause. Jainan gave Kiem a quizzical look. "I'm blocking."

"What if I miss?" Kiem said. Swinging something heavy around had been kind of fun, but now he remembered why he'd never taken well to martial arts.

Jainan lowered the block. "I see. Gairad, why don't you hit, then. Kiem, you can pull your strike."

"Right," Kiem said. Jainan politely hadn't mentioned that there was no way Kiem could get past his guard, but Kiem still felt obscurely relieved. On Jainan's snapped, "Five!" Kiem swung halfway. Gairad lashed out, and her staff hit Jainan's with a violent *crack*.

"Again," Jainan said.

They did it a few more times, until Kiem accidentally stepped in front of Gairad as she started her spin. She tripped over his ankle, said, "Shit*fuck*," and crashed forward into the ground.

Kiem tripped as well, catching himself with his hands as the impact jarred all the way up to his shoulders.

Jainan was there immediately, offering Kiem a hand up. Kiem took it and was about to make a joke before he noticed how strained Jainan's expression was. "I'm sorry," Jainan said. "Are you hurt?"

"I've got bruises," Gairad said. She rolled over and knocked snow off her knees. "*Legendary,* Prince Kiem."

"Gairad, apologize," Jainan said as Kiem pulled himself up.

Gairad frowned and opened her mouth, but Kiem forestalled her. "My fault," he said. "Totally my fault. I think I need to divert my legendary skills into something else. Maybe bull wrestling." He picked up his dropped quarterstaff and handed it back to Jainan with a rueful grin. "I've got an appointment. Let's try it again another time."

That seemed to fractionally relax the strain on Jainan's face. "As you like. Of course."

Kiem left them to it. He could see them through the windows as he closed the door behind him. The lesson was obviously going a great deal more smoothly without him there. Gairad wasn't bad, but Jainan had been training longer, and Kiem could tell every time they clashed; however much force she put into her attacks, they glanced off his defenses. Jainan's face was intent, the same way he looked when he talked about engineering, as if there was *nothing* you could put in front of him that he couldn't take apart. Kiem looked away and firmly reminded himself that he had an appointment.

The sunlight today was bright and thin. It was melting sad green patches in the snow, which would last maybe a day before a new fall covered them up. Kiem glanced up through the glass roof of the connecting walkway as he left the Courtyard Residence. The trees were dripping slush.

He met Vaile in the Emperor's Wing, where she looked entirely at home in her elegant receiving suite. The view from the window showed only the snowy gardens and the nicer palace buildings. She had managed to get one of the prized fourth-floor suites just below the Emperor's own rooms; Kiem had never quite figured out how Vaile managed things like that.

"Every time I need you, you're on Rtul," Kiem said. He threw himself across one of Vaile's armchairs with his legs over the arm and watched her pour two coffees from an ornate pot. The syrup she added to it smelled of flowers. She was carefully dressed as usual: today's bracelets were set with Eisafan bluestone and matched the flint-studded gold bands that secured her braids. She might look as if she had nothing better to do than have a chat, but Kiem knew that was an illusion. Her calendar right now said *Kiem* and her aide had only given him ten minutes.

"Kaan this time, darling," Vaile said. "Why do you think I'm slipping brandy in my coffee? You never need me these days, anyway. You haven't gotten yourself arrested for ages." She ignored Kiem's protest that he'd never technically *been* arrested and continued, "You're taking this better than expected."

"Which bit of it?" Kiem said. "The bit where Internal Security is investigating my partner? Or the bit where he casually breaks it to me that we've stopped him from talking to his family for *two years*?"

Vaile frowned delicately. "I haven't kept tabs on Thean affairs at all, but that does seem odd. No, I meant the part where the Emperor married you off to someone three weeks before the Resolution renewal, and Internal Security didn't tell you he was under investigation. I wonder if they told the Emperor. They're not known for their frank and open communication."

"This has been a massive screwup, and it's all a horrible mistake," Kiem said. "Jainan just needs some space. What I want *you* to do is explain to the Emperor that Rakal's people need to back off and find another way to settle the Auditor."

Vaile gave a musical laugh, then put her cup down and said, "Oh. You're serious."

"You're on the Advisory Council," Kiem said. He had very little idea what the Advisory Council actually did. He was starting to realize he had very little idea how any of the Empire's machinery really worked. It had never been his problem until now.

"Internal Security has never reported to the Advisory Council," Vaile said. "They're like the military; they go straight to the top." She shook her head regretfully. "Kiem. I know you don't really pay attention, but do you know what's going on at the moment?"

Kiem thought he had a fair handle on it—*we're about to sign a Galactic treaty and it turns out one of our representatives was murdered*—but that, from Vaile, was a loaded question. "Probably not as much as I need to, huh?"

Vaile gave him a sudden assessing look, her head tilted, but it was so quick that Kiem might have imagined it. "You know about the Resolution treaty renewal. Are you aware that, behind the scenes, *all* the vassal treaties are being frantically renegotiated right now? There are teams of diplomats arguing over commas while we all smile at each other over coffee."

"I thought we just rubber-stamped the treaties we already have," Kiem said, somewhat bewildered. "This whole thing is only a ceremony."

"The renewal ceremony *seals* them," Vaile said. "The Resolution wants a sector frozen in amber. You can understand, really; it has thousands of worlds to deal with. So we make terms for each renewal, then everyone is largely stuck with them for the next twenty years, under threat of breaking with the Resolution. Of *course* the vassals are agitating for better terms. They always do. It's just that Thea's flare-up is so recent and the dratted newslogs seized on it, and that makes it so much harder to get any serious negotiations done."

Kiem realized his leg was moving restlessly, but the movement felt wrong in Vaile's delicately arranged apartment, so he made himself stop. Vaile was a politician through and through; that had been obvious since she was fourteen. Kiem accepted that she knew more than him, but however he tried to make the puzzle pieces fit, there were still some missing. He could feel rusted parts of his brain trying to move. "So they're renegotiating," he said. "But—we don't have a Minister for Thea, do we? The Thean Ambassador told me."

"Poor old boy," Vaile said briefly. "Faculties failing even before he retired. I met him last year."

"So who's doing the negotiating?" Kiem said. "How can Thea get different terms if there's no one in that post?"

Vaile hesitated. "I honestly don't know," she said. There was a layer of careful politeness over it. Vaile had always been able to turn her various manners on and off like a switch. Kiem used to know how to get past it to her unfiltered self, but he seemed to have lost the knack as they grew older. "I haven't paid much attention to Thea. I assume the Emperor has it in hand."

That was a nothing answer if Kiem had ever heard one. "So you can't help," Kiem said, more of his confidence draining away. He'd been relying on her more than he'd realized. "Well, can you . . . I don't know, recommend a lawyer for Jainan?" There was already a list of lawyers on his wristband; Bel had left it there ten minutes after he'd told her what was going on.

Vaile picked up her coffee cup and ran her finger around the curve of it. "There are many fine legal firms that work with the palace. If you think about it, though, it might be better to distance yourself from the entire thing. Have you both considered a holiday? The north wetlands are quite bearable at this time of year, if you don't want to go off-planet."

"Vaile," Kiem said, cajoling. "Come on, you don't really think the wetlands are nice."

"They have a certain bleak beauty."

"*Vaile.*"

She made a soft, frustrated noise and pushed her cup away with a clatter. "All right, Kiem. If you want my real advice, *dearest* cousin, you won't go near a lawyer with a ten-foot pole."

"Why not?"

"Kiem," Vaile said, with a bluntness that meant Kiem was finally getting a real reaction. "The treaty is on a knife-edge. Whoever is playing games—and I honestly don't know who is, but I suspect it's everyone—knows these are high-stakes negotiations that won't come around again for another twenty years. We *will* sign a treaty, or the Resolution will step back and we'll find some real empire like the High Chain swarming through our link before the year is up. Nobody should be willing to go that far. But the moment—the *moment*—you engage a lawyer without consulting Her Majesty, you are setting yourself up in opposition to the Emperor. She has the legal system, the police, the secret agencies, and to some extent Parliament under her command. What political base do you have?"

Kiem automatically took a gulp of his floral coffee. It was syrupy and tasted of dead plants.

"Exactly," Vaile said. "The only advice I can give is this: sit tight and don't make waves. It will sort itself out. If you want to do something, get Count Jainan to write down everything he remembers. He may need it for his defense." A discreet chime came from her wristband. "Bother. I have to go to Council."

"Ugh. Okay, okay, I get the point." Kiem felt rather like he'd just been slashed up with an ornamental hatpin, but he had asked for it. He swung his legs back to the floor. "No dramatics."

"I'm not sure you could get by without dramatics," Vaile said. "But be careful, Kiem. The water gets deep very fast."

"Don't worry, I'm not going to make trouble," Kiem said. He got to his feet as Vaile's aide poked his head around the door to end the appointment. "I just want some answers, and nobody's given me any yet."

CHAPTER 13

There were fifteen days before Unification Day, and Jainan was sleeping badly again.

He was aware he was a liability, though Kiem was polite enough not to voice it, and he was also painfully aware he could do nothing about it. Internal Security would continue to investigate him whatever happened. Until they cleared him, the Auditor presumably wouldn't instate either of them. He could only imagine the Emperor had discussed the possibility of replacing him, replacing Kiem, appointing a whole new couple—but that would change nothing. Prince Taam was dead, and Thea was unhappy, and until Iskat produced some answers, the Auditor wouldn't instate anyone.

Jainan still had the College project to complete, and part of him held on to the vain, quixotic hope that showing Operation Kingfisher an easy way to fix their mechanical problems might calm some of the tensions between Iskat and Thea. And Kiem had indicated it was good social capital for him personally: at least Jainan could be useful there. The day after the disastrous quarterstaff practice, when Kiem and Bel were out, Jainan moved his research into the main room. He'd spent long enough on the pure mathematics. It was time to go into the Kingfisher files.

The data coin Gairad had handed him at the embassy contained an absurd amount of raw material. Professor Audel had asked Operation Kingfisher for their unclassified materials, as the Imperial College was traditionally permitted to do, and the military had responded by burying them in a mountain of largely useless information. Jainan knew this was Empire politics. The military didn't like to be questioned.

On one level, Jainan knew he had been putting off this work because it was more complicated. He moved the file dumps around the desk, trying to make some sense of the material. Professor Audel wanted him to go through and see what he could find out about the extraction methods the military was already using, because she wouldn't be able to make the case for her new method without that. Gairad thought she could reconstruct them if she could just find a plan of Kingfisher's spaceside refinery; Jainan was meant to try other angles. It would be detailed, painstaking work, but he had done that sort of work before.

The other reason he had been putting it off was that this was Taam's operation.

The files mentioned Taam a lot. He was somewhere on every major document, usually on the clearance list. Seeing his name gave Jainan a minor jolt every time, as if someone's hand had just brushed against the back of his neck.

He was in the middle of a particularly tricky calculation when the door slid open. "Wait a *moment*," he said with some exasperation.

The door shut. It took only a split second for him to realize he had just snapped at someone. Jainan's heart hammered as he reflexively cleared the wall and turned around. It wasn't Kiem, but it wasn't much better: Bel was watching him quizzically. She said, "Didn't mean to disturb you."

"I thought you were at that school fete with Kiem," Jainan said. Bel was carrying a large cone of cotton candy and a novelty balloon. Jainan took a moment to register them.

Bel looped the string of the balloon around a chair arm and gingerly placed the cotton candy cone on a side table. "He won the raffle," she said. "Be glad he found someone else to donate the twenty boxes of smoked fish to."

Jainan's mind was still half in his calculations and half preoccupied with the panic of realizing he'd snapped at his partner's aide. He couldn't remember how to hold a normal conversation. He swallowed. "Good?"

"I should warn you, I left him trying to find a design you'd like at an almond-cake stall run by thirteen-year-olds. Do Theans eat almond cake?"

"Yes," Jainan said. He cleared the desk as well and waved a command sign to wipe the filter he'd put over the windows, hastily getting rid of all signs he'd occupied the room. "Doesn't everyone?"

Bel shrugged. "I'm space-born. Home baking makes my skin crawl. Think of all those hands that have touched it. Are you all right?"

Jainan's head was still too full of equations for the question to really sink in. "Yes," he said. "I was just working on . . . on Professor Audel's project."

"I'm going to get some paperwork cleared," Bel said. "I'll leave you to it."

It was only when she disappeared into the study that he realized she had not objected to his use of the main room even though he'd snapped at her. Kiem probably wouldn't mind if Jainan was using the space for the Imperial College's project. Jainan's clan flag took up half the wall here already. He felt an odd feeling of *space,* at that, and he wanted to stretch out his arms and marvel at the freedom of the empty room. He pulled up his files again.

After some more meticulous trawling, he straightened his back and sighed. The military had redacted swathes of every useful document. There wasn't really enough here to put together a complete picture.

He idly pulled all the financial documents onto the table instead and ran through them: many of the suppliers had figures for their equipment listed on the open net, or he could make educated guesses. There was at least more to work with there.

Ten minutes later, Jainan raised his head and frowned at the wall in front of him.

What he was reading didn't make any sense. He wasn't an accountant, but he was numerate and used to reading closely for detail, and he couldn't make any of this add up. There was a lot of funding money going in that wasn't accounted for in the outputs, even by the most generous estimates.

Of course, there had been disasters. Jainan scanned the incident reports. He had seen Taam come home in a vile mood more than once after a bad day. Jainan had tried not to disturb him at times like that, but sometimes Taam let hints drop, and once, Jainan had seen a newslog report about a piece of rig that had exploded and set back work by months. But even the disasters wouldn't account for this.

Taam had cleared every document.

Jainan brought some of the files onto the table and paged through them. Usually work was a distraction, a pleasant way to lose himself in something during his solitary hours. But now all he felt was underlying discomfort and something else, something like nagging curiosity. He caught himself looking over his shoulder— Gairad was right, it had turned into a tic—and made himself turn back to the table. Kiem was out. Bel was in the study, and Jainan was alone. He could read what he liked.

He set himself to track every credit he could. The space by his elbow filled up with notes and copied fragments of text. There was a peculiar, visceral appeal to working like this, with his heart in his mouth and bile at the back of his throat. He tried chasing different strands, specific funding allocations. Most of them petered out somewhere in the stack of documents.

The money wasn't necessarily missing. It might have been classified. The military wasn't required to hand all its secrets to academic engineers with bright ideas. But if it was missing, someone should have caught it.

Taam had been in charge of Operation Kingfisher. *Taam* should have caught it.

Jainan pushed back from the table and rose to pace across the room. There was a word for what he was doing right now, and that word was *betrayal*. He shouldn't have agreed to scrutinize these files. The inner workings of the military were none of his business, even if it hadn't been his own partner running the operation. And anyway, the military was huge and presumably run on a tight rein. What were the chances he could spot something from an incomplete pile of files that had never been seen before? He must be missing something.

He looked down at the slim silver band around his wrist. It pulsed with soft light as he worked. Bel had saved most of the data on his account, so Taam's backup account was still there on his wristband, sat unobtrusively in a back layer.

Taam had never given him the passphrase. But Jainan had lived with him for five years, and—thinking this felt like more of a betrayal than the rest of it—Taam had not been an imaginative man. Jainan had a fairly good idea of what his passphrase might be. He tried it.

A stream of nonsense text covered the wall. Jainan recognized the format; it wasn't a backup. It was a message channel. He stared at the garbled text, feeling simultaneously like a criminal and sick with disappointment. It was wrapped in its own layer of encryption, of course. Taam wouldn't leave sensitive data in the clear. The only things that were even half-readable were the destination addresses, and they weren't the neat form entries that might note which planet or organization should receive the message. They were strings of anonymous characters, which Jainan could only guess was some sort of encoded military relay.

"Not that I want to pry into your business," Bel's voice drawled from the study door, "but want to explain why you're using Sefalan raider relays?" She folded her arms and gave him a smile that showed her teeth. "Your Grace?"

Jainan had let down too many of his protective barriers to hide his shock. "*Raider* relays?"

Bel frowned. "These aren't yours, then." She stepped farther into the room and looked over the documents on the walls before Jainan could pull them down. "Those are Taam's messages?" She flicked one of the projections with the back of a fingernail. "Wonder why he was talking to raiders. Those are fence drops. Don't suppose you saw any of his valuables going missing?"

Significant amounts of Kingfisher equipment had gone missing. Jainan sat back down abruptly. "I need to send this to the authorities," he said. "Now. Yesterday. I—" He put his head in his hands. "You're taking this straight to Kiem, aren't you?" The files on the walls seemed to be closing in. Causing a scandal of that magnitude for the Imperial family, fifteen days before the Resolution treaty had to be signed, would be the most damaging thing he could possibly do. It would destroy Taam's reputation, damage Kiem, and affect the chances of treaty renewal. Kiem would blame him.

"I'm not his enforcer," Bel said. "I'm not your enemy either, so you can stop looking like I've got a capper at your throat. Are you seriously just going to send it all to Internal Security?"

Jainan lifted his head and swallowed down bile. "This is—" He couldn't say *embezzlement*. That was a crime. He could feel Taam in the room beside them, incredulous and impatient. "This needs official attention."

"That's virtuous of you," Bel said. "Listen, I know how law enforcement works. Think about it. And if you really have to do it, keep a copy."

"A copy," Jainan said. He looked down at his wristband. Every wheel in his mind was spinning wildly. A forensic copy. That would be a logical thing to do, though he could barely focus on any thought that wasn't *Taam* and *embezzlement* and *Kiem*. He could not stop his mind spinning in panic. "You're not going to tell Kiem yet?"

"I'm not in the business of spreading around other people's

secrets," Bel said. "I'm going to finish my paperwork." She gave him an ironic salute and closed the study door behind her.

Jainan spent some time remembering how to take a forensic image while his mind pounded with a drumbeat of panic, then sat frozen for a good thirty seconds before the final gesture that would send it to Internal Security. They already had the encrypted file—Jainan had sent it himself, what seemed like a lifetime ago—but the bio-key was Taam's passphrase in Taam or Jainan's voice. Jainan doubted Taam had kept a backup key. Internal Security hadn't seen the contents.

The suspicious activity had all come from Jainan's device. Taam hadn't risked his own account: he'd used his remote access to Jainan's wristband. If Internal Security had been interested in Jainan before, this would be the final straw and would give them more than enough grounds to hold Jainan for questioning. Kiem would find out. The newslogs would get hold of it.

He stood up. He retrieved Taam's messages. He retrieved the Kingfisher files. He threw up more and more documents and scraps on the wall until the whole room was a frantic mess of projections and numbers. None of it made sense. Of course Internal Security was looking into Jainan himself: he had the skills to sabotage Taam's flyer and, apparently, a motive to cover something up. The messages had come from his device. It looked like Jainan had been embezzling from his partner's project.

He stared at the stream of Taam's encrypted messages. Why would Taam contact Sefalan raiders? There was no more reason for Taam to do that than for Jainan himself. Had Jainan had a psychotic break and committed a crime, or helped Taam commit one? His head certainly wasn't quite right; he felt he had not been able to *think* for—for years, maybe. Since he came to Iskat. *You're always so paranoid.*

Was he mad? *Had* he done something to Taam?

Jainan's strained hearing caught the sound of the door sliding open in the main room. He didn't even think before he killed all the files, wiped his notes, and pulled the data coin off his handheld. As the study door slid open, he turned toward it with the coin hidden in his pocket, as composed as he could make himself. He only just remembered to control his breathing.

It wasn't until he saw Kiem's face that he realized he had been expecting Taam.

"How's it going? Sorry it got a bit late . . ." Kiem broke off, belatedly taking stock of the empty room and Jainan standing in front of him. "Uh. Were you just finishing, or did I interrupt?"

Jainan knew enough to take hold of a lifeline when one presented itself. "I was just finishing," he said. Could Kiem read his discovery on his face? "How was your . . ." He stopped. He had forgotten what Kiem had gone out to do.

"Fete," Kiem said helpfully. "Jakstad Prime School fete. It was good, thanks. I came in to ask you if you wanted to come on a trip to their sister school in Braska on fifth-day? They're having a graduation festival. I've already booked to go, but I could add you. Not that exciting, I know, but I thought we could go over the mountains, it's a nice flight—I'm talking too much again, aren't I."

"Yes," Jainan said, without even really hearing the question. "Thank you."

Kiem glanced at the table uneasily, and Jainan flinched as if he'd left his documents projected over it. That just made Kiem's eyes snap back to him. "Are you all right?"

It was a much slower, more hesitant inquiry than Bel's—and more dangerous. Jainan's fingers clenched convulsively around the data coin in his pocket, his mind still spinning, and he groped for an answer. "Fine."

"Okay," Kiem said, still slowly. His eyes didn't leave Jainan's face.

Jainan's thoughts were a frantic whirl. Kiem would jump to the conclusion that Jainan had been involved. It was the only logical outcome. Jainan couldn't trust his own memories. He didn't know where his duty lay, and that was the most terrifying thing of all.

"I know you don't like asking for help," Kiem said carefully, "but you could keep in mind that I've got a duty to you too. Think of it like . . . a credit account you haven't drawn on yet. I'm just saying that if there's something I can do—"

"Stop," Jainan said abruptly, unable to bear it any more. It was a timely reminder that the last contract he had signed bound him to *Kiem*, not Taam, and keeping this from his partner was also a betrayal. "Sit down."

His manners had deserted him, as they sometimes did when he was agitated enough. As usual Kiem didn't seem to notice. He took the chair by the sofa and looked at Jainan expectantly, his hands resting on his knees. Jainan realized he was watching Kiem for signs of tension and deliberately turned to the desk. It wasn't his business how Kiem took the information. "I may be incorrect about this," he said. He brought up the documents again. "But I must tell you something."

It took time. Jainan was less able than usual to explain clearly. He used too much detail; he forgot Kiem was not a mathematician; he lost the thread and had to go over things twice or more. His voice was harsh in his own ears and broke on some words without warning.

Kiem didn't understand, and still didn't understand—and then the frown faded from his face and was replaced by dawning horror. Jainan doggedly continued, laying out every piece of evidence he had found, until he ran out of things to explain.

They sat in silence. Jainan didn't try and add anything.

"Well, shit," Kiem said, finally. "Taam was committing a crime."

Jainan clenched his hands on his knees. "I could be mistaken about the finances. The only criminal activity is on my account."

"You said Taam had access to your account," Kiem said.

Jainan couldn't bear to look at him. He rose to pace across the room and examined the encrypted projection. "Why would Taam bother to send messages through me? I thought the account was just a data backup." His voice cracked in the middle of the sentence. "Of course Internal Security is interested in me. The simplest explanation is that it *was* me." He turned back, tapping each projection compulsively. "I am going mad. You should alert the authorities."

Kiem raised a hand as Jainan passed his chair. "Jainan."

Jainan stopped dead, but all Kiem did was spread out his fingers in midair, level with Jainan's chest. Jainan breathed out. "You must consider it logically."

"You're not going mad," Kiem said.

"How do you *know*?"

"Because I've been living with you, and I'd be able to tell," Kiem said. "I think you're just really stressed. And you said money is missing from Operation Kingfisher, which you weren't even involved in." He frowned. "And didn't Internal Security say someone tried to hack into Kingfisher *recently*? You didn't do that. Neither did Taam."

Jainan sat down and pressed his hands against each other until he could feel the blood beating in them. The relief he felt was false: Kiem hadn't yet thought it through. Kiem was not devious. Jainan wasn't sure what it said about his own character that he could see the future very clearly.

"Kiem," he said. "Please think through the consequences of Taam being accused of embezzlement. Consider the damage it will do to you."

"Damage." It was more a question than a statement.

Jainan's stomach was tying itself up in knots again. He was going to have to spell this out. "The backlash from the scandal will hit the whole royal family, especially this close to the treaty. I will be directly implicated in his actions, and you will be dragged into it by association with me. You will be asked what you plan to do about your marriage and the treaty. There will be reporters trying to confront you for weeks. The Auditor will take it as further evidence of instability. We only have fifteen days to convince the Resolution to instate us and let us sign the treaty."

"Okay, obviously we don't want to tell the Auditor just yet." Kiem reached out distractedly and moved some of the files on the table, apparently at random. Jainan folded his hands in his lap and suppressed the fierce itch to move them back. "But you didn't do anything. We just need to make Internal Security prove that and find out who did. Even if it was Taam—sorry, I don't mean to speak ill of the dead—he must have had help. He couldn't be doing all that on his own."

Jainan's next argument died off in his throat. *We.* Kiem said it so casually, as if he weren't positioning himself as an ally to a political deadweight, a foreigner under investigation. Kiem crossed his ankle over one knee, flicking aimlessly between projections on the table. Jainan watched him and felt oddly weightless.

"What about Lunver's people?" Kiem said suddenly.

Jainan was taken off-balance. "What about them?"

What was dawning on Kiem's face was, incredibly, the start of a grin. It was impossible to depress him for any length of time. "They have all the data on Kingfisher, don't they? They might know something about the hacking attempt. And your friend Aren seemed reasonable, even if Colonel Lunver isn't."

A frisson went through Jainan like water down a pane of glass. "Aren's stationed in the main Kingfisher offices now," he said. "The remote one. Hvaren Base."

"Taam's flybug was military issue, wasn't it?" Kiem said thoughtfully. "Maybe they'll have the real crash data. Taam's former partner and General Tegnar's son. I bet we can swing a visit."

The air tasted different. Jainan recognized it from when he'd been a practicing researcher: it felt like the moment before he flipped the switch on a combustion experiment. Kiem's eyes were on him. "That would not be out of the question."

"Then that's what we do," Kiem said. "Let's give Internal Security something to really investigate."

CHAPTER 14

By the time they'd set everything up, Kiem was itching to get out of the palace. He had never been good at just sitting there waiting for the other shoe to drop, and Internal Security was presumably cobbling together some fairly hefty shoes. Better for him and Jainan to try and do some shoe-tossing of their own.

He was so keen to get going, he had his bag packed and in his flybug before he realized he was ten minutes earlier than the time he'd told Jainan. He leaned against the side of the flybug in the dim confines of the docking hangar, surrounded by gleaming ranks of flyers, and killed some time by checking the dartcar results. It wasn't easy to concentrate.

Damn you, Taam, Kiem thought, not for the first time that day. Jainan really was a mess, as far as Jainan ever let himself be a mess. Half the time he didn't hear you when you spoke to him and the other half he jumped. Kiem still hardly believed Taam had been reckless enough to embezzle money or get involved with raiders—Imperial Princes got a generous stipend—but involving Jainan's account in it was unforgivable. Kiem couldn't say that out loud, though, because Jainan wouldn't hear it. The one time he'd mentioned that it was the act of a complete coward, Jainan had nearly snapped at him, so now Kiem made an effort to keep his feelings to himself. Something had been going on at Operation Kingfisher before Taam's untimely death. Maybe they'd find some answers at Hvaren Base.

"Ready for your holiday?" Bel appeared at the elevator by the walkway, carrying some sort of case.

Kiem closed the dartcar rankings. "Packed my sunscreen," he said. "What's in there? Have we got the base security codes?"

"Major Saffer sent them through last night. Don't forget you're going to Braska Prime School for their graduation straight afterward. This is the trophy you're handing out to the kid with the best finger painting or whatever children do on Iskat." She handed over the case. "It's just back from the engravers, and I said you'd take it up, since you're going. Don't lose it."

"Right," Kiem said. He took the case and snapped it open out of curiosity. The thing inside was golden but didn't look much like a trophy. "Uh, this is a trowel."

"Traditional," Bel said. "Farming area. Have you got everything you need? Message me if you need anything sent. You've got my contact."

"Bel, of course I've got your contact," Kiem said. He stowed the box in the flybug's hold. "You're my aide. We've messaged each other a dozen times a day for the last year."

"All right," Bel said, "I'm just checking. Have you got everything?"

Kiem looked at her more closely and didn't say, *You already asked that.* It was an automatic question, but Bel didn't get distracted like that. She'd already shifted from one foot to another a few times. "Is something up?"

Bel glanced at the walkways around them and grimaced. "Sort of," she said. She cast another look at the elevator. "I just heard my grandmother's ill."

"Oh, shit, I'm sorry," Kiem said. Bel's family was all on Sefala, as far as he knew, which meant a journey of ten days to reach the planet without even adding however long it would take at the other end. "You'll want personal leave, right?"

"So I was going to ask—" Bel said, then caught herself as she heard what he'd said. It didn't seem to make asking any easier, though; her mouth twisted. "Not just yet," she said. "But I might need to make a sudden request later. I'm just letting you know in case."

"Take it now," Kiem said. "You should go home. Don't wait."

"Stop making this hard," Bel said sharply. "You need someone to do this job."

Kiem raised a hand in apology but didn't back down. "Yeah, but I can find cover from *somewhere*. They might not be as good, but this is kind of important!"

Bel worried at the embroidered threads on her sleeve with a fingernail—something Kiem had only ever seen her do at three in the morning in a media emergency. "She's not in immediate danger," she said. "It could be that nothing happens for months."

"Then take months."

"I'll tell you when I need to," Bel said. She turned her head as the elevator opened for Jainan. When she stepped back, something in the set of her shoulders looked like relief that the conversation was over.

Jainan's eyes went to her as he drew nearer—he was observant enough to pick up when something was even slightly wrong—and his hand gripped his case a little more tightly. "I'm late," he said. "I'm sorry."

"Nope, you're early," Kiem said easily, taking Jainan's case off him. Kiem would have to ask Bel later if he could tell Jainan, but Bel was intensely private with her own life, and he wasn't going to air anything without asking. "Let's head off, and Bel will breathe a sigh of relief and get some work done without us interrupting."

"Don't pretend Jainan's as bad as you," Bel said dryly. "Jainan, feel free to ditch him somewhere over the mountains if he's a nuisance."

Jainan didn't smile, just paled. *Damn* Taam. "Hey," Kiem protested, "do I pay you to gang up on me? Jainan, mind if I fly?" Jainan nodded silently and got into the passenger seat.

Bel waved from the walkway as if they were leaving at a shuttleport. "Have fun with the kids at Braska," she said. "I can send you some thumbscrews if you need them for the military officers. See you in three days."

"You should be sending me armor for the kids!" Kiem called, while Jainan flinched at the thumbscrews joke. "Later!" He set the flybug to automatic to get out of the hangar and keyed up the tractor beam.

The dome closed them into a pool of quiet. Jainan stared straight ahead while the tractor field inched them delicately out of their docking space. The sky was opening up above them, icy and pale blue: a good day for flying. Kiem sighed and settled back into his seat, resting his hands in the mesh of filaments that controlled the flybug.

"Right," he said. "Tell you what, we'll free-route the first bit overland. We can join the tunnels when they come up from the coast."

"The tunnels?" Jainan asked.

Kiem had heard that tone before. He didn't know if Jainan was tense because of the treaty or because of this bloody Taam thing, but he was helplessly out of answers for both. "The commercial routes," he said. "You know. You'd have taken them any time you left Arlusk's city limits." Jainan looked blank. It must be a cultural thing. "Light-tunnels for high-speed freight. Like the city networks but bigger."

"Oh," Jainan said. "Yes. We had something similar on Thea."

"We'll just hop over the mountains for the first bit, then," Kiem said hopefully. "I learned to fly around there. Peaceful. Dramatic crags, snow, that sort of thing."

"Snow," Jainan said, leaning forward to survey the early winter city skyline as they rose into the air. "You do surprise me."

It took Kiem a moment to catch on, and then he grinned in relief. He pulled them into a vein of light that would bring them out of the city traffic network. "Feels good to get out, huh?"

"Mm," Jainan said. His voice had gone colorless again. He was watching the city recede under them, giving way to the foothills to the west, now covered in deep snow. True winter was setting in. The spine of the range loomed up in the distance. "I haven't been this way before. Taam liked to go the other side of Arlusk for skiing."

"There's an idea," Kiem said. "We should have brought skis. Dammit. Think it's too late to go back?"

"I preferred the flying to the skiing," Jainan said. His eyes were starting to gleam with curiosity as they skimmed closer to the first of the real mountains. "Can you go a little lower?"

Kiem grinned. "Can do," he said. "Tell me if you want me to veer off." He switched the controls to a more sensitive setting and dived down.

They skimmed around the sheer cliffs and into the first of the ravines. This one was too close to the city to be really wild and there were a couple of cabins nearby, but when they shot out of the first valley and into the next, Kiem got the reaction he had been hoping for. Jainan took an audible breath.

The ground fell away beneath them into a deep gorge. A river crawled far below between dark pines that weren't yet snowed over, and mountains climbed up dramatically on either side. "It's beautiful," Jainan said.

"Glad you think so," Kiem said. "Made it myself, obviously. It took me ages to get all the trees in the right place."

"I see," Jainan said. "What a shame you couldn't get the river straight."

"It's supposed to be crooked," Kiem protested. "It's artistic."

"Is it," Jainan said. A smile was threatening to tug up the corner of his mouth. He leaned forward to get a better view of the rushing torrent below. Kiem brought them down until they could see the white foam and the chunks of ice tumbling through the current from higher up the mountains. "There's an unwise thing teenagers do on Thea," Jainan said, apparently as a non sequitur.

"What's that?" Kiem said.

"They take the flybug down as close to the water as possible and turn it sideways to try and dip the fins."

"That's a terrible idea," Kiem said. He eyed the water speculatively. "We're definitely not going to do that."

"No," Jainan agreed, in exactly the same tone. Out of the corner of his eye, Kiem saw his hand go up to tug his safety harness tighter.

"How long do you have to keep the fin touching the water for?" Kiem said, in the spirit of inquiry.

"I used to be able to do four-second runs," Jainan said. "Some people got up to five."

"Right," Kiem said. He took a hand out of the dash to check his own harness. "Haven't tried to flip this thing in years."

"Don't worry," Jainan said. "You only need to get it halfway to a full flip and balance it there."

"Oh, well, that's all right then," Kiem said. "No way this can go wrong."

"If the trees look like they're pointing downward, you've gone too far."

Kiem reached up to flick off the stabilizers. "You realize Bel is going to kill us if we crash out here without her," he said, but then his hand froze as he thought about that. He glanced at Jainan, remembering the last time Jainan's partner had piloted a flybug. "Uh. Maybe we shouldn't."

Jainan shook his head. "This is relatively safe," he said. "You can't turn off most flybug safeguards. You would have to break them. But if Bel would object—"

"No, I mean, she'll kill us because we didn't let her join in. Bel has speeding tickets from every subdistrict in the city." Kiem flicked off the last of the automatic stabilizers and firmed up his grip in the steering mesh, feeling the filaments all around his hands. "Are you holding on?" He gave Jainan a moment to grab on to something, and then dived.

The river came rushing up to meet them. Kiem had turned the filaments to the most sensitive setting and could feel every buffet of air against the flybug's shell through the tingle in his hands. He gripped the steering, a surge of adrenaline going through him that he hadn't felt in a while, and turned to veer sideways across the river. They tore straight at the oncoming forest.

"Tree," Jainan said.

"Noted!" At the last second, Kiem yanked them around to bear straight down the course of the river. The sharp turn took the flybug diagonal, and Kiem slammed on the manual tilt with his foot at the same time. They swerved wildly. Kiem's harness dug into his side as the world spun in front of him. He frantically kicked it back the other way as he felt them flipping and tried to steer downward at the same time.

The side fin hit the water with a shock that echoed through the filaments and up his arm. Kiem whooped, but he could only hold it a moment. The buffet of the water surface on the fin physically hurt his hands through the mesh—the flybug was reaching its limits and was letting him know.

They plowed into an eddy, bounced off a piece of floating ice, and flew in a sickening arc upward while Kiem fought for control. He just managed to pull them up in time to avoid the trees.

The flybug skimmed the treetops and climbed slowly, while Kiem let his head fall back and realized he was laughing.

Jainan let go of the dash in front of him. He flexed his fingers, his attempt at a thoughtful expression completely failing to hide his smile. "One and a half seconds."

"I've got the hang of it now," Kiem said. "Next one will be at least three seconds."

He half expected to be told there wasn't going to be a next one. But Jainan was clearly as bad as Bel about flying, because all he said was, "I think the next valley may have another good river for it."

"How am I the most sensible pilot in this household?" Kiem said. "How did that happen?"

"I don't know what you mean," Jainan said mildly. "I'm sensible."

"You only pretend to be sensible," Kiem said.

"I never pretend," Jainan said. "Perhaps try a little more speed next run."

"Do you want a go?"

Jainan hesitated. "Maybe."

"Maybe?"

Jainan looked torn, as if he was getting away with something. "Yes."

At the next valley, Kiem switched the flybug's controls to Jainan's seat. Jainan's first failed try turned into a four-second run on the next pass, which Kiem completely failed to beat in several subsequent attempts. The next ravine brought them to a system of canyons filled with glittering tunnels of light, where they realized at the same moment that they'd been stunt flying all the way to the tunnels and shared a mutual sheepish look. The moment their eyes met, Kiem broke into a snort of laughter, and Jainan reverted to his poker face.

Kiem took them into the tunnels. A diffuse light flooded around them, the pale color of eggshells, and the flybug shifted of its own accord as the tunnel slotted them into a traffic pattern. Blocky freight flyers zipped around them. Kiem took his hands out of the steering mesh and flopped back against the seat.

The tunnels were dull, and there wasn't anything else to do, so they started to talk idly. At least Jainan talked idly, and Kiem, who was now aware of the rarity of that, listened with a feeling in his chest like he had been thrown a ball made of glass and tried frantically to make his own answers casual. They talked about Iskat and Thean culture and what they'd grown up with. Somehow they got into Thean music, and Jainan went as far as attempting to find some song he knew on the flybug's system before discovering the signal was unusably bad.

"Oh, yeah," Kiem said, mentally cursing the signal for putting a wrench in the conversation. They were in an overground section of the route, weaving through a dry gorge. "Sorry about that, there's a big dead zone over the mountains, and we're on the edge of it here. Tacime deposits near the surface."

Jainan raised his eyebrows and looked at the ground below. "Tacime?" he said. "Ah. I forgot Iskat is swimming in it. Still, I would have thought you'd have stripped it out."

"It would have ruined the mountains if we stripped it out for every tunnel," Kiem said apologetically. "We just kind of deal with the dead zone." In its processed form, tacime did a great job at fueling spaceships, but in its natural form, its main property was blocking communications. It probably did other things; Kiem wasn't a scientist.

"It's not a problem," Jainan said. He turned to the stored music. The upbeat chiming of a popular track from some time ago came out of the hidden speakers. As soon as he heard the first few notes, Kiem pulled one hand out of the steering mesh and clapped it to an ear, groaning.

Jainan looked at him quizzically. "Sorry," he said, turning it down.

"No, it just takes me back," Kiem said. "Not in a good way. I must have been back in university when I put that in the system."

"It brings back . . . bad memories?" Jainan said.

"Not really," Kiem said. "Just, you know." He waved a hand. "I got into a lot of scrapes back then. This was playing everywhere at one point. It was probably on the speakers when I got exiled."

"What did you—" Jainan said, and then stopped himself.

"—get exiled for?" Kiem said, completing the question. "Uh, there was a. Um." He tapped his feet on the floor. This was surprisingly hard. "We may have started a fire on a night out."

"How?"

"By accident. With fireworks. Nobody was badly hurt." Kiem paused. "We were drunk."

Jainan didn't say anything.

"I'm not proud of any of that," Kiem said, mainly to fill in the silence. "I don't do that kind of thing anymore."

Jainan was silent for a while longer and then said, abruptly, "No, I can't see you doing that now."

"No," Kiem said, immensely relieved.

"But it fits with . . ." Jainan trailed off. Kiem winced internally, knowing that Jainan must have picked up some of Kiem's history from the newslogs. "Why did you change?"

Kiem had a whole repertoire of jokes to smooth over that kind of question. It was easy to deflect, because he *hadn't* changed—he'd just been an irresponsible teenager with more rank than sense getting on everyone's nerves, and now he was an irresponsible adult who tried not to. That didn't excuse anything. But Jainan hadn't meant that.

He stared ahead at the snow-covered canyon and said, "I started acting out fairly early. You know how my other parent was Prince Alkie? They passed when I was fourteen. Neurological disorder. My mother didn't cope very well, and neither did I, and somehow we made each other even worse when we tried to talk about it. Or about anything else, really."

"I'm sorry," Jainan said.

Kiem flashed him a sideways grin out of habit. "Don't be sorry." Jainan's returning glance was grave and thoughtful. Kiem's smile felt too fake to keep up; he let it disappear. "It took me a few years to realize I was just playing things up for attention. You know, it really hurts when you realize you're doing what millions of teenagers have done before, especially when it takes you until your early twenties to realize it. I dropped out of college after that, stayed away from bars, then I got Bel."

"Mm," Jainan said. He didn't sound censorious or pitying. He didn't come back with a flurry of probing questions either. Kiem usually floundered when he had to talk about his parents, but this felt oddly like touching bedrock. Jainan said, "What happened with Bel?"

Kiem seized on the change of topic with some relief. "She came about a year ago from one of the programs I worked with," he said. "You know, bright people who don't have the qualifications for whatever reason. I was starting to get asked to the odd event by charities and other people, but when Bel turned up, she figured out that was where I could actually be useful and packed my schedule full of it. Turns out she was right." They were skimming near the edge of the tunnel, close enough to see the unevenness of the rock wall beside them. "The job was just supposed to be a reference while she found a more permanent place."

Jainan frowned. "I didn't realize that."

"Well, she hasn't said she wants to go yet, and I'm not bringing it up if she doesn't." Kiem drummed one of his feet on the flybug's floor shell. "Hey, is that the exit?"

It was. Kiem lunged for the route indicator to bring them out of the tunnels. They shot out into the open air, the flybug slowing to a coasting speed, and both of them fell silent.

Below stretched a singly uninviting expanse of barren tundra. The spine of mountains rose up behind them like fangs splitting the landscape from beneath; Kiem hadn't been to this area before and wasn't regretting that choice. "Scenic, huh?"

"There," Jainan said. "Is that it?" He pointed to a toy-sized sprawl of buildings a couple of kilometers away at the same time as a blaring siren came through the flybug's audio.

"Hah, the good old military hello," Kiem said. "Mother uses that as her morning alarm." He keyed their security codes into a response burst.

Ten minutes later they were gliding into the depressing confines of a standard Iskat military base, pieced together from gray fly-and-drop sheds, rows of generators, and a training ground hacked out of the ice. Kiem parked their flybug and waved to the guards who came to meet them. They were handed over to a helpful young trooper who looked about sixteen, had a strong plains accent, and had clearly never done anything quite as exciting in her life as check in two civilian visitors.

Hvaren Base was bustling. Every desk had a soldier at it. Jainan scanned the walls, which had a firework display of different visualizations that presumably had something to do with engineering, while Kiem listened to the trooper breathlessly recite base safety procedures.

"Uh, we were supposed to meet Major Saffer," Kiem said, when the trooper stopped to heave in a breath. "Is he around?"

"Scheduled for eleven hundred hours, sir!" the trooper said. "I will take you on a tour of the base so you're not bored!"

"Gosh," Kiem said. "Can't wait."

He hadn't reckoned with the effect of offering an engineer a tour of an engineering operation. "I would like that very much," Jainan said, a gleam in his eye that Kiem recognized. "May we speak to the unit responsible for the propulsion design on the screens?"

The trooper looked slightly taken aback and then doubly enthusiastic. They'd done it now. Kiem followed Jainan to the engineers' corner. Luckily Jainan could have carried that conversation in his sleep, and at least it got them away from the unit on the other side of the room who had the intimidating look of people who wanted to talk about Trade and Export.

As Jainan got deep into the details of however mining worked—he hadn't mentioned the Imperial College project, which was probably the best approach—Kiem started to count the people in the room. There were only a few dozen, but he saw insignia from three separate divisions, so either the army had started splitting divisions or Kingfisher had about three hundred people, and most of them weren't in this room or at the palace. The Kingfisher emblem, a jagged silver badge that could just about be a bird midstrike if you squinted, was more prominently displayed than any of the division insignia. There was another memorial photo of Taam at the back of the room, wreathed with gray flowers.

Jainan turned from one of the screens to a holo-abacus floating above one of the desks. One of the engineers had gone to find the person who made it. "You're having fun," Kiem said under his breath.

Jainan looked sideways at him, startled. "No, I'm—" He stopped.

"Sirs!" the very helpful trooper said, popping up like a weather alert. "Major Saffer has arrived back at base. Please follow me!"

It was an unnecessary announcement. Just behind her, Aren was removing a heavy outdoor coat. He strode past his trooper, extending a hand. "Jainan! And Prince Kiem. Good to see you. I was hoping to catch you a bit earlier, but I got delayed, sorry about that. You had some questions about Taam and Kingfisher?"

Time to get to work. Jainan had frozen; Kiem automatically shook Aren's hand. "Good to see you, Aren. Have you got somewhere we could talk?"

CHAPTER 15

"Embezzlement?" Aren said, stopping in his tracks. "That's impossible."

They stood in a snowy, windswept gravel yard outside the gray monolith of the base. Aren had taken Kiem's suggestion they talk somewhere quiet and invited them to see the hangar, an enormous shell of a structure large enough to hold a small spaceship.

Kiem pulled his coat around himself in the cutting wind. "Yeah. I know," he said. "But I've seen the evidence. We can show you."

Aren didn't immediately ask for proof. He took off his uniform hat and tugged at his hair, disordering the pale curls. "I would have seen—I mean, Taam dealt with the budgets, I'm only on personnel and logistics, but I can't believe I could have missed it."

"We should take this inside," Jainan said quietly. "This is not something any soldiers should overhear."

"No," Aren said. "Fuck, no. Let's get inside."

He gave the hangar door his bios and ushered them in, rubbing his forehead every couple of seconds as if he'd been physically stunned. They stepped into a dim cavern.

Despite the situation, Jainan let out a low, soft breath. A scale model gleamed above them, suspended several meters above the ground and ringed with an observation catwalk. To Kiem's eyes it looked like a space station, but he could see REFINERY MODEL 002 stenciled on the side, along with another jagged Kingfisher logo. There were other models, some in their own vacuum units:

engines and odd combinations of pipes and liquids. Jainan couldn't keep his gaze away from them.

"Our design models," Aren said absently. "I was going to give you the tour, but that's just become a lot less relevant." He stopped at the foot of some catwalk stairs and turned, leaning against the railings. His face was pale and determined. "Okay. I'm listening."

It was the wrong place to lay out Jainan's painstaking evidence trail, so Kiem kept it short: the equipment. The obfuscated finances. The encrypted messages sent over relays that Bel had identified as fence drops used by Sefalan raiders.

"But why?" Aren said, sounding baffled. He focused on Jainan. "I mean, don't get me wrong, I'm not saying you're lying. But why would Taam risk it?"

Jainan had rested a hand on the railing beside him, and his knuckles were clenched tight around it. "I don't know," he said. "I may—I may be wrong."

Aren's silence left a gap open, and in it Kiem found himself turning over in his head what would happen if they *were* wrong. None of this chaos would help the Auditor decide that Iskat and Thea were voluntarily entering into the treaty. And even if they were right, they were no closer to an answer—embezzling or no embezzling, Taam was dead. If it hadn't been an accident, then someone had killed him.

Aren shook his head. "You know," he said, "this would explain something, as much as I don't like it. Internal Security has been on my back for the past two weeks. I've had to turn over half my operational files—I thought they were worried about our flybug maintenance team. I've had unexplained cuts in my purchasing budget as well, several times. I just—" He looked up at the model gleaming in the shadows above them, as if it might have some answers, and sounded lost. "I just—*Taam*? I knew him." He straightened his shoulders, pushed himself away from the rail and focused again on Jainan. "You want to look at our records."

Jainan swallowed visibly. "I know as civilians we have no right of access."

"I'll waive that," Aren said. "Internal Security combed through them already, so why shouldn't you get a shot? I'll set you up with a room in the base and get you permissions."

Jainan was staring at Aren as if this was profoundly unexpected. It wasn't the way he reacted to Kiem, as if Kiem was a puzzle, but instead the reaction of someone who'd put their hand into an ice-covered river and found it running hot. "You don't have to do that."

"I know," Aren said, waving a casual hand. "Thank me later. I want to know too."

It was just a pokey meeting room with a plastic slab of a desk, but Jainan seemed to think it was adequate. All his attention was trained on downloading vast amounts of Kingfisher data and heaping it in abstract pools and graphic visualizations all over the desk. Kiem tried to help out, and not stand there watching the way research turned Jainan intent and whetstone-sharp.

Kiem wasn't going to be a lot of use anyway. Jainan seemed to know what he was doing and dived into Taam's files immediately, comparing equipment readouts and purchase orders. Kiem stared at a list of numbers under a code name until they blurred, then stood up restlessly and started to pace.

Jainan finally looked up. "Are you going to do that . . . continuously?"

"Sorry," Kiem said. He propped the door open instead, which led onto the main open-plan room, and wandered out to see if he could find some coffee.

He found coffee—and some military rations, which he sampled indiscriminately—at the kitchen station. He also found a corporal to explain the code-named list of numbers, which was apparently a registry of flybug models, and brought her back to the meeting room so she could explain this to Jainan. Jainan, after a moment's startled wariness, started asking her about fuel logging and maintenance schedules.

Kiem strolled back out among the bustling desks. The restful thing about soldiers was they didn't ask awkward questions like: *Why are you looking at our records?* Kiem and Jainan had arrived with Major Aren and been given all-system privileges; that meant they were some sort of inspectors as far as the soldiers were concerned. Kiem hung around various desks and sent some of the soldiers in to Jainan if they seemed to know anything about flybugs or finance. He got some dartcar betting tips off a lance corporal.

The tinted base windows faded as the mountain sky turned toward dusk. Dozens of soldiers came in and out of the room as the day shift handed over to the evening shift. Jainan showed no inclination to move from his piles of data.

Kiem eventually found two box meals and two cans of something sugary and took them in to him.

"How's it going?" Kiem said. "It's getting dark. Shift's changing."

"Is it?" Jainan said vaguely. "I hadn't noticed."

Kiem put the meal at Jainan's elbow. "Found anything?"

Jainan focused on him. "A lot of confirmation," he said, sounding tired but blank, as if Taam were just a name rather than his ex-partner. "I've been sending it to Aren and Colonel Lunver as I go. I hope you don't mind."

"No, you should," Kiem said. "Trying to hide anything at this point would look really suspicious. Is there anything new? Like what Taam was, um, doing with the money? Or who might have . . ." He hesitated. *Killed him* sounded awful. "You know. Who might have been upset with him? What about the raiders he was selling to?"

"That would be a neat answer," Jainan said without emotion. "Unfortunately, I can't break the message encryption without the keys, and I can't find those on any Kingfisher system. Though there are some oddities in system activity. Internal Security might be able to find out more."

"Agent Rakal will be over the moon," Kiem said. "What oddities?"

"I'm not sure yet." Jainan frowned at something in front of him. "I don't know where you're getting these people that you keep sending over—"

"They're right there," Kiem said. "They all work about ten meters away."

"—but can you find me a network engineer?"

"Probably," Kiem said. "Systems team sits in the corner."

"A network engineer? What for?" Aren said from the doorway. He leaned on the open door frame, apparently amused. "I come back to find you've flooded my messages and lured half my staff away from their jobs, Jainan. You never did that when Taam was in charge."

Jainan tensed. "Don't worry," Kiem said, before Jainan could apologize. "We sent them back."

"Oh, that's all right, then," Aren said, half laughing. Kiem could never figure out who the amusement in his voice was aimed at. "Sorry I've left you to your own devices. I was briefing Colonel Lunver. She's going to come out to the base tomorrow. What's this about a network engineer?"

Jainan's focus had faded completely. He sounded more normal—diffident and circumspect—as he said, "Your system logs have been accessed from outside military networks. Someone was trying to break in. I think this has happened every few days since before Taam died."

"Agent Rakal mentioned it when we met them," Kiem said. Aren tilted his head to one side, quizzical. "Network intrusion. Did they tell you?"

"Oh, we get attempts like that all the time," Aren said. "Usually it's petty criminals or idealists who've bought cracking kits from Sefalan gangs. They don't get through."

Jainan looked down at his work. "Don't they?" he said quietly. "I see."

"Surely it can't hurt to check," Kiem said to Aren. "Taam obviously had something going on that you didn't know about. This could be related. Don't you have a Systems team?"

Aren's expression cleared. It was something of a relief working with Aren after trying to make progress with Rakal, Kiem found. Aren at least wanted to cooperate and was more concerned with finding out what was happening than perfecting an impression of a stone wall. "Better than that," Aren said, "I have a Systems night shift. I'll tell them to look into it right now. But I came with a message from the palace—Kiem, they say you have a PR thing at Braska? If you need to get back, Jainan can stay as long as he likes to dig into this. We have spare quarters."

"No, I don't need to—" Kiem began.

"Yes," Jainan said, looking strained. "You should. If not now, then in the morning. I don't want to disrupt your entire schedule. The school is expecting you, and I have embroiled you in this far enough."

Aren was looking between them curiously. Kiem, suddenly aware that they were in public, shut his mouth on a refutation. He was no judge of what was appropriate, but he could read a conversation that far, and it wasn't as if he was much help at trawling through data. "Right," he said. "Take your time. I'll come back here after—or I can meet you at the palace. Whatever works. I'll go in the morning."

"That's settled then," Aren said. He gave them a wave as he turned. "I'll alert the Systems team. Jainan, send over your findings about the hacking attempts, would you?"

Jainan turned back to his report the moment Aren left. Kiem dozed off in a chair, then unstuck his eyes and went to sort out their sleeping arrangements.

All the base offered to house guests were tiny rooms with cots the size of coffins, so Kiem took one room for himself and another for Jainan. They were hours away from the nearest journalist: Hren Halesar never had to know. He eventually had to drag Jainan away from his work to get some sleep. He tried to do the same himself, but the cot's mattress was hard and thin, and he slipped into an uneasy doze while hazy visions of soldiers and Internal Security went through his head.

The next day, Aren pinged them both to his office before Kiem was properly awake.

Aren's entire demeanor had changed. Before, he had given off a bright energy, as if he still hadn't quite processed that his previous commander might have been murdered. Now, he was sober, with a pale face and dark shadows ringing his eyes from lack of sleep.

"I have had a *bad* night," he greeted them. "Colonel Lunver's on her way out here, and she isn't happy. Apparently I shouldn't have let you into our systems but, honestly, fuck that. I need answers." He threw a screen up to hover above his desk. "Here's the really bad news."

Kiem didn't know what he was expecting to see, but it absolutely wasn't a picturesque shot of the gates outside the Imperial College.

"Please tell me this isn't some kind of military joke," Kiem said. Jainan looked as baffled as he felt.

Aren gave him a humorless slash of a smile. "We traced the network intrusion," he said. "We had to go fairly deep into the comms grid, but we found the identifiers. It came from the Imperial College networks."

"Nobody at the College would hurt Taam," Kiem said. "He didn't study there. He went to officer academy. Nobody even *knew* him at the College."

"Wish that were true!" Aren said. "That would make my life much easier. But there is a connection."

He made a sharp-angled gesture toward the screen, and something else appeared: a picture of a person. Kiem blinked.

"Not possible," Jainan said sharply, at the same time as Kiem said, "Isn't that Professor Audel?"

It was Audel. Kiem had only met her in person once but remembered her face: the engineering professor with straggly white hair who had watched Jainan sharply at the College reception then asked him to join her project. "Come off it, Aren," Kiem said. "You're looking for a student with too much time on their hands, not an Imperial College *professor*."

Aren laughed, short and sharp. "Am I?" He made a second gesture, and another photo appeared: Audel, only a few years younger. She wore the blue uniform and silver tabs of a military captain.

"She was recruited as a technical expert," Aren said. "We bring in people from various industries—she's been in and out of academia and commercial mining for years. I found her resume. Her military career stops there, though. Because she made a complaint about Prince Taam, who was only just out of officer academy then, and he made a counter-complaint to General Fenrik. She was discharged as incompetent for her role."

"*What?*" Kiem said. He shot a glance at Jainan. "You didn't know anything about this, right?"

"This is absurd," Jainan said, his composure showing rare cracks. "She mentioned military experience, but I don't believe it was—she didn't know who I was when she met me. She can't have been holding a grudge against Taam. This is preposterous."

Aren slumped back in his chair and sighed. "Look at it from my point of view," he said. "The Auditor wants some straight answers. Internal Security hasn't found anyone to take the blame. It looks like this professor tried to illegally access the Kingfisher network, *and* it turns out she had a grudge against Taam. This is the only person we have real evidence against—and at least it's not a Thean."

Kiem hadn't been happy since they walked into Aren's office, but his whole body recoiled at being complicit in that. "We're not just looking for someone to turn over to the Auditor," he said. "We're looking for what really happened."

Jainan stared at the floor. "I don't think she was involved," he said. "I don't have proof. I just don't think so."

Aren looked at them both dubiously, then at his screen.

"Let me have another look at your network logs," Jainan said. "Please."

There was something defensive in it, as if he expected to be turned down, but Aren made an expansive gesture and said, "Carry on. Lunver's not here for a few hours. Might as well knock yourself out."

Jainan was quiet as they left Aren's tiny office. Kiem stopped himself from saying three different things, all inappropriate, and settled for "I should set off for the school." He opened the door to their makeshift guest room. "I'll just grab my trunk. See you at the palace."

Jainan blinked, as if he'd forgotten Kiem was going to Braska. "Oh—" he said, then looked down at his wristband, which was pinging, and went very still.

"Who is it?" Kiem said, but Jainan was already opening the call, with an expression as if the prompt were a nesting bird about to attack.

The face that hovered in front of him was familiar: Kiem had just seen it above Aren's desk. An older female academic with clips holding back her graying hair. Of course. Kiem had seen Jainan talking to Audel and her students nearly every day.

"Jainan," Audel exclaimed in apparent pleasure. "I was trying to get hold of you."

Jainan swallowed and opened his mouth, but nothing came out. He nodded.

"Good to see you, Professor." Kiem stepped into view so Jainan's wristband would pick him up. "We're out in the mountains." *Was it urgent?* he was about to say, but changed his question midflight, on a hunch: "Can I ask you a quick question?" he said easily. "Did you know Prince Taam?"

Audel frowned. "*Un*fortunately," she said. "Why? I suppose Jainan could have told you that."

"You don't seem to have told him," Kiem said.

"Oh," Audel said vaguely, "I thought I had. But of course—who do you think the project applied to for the data? It was all a bit awkward, of course, given my last job. I still don't think the man could get drunk in a distillery—I *beg* your pardon," she said, breaking off contritely. "I'm sorry, Jainan, I forgot you were there."

"You were discharged from the military," Jainan said, his voice rough. "Why?"

"Well," Audel said, still looking uncomfortable. "Technically Prince Taam, you know. He questioned some of my results; they made his unit look bad. But Prince Taam wasn't actually the root cause. I knew I wasn't suited to it from about week two. A bad decision on my part, but they *do* have all the funding. I tried to resign several times. The last time was a month before it all kicked off."

"You . . . were trying to leave the military anyway?" Jainan said. "It wasn't because of Taam?"

"No, it was honestly quite a relief when they kicked me out," Audel said. "I was more than ready to go. The military doesn't nurture intellectual freedom; I imagine that won't come as a surprise, but I was seduced by not having to write grant applications."

"Ah," Kiem said, with a wash of relief. He didn't particularly want to get one of Jainan's friends in trouble. "Professor Audel. I don't suppose you have a . . . copy of that resignation? *Before* Taam's complaint?"

Audel thought, frustratingly not seeming to give it much weight. "Yes, I suppose so, somewhere," she said. "Why do you want it?"

"It would be really helpful," Kiem said. "Resolution business—don't ask, it will do your head in, and I think it's confidential. But right now would be good."

Jainan looked a little less ill when Kiem ended the call. He sat on one of the room's two stools and raised one finger to his temple, rubbing a tiny circle. "I don't like this," he said tonelessly.

This, Kiem was starting to recognize, was the equivalent of a less controlled person sinking to the floor with their head in their hands. "No," he said. "I'm not a huge fan either. At least this stops Internal Security from going after you, I suppose. Or it will when Aren sends them the evidence. *You* didn't try and hack into their systems."

"It absolutely won't stop them," Jainan said, his voice strained. "They will want to investigate both possibilities. And we have not been cooperative. They will find out I didn't tell them about Taam's secret message account. They will find out we have been here."

"Then what do you want to do?" Kiem said. "Just call up Internal Security and have a friendly chat about everything we know?"

Jainan didn't answer. His wristband flashed with a message, and Kiem's did at the same time. Kiem looked down long enough to see it was Audel's note, then looked back up at Jainan.

"You do, don't you?" Kiem said slowly. "You think we should do that." He dropped onto the bunk mattress and swung his feet up onto the other stool. "Okay, let's be good citizens. I'll give Rakal a buzz."

Jainan raised his head, startled. "You will?"

"Now that sounded like a dare," Kiem said. He couldn't quite believe he was at the point in his life where he had Internal Security on his regular contact list, but here he was. "Agent *Rakal*," he said expansively, as their face flickered up on screen. Rakal, a now-familiar collection of sharp angles and hostility, gave him an impressively stony stare from behind their desk. "How are you? How's the secrets business? Have we got some exciting things to tell *you*."

A few minutes later—Kiem had drafted Jainan in to explain the finer points of his research into Taam's finances, which Jainan did in the sharded-glass voice that came out of him under severe pressure—Rakal unbent enough to give them a single nod. It was a lot easier to explain this stuff to someone easygoing like Aren, but Kiem would take any acknowledgement he could get. "You've done the right thing bringing us your information," Rakal said crisply. "We were aware of significant parts of it. I would like to interview both of you."

Internal Security preferred to do things in person. Kiem assumed it was because it was harder to intimidate someone over a net link. "Great," Kiem said. "Well, we're kind of on a trip right now. I'm scheduled for a school visit this afternoon, and Jainan's staying—"

"Cut it short," Rakal said. "Return to the palace."

Kiem cast a glance beside him at Jainan, out of the visuals. Jainan's head was bowed, his hands clenched into fists on the table. "You'll have to wait a couple of days. We're busy."

"Prince Kiem," Rakal said, not shifting their expression by as much as a millimeter. "I am loath to do this, but this is a command in the Imperial Voice."

Jainan took a quick breath. "A what?"

Kiem took his feet off the stool in front of him and sat up. He wouldn't put it past Rakal to bluff. "Prove it."

Rakal picked a metal lump out of a case on their desk and touched it to their wristband. A blob of something gold and wax-like started in the middle of Kiem's screen and expanded like liquid. Kiem's wristband started to buzz. The gold reached the edge and, through some hypnotic effect, seemed to bleed onto the stool below the screen. It coagulated into an intricate woven pattern.

When it was done, an Imperial crest sat over the screen like a spider. A smaller version had crept over Kiem's wristband itself. Kiem groaned.

"What is that?" Jainan muttered.

"The Emperor," Kiem said. "She's given them a seal to carry out things in her voice. I wonder when she started to take an interest? Either way, we don't have a bloody choice now."

Rakal's face appeared again as the golden crest faded. "I trust that makes things clear," they said. "I will send details of the interview to your aide. Report as soon as you return to the palace."

The screens flickered out of view. Jainan let out a long breath and unfurled his clenched hands finger by finger, flexing them as if to check they still worked. "I am sorry."

"They were obviously going to do that anyway," Kiem said, though he had the uneasy feeling things were getting out of control. He and Jainan would have to cross that bridge when they came to it. "Let's tell the Kingfisher lot that we're leaving."

Aren took it in his stride when they found him in the main office. "Nothing to hide and nothing to fear, eh?" he said. "At least let Jainan stay to talk to the Systems team."

"I must go," Jainan said. He had the odd, choppy rhythm that meant most of his mind was on something else. "We must both go."

"Can't disobey the Imperial Voice, you know?" Kiem said. He tried to make it casual, because it was that or admit to a growing frustration with the whole palace establishment that his mother would have dubbed *sulking.* "Thanks for your help. If the Auditor asks you, tell him we're trying to get him some answers."

The first five minutes after leaving the base, Kiem and Jainan sat in the flybug in total silence. The buildings grew smaller in the tundra underneath them. Kiem bit his tongue every few seconds, aware that being annoyed at Internal Security wouldn't help and that Jainan probably wanted space to prepare for the interview. He took one hand out of the steering mesh to file their new flight plan.

"How long will it take us to fly back?" Jainan said abruptly.

"We'll be back by midafternoon," Kiem said. "If we take the fastest route, that is."

Jainan's profile was very sharp in the pale, snow-reflected light. He stared straight ahead, expressionless. "Do we have to take the fastest route?"

So this was what Jainan looked like when he was angry. Kiem, caught off guard, made a thoughtful noise. Taking their time would at least tell Internal Security that Kiem and Jainan weren't their subordinates to order around. They could stay within the letter of the law and still make a point. "The freight routes are pretty dull, really. Didn't you want to see more of the mountains? It takes longer, but I'm sure Rakal has time in their schedule."

"I could see some mountains," Jainan said.

Kiem adjusted the steering mesh settings to give them more sensitivity, his bad mood fading, and veered their direction setting to the east. A spine of mountains marched between them and Arlusk, pure and clean and a long way away from bloody Internal Security and their bloody interviews. "Course changed!" he said. "Let them wait."

The atmosphere in the flybug shifted. Jainan's shoulders relaxed. Kiem leaned forward, gleeful over their small rebellion, and scanned the foothills ahead. It would do Internal Security good to remember they couldn't just snap their fingers and summon them.

The flight turned into a long, aimless meander deep into the mountains, dipping into valleys and investigating anywhere that looked interesting. Jainan had never done proper mountain flying, so Kiem handed over the helm and showed him how to use the updrafts and wind patterns that snaked around the crags. They found a frozen waterfall; Kiem was at the controls, and he brought them close enough that they could have opened the dome and touched it.

"Gonna take us down a bit," Kiem said. "This thing wasn't built for hovering."

They drifted past the crag at the slowest possible speed. Jainan leaned back and said, "There was something else I wanted to talk to you about."

"'Course," Kiem said, distracted and fiddling with the map on the dash, which he should probably stop ignoring.

"Professor Audel's project," Jainan said. "How would you feel if I withdrew?"

Kiem stopped looking at the map and also stopped looking where he was going. "Withdrew from the *project*?" he said. The steering mesh vibrated a warning, and he had to yank the flybug up to avoid hitting a protruding rock. "But . . . aren't you kind of vital by now?" He pulled them up to drift at a slightly safer height. "If it's this thing with Professor Audel, she basically gave us proof she wasn't involved. Can't you just do the engineering side and stay away from the political and military bits?"

He had said the wrong thing. Jainan's shoulders hunched. "I have made this whole situation worse by working on it," Jainan said. His speech patterns had turned formal again, which was a bad sign. "It was a mistake for me to agree to it in the first place. Internal Security will see it as suspicious. I should not have taken part in something so political."

"I thought you enjoyed it," Kiem said. "Before the whole embezzlement thing, I mean." He cast his mind back to the times he'd seen Jainan working on his diagrams—Jainan had been relaxed, engaged, willing to explain parts of it with very little prompting. He knew he wasn't good at reading Jainan, but surely he couldn't have gotten things that wrong.

"I have some alternatives," Jainan said, "if you would be willing to consider them."

Kiem didn't see what he had to do with it. "Go ahead."

"I know you need to keep your influence in the Imperial College,"

Jainan said. "There are other ways I could be useful to you. The engineering department is also conducting vacuum tests I could consult on, which would gain you capital with higher-ranking academics. I could find out if the mathematics department has any relevant projects. I know this isn't what you hoped for from it, but—please."

Kiem had taken the flybug off its most sensitive setting some time ago, so when the shock made both his hands clench in the steering they didn't veer off course. If he hadn't switched it back they probably would have crashed.

He realized the next instant and relaxed his grip again, but it was a struggle. He felt as though someone had just taken a scene he was looking at and forcibly pulled it around to a new angle. "What *I* hoped for?" he said. "This is your project!" He hadn't made Jainan take it on, had he? He tried frantically to remember the reception where Jainan had agreed to do it. Had he said something?

"Yes," Jainan said uncertainly. "But these are your goals."

Again, Kiem felt that lurch, as if everything were shifting around him. He took both of his hands out of the mesh and set the controls to autofly, clumsier than he should have been. "They aren't," he said, trying to make his voice level. "I mean, I've got interests in the College, yes, but that doesn't affect *you*. I didn't want you to help out Professor Audel for my sake, and you don't bloody need to—to make up for it or whatever you're offering!"

Jainan drew back from him. "I don't know what you want from me," he said, in a thin, blank voice that made Kiem realize he'd been raising his. "I'm sorry."

"I—what? I don't want anything," Kiem said, keeping his voice down with some effort. "That's the point."

The flybug beeped a warning, coming up to a sharp rise that the autofly couldn't deal with. Kiem lunged for the controls again.

"You're angry."

"I'm not," Kiem said, concentrating on the steering. It was true—at least it was true he wasn't angry at Jainan. He wasn't entirely sure who he was angry with.

Jainan said nothing, but the quality of his silence was as good as a formally countersigned memo of disbelief.

"I'm not," Kiem said again. "I'm—upset." That felt accurate. "I'm upset that you'd think I'd—I'd use you like that."

"It isn't unreasonable," Jainan said sharply. "I represent the junior partner in the treaty. I have caused you nothing but trouble so far. It is reasonable to expect my help."

"No, it's not reasonable!" Kiem said. "That's messed up! We're married—even if it's a political marriage, that doesn't mean one of us is in charge!"

"I—of course not," Jainan said. "No."

Kiem raked a hand through his hair. "Expect you to do my work for me?" he said. "Where the hell did that come from? Taam?"

"No," Jainan said, his voice suddenly harsh.

Kiem raised a hand in apology. "No, I didn't mean that," he said. "Sorry. Tactless." He tried not to let himself be hurt that it wasn't okay to imply it of Taam, but apparently it was okay to imply it of Kiem himself. Jainan had been close to Taam; Kiem was the one he had been forced into a rushed remarriage with. It was different. It was understandable.

Jainan cast him a wary glance, "I would still like permission to withdraw from the project."

"*You don't need my bloody per—*" Kiem started to say, but was stopped by a muffled *bang* that shook the whole flybug.

Both of them broke off. "What was that?" Jainan said.

"No idea." A beeping noise started to blare: an alarm Kiem didn't recognize. He grabbed for the steering with one hand and keyed up the display with the other. "It's not—shit, it's not responding." The filaments were dead and inert around his hand. And both of them felt it at the same time—the slow curve of the

flybug as it lost its forward momentum and started to point inexorably downward.

"Hell!" Kiem yanked at all the backup controls, trying to get
some sort of response.

"That patch of snow," Jainan said, leaning forward intently.
"Can you land—"

"We're too far up," Kiem said grimly, as the sickening feeling
of an uncontrolled drop took hold. "I'll aim for it, and maybe if
the landing brakes are still—"

He didn't even make it to the end of the sentence. Another
shattering blow flung his head forward. The snowy ground spiraled up in front of him, but he wasn't aiming, he couldn't make
his arms move. He didn't feel the crash.

CHAPTER 16

Pain had its uses, Jainan thought. It put things in perspective. There was something clean about the way it cut through the emotional tangles and reminded you that things could be worse.

He hurt quite a lot. It took him some effort to ignore it, but eventually he noticed something clammy pressing into his shoulder. He stared at the short expanse of snow in front of him—which was inexplicably sideways—and at the icy-blue sky beyond it. It took him a while to realize that the wetness pressing against his shoulder was also snow.

Once he had realized that, everything else rushed in. The flybug was a mangled wreck around him. He was still strapped to a seat that lay among a crystal pile of safety glass shards, and his security harness was a line of pain across his chest. He drew in a breath of freezing air and attempted to release the harness; he was shaking so much he couldn't press the button. His shoulder ached fiercely.

On the second try, he managed to release the catch and tumbled the last couple of inches into the snow. The last of his breath went. He rested his forehead in the snow and reminded his lungs how to expand.

The cold wasn't making it any easier, but it did him a favor in making the discomfort of his rapidly soaking clothes so unendurable that he had to push himself up. He was already starting to shiver. He turned and looked for Kiem.

He wasn't there.

Jainan stared at the wreckage of the flybug's dome and empty seat for a full three seconds before he looked farther and saw a dark form lying at the end of a track gouged in the snow. It was suddenly very hard to breathe again. His head must still be hazy, because there didn't seem to be any time at all between spotting Kiem and kneeling down next to him, shaking so badly he had to stop with his hand an inch from Kiem's face. Kiem's eyes were shut. It wouldn't help to touch him. What would help? Jainan was useless.

As if he felt the heat from Jainan's hand, Kiem stirred. His eyes opened and he raised his head, pushing himself up on one elbow. "Ouch."

Jainan crouched back so suddenly out of relief that he sat down in the snow, saving himself with his hands. "Kiem."

"Urgh. Here," Kiem said. "At least, I think I am. Ow." He sat up, in spite of an involuntary noise of protest from Jainan, who was thinking about broken ribs and internal injuries. But the movement didn't seem to cause Kiem any more pain. He rubbed his head, looked around and said, "What h— Oh. Shit." He jerked forward, drawing another half-formed protest that Jainan hadn't meant to make, and grabbed Jainan's arm. "Are you hurt?"

"No," Jainan said, and Kiem released his grip. Jainan looked Kiem over closely. He raised his hand to a red graze on Kiem's temple, not touching it. "You went through the dome."

Kiem started to say something but seemed to stutter. His eyes went to Jainan's hand, and Jainan became aware he had brushed the hair away from Kiem's forehead as if he had some sort of right to. He drew his hand back.

Kiem cleared his throat. "Yeah," he said. "Yeah, that wasn't in the plan. It's just a graze. Could do with a stim tab, maybe." He pushed himself to his feet, and dismay wrote itself across his face as he looked at the flybug. "Tell me this wasn't because of the stunt we pulled with the river."

Jainan stood as well, finding his limbs unexpectedly clumsy.

It was hard to balance. "No," he said. Planetside craft weren't his specialty, but he knew the basics. "Nothing the stabilizers are linked to would have that effect."

They both looked in silence at the remains of the flybug. The bulk of the shell was intact, but the front had been comprehensively smashed by the sheet of rock below. Much of the crumpling would have been intentional, built into the structure, but it was still only chance that they had survived.

"We got lucky," Kiem said. "We were flying very low."

He was right. If they'd been at a normal flying height, or in the tunnels, they would have had no chance. "Yes," Jainan said. He didn't want to think of the implications. The cold wind felt like it was boring into his bones.

"It was . . . an accident?" Kiem said. He sounded as if he would like that to be true but wasn't holding out a lot of hope.

Jainan jerked his head around to look at Kiem. Of course, Kiem wasn't an engineer, and he wouldn't have understood the sound and location of the explosion. "It was a compressor failure."

"Is that what took out—"

"—Taam's flybug?" Jainan said emotionlessly. "Yes."

Kiem winced. "I'm starting to hate flybugs." He leaned over it and thumped one of the crumpled panels, which broke off. "We've clearly pissed someone off. Shame we have no idea who."

Jainan shook his head mutely. If someone had set the explosion on a timer, the explosion could have been caused by anyone at Hvaren Base or anyone in the palace. The garages at the palace were secured, but only from the public, not from the palace's own residents. Jainan tried to shake off the feeling that it was his fault. He had been the one to stir up the hornet's nest by going into Taam's private files.

Kiem gave a crooked smile. "I suppose there's not a lot we can do about it from here, anyway," he said. He pulled aside a twisted panel and dislodged the first aid box, a bright red stain against the snow. He made an *aha* noise, pried out the sleeve of stim tabs, and shoved three on his tongue. He held them out to Jainan. "Probably don't take three."

The tabs would give him a slow-releasing drip of artificial energy and reduce the pain in his shoulder. Jainan took the sleeve and detached one. One might not have a great effect, but he was wary of anything that interfered with his perceptions, and he disliked stim hangover. It dissolved into bitterness on his tongue.

Kiem tramped over to the flybug and rested a hand on the intact part of the curved hull, looking into the interior. He shook his head, shot Jainan a rueful glance, and looked up ahead. "Well."

Jainan came up beside him and followed his gaze. His heart sank.

It was a stunning view, objectively. The patch of snow they had crashed on was halfway up a mountainside. The ledge dropped away ten meters or so from the crash site, and beyond it lay a tumbled progression of black rock ledges half-covered in snow drifts—and beyond that, a panorama of towering peaks and pine-clad valleys. They'd left Hvaren Base at least a hundred kilometers behind them, and it must be double that again to Arlusk. This was untouched wilderness.

It wasn't hopeless. Jainan rubbed his upper arm convulsively, hoarding the sliver of warmth. Bel and Internal Security were both expecting them. Even if they'd changed their flight plan, it would be fairly easy to guess where they'd gone, and the crash was visible from the air. There would be shelter in the flybug.

Kiem still hadn't said anything. Jainan risked a glance at him.

Kiem was staring at the expanse of wilderness with a thoughtful frown. He caught Jainan's glance and shook himself. "Well," he said again, "we definitely bought ourselves time to appreciate the scenery."

"Mm," Jainan said, gripping his other arm.

"Oh shit, you're freezing," Kiem said, turning to him. He

made to lift his arm as if to put it around Jainan's shoulders, then seemed to think better of it. "*I'm* freezing, come to think of it. I'm standing here like an idiot, sorry. There are clothes in the flybug. Let's kit up, then we can think about moving."

Clothes in the flybug. Of course there were. Their outdoor coats were packed in their luggage, for a start—how had Jainan not remembered that? He must be mildly concussed. Jainan moved mechanically back to the flybug, feeling his limbs loosen as the stim tab released into his blood, and watched Kiem wrench the hold open. Taam would have been in a towering rage by now. Kiem . . . wasn't. Yet.

"Hey! Jainan!" Kiem waved a bundle of fur above his head. "Found your coat!"

The *yet* echoed oddly in his mind. Jainan put it aside and went over, holding out his hands.

Kiem tossed the coat over. Jainan noticed him grimace after, because apparently even three stim tabs didn't cover all his muscle pain. For some reason Kiem had pulled all the luggage out of the flybug and onto the ground, and now he half climbed into the hold through the bent hatch, so far that his feet dangled in midair. "Nearly got it," he said, his voice slightly muffled. "Just a—ah, here we are." There was a scraping noise, and Kiem drew back out of the hatch with a piece of hold casing in his hand.

Jainan leaned over to peer in, his breaths coming short in the cold. "Why is there a hidden compartment in your flybug?" he said. It was filled with fluorescent fabric packs.

"Huh?" Kiem gave him a puzzled look. "This is just the—wait. I forgot you didn't grow up here." He reached in again and pulled out a square orange pack. "You missed the survival modules back in prime five. I guess Thean schools don't do them? All flycraft have this stuff built in by law." He pulled a tab at the corner of the pack and orange fabric cascaded out, morphing into a padded, waterproof overjacket. He dropped it on top of the scattered luggage and dived in for the other packs. "Tent," he called, throwing out another, larger pack. "Food—it's going to taste like industrial waste, but it's that or pine needles. Hey, a backpack! Only one, though." He pulled himself half out and looked around. "Sorry, this is going to take a little while. Pick out the warmest jacket. Uh . . . you should probably change first."

"Change clothes?" Jainan said. It was below freezing, and though the breeze was slight, it was turning the cold from a blunt weapon into a lethal one. "But—" He clamped his mouth shut on the last word. Iskaners from this region were experts on winter weather. Kiem didn't need questioning.

"Your inner layer's soaked from melting snow," Kiem said. "That's why you're still shivering. We've got dry clothes, might as well use them."

"Oh." Jainan looked down at his coat and realized that his clammy clothes were making the relentless cold even worse. He took a breath, pulled off his coat, and made himself strip off his shirt.

Kiem turned his back, crouching down to inspect the pile of equipment. Jainan wondered if that was politeness or just a disinclination to look at his body.

Jainan made short work of it, despite the trembling and fingers that fumbled catches. He had to double-layer some thin fabric; he had packed for short spells outside, not the winter night that was on its way. A few meters away, Kiem's polite detachment had turned into a flurry of activity as he checked fabric for holes and tested straps. Jainan finished dressing and stepped away so as not to distract him.

The breeze was numbing Jainan's cheeks. He had found his outdoor gloves in his luggage; they made his hands too bulky for his pockets, so he clamped them under his arms as he crouched down to examine the remains of the engine.

Several minutes later, Kiem popped his head over the hull. "I think we're good," he said. "This stuff hasn't been checked in a while, but it looks okay. We're still in the signal dead zone, so

I suppose the emergency beacon's useless. The dashboard map's not still working, is it?"

Jainan turned from the wreckage and opened his hand to show the glowing hemisphere of the flybug's map resting in his palm. "I was just thinking that," he said. "It has some charge, though no signal. I don't know where we are."

"Untracked wilderness," Kiem said, incongruously cheerful. "Kind of illegally, too, since you're not supposed to land in landscape reservations. Some hikers would kill to be us." He inspected the miniature map in Jainan's hand more closely and tried a command sign, but its sensors had died. He poked it instead. "I didn't know they disconnected."

"It was brute force," Jainan said, gesturing at the bits of wreckage he'd used as makeshift tools. "I salvaged the pyro from the engine and melted the connectors. It doesn't project anymore."

"Neat job," Kiem said. He examined the tiny crystal screen. "Okay, I think I have a plan." He pointed to a line across the map that Jainan had to look closely to see. "That has to be the rail line. It cuts east-west, so if we're in the general area I think we are and we head south, we should hit it within two or three days. They strip out the tacime alongside it so passengers can have signal. Our wristbands should pick up the moment we get in range. Then we call for help."

Two or three days. They had ten days before Unification Day. The ceremonies were taking place on Carissi Station, a space habitat in orbit around Thea, and it would take seventy-two hours on a shuttle to get there from Iskat. They could still make it in time. Jainan didn't want to think about the consequences if neither of the treaty representatives turned up to the ceremonies. "Yes," he said. Kiem looked at him. After a moment, Jainan said, "Was there something else?"

"Uh." Kiem cleared his throat. "It's just. I'm not sure if that meant 'Yes, that sounds good,' or 'Yes, I suppose we could ignore the glaring holes in that plan.'"

Despite the coat and overjacket, Jainan felt suddenly vulnerable. "Pardon?"

Kiem seemed to find the toggles of his wrist cuffs very interesting. "You say *yes* like that a lot," he said, not looking at him. "I. Uh. I think I might be missing some cues."

He thinks I'm lying to him, was Jainan's first, panicked thought, but he clamped down on it. Kiem said what he meant, he knew that. But what he meant was bad enough.

"Sorry," Kiem added. "I'm kind of slow about some stuff."

Jainan couldn't even make himself say anything to contradict that, though it wasn't true: Kiem being too astute was how they had ended up here. "I think—" It was unexpectedly hard to continue. Jainan took a deep breath and said, "Should we really move?"

Some part of him was still waiting for Kiem to blow up at him. But Kiem scratched the back of his head. "Normally I'd say no, but we're in the signal dead zone. And if it wasn't an accident . . . well, we're sitting ducks, here."

Jainan had known Kiem would take the challenge calmly. He *knew* that, and his irritating subconscious had still not let him believe it. What was wrong with him? He had an odd moment where he felt he could see that part of him, dispassionately, like some kind of cowering animal behind glass. He hated it.

Kiem looked at him expectantly. Jainan realized he was looking for an opinion—Jainan's opinion. "Then let's move," he said. It was easier to sound decisive than he thought it would be. "No point waiting to run out of food. The sooner the better."

"Right!" Kiem said, shouldering the backpack before Jainan had a chance to question why he was the one carrying it. "We can't die, anyway, we have to be at the press conference that kicks off the whole Unification Day circus. If we froze out here the Emperor would dig up our bodies in two big icicles and prop them up on the podiums." Jainan choked. Kiem was unrepentantly cheerful. "Let's get down to the valley floor. I'll go first. Might be easier to follow my tracks when it's deep."

Kiem sat on the edge of the ledge they'd crashed on and looked down at the tumbled progression of boulders and slopes that formed a sort of natural path. "Doesn't look too bad." He slithered down to the next ledge, landed in the crust of snow up to his knees, and made a face. "I take that back." He kicked his way through the drift.

Jainan followed exactly where he'd gone. Kiem waded up front through the drifts, kicking lumps of snow aside to clear a route for Jainan as he slid down onto each ledge. "You know what they don't put in that bloody survival kit?" he called behind him. "Snowshoes. You okay?"

"Yes," Jainan said. "You're making it easy."

Kiem threw a grin over his shoulder. "I always wanted to drive a snowplow when I was a kid," he said. "Careful, it gets a bit steeper from here."

The breeze had dropped completely. When Jainan paused to look behind him, the sky was a vast blue dome, clear and pristine, like some great hill reaching far above the jagged peaks. Jainan's breath caught in his throat. He knew Iskat was beautiful on an intellectual level: there was a reason the first colony ship of Iskaners had established the capital here and protected it with national parks, but this was the first time he'd really understood why.

The next ledges were acutely sloped and more difficult. They stopped talking. Kiem had the hiker's knack of finding the easiest way down; he skirted drifts and found unexpected flat rocks where there shouldn't be any, so Jainan could stop thinking and concentrate instead on where he put his feet. Kiem's occasional clumsiness indoors translated into something much more graceful out here; his extra bursts of energy just helped him kick his way through the snow and land on a hidden foothold underneath. Jainan found himself watching him more than he really had to.

Kiem looked around to check on him as Jainan slid down to

land on the next patch of rock. Jainan felt a sudden intense gratitude for Kiem's existence: for his easygoing manner, for his ability to take everything in his stride, for how he seemed to think Jainan's opinion was important.

This was hardly new, though: Jainan knew that Kiem was too charming for his own good. As Kiem turned back around to resume the trek, Jainan realized with dismay that it was having more of an effect on him than he'd thought. Kiem obviously couldn't switch the charm off, because he had inadvertently pointed it at Jainan multiple times. Jainan was getting attached to someone who had only ever wanted the appearance of a marriage. Kiem had outright told him so the first time they'd met.

Jainan gritted his teeth and slithered down the next drop. He clearly needed to watch his behavior, or he was going to end up being needy and embarrassing both of them. He had to keep a tighter hold on his emotions. They were already on a knife-edge with the treaty. There was no room for error.

Up ahead, Kiem stopped and looked down at his feet. Jainan put aside his churning thoughts and increased his pace, slipping and sliding, until he caught up. He stood beside Kiem, slightly breathless in the cold, and looked at the sheer drop in front of them. "Oh."

"This one might be a bit tricky," Kiem said.

They had come down a long way already, but they were still about fifty meters above the valley floor, where the snow was patchy amid pines and clumps of stranger Iskat trees. There was possibly a way down, if you squinted. It would require climbing.

"We can make it," Kiem said. He pulled off the backpack and, before Jainan realized what he was doing, dropped it over the edge. It fell, rolling against the rock face for what seemed like a disturbingly long time until it hit the ground far below, where it bounced.

"We'll have to, now," Jainan said. The backpack rolled to a halt. "I hope you wrapped up the family glassware in that."

"Like a baby," Kiem assured him. He was moving with a nervous energy that Jainan suspected was the result of the three stim tabs. "Ready?" Kiem pulled his heavy-duty gloves off and stuck them in his pockets, leaving himself with only the thin, flexible inner ones. Jainan did the same.

Kiem went first, by unspoken agreement, so Jainan could see what route to take. He spread himself like a spider over the rock face, clumsy in his boots but somehow balancing. Jainan crawled to the edge to watch, but Kiem was making such good progress that Jainan started to relax. Then Kiem reached a part near the base of the cliff—one that looked the same as all the other parts to Jainan's unpracticed eye—and got stuck for several agonizing minutes.

"Above your head to the right," Jainan called, when he couldn't stay quiet any longer. Kiem looked up, saw the ridge, and made a grab for it. It was just enough to get him onto the next shaky foothold. Then he went for one to the side of that—not even a ledge, more of a vertical groove—and his foot slipped.

Jainan gripped the ground in front of him convulsively as Kiem slithered down the remaining distance. The base of the wall didn't end cleanly but broke off into a shallower slope of fractured rock and tumbled boulders, and Kiem hit them hard. He fell off one and landed on the one next to it, catching himself with his hands. After a moment, though, he pushed himself up and held his thumbs up. Jainan sat back on his heels weakly and raised his hand in response.

"Not too bad!" Kiem shouted. "Keep to the left-hand side and don't worry about the last bit!"

He was right, worrying wouldn't help. Jainan was at least very good at doing what had to be done. He let himself down carefully over the side and felt for the first foothold.

It was not easy. Jainan had never climbed seriously and wasn't accustomed to testing footholds to see if they would hold his weight. His back and shoulder twinged in a way that told him he was starting to build up stim debt. The cold air tasted like metal in his mouth as he took his foot off one hold and slid his boot across the rock face, feeling for another foothold he couldn't see. He had never been so grateful that he had kept up his quarter-staff training. Even as it was, his arms were shaking by the time he reached the part that had defeated Kiem.

He looked down. If Kiem couldn't make it, Jainan doubted that he could. The ground below offered no good landing place; Kiem had been lucky not to twist an ankle. And in any case, Kiem himself was standing in the way. Jainan clung tighter to the ridge through his gloves and tried to make himself think.

"Jump!" Kiem called. He was holding his arms up. "Just let go!"

"I . . ." Jainan said. The word got lost in the cracks of the rock in front of him. "What?"

"I'll catch you!" Kiem's voice was going hoarse from shouting up advice. "It'll be fine!"

It was not going to be fine. Jainan made himself pry his fingers off the handholds anyway. He let go.

He didn't fall, just as Kiem hadn't fallen—it was more of a slide, painfully scraping across the rock face and gathering speed. He only had time for a moment's panic before he crashed down on top of Kiem. Kiem staggered, but his arms encircled Jainan, and his footing on the boulders held. Jainan had enough of his wits about him to jam his elbow into Kiem's back so he stayed balanced over Kiem's shoulder and they didn't both fall.

There was nowhere immediate for Jainan to get down. It was not easy for a grown man to carry another one; Kiem took a couple of wobbly steps across the boulders while Jainan held on and tried not to move. His face was buried in Kiem's shoulder. Kiem's hair pressed against his forehead, the smell and feel of it distracting in a way they really shouldn't be. Kiem was holding him close—for balance, for *balance*—and Jainan could feel the press of his body even through all their layers.

Kiem came to a halt on flat ground as the boulders petered out. It took Jainan a moment to react, then he realized Kiem was trying to put him down and he was still holding on. He rolled off Kiem's shoulder and half fell, landing on his feet. Kiem stepped back very quickly.

Jainan caught his breath. Kiem looked more shaken from the climb than Jainan had realized, and his hand appeared to be trembling as he lowered his arm. Was that the effect of the stim tabs Kiem had taken, or had Jainan's thoughts shown on his face?

Kiem rubbed his neck where Jainan's hand had rested. Jainan gathered his defenses and swallowed the whole incident down, burying it where it wouldn't affect either of them. "I'm not sure climbing is a sport I'm going to take up any time soon," Jainan said lightly. "It's getting dark. How much farther do we go today?"

"Right," Kiem said, shaking his head a little and coming back to the logistics. The mountains had long twilights even by the standards of Iskat's long evenings, but now the deep blue above their heads was turning into dusk, and clouds were creeping up from the farthest peaks. "We should camp. Maybe not here though—the snow's pretty deep." As he turned to scan the shadowed valley, his eyes skated past Jainan awkwardly. "We could probably reach that overhang in half an hour." He shouldered the backpack again. Jainan fell in beside him, not too close.

The boulders at the base of the mountain gave way to rock and earth in patches visible under the thin layer of snow. This part of the small valley was more sheltered than the higher reaches, though the snow lay in smothering drifts on the other side. They didn't talk.

The snow was still deep enough to crunch beneath their feet. Jainan's breath crystallized in front of him in white clouds in the still air, which hung and then dissipated. He found himself sinking into a rhythm of walking, eventually warming up enough that he unfastened his coat and let it flap open. Every now and then, a breath of wind chilled his face.

The stillness was the stillness of a shrine. None of the palace politics seemed important: even Internal Security and the Resolution felt toothless out here. Apart from the brush of their footsteps and their laboring breath, absolute silence reigned. The cold against Jainan's face was clean and purifying; he felt detached, but in a strange way, as if he could see his tiny, insignificant form moving at the center of the huge spaces around them. Something in the space and silence was trickling into his bones, gradually filling them up with an itchiness like shoots of grass unfolding. It came with an aching feeling, and for some reason, the ache felt like loss.

There is something wrong with you, he told himself, because there was no loss, and now he was sounding quite insane. But it was like an echo of someone else's voice.

"Here?" Kiem said, startling Jainan out of his reverie. Jainan turned, slow to react, and realized Kiem had stopped a few paces back to inspect a patch of earth sheltered by a cliff face.

Jainan gestured assent. "Give me the tent."

Kiem unshouldered the backpack and tossed over a dense, knobbly pack with a handle at the top. When Jainan pulled the cord, the pack exploded into a pincushion of plastic tubes that pistoned out like spikes, and a waterfall of fabric that chased them and covered the surface of the structure until he was holding a rigid pod. It was noticeably small for two people. Jainan decided not to think about that. "Is there a heater?"

"Yes, but only three canisters," Kiem said. "I thought we should save them. There's food if you want it." As Jainan finished securing the tent and came around the front of it, he saw Kiem had laid out several foil packs on the snow by the sleeping bags. "Finest gourmet choices: you can have brown sludge, brown sludge, or grayish sludge. The gray one says it's strawberry, but I'm not sure I believe it."

Jainan picked up a piece of the brown rations. It was more like a hard cake than sludge, and it crumbled like a cookie; a square broke off in his hand. He tried a mouthful and then broke off a square of the gray one on the working hypothesis that it couldn't be worse. It wasn't, quite. He sat next to Kiem in front of the tent, his outdoor clothes rustling as he settled down. The valley they had just trekked down folded out in front of them.

Kiem stared at the red-tinged snow where the sunset light came through a break in the fiery crags, absently eating square after square of the horrible rations. "Jainan," he said. "What happens if both the treaty representatives die in a crash just before Unification Day? Does the Resolution appoint new ones?"

"I don't know," Jainan said. If he thought about it clinically, as a diplomatic puzzle rather than a sector-wide disaster, he could just about treat it logically. "Under normal conditions, maybe. Given the Auditor already suspects Taam was murdered, it seems likely he would take this as a further sign that Iskat and Thea are not stable enough to sign a Resolution treaty."

"So that would be a great way to screw things up," Kiem said grimly. "Even better than killing Taam."

Jainan shook his head. It gave his stomach a painful twist to even consider the idea, but he couldn't fault Kiem's logic.

Kiem broke another square off with his teeth. "Did you see anyone near our flybug at the base?"

"No."

"I guess we were inside most of the time. And Heaven knows I don't keep tabs on my flybug at home."

Jainan glanced at their tent and noticed for the first time that Kiem had picked a site where they weren't that visible from the air. The overhang provided some cover. "For what it's worth, it would have been easier to carry out the sabotage at the palace,"

Jainan said. "More people come and go from the garages there. But it could have been either."

"Or it was an accident."

"Yes." Jainan didn't bother saying any more.

Kiem thoughtfully flicked some crumbs off his leg. "I hope Internal Security does a better job with this investigation than the last one."

He broke off another ration square and leaned against the backpack, which shifted to reveal something poking out of the top. It was wrapped in Kiem's spare sweater. The part that was sticking out glinted.

Jainan leaned over and disentangled what looked like a trowel. It was either made of gold metal or convincingly gilded. He raised his eyebrows at Kiem. "Gardening?"

"Ah," Kiem said. He looked faintly guilty. "Um. That's the school prize. I thought we'd better not lose it."

Jainan weighed it in his hand. It had a solid heft and must have contributed to the weight of the bag. "So we are instead . . . carrying it over kilometers of trackless tundra?"

"Well. It belongs to the school."

"They could get a new one."

"But this one has all the names on it, see?" Kiem took it and turned it over. "It might be important to someone."

"A school prize."

"Just because it's not important doesn't mean it's not important to *someone*," Kiem said. He must have mistaken Jainan's look for doubt, because he looked faintly stubborn and said, "I'll carry it."

"Mm, no," Jainan said. He took the trowel back, wrapped it up in the sweater, and stowed it carefully back in the rucksack. "I think it's a good idea." It would not have occurred to him to do it. It had obviously not occurred to Kiem not to do it.

Kiem sat back, more relaxed, and tilted his head to look up at the sky. His breath misted in the freezing air. It was absurd to be content, when Jainan's shoulder still ached and they were in the middle of nowhere, in snow and treacherous terrain, relying on reaching a rail line to get back to civilization. More absurd when Jainan thought about the wreckage of their flybug behind them and all the people at the palace or the base who might have had access to sabotage it. He felt it anyway.

Jainan shifted position to cross his legs, and his knee came into contact with Kiem's. He didn't even realize he'd done it until Kiem twitched and drew up his legs to put space between them.

The contentment receded. Jainan struggled to hold on to it, then realized it was in vain, and let it go. He let out a breath and let the twinge of humiliation recede with it. "It's been a long day," he said, because it seemed the least awkward way to apologize.

"Very long. So long," Kiem agreed, though he was still holding himself awkwardly to avoid touching Jainan. He turned it into a scramble to his feet. "You know what! I think I'm going to go to bed."

"Yes," Jainan said. He got to his feet as well. "Do you want—"

Kiem had already grabbed one of the sleeping bags. "There isn't enough room in there," he said. "I'll sleep out here."

"What," Jainan said blankly.

"These things are rated for outdoors, and there's no wind," Kiem said, unfolding the sleeping bag. "Perfect conditions."

"Oh," Jainan said, feeling leaden. It was a reasonable solution; sleeping in the same small tent would have been extremely awkward. "No, I have the bedroom at home. Take the tent."

"This is not your problem," Kiem said, intently not-looking at Jainan. "You're not sleeping outside because of something that is *in no conceivable universe* your problem."

It wasn't worth fighting about. "All right. Yes."

"All right," Kiem repeated. The relief was unmistakable; Kiem always wore his emotions on his sleeve. "I'll just get some water. I think there's a stream still running over there."

Jainan turned away and crawled into the tent. He could identify the odd sadness now. It came from the same source as the joy: life had been good to him, unexpectedly, but it wasn't fair to try and stretch it out. If he had any regard for Kiem, any gratitude, he would have to try and think of a way out for him—some way that Kiem could live his own life, not shackled to someone he wasn't attracted to. This couldn't go on.

CHAPTER 17

Kiem was already sitting up and taking stock when the dawn sky started to lighten.

He still hadn't managed to come to terms with someone wanting him or Jainan dead. He could go over the facts as much as he liked—someone had swapped out Taam's crash data, someone must want the treaty in trouble—but even though he kept listening out for the drone of a flybug coming after them, he couldn't make himself *believe* it. Nobody had ever had a grudge against Kiem. He didn't really make enemies.

They were doing as well as they could, given the circumstances. It wasn't Kiem's fault that Taam had been up to his ears in shady transactions, or that the Auditor wouldn't instate them yet. It wasn't his fault their flybug had crashed or that someone might have enough of a grudge to sabotage it. Maybe if Kiem hadn't taken them off their scheduled flight path, they wouldn't have to trek to find help, but they were doing all right at the trekking. The only problem that was really, indisputably his fault was Jainan.

It wasn't fair to phrase it like that. The problem wasn't with Jainan himself; it was all on Kiem's side. If Kiem had managed to be less weird last night, they might still be almost friends, or whatever it was they had been recently.

Kiem absently dug up a handful of the snow beside him in his gloves and packed it into a ball. He needed to get a grip on himself. He and Jainan had managed to reach some kind of fragile stability, and if Kiem carried on like this, he was going to screw it up for both of them.

"Is this the prelude to a snowball fight?" a voice said from behind him. "I should warn you: unlike your usual school fete opponents, I am not five years old."

Kiem grinned and tossed the snowball in his hand, banishing the introspection. "So much the better," he said. "Have you ever faced twenty five-year-olds? They're terrifying." He tossed the snowball again, but it fell apart when he tried to catch it. "Dammit."

"Structurally unsound," Jainan said. "Blame the contractors." One corner of his mouth was pulled up in a smile, but there was a tension underneath it. Kiem hoped he was hiding his own better. "How are we set for today?"

"Right." Kiem scrambled to his feet and started compressing his sleeping bag. "If the terrain's not too bad, I think we should get to the rail line today or tomorrow. We could get going and have breakfast later, if you've slept enough."

"I'm not sleeping any more," Jainan said. He sounded as resigned to it as Kiem had felt at four that morning. "Let's start out." He turned away to collapse the tent.

The shadow of the mountain bowl kept the snow around them dark even while the sky above lightened to powdery gray. On the far cliffs, the dawn light glinted on the flybug wreck, small by now in the distance. Kiem looked at it ruefully.

No point crying over spilled milk, and it was too cold to hang around. He and Jainan consulted over the map, which had no idea where they were but handily told them which way was south. They picked the likeliest-looking pass they could see and set out.

They ate breakfast while walking by unspoken agreement. Kiem had been hiking in winter before, but he would be lying if he said he was *happy* to be stranded out here on an unplanned survival trek, not knowing if someone was after them. They'd been lucky: they were kitted up, and technically the rest of the journey should just be a matter of putting one foot in front of the other, but still, the more distance they could put behind them the better. Jainan seemed to feel the same way.

Once the light broke over the top of the mountains, midway through the morning, they both relaxed a fraction. Kiem was trying not to brood and also trying not to mention anything that would make the stress worse. He and Jainan traded comments and absent half jokes that didn't really lead on from each other.

By the afternoon Kiem was feeling the walking in the complaints from his thigh muscles, though it was hard to distinguish the aches from the bruises he'd taken in the crash. He came to a halt as they crested another ridge. "Break?"

A weight lifted from his back as Jainan took the backpack. They'd been trading it all day. Kiem slipped out of the straps without argument. "Sorry," Jainan said. "I should have noticed. What hurts?"

Kiem made a face. "Nothing important," he said. "Twinge in my hip. It'll hold."

"Sit down," Jainan said abruptly.

Kiem was familiar with Jainan's way of offering concern by now and was touched, but that seemed like a bad idea. "It's going to be hard to get up again," he said. "How about we just stop for a moment? View in a million, right?" He gestured ahead of them, where the ridge they had painstakingly labored up dropped away again into a series of valleys and more snowbound peaks. "I mean, apart from all those other ones like it that we've seen."

"I have filled my quota of beautiful mountain scenes for the year," Jainan said. "Possibly for the rest of my life." Nevertheless, he joined Kiem on the promontory, a step back from the edge.

There was a long silence while they both contemplated the view and the relief of not walking, the wind occasionally gusting around them. Kiem rolled his shoulders.

"Kiem," Jainan said.

"Yeah?"

"I was thinking—if the treaty goes smoothly. If we have twenty years until the next one. I was thinking about monasteries."

"What about them?" Kiem said, startled by the sudden change in direction. "Is this about the time I got sent on a retreat? I haven't done anything recently."

"No!" Jainan said. "No. That's not—it's quite normal for people here to go on long meditation retreats and, and contemplation and that sort of thing, isn't it?"

"Well, it depends on your sect," Kiem said dubiously. "I mean, the meditation stuff is pretty general, but some sects have strong ideas about gods. Does yours? Uh. Sorry. That was kind of a personal question."

"No. It's fine," Jainan said. "My faith group is quite generalist." He looked up ahead. The wind gusted again; Kiem had to squint to see Jainan's face through the sudden water in his eyes. "Once the investigation is over, I could give us both some space by going on a retreat. I could do it regularly. I'd be out of your way."

It took Kiem a couple of moments to understand what he was saying. "Right," Kiem managed, not quite knowing how to form a coherent sentence. He should have expected this. Jainan wanted a space where Kiem wasn't there—that was completely understandable. "Right."

Jainan was still watching him in that sideways way he had. Kiem raised a hand to his face, not knowing what he was doing, and changed the aimless gesture into trying to rub some warmth back into his cheeks. He was supposed to be good with people, dammit. He shouldn't be blindsided by things like this.

"It might not work," Jainan said. "It was—it was just a thought. We can talk about it later." He looked like he might have said something more, but at that moment, his eyes narrowed. He jerked his head around to look behind them.

Kiem was slower to react, still stuck on the thought of Jainan leaving, but he heard the second sound. It wasn't coming from the ridge Jainan was looking at but from a row of trees straggling along to the side.

"There," Jainan said, turning his head again as he triangulated. "What—"

They both saw the black shape detaching itself from the shadow of the trees at the same time. It had its head down in a gesture you never wanted to see in a bear, one that meant it was speeding up to charge. Kiem's mind seemed to move slowly and his body was sluggish. He heard himself shout "Bear!" then desperately backed into Jainan, grabbed him, and threw them both off the promontory.

They landed a few feet down the slope in a thick layer of snow and rolled. The snow sheared off with them as they tumbled, clutching at each other. Snow. Sky. Snow. Sky. Rock. Kiem heard himself yelling. On one frantic, painful rotation he caught sight of the black shape shooting through the air over them—it had miscalculated the tackle. He tried to yell again, but one of the rocks knocked the breath out of his lungs. On his next glimpse he saw the bear land on the snow and scuttle away into the trees.

Jainan pushed himself up the moment they stopped, a stone's throw from a stand of trees. "What *was* that?" he said, fighting for breath. "It moved like a lizard!"

"Bear," Kiem said, looking around warily for anything that could be used as a weapon. "Let's back off slowly—it's got our scent now, it'll come back."

"That's not a bear!"

"Pretty sure it couldn't be anything else!" Kiem said. "Quick, we need a rock, or a—"

"Here." Jainan pushed the end of what seemed like an entire fallen tree branch into Kiem's hand.

"What—right," Kiem said. He examined the branch, keeping a wary eye on the trees where the bear had disappeared. "I guess we can wave sticks. If we're threatening enough, it should leave us alone—Jainan?"

"Just over here," Jainan said, from a few yards away. He had picked up another branch and was methodically stripping it of twigs and leaves.

Kiem spun around at another sound, but it was just snow shifting in the groove gouged by their fall. "Okay, I think we should really get away from the trees." The back of his head hurt and he'd pulled something in his leg. The bear was presumably skulking somewhere in the copse, but they hadn't hurt it, so it would still think of them as easy prey. "Into the open. Down here." He pointed down the slope, where a wide swathe of open space stretched between two straggling edges of a pine wood. There was a frozen river running along one side of it.

Jainan came away from the trees, weighing the branch in his hands. "Is that ice going to hold us?"

"We don't have to cross it," Kiem said. "Just follow its banks so it can't come up behind us. Let's go." He waved Jainan in front of him and followed him, checking back over his shoulder every couple of steps. "If you see it, yell and look threatening. It's not that dangerous if we can scare it off."

"Not that dangerous," Jainan repeated. He grounded the end of the stick beside him as he walked, while Kiem kept his—still with the leaves on—raised by his side, in the hope that looked threatening. "But that one attacked us. Do these things kill people?"

"Sometimes," Kiem said. "Occasionally."

"So, yes," Jainan said. His hand moved over the branch restlessly. "You could have mentioned these before."

"I didn't think we'd meet any!" Kiem said. "They're pretty rare this far north. Don't you have bears in the mountains on Thea?" He paused to turn back and stare at a patch of shadow by a bush that caught his eye, reassured himself it was just a shadow, and turned back.

Jainan waited for him to catch up. "Bears where I grew up are shy and retiring unless they have cubs," he said. "Also they have *fur* and *four legs*. That thing is an oversize reptile."

"What kind of bear has fur?" Kiem thought he heard something and turned back to scan the trees again.

"Kiem," Jainan said sharply.

Kiem spun around. Jainan pointed to the side, far from where Kiem had been looking. A black shape was frozen just shy of the tree line, low to the ground, its blunt, scaled snout pointed toward them.

"Shit," Kiem said. "Let's, uh, let's move back slowly." It only took a few steps to put himself between Jainan and the bear. He held up the branch in front of him. The leaves swayed on the twigs; he had a bad feeling the bear wouldn't find it that threatening. "If it comes nearer, get ready to yell."

"There's not much room," Jainan said from behind him, tense. "If we move back much we'll hit the river. The ice looks thin."

"Then . . . sideways," Kiem said, trying to keep his eyes on the bear, which was raising and lowering one of its hind legs as if testing the ground. "We heroically retreat . . . sideways."

"Yes," Jainan said. "We should separate." His voice was farther away than it should be, and Kiem realized he was striding away at a tangent, widening the gap between them, on a trajectory that took him diagonally away from the river.

"Wait, not closer to it!"

"We can confuse it if we're in different places!" Jainan called back.

"Wait! Jainan!" Kiem moved his head, and at that moment, the bear charged.

Kiem stumbled, caught off-balance as he ordered his body to sprint. He saw, as if in slow motion, Jainan stop, turn toward the bear, put up his tree branch in front of him. Kiem pushed forward as if moving through treacle. Only then did he turn his head to see the bear trundle and curve in its charge.

It wasn't going for Jainan. It was going for *him*.

He didn't have time to shout. The bear was on him: a shattering impact of scales and teeth, a blast of foul breath. Kiem thrust the branch desperately between them as the impact threw him back. He tried to catch his footing, but he was already falling.

He hit the ground. There was a jarring, splintering crash that he thought for one horrible moment was his bones, but he couldn't feel pain. Then he registered *ice* at the same moment the cold water hit him like a weapon.

He gasped and flung himself forward at the river bank, dropping the stick. The cold was viscerally shocking, nearly stopping his heart, and for a moment he forgot about—

—the bear. The bear should have been on him. But there was no ripping pain, not yet. Instead it was several feet away, *by Jainan*, in a blur of movement. Kiem heard a grunt of rage as his brain caught up with his ears. Jainan stepped back out of reach of the armored claw, spun for momentum, and brought his make-shift quarterstaff around for another blow.

The bear reeled back. One of its paws came up to its snout while it scrabbled itself back with the other five. It and Jainan regarded each other warily.

Kiem tried to hold still in the water as he got his footing on the rocks below, panting in shallow gasps from the cold. The bear moved, but Jainan was quicker: he lunged forward and cracked the stick with surgical precision across one of the bear's eyes.

A screech of animal pain filled the space between the trees. The bear stumbled back on its six legs, ducking its head away from Jainan. Jainan was in a defensive stance, as if he expected it to spin and attack, but it was already skittering away across the snow.

Kiem pulled himself up the bank. His teeth chattered and he still couldn't breathe properly, but he managed to get one sodden leg out of the water. And then hands were under his arms, dragging him out until he lay on the bank in the snow.

"I'm sorry, I'm so sorry." Jainan fell to his knees beside him. "Kiem, I'm so sorry, I thought it would go for me if it saw me moving."

The note in Jainan's voice galvanized Kiem into moving. He sat up, shivering, and resisted the urge to curl up. "Y-you *meant* it to go for you?"

"No," Jainan said. "Yes. I don't know. I thought I could draw it off. I didn't mean it to be anywhere near you. I'm sorry. I'm sorry. Take my gloves."

Kiem tried to wrap his arms over his chest, but it wasn't helping. "Jainan," he said, "that w-was incredible. You just fought off a bear. Shit, it's cold. I d-don't want your gloves," he added, as Jainan tugged Kiem's soaked gloves off his hands and replaced them with his own.

"Mm." Jainan's talkativeness had apparently run out. He gripped Kiem's wrists and pulled him to his feet. Kiem followed the direction clumsily, too cold and soaked to do much thinking, and wasn't expecting a full-on embrace.

He was too surprised to move. Jainan wrapped his arms around him, heedless of the fact that Kiem's dripping coat was probably soaking river water into his own clothes. Kiem was too cold to feel much. It wasn't even noticeably warmer, except on his face, where Jainan's presence created a shelter against the breeze. Kiem just shut his eyes and drank in the feeling of Jainan close to him.

It lasted only short seconds. Jainan let go and said, "We'll need to set up the tent. At least we saved the heating canisters."

"R-right," Kiem said. He resisted the urge to wrap his arms around himself again and forced himself to think. "Right. Okay. Maybe not here. Let's get a bit farther."

"Will it come back?" Jainan said. He picked up the backpack—Kiem hadn't noticed him shed it to fight—and hovered by Kiem's side.

He was obviously waiting for Kiem to get his shit together and actually start walking, however much Kiem's whole body ached. Jainan had just fought off a bear. Kiem was only cold. "Shouldn't," Kiem said, finally clearing the lowest bar for effort and putting one foot in front of another. "You scared it off. They only go for prey that doesn't f-fight back." He clamped his jaw shut to stop his teeth chattering.

Jainan fell into a tense silence. Kiem stopped himself from talking. He pretended it was easier to keep walking once he'd started and tried to ignore the way his energy seemed to be seeping away with every step, like his soaked and freezing clothes were bleeding it out of him.

"Here," Jainan said. Kiem stopped, pulling himself out of something close to a fugue state. He glanced around. They were some distance from any trees, under an overhang at the top of a shallow slope.

"Looks good," Kiem said. He held out his hands for the backpack. "Let me—"

"I've got it," Jainan said, already laying out their spartan camping gear. Kiem took the sleeping bags to unpack, but his fingers were numb and clumsy, even when he slipped his hands out of his borrowed gloves. He fumbled a toggle time and time again because his hands were shaking too violently to control.

It slipped out of his hand for the tenth time. "Argh!"

"Are you all right?" Jainan called.

"Yes. F-fine. Ignore me," Kiem said. He finally tugged the string free on about the eleventh try and straightened up with some relief.

When he looked over his shoulder, Jainan already had the tent up and anchored—about twice as fast as he'd done it the previous evening—and had stowed most of their things inside. He came back around the front and handed Kiem a stim tab, already unwrapped. For all that Jainan hadn't grown up in this climate, he was remorselessly efficient at getting things done, while Kiem fumbled around here like he had a faulty connection.

Jainan caught his expression. "Is something funny?"

"I was just th-thinking," Kiem said, "that it's lucky *one* of us reacts to danger by actually being competent, rather than f-falling into the nearest river."

Jainan's face went blank. "I am sorry if I gave the impression—"

"What," Kiem said. "Jainan, you f-fought off a *bear*." He tried to shove his hands back into his pockets; one of his nearly numb fingers caught on the fabric, and he suppressed a grunt of pain.

A complicated mix of emotions had risen on Jainan's face, but that wiped them away and replaced them with concern. "You should get inside."

Out of habit, Kiem said, "We should eat out here where there's space—"

"*Inside*," Jainan said, with an edge to his tone that Kiem hadn't heard from him before. Kiem half grinned through another convulsive shiver and did as he said.

It was no warmer in the tent, but the two sleeping bags Jainan had laid out covered the floor and made it look so inviting, Kiem's tiredness was suddenly impossible to fight. He gave up wrestling with the door flap and fell from his knees facedown on the cushioned fabric. It was damp with melted snow. He didn't care.

Behind him, Jainan was politely trying to move Kiem's feet so he could fasten the door flap shut. Kiem groaned because moving seemed like a mountainous effort, but he recognized he was being a pain. He managed to roll over, sit up, and make a half-hearted tug at his boot. His hands still weren't working; it slipped out of his grasp. The friction hurt. That was when the tired misery he'd kept at bay tipped into something like panic.

"Let me."

Kiem opened his eyes from his frustrated grimace to say, *What?* but Jainan was already crouching over his feet and freeing the fasteners. His hand slipped around Kiem's ankle and held it while he tugged the boot free. Every movement was gentle.

You don't have to do this was on the tip of Kiem's tongue, but he couldn't say it. He'd be in serious trouble if Jainan had decided not to come along on the trip in the first place. He couldn't even make his bloody fingers work properly, and if he didn't warm up soon, he was in the danger zone for frostbite and hypothermia. Instead he said fervently, "I'm *really* glad you're here."

Jainan stopped momentarily in the act of setting Kiem's boots aside. Kiem worried he'd just offended him, but Jainan's glance at him was thoughtful and somehow pleased. "Mm," he said. "You're not going to get any warmer lying on top of the cover."

Kiem took the hint. He managed to strip off his wet trousers and underlayers himself—it hurt, but there was no way he was going to make Jainan feel he had to do that. Besides, pain was probably a good sign; at least his hands weren't entirely numb. His legs felt like lead. He climbed into the sleeping bag and zipped it up behind him through sheer force of will.

That was the last effort he could make. He lay down on his stomach and let his face press into the cushioned ground. The dry fabric of the sleeping bag was smooth and warm against his bare skin, and it felt almost good. His limbs were too heavy to move. He shut his eyes.

After a while Jainan started moving around. Kiem heard the rustling of waterproof fabric and clothes, and then a click and a low buzz that he recognized. Jainan had set off one of the heating cylinders. Kiem still couldn't get up the energy to move, but he felt the warmth on his face a few moments later, way before it could get through the insulation of the sleeping bag. He kept his eyes shut and let himself just exist. He would warm up eventually.

"Kiem!" Jainan said sharply.

It took Kiem a moment to realize that wasn't the first time Jainan had said his name. He resented being pulled out of the fog of weariness. "Mmrf?"

"I said, can you eat something?"

Kiem managed a negative grunt. "L'ter."

From the sound of it, Jainan was leaning over him, rustling around near the foot of the sleeping bag. "This isn't—" he said. "How do I turn this up? The heater."

"Don'," Kiem said, his eyes still shut. "Runs out sooner."

"That is *not important*!" There was the same edge to his voice as when he'd told Kiem to get inside the tent.

Kiem opened his eyes. "'S fine," he said, because apparently he wouldn't get enough quiet to sleep until Jainan was reassured. "Warming up. Bear's gone. No reason to be worried."

"Yes, there is," Jainan said. "You've barely said anything in the last half hour."

"Damning evidence," Kiem mumbled into the bit of cushioning that served as a pillow. He could feel the ground through it. He was too tired to solve this; surely it could wait.

More rustling, while Kiem closed his eyes again. Then Jainan said, "Excuse me," and he felt the sleeping bag move. The zip at the side opened, and then there was the glorious warmth of someone right next to him. Kiem turned without even thinking about it and pressed himself closer. He had a horrible, nagging feeling that there was some reason he shouldn't give himself up to the comfort of this. He ignored it.

"All right," Jainan said quietly, somewhere that sounded very far in the distance, though the voice was right next to his ear. "Please be all right."

Kiem tried to tell him that everything was fine, more than that, everything was for some reason perfect, but sleep was too close to claiming him. He let himself sink into it.

CHAPTER 18

When Jainan woke, he was warm. Faint gray moonlight filtered in through the tent roof. He had a collection of small aches and pains trying to make themselves known, but for some reason he felt at peace.

Then he realized he was tangled up with Kiem, his bare arm over Kiem's naked back, and he froze.

Even as Jainan's brain raced headlong toward panic, Kiem's eyes opened. His gaze was unfocused and sleepy. Jainan took a breath, and that was all it took for Kiem to realize they were touching and flinch back as far as he could in the sleeping bag.

Their legs were still touching. Jainan was very aware that he was only wearing a shirt and underwear, and Kiem even less than that. He tried not to let the awkwardness come through in his voice. "Better?"

Kiem cleared his throat. "Uh, yeah." He sounded more coherent than he had last night. Jainan tried not to think about the agony of mixed comfort and embarrassment that last night had been. "Yeah. Yes. Much better. See, no shivering." He moved his hand as if to demonstrate, but that nearly brought them back in contact again, and he stopped and held unnaturally still. "Um. Thanks."

Jainan suddenly realized the fastenings were on his own side. He was an idiot. He wasted no further time in unzipping the side of the sleeping bag, rolling out, and retreating to his own cramped half of the tent. His skin felt tight with mortification even at this distance. He crossed his legs, attempting to compose himself, and focused on unwrapping a ration pack.

Kiem slowly sat up and rubbed his shoulder. There was a red mark across it that must be from where he'd lain on Jainan's arm.

"I am sorry I took the liberty," Jainan said, focusing with all his might on the wrapper. He folded it back in small, neat squares. "I thought you were in danger of hypothermia. I may have been wrong."

"Er, no, really, don't be sorry." Kiem said. He was talking slightly faster than normal. "I was definitely getting that way. You did everything right—actually, my prime five teacher would be pretty proud of us, I guess. Of course, she never taught a module on how to win fights with bears."

Of course Kiem knew how to paper it over. Kiem was good at smoothing away awkwardness. "No," Jainan said, making sure he was still looking down at his hands. He folded the wrapper back over itself again into another neat square.

Kiem grabbed the other ration pack. "I'm just gonna have a quick look around," he said. "Scout the next move. Back in a moment." He pulled on his trousers and coat—they looked almost dry from the warmth of the heater—and climbed out of the tent.

Jainan looked up as he left. *Sorry,* he wanted to say again, but his tongue was clumsy and slow. However sensible sharing their body warmth had been, he had been wrong to find it pleasant. He had taken advantage of Kiem's incapacitation. No wonder Kiem wanted to take some time outside.

The heating capsule had run down in the hours since they'd fallen asleep. He occupied himself with changing it and organizing the detritus of their bag. The stim tabs were missing; Kiem must still have them in his pocket.

It was just unfortunate, that was all. They lived in close quarters at home and they had been forced into closer quarters here. If Kiem could get the space he needed, they could go back to what had developed into an almost comfortable equilibrium.

Jainan activated his wristband automatically to look up more about monasteries, but of course they were out of range. Never mind. He could ask Bel when they got back.

Jainan looked up from the heating capsule when Kiem returned. It was working now: the tent was so warm that Kiem shrugged out of his coat the moment he came in. "I thought we might as well use another one," Jainan said in explanation. "I'm not sure when you want to set off, but I assumed we would wait at least until it was light enough to see, so we may as well keep warm. And I think we may be able to use this to warm water?"

"Good idea," Kiem said. "There's coffee powder somewhere, did you find it with the food?" He seemed more energetic. He must have taken at least one more stim tab.

"Yes," Jainan said. He shook some powder into the cup attachment, which Kiem took outside and filled with snow. Jainan paid more attention to melting it than necessary, but once it was fitted to the canister and warming, he ran out of things to do to keep from looking at Kiem. He found himself locking his hands together in his lap and inspecting them.

The awkward silence stretched out for long minutes, until Jainan heard Kiem take a deep breath. "So, uh," Kiem said, sounding as if he had reached some sort of conclusion when he was outside. "Can we talk for a moment about . . . stuff?"

"Stuff," Jainan said blankly.

"I've been thinking about what you said about the monastery. I think I know why you brought it up." Jainan's back started to knot up with tension; so it was going to be that kind of conversation. Kiem carried on, "It's about having your own freedom, right? I understand. I know you didn't choose this marriage. But, you know, long-term, it doesn't have to be so much like a marriage. I mean, we're—we're friends, right? Sort of?" He stopped. *Sort of friends* echoed in Jainan's head. It was a relief to hear it confirmed, and more than he should expect. It shouldn't hurt. Jainan didn't know why it did.

Kiem was still waiting. Jainan realized he was expecting an answer, and gave a slow nod.

"Right! Yeah," Kiem said. "So we can just stay like this, can't we? Being married won't stop you doing anything you want to do. If there's someone you—if either of us was to start seeing someone on the side, that's—that's fine, right? We can both keep it quiet. So we can make sure the marriage doesn't get in the way of, of either of our lives."

Someone on the side? Jainan realized he was staring at Kiem, groping in vain for some sort of response, and made himself look back down. "I see." It was not his business if Kiem wanted to see someone else. He must get offers all the time. At least he was being honest about it.

"Right," Kiem said. There was more uncomfortable silence. Kiem reached for the open ration pack and wrapped it up to put away.

Someone else. It was like an invisible splinter: Jainan didn't want to press at it, but at the same time he couldn't leave it alone. "This is an impolite question," he heard himself say, "but may I ask who it is?"

The wrapping in Kiem's hands ripped.

"What? *Me?*" he said. "No, wait, there *isn't* anyone! This isn't me telling you I'm seeing someone!"

"Why not?" Jainan said. It was easier to sound calm and reasonable if he didn't look at Kiem's face. "Your marriage isn't fulfilling. I don't mind."

"It wouldn't be fair to them," Kiem said. He sounded baffled, which didn't make any sense. "It wouldn't be fair to *you.*"

"I see," Jainan said. He didn't. Kiem seemed to be undermining his own argument. Jainan felt like he was trying to unravel a mathematics problem, but he cared about it too much to have any chance of solving it. "So you would like to see someone in the future."

"I just thought—I thought *you*—" Kiem opened one hand in a

frustrated gesture. "Look, it's better than you going off to a monastery."

Something unreasonable shot through Jainan's chest like an energy cutter. He looked down at the coffee to conceal it. It was starting to boil, but he couldn't seem to move his hands to do anything about it. The orange light flickered on Kiem's face, highlighting his expressive eyes and the consternation there. Jainan had somehow hurt him. He didn't know how to fix it.

"Sorry," Kiem said.

He apologized to make Jainan feel better when it wasn't even his fault. Jainan's chest hurt. Kiem meant well; if only Jainan weren't so inadequate. If only Jainan could be good enough for anyone. He shut his eyes. It was his cardinal rule not to ask questions in a situation like this: they tore away more remnants of his dignity and they irritated his partner. But Kiem said everything he thought, and Jainan had to try. "Is there anything I can do," he said, his voice coming out flat and toneless, "to make myself less repellent to you?"

"Repellent," Kiem said, and stopped.

Jainan tried not to pay attention to the shriveling feeling inside him. The moment's pause stretched out to eternity.

Then Kiem said, *"What?"*

They should never have gotten into this conversation. Jainan wished he could erase the last five minutes from existence or somehow switch to a continuum where he had not asked the most inappropriate question possible. He turned away to take the water off the heater. "It doesn't matter."

"Where the—what the—*Jainan*." Kiem leaned forward on his hands in the tiny space. Jainan stopped in the middle of screwing a lid on the water cup. He had seldom seen Kiem reduced to stuttering. "What do you mean, *repellent*? You can't mean you. We're not talking about—" His hand gesture included Jainan from head to toe, but he seemed to realize what he was doing and snatched his hand back.

Jainan put the cup down and tapped the heating canister, which was quietly hissing. He couldn't make himself meet
Kiem's eyes. "I know you've tried to spare my feelings, and I am
grateful. But you don't have to pretend."

Kiem didn't say anything. Jainan had handled this so badly
that even *Kiem* couldn't think of anything to say. He was just
looking at Jainan as if Jainan had hit him over the head. Jainan
opened his mouth, ready to take it back, but then stopped. It was
better to have it in the open.

Kiem groaned and dropped his face into his hands. "Jainan,"
he said into his fingers. He pulled his hands down until his dark
agonized eyes met Jainan's. "You're *beautiful*."

The world twisted sideways. "What," Jainan said.

"It's really distracting," Kiem said. Then he added hastily, "Not
that that's your problem. That really isn't your problem, sorry, I'll
get over it."

"I don't understand," Jainan said. "If you think I'm—" He broke
off, and his mouth moved but nothing came out. He tried again.
"If you think—that, then why—" Another sentence he couldn't
see how to finish. "Then why?"

"You were grieving!" Kiem said. "Are grieving, I mean."

Jainan's thoughts were transparent and slippery, and every
time he tried to face one, it fled. All this time he had been trying
to figure out Kiem: what he wanted, what he liked and disliked,
what made him angry. Jainan felt as though he'd been asking
himself the wrong questions the entire time. Kiem wanted him.
It was true he was in mourning; had *that* held Kiem back? When
he looked back Kiem's eyes were still locked on his, and a jolt ran
down his back—not fear, but something foreign or forgotten. He
knew fear. This was something else entirely.

"I haven't stopped living," Jainan said. He meant it as an explanation, but it somehow came out more like a challenge. Kiem
had already had a chance and had turned it down. "You left. The
night we were married."

Kiem hadn't taken his eyes off Jainan's. Jainan could see the shallow rise and fall of his chest. "I thought you were just doing your duty," Kiem said. His hands had clenched where they rested on his knees. "You were shaking. You had to force yourself to touch me. I might be slow, but I can tell when someone's not interested."

Oh. Jainan hadn't expected that. Whatever was happening between them felt like pebbles gathering speed at the start of an avalanche; a voice in Jainan's mind told him *stop,* told him that he was misreading Kiem's intent. He deliberately blocked it out. He didn't even let himself listen to his own voice as he said, "I'm interested now."

He saw Kiem's throat move as he swallowed. The sight of it sent a curl of warmth to Jainan's stomach.

"So . . ." Kiem said. He trailed off. For once he didn't seem to know the right thing to say.

"So," Jainan echoed. The shadows of the tent wavered. Jainan took his courage into both hands and plunged over the edge. "Come here."

Improbably, unbelievably, Kiem moved. He was drawing closer even before Jainan's voice died away, as if his words had weight enough to make this happen. Jainan knelt up in the cramped space to meet him. Kiem's mouth on his was warm and sure. Jainan didn't remember it feeling like this. He barely recognized this feeling in himself at all, not this hunger for another body pressed against his. Kiem's hands had crept around to the small of his back, but lightly, as if he wasn't sure he would be welcomed. Jainan leaned forward in an experiment, pressing their bodies together, and Kiem's hands tightened convulsively.

Jainan felt his breath constrict, his blood starting to thump. He tugged at Kiem's shirt, and after a moment Kiem realized what he was doing and stopped kissing him just long enough to get it over his head. Jainan felt a spike of victory which he capitalized on by putting his arms around Kiem, feeling his glorious, solid weight and the warmth of his skin, and pulling him down with him. They fell into a tangle on top of the sleeping bags, barely cushioned from the ground below. Jainan didn't remember consciously *wanting* anyone to touch him—he'd spent so long avoiding it—so he didn't understand why the heaviness of Kiem's body against his was like water after a drought. He pulled Kiem closer.

"Jainan—" Kiem caught himself with a hand on either side of Jainan's head, not quite on top of him. It cast a shadow over Jainan's anticipation. He had misunderstood something again, somehow. Kiem was going to stop. Jainan shut his eyes as if he could change reality by ignoring it.

He felt the fabric of his shirt move just before he felt the warmth of Kiem's hand resting on his bare hip. It took him a moment to realize the shaking wasn't coming from him. Kiem was trembling.

Jainan opened his eyes as something coursed through his body like molten metal: shock and need, his own desire casting off its last restraints. Kiem's face was very close to his and his eyes were dark. Jainan said without even thinking, "You really do want me."

"Oh, fuck yes—*please*—Jainan, I'm losing my *mind*—" Kiem broke off and swallowed, his touch still a pool of heat on Jainan's skin. "Not if you don't want it," he said. "And not for duty. Never for duty."

Jainan had spent so long not knowing what to do. He had spent so long misunderstanding Kiem, *wasting time,* that it came as a surprise to find he had no doubt anymore. He covered Kiem's hand with his own. "Yes," he said. He could hear his voice come out rough and edged. "Kiem. I mean it."

That was all Kiem needed. He kissed Jainan and eased up his shirt, and Jainan lost the ability to string together words under the touch of Kiem's hands. Shivers of pleasure went through his muscles; Kiem's touch was light, almost wondering, and Jainan's body answered it without Jainan even having to think. Kiem talked in fragments that were barely audible, *can I,* and *you're beautiful,* and *Jainan, Jainan,* his name whispered against the skin of his neck over and over like a prayer.

Jainan's hair was still bound back, out of the way. He hadn't thought of loosening it so far, but Kiem's hands seemed to stray there often, running over his hair, or his fingers stroked the short strands at the back of Jainan's neck. On impulse Jainan unwound the cord that held it. He didn't have any time to regret it: Kiem's breath caught and his eyes widened as if this was a revelation. When he kissed Jainan again, his hands were buried in Jainan's loose hair.

Jainan had forgotten. It was *supposed* to feel like this.

He only realized then that he had done almost nothing for Kiem in long minutes. It took him an effort to find his voice. "Kiem," he said. "Should I." Kiem raised his head from Jainan's chest and didn't seem to comprehend. "I don't want to be selfish."

"What," Kiem said. He propped himself up on his hands. "What do you mean *selfish,* this is—you're just—I'm babbling, aren't I, please stop me talking." Jainan felt astonishment, which turned into something like a laugh, which was absurd; this wasn't something you were supposed to take lightly. But he felt light and giddy enough to float off the ground. "Jainan, please, anything you want," Kiem said. "Tell me what you like."

The question took Jainan off guard. "What?"

Kiem caught Jainan's hand and laced their fingers together. "We'll do what you want. What do you like?"

Jainan only just stopped himself from saying, *I don't know.* He couldn't remember being asked. But he could feel Kiem's expectation and his stirring of surprise when Jainan didn't have an answer. Something dark and defensive rose up inside Jainan; it would be easy to make Kiem move on by bringing up his last partner. He could ask if Kiem wanted to be compared. He didn't know any other way out.

But he didn't want to. Let Kiem think he was strange. Let him ask awkward questions tomorrow if he had to. Maybe tomorrow Jainan would find out that Kiem didn't mean any of this as he seemed to, that he hadn't meant to look at Jainan as if Jainan were the only source of beauty in the world. But tonight Jainan owned Kiem's gaze and the touch of his hands, and everything else was irrelevant. Tonight he could do nothing wrong.

Kiem was still looking down at him, a hint of uncertainty in his eyes. Jainan reached up and touched his cheek, which seemed to stop Kiem's breathing. "We could . . . find out."

It was too short a time before the sky lightened around them. They were quiet and content, lying side by side half under a sleeping bag. Jainan felt the exhaustion of yesterday in his limbs, but the heating capsule filled the tent with warmth, and nothing could affect his deep well of happiness. Kiem had his head propped on Jainan's shoulder. He was pressing against Jainan's arm—or maybe Jainan was pressing against him, because he didn't want to leave space between them. "Mrm," Kiem said, half into Jainan's shoulder. "Y'know, your elbow. 'S perfect."

Jainan shifted his head and made an inquiring noise before he had time to realize that Kiem was still half-asleep, or might even be talking in his sleep. But Kiem woke up further and seemed to take that as a request for clarification. "I mean, probably both your elbows. Can't see the other one. Everything's perfect."

It took Jainan a long, startled moment to absorb that—which was absurd, because Kiem had said that and a hundred things like it last night. Jainan hadn't realized he would keep doing it the next morning. And he knew what Kiem said was what he thought. "Really," Jainan said aloud, his thoughts unguarded, "I think you just verbalize *everything*."

"Sorry," Kiem said, raising his head. "Stopping! Stopping. Promise."

Jainan turned over so they were nested beside each other, his head in the hollow between Kiem's head and shoulder. Helpless amusement settled around him like warmth. "No," he said. "I like you talking."

Kiem smiled that ridiculous, unfairly stunning smile. "Did I say thank you, by the way? You know, for saving my life. Possibly twice. I must have said thank you."

Jainan just wanted to store that smile in his memory forever. He groped for a reply. "I didn't save your life."

"You did. You fought off a bear."

"That was chance."

"Fine, play it down," Kiem said. "I'll sell the story to a vid-maker, then you'll see."

The helpless amusement was getting worse. Jainan held his grave face with an effort. "It's hardly vid material."

"It'll star me, falling into a river. In my undershirt. The ratings will be off the charts."

Jainan's felt his face crack into a smile. "I might watch it for that."

Kiem let his head drop back, as if Jainan smiling was all he needed to be supremely satisfied. The fabric of the tent was luminous from the sun outside. "Day's getting on," Kiem said lazily. "We should . . . go and do something."

"*Something,*" Jainan said. "You mean: seek rescue from our stranded situation and attend the treaty signing." He pushed himself up to a sitting position. Kiem made a noise of protest when he moved.

"Well, I dunno," Kiem said. "I mean, being stranded: not too bad, right? Look at us."

"So maybe we should just stay here," Jainan said. "Just you, me, acres of snow, the bear . . ."

"Bears often hoard rose petals to strew on hiking couples. Little-known romantic fact."

Jainan couldn't stop the chuckle that came out. "Even so," he said, once he had control of it. "I would like to eat something that doesn't taste of plywood and perhaps reassure my sister that I'm not dead." He reached for his clothes.

Kiem groaned and rolled over. "Point. Argh. Why is moving so hard?" He pulled his undershirt over his head and got his arm stuck in the neck hole. "Civilization is overrated," he said, his voice muffled. He waved his arms until he somehow sorted out the tangle and his head emerged. "We could just start again out here."

"You will find it hard to get the dartcar results from here," Jainan said. Kiem's hair was disordered, and Jainan's fingers itched to neaten it. He didn't let himself; they weren't in bed anymore.

"I could live without them." Kiem picked up the heating cylinder and reluctantly snapped the inner sleeve away.

"I'll get water," Jainan said. He pulled on his boots and coat. When he emerged from the tent, it was into a glorious landscape where the sunlight reflected blindingly from the snow. He drew in a lungful of cold, fresh air, raised his hand to cover his eyes, and squinted in the direction they were traveling.

"Oh," he said, startled. "Kiem!"

"What?" Kiem was already sitting in the tent entrance, fully clothed and putting on his boots. He followed the direction of Jainan's pointing arm.

The dawn sun had burned off the fog. In the cleft between two valleys, just visible past a rocky shelf, pylons stretched out of the mountains like metallic trees. A silver thread of magnetized cable gleamed between them. They'd reached the rail line.

CHAPTER 19

The rescue flycraft descended on the peaceful mountain scene like an invader, its hover drivers filling the valley with an ear-splitting whine. Its orange bulk would have been easy to spot kilometers away even if it hadn't been constantly sweeping its surroundings with a rotating white light.

Jainan watched it descend with mixed feelings. His emotions were raw in every way, singing with exultation and tension like taut wires—he could barely deal with Kiem's presence next to him, let alone anyone else. He didn't want to let the rest of the world in. Part of him perversely wanted to stay here with Kiem in the solitude of the snow and the mountains so he had the space to sort out his bubbling feelings. He wasn't *ready* for them to be rescued.

"Urgh," Kiem said beside him. "Do you think we're going to have to stand up?"

Jainan turned. They'd been sitting on a rock shelf for the last hour, resting while they waited. Kiem had been unusually quiet after the first twenty minutes, but Jainan had just assumed he was tired from the trek. Now, though, he saw Kiem had let his head flop forward onto his knees, and Jainan realized this was more than muscle ache. "You're stim-crashing."

"Maybe," Kiem said into his knees.

"How many tabs did you have?"

"Five? Uh. Six." It sounded like it was taking him some effort to talk. "Should probably take another. Get through getting rescued."

"No," Jainan said. "Absolutely not." His mixed feelings abruptly disappeared, replaced by sheer relief that Kiem's stimcrash hadn't happened any earlier. He raised his hand and waved needlessly at the descending flycraft.

The rescue craft had no need for a clear landing ground. Its whine was deafening as it finished its descent; Jainan clamped his hands over his ears, but it didn't help much. Then the whine changed, and it came to a halt in midair, only a couple of meters from the snow. A hatch opened and a ramp extended from it. At the top, two figures looked like they were arguing, one in the same army uniform everyone on Hvaren Base had worn, and the other—that was Bel.

Jainan pulled Kiem's arm around his shoulder and helped him stand. Bel jumped onto the ramp as it was still extending, and as the soldier flung out a cautionary hand, she ran headlong down it and leapt off. "Two days! You idiots!" she said and hugged both of them.

Jainan froze. Was she glad to see him as well? Kiem didn't seem to have noticed Jainan's reaction; he just gave Bel a weak grin and said, "Didn't mean to worry you."

Bel had already realized something was off about Jainan's response; she drew back. Jainan couldn't look away fast enough. Too late he realized that he was abnormal. He couldn't even manage to gracefully accept a friendship.

But Bel said nothing and instead rounded on Kiem. "If you don't want to worry me, try not crashing your flybug!" she said. "You fly like a pensioner! How the f— How in Heaven did you crash?"

"It was only a small crash," Kiem said. Bel dipped her shoulder under his other arm, taking some of the weight off Jainan as they made their way up the ramp. "A crash-let. A microcrash. Can I sit down now?"

The soldier reached them with a stretcher hovering behind him. Jainan and Bel let Kiem down until he was sitting on it. Bel followed the stretcher to give Kiem facts about abuse of stimulants, which Jainan suspected was relieving her feelings.

"Is he conscious?" The person striding out from the mouth of the flyer was the upright form of Colonel Lunver. "Get him in the flyer."

It shouldn't have been unexpected. Of course Hvaren Base had scrambled its rescue flyers to find them, and of course their senior officer would join the search for a member of the royal family. Jainan was surprised at the unpleasant frisson that went up his back. He had always known he should be grateful for any help that Taam's officer colleagues offered, but he hadn't realized seeing one of them would jolt him out of his hard-won equanimity so quickly. He found himself remembering his conversation with Kiem: *Did you see anyone near our flybug at the base?*

"What happened?" Lunver said.

Colonel Lunver had not wanted them to see the Kingfisher files. Jainan, feeling unusually obstructionist, met her eyes with a blank look. "I don't know. We crashed."

"I see," Lunver said. She didn't challenge him. Of course she wouldn't: Taam's colleagues had never expected Jainan to have anything useful to add. "Stay with the medics." She turned back to the cabin, presumably to report they'd been found.

The second medic was a civilian, which made Jainan slightly more relaxed. The palace had clearly flown out their own people—including Bel—to help with the search-and-rescue effort, which meant this wasn't just Lunver's operation. The medic handed Jainan a hydration sachet and ran through some questions, which Jainan apparently answered to her satisfaction. "We'll be launching in a moment," she said to Jainan. "You may be feeling reasonably fine, but I strongly recommend you lie down—"

"I told you, I'm fine, check Jainan!"

"—as we apparently can't get his highness to do," the medic

finished, as they entered the small body of the craft. "Prince Kiem, please. Lie down."

"Not until you check—"

"I am right here." Jainan crossed to the shelflike bed, followed by Bel, and pressed two fingers against Kiem's shoulder. "Lie down. You are being stubborn."

He didn't realize until the words had left his mouth that he was touching Kiem—easily, naturally—and all that happened was Kiem stopped talking and lay down. Kiem's face was ashy with exhaustion by this point, which was probably the reason he said, "Mm," and nothing else. But he caught Jainan's hand, and Jainan didn't even get around to wondering why before he squeezed it and let it go.

On an impulse, Jainan rested his hand on Kiem's head. The hair was soft under his hand. Kiem's breath caught, and then he relaxed all at once, like an animal stretching out before it went to sleep. Even the lines of tension on his forehead smoothed out.

The strange feeling that had settled around Jainan like a combat shield since this morning was still there, and he found he had no fear of anyone's disapproval at all. He sat beside Kiem's bed in one of the medic chairs and slipped the harness over his shoulders.

The military medic eyed both of them and apparently decided this wasn't a fight worth picking. "Sleep and nutrients," he said. "Don't let Prince Kiem get up. Bel Siara, Colonel Lunver will have the coordinates you wanted to report to the palace." He held the door to the front cabin open, and Bel gave them a wave and followed him through.

Jainan sat by Kiem in the suddenly quiet cabin and kept his hand resting by his head, idly touching his hair, as the flybug rose. The floor under his feet juddered as the hover engines fought with the wind. He could vaguely hear Bel's "professional" voice replying to Colonel Lunver through the cabin wall. Jainan felt strangely at peace.

What did it mean, what had happened that morning? Had Kiem *meant* anything by it? Jainan reminded himself that Taam had seemed to enjoy some of the times they'd slept together, though they hadn't been like that. He tried not to think too hard about where it left him and Kiem—it felt like something delicate, something he could damage if he examined it too closely. He should just be thankful Kiem had seemed to enjoy himself and not worry about whether it would happen again, or entertain pointless questions about the future.

After some length of time, the sound of the door opening shook Jainan out of his reverie.

"Oh, good, he's resting," Bel said. "I've sent the report off. The Emperor can breathe easy. Not that I think she was that worried, but one dead prince could be an accident. Two dead princes in three months—no offense—starts to look like a body count."

"Yes," Jainan said.

"Mrh." Kiem stirred, opening his eyes, and made an effort to sit up on his bed. "I'm taking *some* offense. Someone just tried to kill us."

Hearing Kiem say it bluntly made Jainan feel colder than at any point on their trek. It didn't faze Bel, though, who gave the kind of smile that seemed designed to worry onlookers. "Did your last school board meeting go badly?" she said. "Or maybe you pissed off a municipal councilor?"

"Jainan found more evidence Taam was embezzling money." Kiem's voice was hoarse, but for once he sounded serious. "You said he was messaging Sefalan relays. We know there's a black market on Sefala. Then someone tried to break into the King-fisher networks, and they're still trying, even after Taam died. Is it possible Taam tried to cheat the raiders and they came after him?"

"Anything's *possible*," Bel said. "I can tell you some of the raider congloms would kill to get their hands on Iskat military surplus—but mining equipment? I can't see them killing anyone over that. They trade in weapons. And why would they come after you?"

"Because we started investigating?" Kiem said. "Come on, Bel, it might have been raiders."

Bel gave him a long look that was opaque to Jainan, as if she was familiar enough with Kiem that she could see something he couldn't. "Why do you want it to be raiders so badly?"

Kiem rubbed a hand through the hair on the back of his head. "It means it was nothing to do with Thea," he said. "It means the Auditor might accept Thea is entering into the treaty voluntarily. It means he might instate us. We just have to tell him Taam was a small-time criminal who cheated the wrong person." He seemed to hear what he'd just said and cast a somewhat guilty look at Jainan. "Sorry."

They could get instated and sign the treaty. Jainan should feel relief, but instead a gap had opened in his chest. He couldn't find anything to say in Taam's defense. Taam had cared about the military. Jainan wouldn't have thought him capable of undermining the whole institution like this—but in some ways, it was becoming clear he hadn't known much about Taam at all. Taam had been talking to raiders. "We would need proof," Jainan said, "and we would need Internal Security to support us. They must be the ones to give evidence to the Auditor. I—we are too involved. We won't be believed."

The grinding noise of the flyer's engines changed to a whine as they stopped climbing and started to glide.

Bel grimaced and looked over at one of the porthole-like windows on the opposite wall. "I could see what I can get from the Kingfisher outward comms. See if anyone else tries contacting those message relays."

"Bel—*no*," Kiem said, apparently catching something from her tone that Jainan hadn't. "You're not in the Sefalan Guard anymore. You can't just eavesdrop on people's comms."

Bel pushed herself off the bed and paced to the porthole. "This is not okay," she said. "I don't know if it was raiders or not, but this is so far beyond okay. I know you like to think everyone's basically nice deep down, but they're *not,* and someday that attitude's going to come back and bite you. I don't have a job without you."

"Come on, you have your pick of jobs," Kiem said, apparently trying to lighten the mood. Bel folded her arms and leaned against the hull wall. "I'm not sure about relying on Internal Security to help us, though," Kiem added. "I'm still deciding if I've forgiven them for the security clearance thing."

"Please don't blow that out of proportion," Jainan said. "They have to do their jobs in order for the system to work. I was calculated to be a risk. I can't be the first."

"A calculation that completely screwed you over!" Kiem said. "They handled you like an enemy of the state!"

"That is not your pro—" Jainan stumbled halfway through the sentence. The look Kiem was giving him now was betrayed; Kiem was fully aware how he intended to end that word. Jainan let out a slow breath. His mind was a train running on a phantom rail; he had to stop this. Ever since the wedding Kiem had treated Jainan's problems as his own.

Trying to work out what was fair treatment of himself made Jainan's head hurt. "All right," he said. "But if we don't cooperate with them, we'll both be held in contempt. We could be arrested. They have the authority of the Emperor."

Kiem slumped back against the hull where it met the bed, as if the burst of energy had exhausted his reserves. "You're a treaty representative. They shouldn't even have any power over you."

"They do," Jainan said tightly. "The Empire comes first. My home planet can do nothing for me without endangering the Resolution treaty. I am not an asset—I am a *liability.*"

There was a sudden silence, as if Jainan had thrown another spanner into the exchange. Kiem's steady gaze was disconcerting. He left a considered pause before he said, "That's not right."

"It's how it is," Jainan said, in a voice flat enough to shut down the entire line of conversation. "We must cooperate."

The door to the cabin clicked open. "Good to hear that," Colonel Lunver said. Jainan sat up straighter, wary, but she had apparently only caught the last thing he said. "Your Highness. Now that you're awake, can you tell me what happened?"

Kiem traded glances with Jainan. Kiem was usually cooperative with everyone, but this time Jainan recognized the stubborn twist at the corner of his mouth. "I was flying and there was an explosion," Kiem said. "Not sure what you want from me, Colonel—believe it or not, it doesn't happen to me on a regular basis."

"This is not the time for jokes, Your Highness," Colonel Lunver said.

"No, I should think not," Kiem said. "Did Aren tell you what Jainan found?"

"Excuse me?" Colonel Lunver said.

"Your operational records are littered with proof that Taam was embezzling from Kingfisher," Kiem said. "And you've got someone trying to hack into your systems as well, though I'll admit that one's probably not Taam's fault—why *didn't* you want us to visit Hvaren Base, by the way, Colonel? That doesn't look good."

It was so amiable, you could almost miss it was an accusation against Colonel Lunver personally. Jainan pressed down a sudden spike of panic. There was nothing she could do on a ship with civilian witnesses.

Lunver frowned, as if her pet cat had suddenly started spouting wild allegations. "Are you going to explain what you're saying, Your Highness?"

"I'm saying that it's a bit weird that *Jainan* was the first person to find out about all the holes in your accounting," Kiem said. "I know you got moved onto the operation after Taam died, but it's been two months. Weird that you didn't find anything."

Whatever burst of energy he'd found was clearly running out; his words were slurring at the edges from tiredness.

"This is absurd," Lunver said, brutally short. "You are stim-crashing and in no state to make allegations. If I were you, I would stop before anyone overhears or you may find General Fenrik makes your mother aware of this wild behavior."

It was a clumsy attempt to shut Kiem down. Jainan, watching the exchange, couldn't help but feel there was something familiar about Lunver's knee-jerk defensiveness. She was worried about her reputation—and not just hers. That of the operation she ran.

"Colonel," Jainan said abruptly. "You have a duty to your unit."

Lunver looked at him in surprise, and her eyes narrowed.

"You are not responsible for anything Taam may have done," Jainan said. "But you are responsible for setting it right. There is someone *else* attempting to hack into your operation." There was also someone else who had tried to kill Kiem and Jainan, but Jainan didn't trust Lunver enough to speak about that. "If Taam didn't act alone, then someone else may be attempting to continue what he was doing. Shutting Kiem down like this will not help."

He'd expected rage. He'd never spoken to Lunver like this. But instead, after one sharp, angry breath, she shut her mouth. Her expression was suddenly distant and introspective.

She didn't seem surprised at the allegations. Of course, Aren would have told her what Kiem and Jainan visited Hvaren Base to do. But laying out that Taam must have had an accomplice—that seemed to be unexpected.

"I need to call my base," Lunver said crisply. "Make sure his highness is taken care of." She got to her feet. "I can assure you, if this embezzlement case isn't solved, it will not be because my unit was negligent in investigating."

"I'm glad to hear that," Jainan said. He bit his tongue on *Let us know how that goes,* but Kiem's expression said it for him. Kiem was bad for him. "I appreciate your reassurance on the matter."

Bel gave Jainan a tight smile and left for the cockpit after

Colonel Lunver. Jainan had neither the energy nor the urge to ask her not to eavesdrop.

Jainan rolled his shoulders, trying to drain the tension from his neck and his back. He was distracted by keeping an eye on Kiem, who must be exhausted; his eyes were flickering shut and his breathing was slowing into sleep. "Think she'll really find out what's going on?" Kiem mumbled.

"I'm not holding out a great deal of hope," Jainan said softly, because Kiem was struggling to stay awake. "Get some rest."

It was unnecessary. Kiem had already lost the battle and sunk into a doze, the lines smoothed out of his face. Jainan couldn't touch him in case he disturbed him; Kiem would need all his energy for the interview that waited for them. Shafts of light lay bright across the floor from the small windows set into the flyer's sides. Jainan lifted his eyes from Kiem's sleeping form to watch the white horizon pass under the pale-blue sky, felt the rumbling of the flyer through his body, and tried to be glad they were returning safely to the palace. They flew on.

CHAPTER 20

Internal Security summoned them as soon as they'd touched down in Arlusk. Kiem refused point-blank to enter the comms dead zone in their working quarters, so instead Rakal ordered the receptionists' office cleared, and they perched uncomfortably on chairs for visitors. Kiem was slumped back across a hard couch, slow and bleary, his fingers resting on his wristband as if to remind Rakal he was recording everything they said.

"You think someone caused the crash to stop you from investigating," Rakal said.

"I make no accusations," Jainan said. His voice was hoarse. He had spent the last hour laying out his Kingfisher research in exhaustive detail. Rakal showed no sign of being tired; they ran the interview like a belt grinding over a gear—the same questions over and over again until Jainan started to doubt his own facts. "We were not subtle about our investigations."

"You should not have been investigating at all," Rakal said, but with curt impatience that said they knew it was too late for that.

"You knew about the hacking already," Kiem said. He'd taken another half of a stim tab when the flyer had landed, in spite of Jainan's objections, so he was at least talking coherently. "You've had days to link it up with Jainan's information. Stop pretending you don't have your own theories. You've gotten much further than we have, haven't you?"

Rakal sighed and touched the bridge of their nose, a gesture so

uncharacteristic that Jainan wondered if he had started hallucinating. "Your Highness," Rakal said shortly. "I am going to ask
you to stop recording so we can have a genuine conversation. I
will ask this once."

Kiem met Jainan's eyes. Jainan nodded. "All right," Kiem said
reluctantly. "We've already obeyed your Imperial Voice command, though, so if you make any threats, we're leaving."

Rakal watched Kiem deactivate his wristband before they
spoke. "There has been trouble with the Auditor since you left."

Jainan felt the Auditor's presence rise up from the back of his
mind where it had been lurking like a storm warning. "What kind
of trouble?"

"Something has upset him and his staff," Rakal said. "They
have all retreated to their ship, with the remnants, and set off
early for Carissi Station. They are not communicating even with
the authorized representatives. The Emperor believes they will
still carry out the treaty ceremony; the Resolution has some ar-
cane protocols we still don't fully understand."

Kiem sank down a fraction in his chair. "So we're even further
from the treaty," he said.

"No," Rakal said crisply. "I know you were not instated. I
know it was because of Taam's murder. This crime must and *will*
be solved. When we arrest the perpetrator, the Auditor will see
Thea and Iskat are in agreement—which they will be, because
the suspect is not Thean—and instate the treaty representatives."

Jainan didn't immediately understand the implication, but
Kiem did, because he sat up. "You've cleared Jainan?"

"Count Jainan." Rakal gave a thin smile. "Yes, Your Grace is
no longer our main suspect. But you can help."

Jainan did not like the way Rakal said *help*. He laid his hands
on his knees, carefully controlling any signs of unease. "I am at
your disposal."

"You still have a professional relationship with Professor Feynam Audel."

Jainan had not known her personal name. "Yes," he said. A bitter relief sat on his tongue. "You want me to withdraw from the project."

"No." Rakal leaned in. "I want you to get proof that Audel murdered Prince Taam."

"Wait, what?" Kiem said. "Your suspect is *Professor Audel*? But we cleared her."

The room blurred around Jainan. He cut off Kiem's protestation. "We told you she could prove she had no motive. Please explain."

"Feynam Audel was behind the attempts at network intrusion," Rakal said. "We have spent the last two days tracing the comms involved, and that much is indisputable. She used not only her own account but also those of multiple students, even one owned by a student who passed away two years ago."

Jainan felt an unpleasant tingle under his skin. Internal Security had no reason to outright lie to them. "If that's true, she's technically committed a crime," he said. "But you can only prove she was trying to get into Kingfisher's systems. You have no evidence she murdered Taam."

"Apart from a clear motive against Taam and against Kingfisher," Rakal said. They put up their hand to forestall Kiem's protest. "Yes—I have seen the resignation letter you copied to us. It is a forgery. The military has no record of receiving it."

Jainan's mouth was dry. "I see."

"The situation is untidy." Rakal said *untidy* with an air of picking up a rotting piece of vegetable matter. "The Emperor has entrusted Internal Security with finding an answer before Unification Day; the evidence must be watertight. We know Audel is traveling to Carissi Station to witness the treaty signing. The Kingfisher refinery is in the same habitat cluster as the station. We believe she intends to make another attempt at illegally accessing Kingfisher's network from there."

"What's that got to do with Jainan?" Kiem said.

"We want you to give her an access credential to the refinery," Rakal said. Their manner was abrasive, but unlike some of the military they spoke directly to Jainan, not through Kiem, with a gaze that seemed to bore through the back of Jainan's skull. "She will try and use it. The device is a honeypot, set up to gather evidence of what she does in the refinery. Once we have proof of sabotage, we can use that to tie this up. It will also clear your name."

"You can't force Jainan to do this," Kiem said. He had switched back to his initial combative tone. Jainan would have appreciated it, but both Rakal and Kiem sounded muffled to him. The enormity of Galactic politics seemed to be pressing on him like a gravity well, as if the unfathomable distance and terrible strangeness of the other Resolution systems were clustering in low orbit above them. The Empire didn't just mean Iskat: the Empire was Thea as well, and five other planets with hundreds of millions of citizens, all drifting away from the rest of the universe like the axial tilt of winter.

"I'll do it," Jainan said. He felt gray and stretched, like an old piece of cloth. There was no choice. There had never been a choice.

"Is it really justice if you're trapping her into it?" Kiem said to Rakal. "I thought justice was the point."

"Justice means nothing without a framework to impose it," Rakal said. "Internal Security is an intelligence agency, not a policing body; we are about *stability*."

Jainan found himself in unwilling agreement. He said nothing.

"Doing a good job there, aren't you?" Kiem said mutinously. "I don't buy this explanation. I don't have a better one, but I don't buy it. Don't tell me *Professor Audel* sabotaged our flybug."

Rakal hesitated. "That has given us something of a headache," they admitted. "It would have been a big risk for her to take. But it *is* a common mechanical flaw, and I understand you were putting unusual demands on the flybug. It could have been an accident."

"I feel so safe," Kiem said.

"I will assign close protection to your flybug—"

"I'm not getting in one of those until this is all over," Kiem said bluntly. "My aide says she'll book a random shuttle for us to travel on to Carissi Station tomorrow, so unless someone wants to blow up the entire shuttleport, they shouldn't be able to do anything. But I don't like trapping Audel like this. I thought Internal Security was at least bothered about the law."

"The state is the law, Your Highness," Rakal said. "I serve the Emperor."

Kiem's expression said, as clearly as if he'd passed Jainan a note, that this was not as reassuring as Rakal thought it was. Jainan swallowed a bubble of hysteria at this perilous swerve toward lèse-majesté. "We understand, Agent Rakal," Jainan said. "We are all dedicated to the Empire."

Rakal turned on their own wristband briskly, a sign the interview was coming to a close. "A representative from Press Office is waiting to speak to you," Rakal said. *Press Office* also came out like a piece of radioactive waste in a pair of tongs. "A local newslog in Braska ran a report on Prince Kiem's failure to attend the school graduation. Whatever story you give them must contain nothing that points to the investigation. Do I need to invoke the Imperial Voice?"

"No," Kiem said. He pushed himself up from his slouch just to slump forward, his head bowed over his knees. "I'll do it. I can handle them."

Jainan had long ago realized that anger was an unsuitable emotion for diplomats and suppressed it, so it took him a moment to recognize the low, cold sensation at Kiem being given a further set of orders. "I hope this has given you what you need, Agent Rakal," he said. "Kiem is suffering from stim hangover; may we leave? You know where to find us."

"You could say that." Rakal gave a tight, unreadable smile. "And if not, I'm sure the newslogs will tell me."

Jainan rose and had to stop himself from reaching a hand out to help Kiem. Kiem would find that embarrassing; Jainan himself would have rather given a tell-all interview to a newslog than accepted physical support in front of Rakal. Kiem was fine, in any case, even if he moved more slowly than usual.

Bel met them at the door to Internal Security's offices, which let into a wide hallway with curved stairs leading down to the entrance of the staffing headquarters. She cast a glance over Kiem that was somewhere between impatient and worried. "There's a palace medic waiting for Kiem downstairs," she said—to Jainan, as if Jainan could do anything about it. "Make him get checked. Press Office as well, but I'll try and head them off."

"I'm okay," Kiem said. "All I want is a shower." When they rounded the curve of the stairs and he saw who was standing at the bottom, he groaned and collapsed on Jainan's shoulder. "Nope, scratch that, I'm definitely too ill to talk."

Jainan offered his arm without thinking. Of the two people waiting for them, one was a palace nurse. The other was someone Jainan had only had very brief, unpleasant dealings with and did not particularly want to be debriefed by.

"Trust you," the chief press officer said. Hren Halesar had his arms crossed and was standing in Kiem's path. "Trust you to fuck up a school visit. You really crashed?"

Kiem stumbled down the last of the stairs on Jainan's arm and stopped. "Urgh," he said. "Yes, we crashed. I fell in a river. Jainan fought off a bear. There were flights of angels. Alien invasions. Can I get my checkup and go to bed?"

"Angels my ass. Have you been talking to any journalists?"

"Yes, one popped out of the lockers on the rescue flyer," Kiem said. He was still leaning on Jainan, and Jainan didn't think it was all theatrics. "I just attract them. Pheromones." Jainan choked.

"They're trying to get hold of you. A couple of outlets picked up that local report about your no-show at Braska. Don't reply. I've been told by the spies that they need this to disappear for the sake of the fucking Resolution"—his expression made it very clear that Press Office wasn't any fonder of Internal Security than Rakal was of them—"so I'll need a statement and a short vid from you."

"Can do," Kiem said. He was clearly trying to put energy into it, but for once it wasn't working. "I'll put something together tomorrow. Leave it to me."

"I'll need some handling detail for the—"

"Hren Halesar," Jainan said, cutting in midsentence with his formal name. "His highness is tired from travel, and we have to take a shuttle tomorrow on Imperial business. You will kindly allow us to shower and rest."

Hren turned on him in astonishment, but his eyes narrowed. "I'm going to need more than—"

"Oh, shit, Hren, actually," Kiem said, interrupting him for the second time, "you're just the person I want, come to think of it." He pulled something bulky out of his jacket pocket and pressed it on Hren.

Hren looked down at the golden trowel in his hands. "The fuck is this?"

"It's a trowel," Kiem said.

Jainan said gravely, "It's very important."

"Get that back to Braska Prime with a good apology, would you?" Kiem said. "Great opportunity for good press. Write them a flowery letter. Oh, and you'd better let them know I'm not dead. Tell them I'll call them—"

"You'll call them when you don't look like death," Jainan put in.

"I'll call them when I don't look like death. Take care of the trowel. Just the man. Knew I could count on you."

"Excuse me," Jainan said to the nurse. "His highness is in poor condition and needs to get to the clinic."

"No kidding," said the nurse, who had been trying to put a blood-pressure patch on Kiem's wrist for the past two minutes. "This way, Your Highness."

"And lice. I think I've got lice," Kiem said mournfully, stepping close enough to Hren to make him take a sharp step back. "Wouldn't get in the elevator with me. 'Scuse me." He disappeared into the elevator with the nurse.

Jainan traded a glance with Bel and followed Kiem. Bel went to take Hren aside and presumably give him enough information to keep him away from Kiem until tomorrow. "Lice?" Jainan murmured as he followed Kiem into the elevator.

"Well-known side effect of hypothermia," Kiem said.

"Of course," Jainan said. "As is talking nonsense, I believe. I'll pick up some of your clothes and meet you at the clinic."

It didn't feel like a triumphant return. Jainan was tired to the point of exhaustion, and the momentary levity had faded into the nagging sense of wrongness that followed him wherever he went. He was embarrassed to be seen by the people he passed in the corridor in the mess of clothes they'd put on after the crash. He forced himself to shut down every thought but the immediate task, but that tripped him up: he was halfway to Taam's rooms before he realized he was in the wrong wing of the palace.

He backtracked, frustrated, and increased his pace back to Kie—to his own rooms. He was almost there when he became aware of footsteps behind him.

"Your Grace!"

Jainan turned. The person following him was a smartly dressed, short-haired woman with fashion-statement silver eye implants. Jainan recoiled automatically before he recognized her.

The woman wore a bright, intent smile. "Sorry to chase you around, I wasn't quite sure it was you." She advanced with her hand out. "Hani Sereson, I'm—"

"A journalist, I know," Jainan said. He didn't take her hand. He was in no mood to fake pleasantries, and there was nobody to demand it of him. "I recognize you from the wedding ceremony."

"Yes, I'm with *Consult News*," Hani said. She dropped her hand in a smooth recovery and gave his disheveled clothes an assessing look. "Unscheduled ski trip, Your Grace? Does this have anything to do with the Auditor suddenly disappearing?"

"No—" Jainan said, then realized he was falling into a trap. If he gave her the slightest opening, his and Kiem's names would be all over the news tomorrow, and even Hren Halesar wouldn't be able to control the damage. "Why are you in here?" he said instead. "Do you have a visitor permit?"

Hani gave a slight, ironic bow. "Yes, Your Grace," she said. "As a matter of fact, Prince Kiem and I meet every month for drinks. Only he didn't turn up today. The public gets rightly concerned when one of our Resolution representatives is nowhere to be found. He's usually so public."

"Prince Kiem is not available," Jainan said. "He is preparing for Unification Day."

"I hope he's not ill?" Hani said. Jainan shook his head. "All eyes are on the treaty reps and the Resolution, you know. I'm covering it from Carissi Station, so if you have any quotes you want me to print . . . ?"

"No," Jainan said. "Please leave."

"Okay, okay." Hani held up a palm in front of her. "I'll consider this conversation off the record." Jainan didn't like the silver sheen on her eyes. It made her harder to read as she stared at him. "But you should know, I'm not your enemy."

You are, Jainan said in the privacy of his head, but instead he gave her a tight smile. "I'm afraid I value my privacy." His wristband chimed, but he ignored it. "Do you need escorting out?"

"I'm going!" Hani said, but Jainan didn't care. He shut the door behind him and was enclosed safe in the calm oasis of Kiem's rooms, finally alone.

He expected to feel relief. He had always counted his time alone in the palace like gold dust. But, somewhat to his surprise, he strode impatiently through the room and rooted through drawers in the bedroom to find Kiem's clothes, not pausing even to sit down. There were still things to be done.

A staccato tapping on the window heralded the arrival of the doves, who had obviously seen movement and hoped for food. Jainan knew it was Kiem who fed them; he had caught him at it several times. Jainan had no time for them right now but the sound was familiar and reassuring.

His wristband chimed. He tapped it to make it stop and glanced at the messages that had come in while he was out of signal. There were more than he'd anticipated: he could ignore most of the College communications, but the flurry of messages from Gairad caused a sharp pang of guilt. She was still messaging him about the project, trying to work out how Kingfisher had set up their refinery.

He sat down and tried to sort out a reply. Gairad had no idea what Professor Audel was doing. It could be dangerous for her to stay on the project. And yet, he had given his word to Internal Security, for the sake of the Empire—for the sake of Thea.

He spun through to Gairad's last message. *I've found some plans I need you to see. I'll meet you on Carissi.*

Jainan's resolution wavered and gave way. He messaged back, *I will see you there.* Then he took his wristband off, opened a drawer, and dropped it at the back for the night.

"Hey," Kiem said from the bedroom door.

Jainan whirled around. "I thought you were in the clinic." *I was coming,* he wanted to say, but Kiem was giving him his best hangdog look.

"I flirted my way out of it," Kiem said. "I was shameless. I just wanted the fuss to stop. Forgive me?" His tone was half-bantering, half-serious, and the serious parts made something odd happen in Jainan's chest.

"Now you're trying it on me," Jainan said as Kiem crossed the room.

"Is it working?" Kiem said, and before Jainan could reply, he kissed him.

It was light and tentative, as if now that they were back in the palace, they had to learn how to do this all over again. Jainan took hold of Kiem's shoulder and deepened the kiss. There was a long moment of intense silence, and then Jainan took a breath and said, "It's working. Are you trying to bribe me into letting you use the shower first?"

"Is *that* working?" Kiem said. There was a laugh in his voice for no good reason. "Promise I'll be quick." Jainan waved him in. Kiem stumbled on his next step, but he quickly righted himself and shot Jainan a grin. "Too much mountain climbing."

As Kiem shut himself in the shower, Jainan occupied himself with undressing. In the heat of the palace his outdoor layers felt grimy and unpleasant. He hung them up in the wardrobe's cleanser and turned toward the bathroom, debating whether or not to get Kiem's clothes. The door was shut, but the light indicated it wasn't locked. It might be an invasion of privacy.

The dilemma was solved for him by an abrupt crash from inside. Jainan opened the bathroom door without thinking. "Kiem?"

"Meant to do that," Kiem said from the floor. He had managed to get his trousers off but was now sitting in a corner—if being half collapsed against the wall could be called *sitting*. One look at his face and Jainan realized Kiem had somehow been managing to hide the extent of his exhaustion.

Jainan took his wrist—Kiem didn't resist—and attempted to help him to his feet. "Kiem," he said. "You're not in a state to wash. Go to bed."

"I'm showering," Kiem said to the towels. "I'm getting in the shower."

"You don't need—" Jainan broke off. It wasn't as if he didn't understand the feeling. He considered whether or not he could take a liberty and decided that he probably could. "Very well. In that case." He pulled Kiem the rest of the way to his feet and let go of him—Kiem propped himself up against the towel rail—and stripped the rest of his own clothes off. He turned the shower on and the sensors lit up. "At least this way we don't have to fight over who gets to go first."

"Right! Right." Kiem caught on to what they were doing and yanked his shirt over his head, nearly losing his balance again. Jainan steadied him. "More tired than I thought," Kiem said, in what might have been an apology. He stumbled into the shower, keeping himself stable with a hand on Jainan's arm. The way his eyes tracked to Jainan's exposed chest was gratifying even though neither of them were in much of a state to do anything about it.

The sensors beeped in confusion when they registered two people. Showers were highly personalized things, and Jainan hadn't been using this one long enough to get to know it, but he managed to wrestle one of the jets into manual mode. Kiem sighed when the water hit him, as if all his breath was running out of him. He dropped his face into the curve between Jainan's neck and shoulder and stood there as the water coursed down his back, his weight against Jainan.

"Kiem," Jainan said. "Really." It felt good in a low-key way, even through Jainan's own fatigue, and though it was thoroughly inconvenient, he couldn't quite bring himself to move Kiem's head.

"Mrh," Kiem said. "You have so much hair." He brought up one hand and ran it through Jainan's rapidly soaking hair—or tried and stopped, because by this point Jainan's hair was badly knotted. Kiem made another wordless noise and shook his head as water ran into his face.

Jainan had to suppress the urge to laugh when it occurred to him that Kiem could very literally drown in his hair. He must be tired if he was finding that funny. He took hold of Kiem's hand and disentangled it, inexplicably gratified. "Try not to fall over for two minutes, and I promise you can go to sleep." Kiem made a noise that might have indicated cooperation.

Jainan did a reasonable job of rinsing them down, given the circumstances, and managed to get Kiem dry afterward. Drying

Jainan's hair was a lost cause even with the heater, but he was too tired to care about it being damp. Kiem was now unapologetically leaning on him to stand.

When they emerged from the bathroom, Jainan was tired, strangely content, and not expecting it when Kiem attempted to pull away.

"What is it?" Jainan said.

"Need to get out the bed," Kiem said.

Jainan stopped where he was. The folding bed. Kiem's eyes had darted to his face as he'd said that, and though Jainan had once thought he would never be able to read Kiem, he could now take a confident guess.

"Kiem," he said deliberately. "You're my partner. Come to bed."

Relief broke over Kiem's face like sunlight. "You mean that? You mean that."

"Obviously," Jainan said. "Apart from anything else, you're going to be asleep before you can even turn over." He guided Kiem to the bed, and Kiem half collapsed on it, tugging Jainan down with him.

Jainan let himself fall. A bone-deep exhaustion rolled over him as he settled beside the weight of Kiem. They had to catch a shuttle tomorrow. They still weren't confirmed by the Resolution, and the whole sector hung in the balance. He was so tired. He turned his face toward the warmth from Kiem's skin and slipped into sleep.

CHAPTER 21

In the vast silence of deep space, Thea hung like the chime of a single pure note. Its ultramarine seas glittered and shifted under a delicate ring of silicate and ice, rotating imperceptibly behind the observation window of Carissi Station. Kiem had seen a couple of the Empire's planets from space—Eisafan, Rtul—but he was prepared to award Thea the prize for first impressions, with a bonus entry for Planet He Might Consider Dating.

"You're humming," Jainan said from beside him.

"Am I?" Kiem hung over the observation railing. He must have picked up the habit somewhere. He couldn't remember where; he was tone-deaf, but the urge was irresistible. "I'm in a good mood." He leaned slightly too far and had to push himself back. Carissi Station kept eight-tenths of full gravity, which made every movement an adventure. They'd been stuck on a shuttle for three days—a budget shuttle Bel had picked for them, which didn't even have real-time comms—and he should be worrying about the treaty, but with Jainan there he'd barely noticed the time pass. Of course, sleeping through the first twenty-four hours might have something to do with it.

Jainan didn't smile, but the line of tension between his eyes relaxed. He rested his hands on the rail to keep himself steady in the lighter gravity and lifted his eyes from his wrist-screen to the five-story-high viewing pane in front of them. The station's Observation Hall was ringed with similar windows. Jainan wasn't gawking like Kiem, since he must have seen this view before, but every time he glanced up his eyes went half-clouded, half-longing. His sister Ressid would be arriving with the Thean planetary delegation in another four days. Kiem got the impression Jainan was nervous.

Congratulating himself on his sensitivity—what if he *didn't* try to make Jainan talk when he obviously didn't want to?— Kiem left him to catch up on his messages and moved around to the next window, where a cluster of blocky industrial habitats were rising into view in the wake of the main station. One of those must be the Kingfisher refinery Aren had mentioned, fed by minerals from asteroids farther out in the sector. Kiem winced at the reminder, and wondered if Professor Audel had made it to the station yet. He still had a fundamental hope things might all sort themselves out—maybe Taam's crash really *had* been an accident—but even he was finding it harder and harder to hold on to that idea.

The rest of the Observation Hall was surprisingly empty. Kiem was keeping half an eye out for the Auditor. Agent Rakal obviously thought they could still find a suspect to satisfy the Resolution, but Kiem was starting to get surer and surer that they didn't have time. At least if they told the Auditor everything they knew, it would be obvious that *Jainan* hadn't killed Taam. Maybe that would be enough to instate them.

The Unification celebrations would kick off in the Hall later, after the Resolution signing, but most of the official contingents hadn't arrived yet, and for now people moved through it in dribs and drabs. There weren't many Theans among them. Jainan had mentioned on the shuttle that the habitat modules of Carissi Station were still considered an Iskaner vanity project, despite its position in orbit around Thea, and Theans themselves only tended to use the docks in the Transit Module where travelers caught connecting shuttles on and off the planet. Kiem still had a lot to learn about the subtleties of Thean current affairs.

Jainan looked up from his wristband. "Your newslog articles

came out while we were on the shuttle," he said. "The ones about the crash."

"Oh yeah?" Kiem said. He leaned forward to catch sight of a wisp from a distant nebula. "Any angry messages from Hren?"

"No," Jainan said. Something seemed to be bothering him. "I didn't realize you planned to blame your own bad flying. This paints you as incompetent."

"Well, it's a narrative they know. Easy to get traction."

Jainan didn't respond. He was frowning at the screen.

"I didn't mention you, did I?" Kiem said, suddenly worried. He had tried to give the impression he was the only one in the flybug.

"No, you didn't," Jainan said. "I just—why do you talk about *yourself* like this?"

That threw Kiem off-balance. Jainan seemed to be expecting a concrete answer. "Er. It seemed like the best way to go."

"Oh," Jainan said. He examined Kiem for a moment, then lifted his gaze to a scruffy figure striding her way across the Observation Hall.

Kiem had approximately two seconds to wonder what Gairad was doing on Carissi Station before he recalled she was Thean, and this was technically her home orbit.

"Are you still alive?" Gairad said to Jainan, by way of a greeting.

"The evidence seems fairly conclusive," Jainan said dryly. He seemed glad to see her as well, in his own quiet way. "Is Professor Audel on station?"

"It isn't as if you got in a flybug crash and then made me worry for two days straight or anything," Gairad said. "No, she's supposed to get here today. Why?"

Jainan didn't look at Kiem. "I need to see her. Are you here to work on her Kingfisher project?"

"No," Gairad said, suddenly morose. "My scholarship says I have to attend goodwill ceremonies with the Iskaners. I *should* be at a protest right now," she added, as if Jainan would understand. "I just can't afford to lose the scholarship."

Kiem saw the tiny shift in posture that meant Jainan's focus had narrowed to Gairad to the exclusion of everything else. "What protest?"

Gairad's wristband buzzed and she opened and shut a personal screen, scowling at it. "There's a big Unification Day protest back in Bita. All my friends are getting at me for being up here with the Iskaners instead."

"Gairad," Jainan said, controlled enough to be a warning sign. "You can't have connections with radicals."

"They're not radicals," Gairad said, as if they'd had the conversation before. "They're my friends from university."

"*Especially* not during Unification Day," Jainan said. "Please. Leave them to it. You have your project to focus on."

The edge of appeal in his voice apparently gave Gairad pause. "Ugh," she said eventually. "I suppose. At least with you and the professor here, we might get some Kingfisher work done. Did you have a chance to look at my mass analysis of their refinery?" She threw up a screen right there, between her and Jainan, which showed a cross-section of a space habitat. After a moment, Kiem recognized the refinery they'd seen a model of at Hvaren Base. "Here. There's something weird about the mass distribution that I can't pin down. Can we go over it this evening?"

There was a sudden shattering, grinding noise. Kiem turned and saw one of the huge bulkhead partitions was moving, folding itself back to reveal another part of the Hall. They must need the full space for the ceremonies. The new part of the Hall had already been set up with a cluster of waist-high stands covered with bubbles of force. Each bubble held a Galactic remnant. Kiem recognized a Resolution staffer adjusting one of the stands.

Jainan only spared the noise a single glance over his shoulder. "Tomorrow," he said to Gairad. "I am at a dinner this evening."

"Advisory Council banquet," Kiem said helpfully. "But we don't have anything tomorrow morning." If he went by Bel's meticulously color-coded schedule, it was easier to ignore that they only had four days to sort out the instation problem or none of the circus would matter. He touched Jainan's elbow. "There's a Resolution staffer over there. We should talk to them."

Jainan caught his meaning at once. If the Auditor wasn't speaking to anyone, a staffer might be the only way in. "Yes. Gairad, I will see you tomorrow."

Gairad insisted on trailing behind him to point out some final things about the mass analysis, which Jainan listened to gravely before pulling himself away, but Kiem was already focused on the Resolution staffer. The bulkhead shuddered back against the wall, revealing another dozen remnants, each on its own stand.

It also revealed the Auditor himself, striding in from a side door, and Prince Vaile, skirts clutched in one hand as she hurried to keep up with him, saying, "Auditor, if you would only *explain*—"

Kiem fell in beside her and slid himself into the conversation. "Hey, Vaile. Explain what?"

The Auditor wasn't answering anyway. Vaile gave Kiem a harassed look. "Oh. Kiem. Of course, you were on a shuttle. Have you checked your confirmation status recently?"

Kiem traded a glance with Jainan and spun up his correspondence with the Auditor's staff. A miniature web of pictures appeared on a small screen above his wrist, with the faces of the treaty representatives displayed above their statuses.

His and Jainan's statuses no longer said UNCONFIRMED. They had been replaced by another tag, glowing red. REVOKED.

Jainan's voice was gray and brittle behind him, as he caught up in time to see Kiem's wrist-screen. "That— I don't understand. That can't be right. Not *all* of them."

In his shock, Kiem hadn't looked at the others. Now he saw

there was red spotted all across the web: the Sefalan representative had also been labeled REVOKED, as had every Iskat half of the remaining couples.

"Yes," Vaile said grimly. "You see the problem. Auditor," she said, raising her voice. "I understand you must work by Resolution protocols, but the Emperor needs to know your grounds so she can respond. *If* you would just stop for one moment and tell me—"

"Here," the Auditor said, stopping in front of one of the remnant stands. Two junior staffers flanked it. Kiem hadn't noticed before, but the Auditor's eye-covering took on a different aspect this close to remnants: a new element crept into the swirling field. It looked like a color, but Kiem's brain interpreted it not as visible light but as a sharp taste in the back of his mouth. The Auditor turned to Vaile. There was no way of telling where he was looking, but Kiem was for some reason sure he had acknowledged him and Jainan. "Prince Vaile, if you would step forward."

Vaile let the hem of her skirts fall back to the floor and moved toward the stand. It was the largest remnant, big enough that Kiem couldn't have fitted his arms around it, and seemed to be made of hundreds of metal sheets melting into each other. Kiem recognized the unpleasant prickling down his back from the ceremony back on Iskat, along with the horrible feeling there might be someone behind you. The stand was surrounded by a bubble of light.

Vaile regarded the remnant like it had personally tried to sabotage her reputation with the Emperor. "I recognize this one," she said. "General Fenrik provided it. The Tau field?"

The Auditor laid a hand on the remnant, reaching through the force field as if it weren't there. The remnant reacted immediately, sharp light running in waves over its surface and clustering hungrily around his hand. His face shield went pure black as he stood there for a long moment, light running around and over his fingers.

"Auditor?" Vaile said, with what Kiem felt was commendable composure.

The Auditor's face turned to her, returning to its normal state. "This is the biggest find we have had from a system as small as yours in quite a while," he said. "I've seen the designs you submitted for a *therapy machine*—a sorely misplaced idea, but even if you were running it continuously, it should barely have drained any of the remnant's energy. I should not be able to touch a sample like this, even with assistive tech, and stay within the parameters of my own mind."

"But you are," Jainan said evenly. "So?"

"This is a fake," the Auditor said.

"That's not possible," Vaile said. "It's been under guard the whole time."

The Auditor gestured to his junior staffers. One of them took out a tool that seemed to be a cutting wheel on a handle, spinning lazily. It looked too slow to do anything, but its rim glowed violet. As the staffer brought it down to touch the remnant, the remnant *split*, like wood beneath an axe. The two halves crumbled gently away from each other, falling off the stand, and froze in midair where they hit the force field.

A small, dense shard clattered to the stand. It was the size of Kiem's thumb.

"That is the only legitimate remnant," the Auditor said coolly. "A shard nestled in a clever fake, enough to simulate some of the effects. We have discovered fourteen other fakes among the materials submitted to us."

"Why would anyone fake a remnant?" Kiem said.

Vaile pinched the bridge of her nose. "I assume so they could remove the real ones without the Resolution noticing," she said. "I cannot think why anyone would want *multiple* remnants."

"Some of the smaller ones have been carved up and used to fake the effect of larger remnants," the Auditor said. "My staff have now tested all of them. Your Emperor wanted to speak to me, Prince Vaile. Tell her I will have the current location of the remnants, or there will not be a treaty."

Vaile stood like a statue, her expression suddenly opaque.

"Hang on," Kiem said. "There can't just not be a treaty. I know you had concerns about Taam and Thea, but we have an answer. We were going to give you an answer."

The Auditor was no longer paying attention to any of them. He had turned back to the tiny remnant, holding it in his hand as his face shield turned black. It was like watching someone in religious communion.

"Excuse me," Vaile said.

"The Auditor has laid down terms," one of the junior staffers said, politely gesturing them to step away. "Please inform the Emperor, Prince Vaile. He will speak to you when you have an update."

"Wait a *moment*," Kiem said helplessly, but there didn't seem to be anything they could do. They had no way to persuade or bribe or blackmail the Auditor; it was like trying to persuade the weather.

Vaile jerked her head to indicate they should leave. "I will deal with this," she said, sounding uncannily like the Emperor. She eyed the glossy, closed group of Resolution staff, obviously discarded further argument as pointless, and strode off. Presumably she had a direct line to call the Emperor.

Kiem and Jainan let the Resolution staffers shepherd them away from the Auditor. Kiem felt stunned, as if the floor under his feet had just opened onto hard vacuum.

"Those remnants must be found," Jainan said tensely. "The entire Taam investigation is pointless if the Resolution uses this to void the treaty."

"Right," Kiem muttered. Their voices seemed to echo too loudly in the Observatory Hall. "The Emperor will have the station turned upside down."

"She would have to start searching on all the planets the fakes came from," Jainan said. "That fake was not a five-minute job. Someone planned this."

Kiem rubbed the back of his head. "What do we do?" he said. "I'm out of ideas, Jainan."

"I have nothing yet," Jainan said, his voice clipped, but it sounded more like frustration than panic. Even that gave Kiem some hope.

Kiem was distracted by the sudden chiming of his wristband. "Bel?"

Jainan frowned. "Isn't she off the clock? I thought she went to the bar."

Kiem checked the message. "She wants to meet up," he said. "She's flagged it *urgent*. I'll see what's up."

"I'll leave you to sort it out," Jainan said slowly. "There's something I want to see about Gairad's work."

As they left, there was a flash from behind them. The Auditor turned. As he opened his hand, the remnant appeared, shattered to pieces. His expression was something like disgust. He shook his head at his staff and stalked away from the remnants and the Observation Hall, disappearing into the closed Resolution offices already established in the bowels of the station. Kiem had a feeling they wouldn't see him emerging any time soon.

Kiem left Jainan to his project and made his way to the Transit Module, where Bel had given her location. It was unlike Bel to be cryptic in her messages.

Bel was standing in front of the huge light-partition that marked the entrance to the shuttle docks when Kiem came out of the airlocks and hurried over to her. Everything was not okay. He looked at the vacuum capsule hovering beside her, and her travel coat, and the expression on her face, and said, "Oh, shit. You heard from home."

"My grandmother," Bel said. "I need to go, today. Now, if it's okay." She brushed her braids back from her face, then did it again when they immediately fell back. "I don't have time to arrange cover. I'm sorry."

The investigation and remnants suddenly seemed much less urgent. "Hey, no, it's okay! Have you got a shuttle ticket? Can I get it? Should I call your family and say you're coming? Can I—"

"*No!*" Bel took a breath. They both had to step back out of the way of travelers hurrying to the immigration gates. "I just need to go. There's a shuttle going to an Eisafan hub tonight, and I should be able to get a last-minute ticket if I camp out at the ticket desk. I can get to Sefala from there."

Her face was even more strained than it had been when he'd arrived. Colors reflected off it from the gates behind them: blue for commercial travel, red for Imperial. Kiem felt helpless and slow. He held out his hand. "Well. Good luck."

Bel clasped his hand. "Give my best to Jainan." Her fingers felt chilled. She pulled away after a split second, all business. "You'll need briefings for the rest of your appointments while you're here. I put together a handover file. It has the current state of everything we know about Taam as well."

"I don't give a shit about my briefings," Kiem said. "Your grandmother—all right, all right." This wasn't the time to start an argument about the relative importance of his schedule. "Give me the briefings."

"Promise you'll read them," Bel said warningly. Kiem's wristband beeped as she transferred the data.

"I'll read them," Kiem said. "Top priority." He wanted to offer to book her a flyer, or something pointless like buy her food for the journey, but she would already have those in hand. There was no point telling her what they'd just learned about the remnants. The treaty would be signed, or it wouldn't, but either way it would take a couple of years for the megapowers to move, and there was nothing either of them could do about that.

She gave him a mechanical smile and something halfway to a

salute, and then turned and started walking to the blue commercial gates. The vacuum capsule bobbed behind her.

Kiem's optimism had been well and truly punctured. He turned away just before she reached the gates.

The Imperial gate had a constant stream of travelers on treaty business. Even apart from the hundreds of guests, there were phalanxes of stressed-looking aides and organizers as well as a trickle of soldiers.

One of them was Colonel Lunver.

Her mind appeared to be on her own business, but she caught sight of Kiem and immediately slowed. "Your Highness," she said, giving him a curt nod. "Leaving the station four days before the treaty? Where are you going?"

Kiem usually liked to be helpful, but something in him bristled at the question. "Seeing off a friend," he said. "Why, where are you off to, Colonel? How's the investigation?" he added, needling slightly.

It had an electric effect on Lunver. Her whole body stiffened, and she stepped in front of Kiem as if she could stop him from going anywhere. "What do you know about the investigation?"

"Your investigation," Kiem said. He wasn't going to be intimidated. "You were trying to find out if anyone in your unit was helping Taam embezzle. You told us you would, remember?"

For a moment Colonel Lunver looked more furious than anyone Kiem had ever seen. "This is unhinged," she said. "You accuse *Prince Taam*—your *cousin*—" Words seemed to fail her, and she had to work her mouth for a split second before she found her voice again. "Where has this come from?" she said. "Why are you bringing it up now? You may think you're above a treason charge, but I assure you that you aren't."

"Wait, what?" Kiem said. He stared at her. "You've known about this for days. We spoke about it in the flyer when your unit rescued us."

"We spoke about nothing of the sort," Lunver snapped. "I remember every part of that flight. I don't know what you would gain from making up something as irresponsible as this."

Kiem was used to the military overlooking unpleasant truths, but this took the prize. "You can pretend it's not happening all you like," he said. "If you don't do the investigation, Internal Security's going to. You can try and cut me and Jainan out of the loop. We'll find out anyway."

Lunver's fury transmuted into something else, something that Kiem could have sworn was doubt. She narrowed her eyes. "You had better not be passing your theory around the station."

"Not yet!" Kiem said cheerfully. "Good day, Colonel Lunver. Let me know how you get on."

The wave of unaccustomed annoyance washed him back to the residential room they'd been assigned in the station proper. Jainan was out. Kiem couldn't remember where he'd said he was going.

It was too early to dress for dinner, and he didn't have any appointments. He could pay some social calls, but for once Kiem didn't feel up to listening to the Minister for Trade talk about his latest longevity treatment. He was perfectly *capable* of operating without Bel. He just wasn't used to it.

He sat at the cramped desk and grudgingly put up Bel's briefings on the wall-screen in front of him. A collection of glowing circles unfolded on the screen, each spilling out text and data. He opened the most prominent, as Bel had clearly meant him to read it first, and realized belatedly what it was: she'd gone into the newslog archives to research Operation Kingfisher. Kiem frowned. He hadn't asked her for this.

He skimmed through the newslog extracts in chronological order. Taam and the High Command had clearly managed to keep most of Operation Kingfisher secret. Even the extracts from Thean newslogs were mainly opinion pieces with no details, but there were snippets in technical journals that might mean something to Jainan.

Disappointingly, Audel's name wasn't mentioned at all. Kiem supposed that made sense, if she'd only been in the military for a short time and wasn't a senior officer, but he'd hoped for something. Maybe something that would make him and Jainan feel better about Internal Security's instructions.

There was a sudden flurry of material from two years ago, after the accident the adjunct at the College reception had mentioned. It was hard to cover up two deaths, though the military press liaison seemed to have done their best. Kiem started skimming faster, then stopped when he got to the faces of the two people who had died in the explosion.

They were both strangers: a young private in military uniform and a Thean civilian with long hair. The Thean had light eyes and a clan neckscarf tied in a way Kiem thought indicated a man; he was smiling for some kind of graduation photo. Kiem felt something in his chest twist. He didn't have the knack of imagining disasters from reports. He hadn't reckoned on being hit in the face with a real person.

Kiem summoned all the scraps of clan heraldry he'd picked up from Jainan and identified the scarf pattern as representing Deralli, one of the largest Thean clans. He scanned the attached text. The victims' photos hadn't been published at the time; Bel had dug them out of some archive. The young Thean man was listed as a civilian consultant, but it didn't say anything about what he'd been doing on the mining probe or where the military had employed him from. Bel had managed to find some history from his name: his family, his clan lineage, his education. Kiem felt nauseous but kept reading. It felt like a duty.

When he'd finished, he pushed the chair back and stared at the corner of the ceiling. Two people had died. Two people not even connected to Taam, with lives ahead of them and families left behind to grieve them. Someone had let these disasters happen, if not engineered them outright. Someone had hacked into Kingfisher's systems; someone had embezzled its funds. *Someone* had killed Taam.

It would be neat if it was all the same person. Kiem spun up a picture in his mind: an embittered saboteur, anti-military, anti-Iskat, looming in the shadows. The whole picture fell apart when Kiem tried to put Professor Audel in it, because he couldn't believe Jainan was so wrong in his judgment of her character. Maybe it was someone else. Maybe someone Kiem didn't know at all.

The thought came slowly, from some cold and distant part of his mind: Internal Security must want that cackling saboteur as well, especially now, four days before the treaty. It would be so *simple* to have an enemy.

He stared at the dead young Thean on the screen. This wasn't really about facts, it was about people. People were many things, but by and large they weren't masterminds. They always wanted something. They always had a reason for what they did.

Something uncurled in his head.

Kiem spun back through the Thean's history. There wasn't much more there: a handful of research papers, memberships of some political groups at his old university. Kiem wanted to go and shake some answers out of Lunver and Agent Rakal, but he'd tried that before and hadn't got far. Perhaps, for once, he should hold off. For *once* he needed to think.

CHAPTER 22

Jainan ended up in Carissi Station's outer control room. He hadn't planned to. He had been thinking deeply about Gairad's mass analysis and the remnants, and it had occurred to him: he was the Thean treaty representative. He was married to an Imperial Prince. Why *not* see if they would allow him into one of the control rooms? The assistant staffing the door had barely batted an eyelid.

Now Jainan was in front of an array of screens and viewports, watching the rest of the orbital cluster as each shining habitat followed Carissi Station in its slow, unending curve around the planet below. The refinery was the last of them, a stately mass of spheres following the smaller modules. He'd spent an hour here already. A shift change buzzer had sounded halfway through, but he'd ignored it, and nobody seemed to realize he shouldn't be there.

It was aesthetically compelling, maybe, but the readings on the screens were more valuable. Gairad had put Kingfisher's official mass readings in her diagram, then scribbled all over it with requests for Jainan and Audel to check her work because her calculations weren't making sense.

She was right. Jainan had spent some time puzzling over the inconsistencies in the readings: Carissi Station's instruments were much more accurate than anything from public sources, and Kingfisher's official figures didn't match what they were telling him. Operation Kingfisher had drawn up plans that showed their refinery as smaller than it really was.

Jainan took a quick look to see if anyone was watching him use station equipment without authorization—Kiem was bad for him—then tweaked the viewscreens to show the Kingfisher refinery in detail. Most of the unexplained mass was concentrated on the underside of the refinery, where the diagrams showed nothing but an outer hull. That was a storage module.

There was no reason to leave a storage module off your official diagrams unless you wanted to hide what was in it. Jainan found it suddenly harder to breathe.

Taam had been buying as well as selling. That was where the money had gone.

But buying what? Jainan stared at the viewscreens until his eyes watered. It gave him no answers. Whatever he was buying must have been significant, to distort the mass readings this much. Where had he gotten all the money? Surely not just from selling surplus mining equipment?

Jainan felt cold. General Fenrik had submitted the remnant they called the *Tau field*. It had been in military hands. Had Taam been in possession of the real one? Had he sold it?

"Sir?" a station official said. "Can I ask what you were doing on the screen—are you all right?"

Jainan moved away from the screen and turned, absently hearing the question like the buzzing of a fly. "I don't need it anymore." He began to walk to the door, barely seeing the rest of the control room. His mind was full of moving parts that ticked over every few moments and fell into new positions. It wasn't only Taam who had something to hide. *Kingfisher* had something to hide.

He tried to call Kiem, but Kiem's wristband was dead. There was no point leaving a message; Jainan needed to talk to him. This whole thing had grown too big for them to keep quiet about it. If he was honest, it was too big even for Internal Security.

Jainan screwed up his courage, activated his wristband, and sent off a brief, formal meeting request to the Emperor's Private Office about discrepancies in Operation Kingfisher.

A cold sweat settled on him as soon as he'd done it. The audacity of it was beyond anything he'd ever attempted. But neither Internal Security nor the military had solved Taam's murder, or what Taam had been doing at Kingfisher, or where the missing remnants were, and time was running out.

He had walked through half the station before he recognized where he was. His subconscious had been problem-solving without consulting him, and he realized his feet had been taking instructions from it just as it presented him with an unwelcome conclusion like a lump of plutonium.

He looked up at the closed door to the Auditor's quarters, which had an ACCESS DENIED sign over it. The control panel glowed red beside it. Jainan reached out slowly and gave his skinprint and retina scan to request entry.

"The Auditor is not seeing visitors," a Resolution staffer said, their face appearing on a screen midair.

Jainan had been prepared for that. "I am a treaty representative," he said. He probably still was, despite the REVOKED status. It wasn't as if they had an easy replacement. "I have information about the remnants."

He had expected he would have to argue. But instead the staffer's eyes tracked something on their eyepiece, and they said, "Enter."

The screen disappeared, and the door opened. Jainan stepped inside.

The room was surprisingly small, even for the station. Like the temporary Resolution office on Iskat, they'd hung some of their odd textile-screens around the walls, but there was only one tiny desk, and all in all the room looked like an afterthought. The staffer was leaning back on a chair behind the desk, looking bored and uncomfortable. "Go on in," they said, gesturing to the opposite wall. One of the textile-screens lifted itself aside as if an invisible hand had pulled it.

It was an airlock. Jainan realized they must be next to the hull of the station. The Resolution hadn't installed themselves on Carissi; they'd just docked their ship and stayed there.

The airlock yawned open. The impression behind it was one of relative darkness; Carissi kept most public spaces brightly lit. Jainan cleared his face of expression and stepped through it.

The first thing he noticed was that the Resolution ship had dispensed with station gravity. Or no—not exactly. Jainan nearly overbalanced in his first step beyond the airlock, but managed to land his foot on the polished black floor and ground himself. Each movement felt supported, as if something had anticipated where he was going to go and was helping him. The air felt treacly around him.

Past the airlock, the passage sloped upward at a sharp angle. Jainan used the odd gravity to help him up, each stride much longer than it would have been on the station. The walls around him lit up gradually as he climbed, glowing a pale, featureless pearl. The slope seemed endless. Every few meters he would pass a closed, arched doorway. He could not see the end of the passage.

As he passed one door, it sprang open, falling downward into the floor. Jainan stopped short. Behind it was the Auditor.

The narrow chamber beyond was set up in a disturbingly staggered way—not completely zero-grav, but furniture hovered at different levels, or was attached to the hull halfway up the wall. The Auditor sat at a desk suspended at the height of Jainan's shoulders, surrounded by streams of light with no meaning to Jainan. The light-streams dissipated and gradually faded away as the Auditor looked down at him in the doorway.

"Come in," the Auditor said. He opened a hand to a chair on roughly the same plane as him.

Jainan considered the problem then gently tested to see if the oddly helpful gravity would get him all the way up. It wouldn't, quite, but a careful step took him to a rug floating at waist height, and from there it was a fairly easy step up to the chair.

The chair was the same pearly shade as the walls outside. As Jainan sat in it, it reformed itself underneath him, holding him gently in place. Jainan lifted a knee experimentally, and it released him. He settled back down.

The Auditor smiled, the last of the light-streams fading around him. "You're a hard person to disquiet, Count Jainan."

Jainan, who felt disquieted most of the time, chose not to answer that. "Thank you for seeing me."

"I assume you have something relevant," the Auditor said. "If not, this will be a waste of both our time."

It would have helped if Jainan could have seen his eyes. "Has Iskat told you what has come to light about Taam?"

The Auditor's lack of reaction just strengthened his feeling that they hadn't. The Iskat establishment preferred to keep things under wraps until they had a result. That would be fine when it wasn't playing with the safety of all their planets—which, of course, was exactly what Jainan was doing now. He made himself breathe out and explained, surprised by his own steady voice. Taam's death. The embezzlement. Internal Security's pressure to find a suspect. Aren and Lunver's investigation. Professor Audel, whose guilt Jainan had never been sure about. The flybug accident. The odd mass readings from the refinery.

The Auditor leaned back in his chair, inscrutable behind the alien field over his eyes. Jainan couldn't tell if he was listening. Now that Jainan looked closer, he could see the structure of the eye-covering in more detail: it was anchored by a pair of black, lacquer-like pieces that attached discreetly to the skull on either side of his head, then the field arced unsupported across his face. The visual effect of the non-colors was undeniable; Jainan's eyes actively hurt examining it.

"You think the remnants are in this mining refinery?" the Auditor asked.

"Would they cause a mass distortion?" Jainan said.

"No," the Auditor said thoughtfully. "Nothing noticeable on the basic sensors you have here."

Jainan forced himself to say it. "I think he may have sold them. They may be on the Sefalan black market." If they were, it would take more than four days to find them. "They may even have already gone through the link."

"Possible but unlikely," the Auditor said. "No ship goes through a link without a scout to pilot it. It takes complex measures to smuggle a remnant on board the same ship as a scout without them noticing, and I doubt this backwater is capable of that level of sophistication: Ah," he added dryly, as the colors shifted on his face. "I have been notified that I shouldn't have deprioritized my etiquette module. Accept my apologies."

"I am not overly concerned with apologies," Jainan said, the underlying dread making him blunt. "What does this mean for the treaty?"

The Auditor folded his hands in silence. As he did so, Jainan was suddenly aware of the absolute, deadening silence in the chamber. On a station there was always the background hum of life support systems, but here it was as quiet as deep space.

"The situation is interesting," the Auditor said. "By not presenting the remnants by the deadline, Iskat has broken our nonproliferation terms."

Jainan's veins ran with acid. He said nothing.

"Thea's representative, on the other hand, is trying to work with us." The Auditor's voice was a soft monotone in the stillness. "If the Iskat Empire is no longer a Resolution signatory . . . other arrangements could be made."

And just like that, the crystal shape of the treaty in Jainan's mind shattered into seven parts. "You mean cut Iskat loose. Draw up a separate treaty."

"It would have to be done fast," the Auditor said. "It is unwise to be outside the Resolution for any length of time."

Jainan was so far out of his depth, it felt like someone had punched a hole in the hull of the Auditor's ship, and he was hanging over the void. "The remnants need to be found. There are still four days until your deadline. You could extend it."

The Auditor regarded him. Then he reached for the corner of his desk and gave it a gentle push; the whole thing slid smoothly out of the way, lining itself up against the wall, leaving nothing in between him and Jainan. He put his hand up and touched one of the lacquered pieces on the side of his head. The field around his eyes changed and faded.

Behind the field—though some distortion remained—his features came into view. His face was spare and space-pale, with prominent cheekbones and shockingly normal dark brown eyes. It should have been reassuring. Jainan was profoundly unsettled.

"You should make terms," the Auditor said. Something about his voice was thinner, as if there had been extra harmonics before. "I say this not as role four-seven-five, or any of my committee roles, but as a human citizen. I'm not supposed to do that, you understand. How much Galactic politics are you aware of back here?"

At the question, Jainan felt like a village fisherman who had never left Thea. He knew of some of the megapowers, but Galactic politics were too far away to be of much concern on Thea when Iskat was right on their doorstep. "Not a great deal."

"You should understand your threats," the Auditor said. "I know the Iskat Emperor does. The megapowers have been chafing for decades—after all the consolidation last century, there are very few tiny sectors like yours *not* protected by a Resolution treaty. Do you understand what that means? Some hungry powers are looking for places to expand, and there is almost no fair game. No new links have opened in the last thirteen years."

Jainan wished Kiem was here to ask questions. He had a knack for picking the obvious ones that clarified things. Why had Kiem turned off his wristband? "Why are they expanding?" he said. "I thought the Resolution was supposed to keep things in balance."

The Auditor laughed—a strange, dry sound, as if he didn't produce it much. "Do you know how big a territory the High Chain rules?" he said. "You're sitting here with seven planets and a total population in the low billions. The High Chain owns a third of the known *universe*. Without assistive tech, the human brain cannot effectively comprehend either their population or the distance between their borders. The Resolution was drawn up by a balance of megapowers. We are a skeleton group overseeing a fragile truce. Do you really think the Resolution isn't, itself, half under the Chain's influence?"

"Oh," Jainan said.

"The Chain is old and slow and may not be your main threat. No—the minute you leave Resolution protection, the powers that will be scrambling fighters and plotting routes are Kaschec and the Enna Union, both military megapowers that need quick victories to prop up their demagogues at home. Kaschec owns territory nearer to your link and has better passage agreements, so I'd expect them to get here first. You might have months. You probably have weeks."

Instead of panicking, Jainan felt he was watching the machinery in his head as it kept ticking over, heavy and relentless, crunching this new information and its consequences. He imagined Thea standing alone in a sector annexed by a Galactic megapower. The Resolution promised stability. How much independence would Thea manage to keep if the rest of the sector was at war? "What if Thea somehow managed to agree a treaty in four days?" he said. "What about the other planets? Sefala? Eisafan?"

The Auditor gave a fluid motion of his shoulders that could have passed as a shrug. The chair shifted under him. "They have not volunteered information as you have for Thea. We don't generally encourage schisms in treaty signatories, but we encourage remnant use and deceiving the committees even less."

Jainan was surprised at his own lack of dread. Everything seemed very clear, clearer than it had for the past five years, as if the beginnings of a breeze had stirred in his head and the fog there were melting away. He barely needed to stop to consider Kiem, and Bel, and Audel and her students. "I need the whole sector to be part of the treaty," he said quietly. "Even Iskat. I have . . . links."

The Auditor gave him a long look, from those disconcertingly normal eyes with their alien political views. He reached up and touched the lacquer headpiece again; the field swirled back over his face.

"Then find me those fifteen remnants, Jainan nav Adessari of Feria." The Auditor's mouth, now the only visible part of his face, curved up in something that wasn't a smile. "You have four days."

A shift change buzzer sounded in the narrow corridors of a hostel as Kiem knocked on the door of the guest room assigned to Professor Audel. The attendees from the Imperial College had been assigned to hostel rooms in the Transit Module; they'd clearly run out of guest suites in the nicer residential areas.

It was the second door Kiem had tried. It was locked, but an occupancy light glowed softly. Kiem tried the bios sensor.

A voice from the speaker said, "Oh, it's you. What do you want?"

The door slid open to show a small set of rooms with a pokey living area cramped by a desk and chair. Several screens were open above the desk. The window opposite the door, sunk in the wall to give the illusion of a view, was currently set to a projection of a beach that seemed faintly alien to Kiem.

Gairad sat on a flat couch under the window, staring discon-solately at the alien beach. There was nobody else in the room.

"Did you want the professor?" she asked, without bothering to look up. "She's out."

Kiem shifted one of the desk chairs and sat down facing her. The room was so small that he took up most of the available width between the desk and the opposite wall, cutting off the route to the door. Gairad's eyes finally flickered to him.

"No," Kiem said amiably, "I don't want the professor."

"Jainan?" Gairad said. She straightened up from her slouch, putting her feet on the ground. "He went to the control room to check my refinery data."

Kiem leaned back in the chair and brought up one ankle to prop on his opposite knee. "Did you know Professor Audel was under investigation?"

"No," Gairad said. Kiem kept his eyes on her face and noted how quickly that answer had come. She added belatedly, "Why? What for?"

"Internal Security is saying she compromised Kingfisher's systems."

Gairad's hands curled around the edge of the couch seat. "Why would she do that? Kingfisher already gave us the data she asked for."

Kiem lifted his shoulders in a half shrug. "Did they? Too tech-nical for me to understand, really." He leaned forward a fraction. "Internal Security thinks she used your account, though. As well as her other students' accounts. That's a shame. Jainan didn't want you involved."

To give Gairad credit, her expression had the same low-key hostility she'd shown Kiem when they'd first met. She wasn't giving anything away, and Kiem wasn't sure of anything, not yet. "She didn't use my account," Gairad said. "She didn't do any-thing."

"No," Kiem agreed. "She didn't use your account. You'd barely trust the average Iskaner to pass you the salt; I can't see you handing your teacher your private keys. On top of that, you're clever and technical enough to keep up with Jainan; there's no way you wouldn't notice if Professor Audel was using your account in secret."

There was no trace of a slouch in Gairad's posture now. "What do you mean?"

"You broke into Kingfisher's systems," Kiem said bluntly. Gairad laughed outright, short and incredulous. Kiem waited for her to finish before he carried on. "What were you after?"

"This is bullshit," Gairad said, squaring her shoulders as if she might start a physical fight. "I don't know where you got that idea from. I'm here to pass my study program and get my shipping license. I already had to come all the way to Iskat for it. Why would I take a risk like hacking an Iskat army system?"

"Good question," Kiem said. "May I use your screen?"

Gairad frowned, looking for the trap, but after a moment she waved permission. Kiem gestured to his wristband and threw up the picture of the young Thean who had died in the accident.

"I don't know who that is," Gairad said.

"Fairly sure you do," Kiem said.

"Why would I?" Gairad said defensively. "That's a Deralli neckscarf. Whoever he is, he has nothing to do with Feria."

"Yeah, I know," Kiem said. "I think that's why Internal Security didn't make the link. Iskaners deal with your prominent clans, because that's who takes up political positions on Thea. We know just enough about clans to *think* we know how Thea works. But not everyone thinks clan society is the most important thing, do they? I read your article."

"You barely read anything," Gairad said. Kiem grinned at her, which didn't lessen the tension but instead spun it out. Gairad took a moment to think, which was the first crack in her defenses Kiem had seen. "What article?"

"The one you wrote for your *Pan-Thean Interest Society* back at Bita Point University," Kiem said. "Fascinating newsletter you guys had. I liked all the cartoons of the Emperor, they really nailed her scowl. Our friend"—he gestured to the face on the screen—"was a member too. From his bylines, it looks like he joined two years before you. You would have crossed over. I think you knew him."

"So I was at university with someone who's now dead," Gairad said. "So what? You don't have proof of anything. Fuck off."

"I'm curious," Kiem said. "And the *reason* I'm curious is because Internal Security wants to bundle this all up together. They'll sacrifice both Professor Audel and Jainan if they have to." It was supposed to be a lie. As Kiem said it, though, it felt close enough to the truth that his chest tightened.

Gairad went white. "They wouldn't."

"Jainan fought to keep you out of this," Kiem said. "He thinks he has a clan obligation to you. I'm not Thean so bear with me—do you have one to him?"

Gairad was silent. She looked away.

There was a small, ordinary noise behind him: a door sliding open. Gairad's eyes flicked over his shoulder. She wasn't surprised, Kiem realized. She'd sent a ping he hadn't seen.

"Your Highness," Professor Audel said, "what an unexpected honor to find you here."

Kiem turned in his chair. He started to get up politely, but Professor Audel waved him back down. "Professor. Not good news, I'm afraid."

She didn't seem to hear. She stood in the doorway, untidy in traveling clothes, with strands of hair coming loose from their clips and a vague look in her eyes. "Gairad, I think I'm going to have to alter the fish nutrients. Do you think she's looking peaky?" She opened a screen that hovered above her wrist, showing a feed to some sort of aquarium.

"Professor," Kiem said again.

"You must be here to find Jainan? I don't know where he is. But I'm afraid I'm going to have to steal Gairad to look at—"

"Don't bother," Gairad said. "He knows."

In the two seconds of silence that followed, Kiem's tentative conclusions rearranged themselves with a swift lurch.

"Ah," Professor Audel said softly. She didn't sound vague in the slightest anymore. "What, exactly, does he know?"

Part of Kiem's hindbrain noted that Gairad was on one side of him and Audel on the other. He stretched out his legs in his chair, smiling, because there didn't seem to be anything else to do. "Internal Security never dropped their investigation into you," he said. "I was just having a chat with Gairad about it. Informally."

Audel stepped forward, closing her wrist-screen briskly. The door shut behind her. "Can I convince you that Gairad wasn't involved?"

"Not really," Kiem said apologetically. "I'd just convinced myself that *you* weren't involved, actually. Did either of you kill Taam?"

"No!" Gairad said, with an indignation that rang true to Kiem's ears. "What do you take us for, murderers? We've been trying to find out who killed him!"

"Gairad has a regrettable tendency to the dramatic," Professor Audel said. "But she's correct. I'm afraid we can't help you with Taam. However—would you mind . . ." She pointed to her wrist.

Kiem looked down at his wristband. He hesitated for a moment, but Bel was in the shuttleport on her way to Sefala, and Jainan could use the station comm system if he really needed to get hold of Kiem. He turned it off. "I wasn't recording."

"Oh, I hope not, but I *am* admitting to criminal access of information," Audel said, "so forgive me my quirks. How did you find out?"

"Internal Security has been after you for days now," Kiem said. "Since you called us at Hvaren Base. They brought us in to help."

"Tch," Audel said. "They really haven't dropped it, then? That makes the next step harder."

"What are you trying to find?" Kiem asked.

"The truth," Gairad said, failing to disprove Professor Audel's character assessment.

Professor Audel didn't answer immediately. She tapped the screen on the wall, where the young Thean smiled in his graduation photo. "Rossan was one of my student researchers. My first one after I left the army, as a matter of fact. When I came back to the Imperial College, I decided to carry on working on regoliths, because I thought it could be done so much better than the military was doing it. Rossan was on one of their mining probes as our first embedded civilian observer in Operation Kingfisher. We fought tooth and nail to get him there. His death was a catastrophe."

"I'm sorry," Kiem said. It sounded completely inadequate.

"It was also very convenient for Kingfisher's officers," Audel said. "But why go that far just to throw off some academic researchers? We weren't a threat to them. That was when I started wondering what else Kingfisher was doing. I wanted to replicate their methods and improve them—of course I did, I'm an engineer. But I also wanted to know why they needed so many non-engineering soldiers on a mining operation."

"Taam was using it as a personal credit source," Kiem said. "He was selling off equipment. Jainan found the money trail."

"Wait, that doesn't fit," Gairad said, with a quick look at Audel. "Stuff's been coming *in* these past few weeks."

Kiem raised his hands in front of him. "Hold up. Go back." He looked at Audel. "You said *next step*, Professor. Does that have anything to do with Agent Rakal saying you planned to hack into the refinery while you're on the habitat?"

Gairad gave his inactive wristband a suspicious look. "Are you sure you're not recording?"

"My dear, making any kind of attempt now seems like a

nonstarter," Audel said. "Gairad and I suspected we had flags on our accounts. Yes, I had a plan to try connecting from a geolocal orbit and seeing what we could find. I used to work on the refinery plant equipment; I know some ways in. But that depended on Internal Security not tracking all our outgoing connections."

Like Internal Security had done to Jainan. It seemed natural for Kiem to say the next thing. "So use my account."

"What?" Gairad said.

"I don't think *mine's* flagged," Kiem said, "and I want to know what's going on."

He didn't let himself think too much about the implications. Of the three of them, he was probably the safest when it came to a real treason charge. It would be embarrassing for the Emperor to have a member of her family arrested. Of course, that might not stop her, but he could cross that bridge when he came to it.

"Well, in that case," Professor Audel said, a gleam in her eye that Kiem had started to recognize in Jainan whenever he had a new data source. "If you'd link up your wristband, Your Highness."

The atmosphere changed immediately. After a suspicious glare at him, Gairad started bustling around the screens, bringing up scripts Kiem didn't recognize. Audel was totally focused on her screen. Kiem had thought it would be complicated, but once he'd linked up his wristband to the input sensors, Audel attached a data coin, and that was it. The screens flickered through interfaces too fast for Kiem to watch. Gairad kept cross-checking the displays with her own wristband and occasionally said things like, "Looks like they took Model 5 offline." Audel just watched.

"Can anyone learn to do that?" Kiem said, forgetting that now was not the time to be fascinated.

Audel blinked, coming out of a trance. "This?" she said. "Sad to say, Prince Kiem, we're doing very little. Most of this is a Kingfisher admin script I took with me when they discharged me. You'd need a Sefalan systems breaker to do this manually. Ah. Here we are."

Kiem looked up at the screens as they began to fill with the square branches of a data map. Gairad handed Audel another data coin, which must have had another script on it, because the data started to flicker and Audel muttered. Gairad was scowling.

"Well, we can't get what we wanted," Audel said, looking up at the screen. "They've rotated the keys."

"But *that's* interesting, isn't it?" Gairad said, pointing at a string of numbers that meant nothing to Kiem. "That's a commanding officer. Who is it?"

"I believe that's General Fenrik's code," Audel said, with an unseemly satisfaction. "How careless. He must have a local storage module. I wonder what he doesn't want to keep on his personal systems?"

Gairad started to grin. "Can I have a look?" Audel gestured for her to go ahead.

Kiem finally realized what they were doing when Gairad started to open things. They were . . . personnel dossiers. Some of them had vids. They were all from officers whose names Kiem didn't recognize, all at colonel rank or above.

"This isn't right," Gairad said. "This doesn't have anything to do with the refinery."

They didn't. The one she had open was about an officer's conviction for petty theft and the affair he was having with a subordinate. Kiem felt dirty even skimming it. "Why would General Fenrik have this?"

Gairad shrugged and moved to the next one. Kiem took a moment to realize this was Aren Saffer's file. "Close it," he said, but Gairad didn't. Instead she expanded it to fill both screens. Aren had been busy, Kiem realized, with a slightly sick feeling. He had gambling debts going back ten years.

"This is blackmail material," Kiem said.

Professor Audel nodded, apparently unfazed. "So there must be a reason Fenrik needed to keep his senior officers in line."

"Here's a file on Prince Taam," Gairad said suddenly.

"*Don't* look at that," Kiem said, but she'd already opened it.

It wasn't a file. It was a vid. Gairad's expression changed as she opened it.

At first Kiem couldn't make sense of what he saw. Then his eyes adjusted, and he realized it was a view of a corridor from the static angle of a security camera. It wasn't a place he recognized, but it had the white walls and polished opalescent flooring of—no, he *did* recognize that flooring pattern, that must be somewhere in the palace. It looked like the Emperor's Wing.

Taam and Jainan stood outside the door of their quarters. Too close to each other, Taam furious, Jainan blank. Somewhere in Kiem's head, the floor gave way.

Blackmail material.

"I . . . maybe we shouldn't," Gairad said uncertainly.

"Give me the vid," Kiem said. He held out the data coin.

Gairad looked at him and did a double take, as if whatever was on his face wasn't worth arguing with. She downloaded the vid and hastily came out of the program.

"We'll carry on looking, then," Professor Audel said, scrutinizing Kiem as if he were a research subject. "You'll want to take that . . . outside."

Kiem wasn't listening anymore. Kingfisher didn't seem important. Nothing seemed important except the slim disc of cool metal he held in his hand.

The door shut behind him. He was aware of passing other people in the corridors, but he didn't see their faces. He realized he was walking too fast; he was probably drawing attention, and attention was the last thing he wanted right now. He stopped in a corner where two little-used corridors met and took the coin out of his pocket. It was warm from his hand; had he been holding it that tightly? He attached it to his wristband.

The security camera feed ran for a handful of seconds without any movement. Kiem focused on it like the mountainside under his falling flybug.

The screen moved, and two distant shapes came into view. Kiem's stomach lurched as he recognized Jainan's slim, straight figure again. Beside him was a man the same height in a gold-braided uniform with close-shaven hair—Taam.

Even though there was no sound, it was clear something was wrong the minute they came in the picture. Taam was saying something with his face distorted into a scowl, and the expression Jainan wore was completely closed-off. Kiem checked the time stamp in the corner—late at night. Both of them were in formal dress; they must have been coming back from an event. Jainan said nothing as Taam pressed in close to him, clearly angry from his jerky strides down the corridor. Taam seemed to grow more and more irritated as they drew closer to the camera, and finally something he said seemed to resonate with Jainan, who turned his head and replied with something short and clipped.

In the next second, Taam had grabbed Jainan's arm, twisted it behind his back, and shoved him against a wall. Jainan said something else. Taam backhanded him across the face.

Kiem's fingers clenched on the insubstantial sides of the projection. He froze it with a violent, instinctive jab, but then couldn't move his hand again. It felt like he had ripped a scab half off.

In the frozen vid, Jainan's expression was one of pure shock. He wasn't even looking at Taam but past him, to the corridor where they'd come from. He was checking if anyone had seen.

The prickling down Kiem's spine wasn't going to stop if he didn't get this over with. He unfroze it.

Taam said something only inches away from Jainan's face. Jainan was fully focused on him now: he held his head stiffly and said something in the gap between whatever Taam was saying—from the shapes of his lips, and because he was expecting it, Kiem could make out *public* and *not here*. Jainan jerked his chin to the door opposite.

Taam stopped. His lips drew back from his teeth, but Jainan

had carried the point. He adjusted his grip on Jainan's arm—Kiem let out an involuntary hiss—and shoved him toward the door. Jainan put up little resistance, only shook his arm as Taam let go as if dislodging something unpleasant. The door opened and he stepped through it. Before Taam followed, he looked around, and his eyes fixed on the security camera. Kiem had the urge to draw back, as if he'd been seen. But he carried on watching as he saw Taam call over Jainan's shoulder to someone already in the room. *That—delete*—Kiem couldn't make out any more.

Kiem recognized the place now. That must be their rooms.

The vid—the security camera footage Taam had called out to delete—ended and shrank back to a dot. That was it. The data coin held nothing else.

Kiem didn't feel shock. That was the worst part. He felt surreal, headachy, as if his muscles weren't under his control, but not shocked. He gestured the replay command by mistake. It started to play again; he jabbed it to stop, and then to start, and then to stop again a second later when he couldn't bear it. His wrist-screen shut off.

All of a sudden, he couldn't stand still anymore. He paced to a viewport and back to the corridor wall. It felt like there were stinging insects moving under his skin, crawling inside his rib cage and pooling in his chest. This made no sense. He raised his wristband, spun through to Bel's contact, and then violently canceled the action. He couldn't call anyone. This *made no sense*.

Jainan had loved Taam. Yes, he had dropped a hint or two that their marriage wasn't perfect, but no marriage was, and the only times Jainan had spoken sharply to Kiem were when Kiem had sounded like he was disrespecting Taam's memory. Would you do that for someone who had acted like *that*? Jainan hadn't fought back in the vid. He could take out a charging bear with a tree branch, but he'd done nothing. His partner was an Imperial Prince.

Kiem compulsively started and stopped another sliver of the

vid. The two figures hung frozen at the far end of the corridor, inexorably headed to their room. Jainan had *loved* Taam.

No, he realized. Jainan had never said that.

It hadn't been grief that made Jainan gaunt and drawn when Kiem first met him. He had looked the same in the vid: pinched and strained and entirely focused on Taam. Like—*fuck*—like he'd been entirely focused on Kiem the first few days after the wedding. Those odd pauses. The messages linked to Taam's account. The way Jainan had *never said no*.

If Kiem had known him as he did now, he would have noticed that. If he'd had the intelligence of a block of wood, he would have noticed it. He was the most unobservant, most world-shatteringly useless—

His wristband chimed with a reminder. His arm jerked as if it had burned him.

Tiny lettering projected itself over his wrist, reminding him he and Jainan were nearly late for the Advisory Council dinner. He stared at it for a long time. The stinging feeling under his skin made it a punishment to hold still.

He shoved his hands in his pockets and turned around. He needed to talk to Jainan.

CHAPTER 23

Jainan dressed for dinner and set off a few minutes early, hoping to catch Kiem beforehand; he must be told immediately about Jainan's conversation with the Auditor and should also know about the refinery. Through the open doors of the station's banqueting hall, Jainan could see there was already a crowd of people at dinner, none of whom he knew. He slipped into one of the empty, elegantly decorated anterooms off the corridor and checked the messages on his wristband while he waited. Nothing from the Emperor's office yet.

When Kiem arrived, one look at his face made everything run out of Jainan's mind like water.

"Kiem?" Jainan dropped his wrist and the screen disappeared. The chair he was in skidded back an inch as he scrambled to his feet, stumbling in the lower gravity. "Is something—what's wrong?"

Kiem didn't answer. He was standing in the doorway, so the door couldn't close.

"Are you ill?" Jainan took a step forward. The lines on Kiem's face were tight and strained. "I'll—I'll call someone." *Sit down,* he wanted to say, but Kiem's expression stopped him.

Kiem tried to speak, but had to clear his throat. "I—Jainan. We need to talk. About." He stopped.

Jainan froze as his mind crowded with all the things he could have told Kiem but hadn't. Some minor transgression—someone he had spoken to or some way he had embarrassed both of them—no, that couldn't be it. He struggled to remember that Kiem wasn't like that. "About what?"

Kiem stepped in so the door shut behind him. "You and Taam."

Jainan had never heard Kiem's voice sound like that before. It could still be anything, he told himself. The air around him felt sticky. It terrified him that he was falling back so often on his last line of defense—*I don't want to talk about it*—but he started framing it anyway. "I—"

"I found out how things were between you."

No. Jainan's next words dried up on his tongue. Cloying shame filled his mouth, his throat; it bound his feet to the floor.

"Jainan?"

"It's not true," he managed.

"*What's* not true?" Kiem said. There was a pause as if, in the natural flow of conversation, he expected Jainan to reply. "Jainan, I saw it!" He must have caught Jainan's flash of panic, because he frowned and said, "You were—you were arguing. It was a security feed." It was obvious he didn't want to say the next bit, but Kiem had never learned to hold the slightest thing back. "He shoved you into the wall."

It's not what you think. It was less than a handful of times. That sounded so pathetic Jainan discarded it. He shook his head, fighting a wave of nausea.

"Jainan, come on!" Was Kiem raising his voice, or was Jainan imagining it? He couldn't tell; his ears were buzzing. "I worked out Taam must have been the one who got your security clearance revoked. See, you're not even surprised. You knew that—oh, for fuck's sake, *Aren* knew, didn't he? Taam's friends knew how he treated you. It was staring me in the face. *Fuck.*"

Jainan stood like a statue, one hand resting on the back of the chair. His eyes compulsively followed Kiem as he paced from wall to wall: he was blurred, a moving shape that Jainan couldn't focus on.

"Aren knew," Kiem said, persevering. "Why did he act so friendly? To—make fun of us or something? To play with our heads? Why didn't you say anything? I had to find this out from Audel stealing a vid from Kingfisher!"

Jainan barely understood his last sentence, but it didn't matter. It blinded him, the sudden, awful image of Audel and Kiem dissecting Jainan's list of private humiliations, Kiem like this—distressed and disgusted at the same time. You couldn't love someone when you had trawled through their sordid problems like this. They were only an object of pity. *He* was an object of pity.

Kiem was still talking. Jainan couldn't make sense of it anymore. He imagined the garbled noise as a river below him, and he himself balanced on a dam that was cracking under his feet. Everything he'd built was falling apart. Everything he had tried to do to save the treaty was rendered useless by his failure. He thought he'd been dignified, he thought he'd been brave—really, he had just been in denial about the fact that *nothing* could save his dignity when people found out. Nothing could make him more than a sob story.

"Jainan?" Kiem said. He had stopped; he was only a pace away from Jainan. "You look—Jainan!" The name was like a whip. Kiem reached out.

Jainan pulled away. His failure, his terror was coming to a point in his head like a storm building. He hadn't even moved consciously. The pressure swelled unbearably, shot through with fury and panic, and what came out of his mouth was, *"How dare you?"*

Kiem's mouth formed the start of *what,* but didn't finish it.

"I asked you not to talk about it! You had no right!" Kiem actually flinched. But he had stopped talking, finally, and Jainan didn't dare let him start again. Jainan was shaking. "This was *my* marriage, *my* past—did you think you were entitled to it just because I married you? How dare you!"

"I didn't—I wouldn't—" Jainan could barely see Kiem through

the haze that blurred everything, but Kiem's voice was agonized. Sweet God, it was so much easier to be angry than afraid.

"I have to go," Jainan said. It sounded lame and faltering. "I have to go and get—I have to go."

He struck out rapidly for the exit. Kiem moved as Jainan did, his arm outstretched to catch Jainan's elbow. "Wait! Jainan!"

Jainan shoved the door aside and burst into the hallway, now crowded with dinner guests. People were looking at them. They were in the way of the exit; Jainan had to stop for an instant, trapped. He turned his head.

"I . . . I understand," Kiem said. The tight lines at the corners of his eyes were back. "I'm, I'm sorry. I'll leave you alone."

And then he was gone.

It happened so fast that Jainan didn't even realize Kiem had really gone until the murmur of chatter started up again. People's sidelong glances were turning into outright stares. Kiem had pushed through the crowd, not toward their guest suite, but deep into the station in the opposite direction.

Jainan looked at the floor, reflexively straightened his shirt, and walked through the crowd without meeting anyone's eyes. The next thing he knew, he was back in their rooms. Their silent, white, empty rooms, with just the ringing memory of what he had done. He crumpled into a chair.

Who would Kiem tell? With Taam there had always been the safety of knowing that both of them would rather crawl over broken glass than shame themselves in public. Kiem didn't care about his reputation. Would he talk to the press? Jainan couldn't stop him. He could not go back to Thea. He pressed his hand over his face and tried not to think about the fact there was no way *out*.

He would have to talk to Kiem later and attempt to salvage something. They still had to try to find some way of fixing the treaty—though it seemed more and more unlikely with every hour. Jainan felt the weight of the station atmosphere on his shoulders as if it had substance and mass, pressing down. Was his marriage dissolved? How likely was it that Kiem would keep up the charade after a scene like that?

The door chimed. Jainan looked up, adrenaline surging through him until he realized that the door would have just opened for Kiem without announcement. He sank back. He was not going to receive company on Kiem's behalf, not now.

The chime sounded again. It cut off halfway through, with a harsh beep, and the door opened of its own accord. An arm slammed against it as it drew fully aside and someone slapped a manual lock on the frame to keep it open.

Jainan was only halfway to his feet by the time the visitors entered. There were five of them: a corporal strode into the middle of the room, and his four soldiers fanned out into a loose semicircle. Their incapacitator guns were out. They weren't pointed, but everyone's attention was on Jainan.

Jainan stopped his instinctive scramble to stand and rose the rest of the way slowly. He was in a place beyond emotion. "Ah. Good evening."

"Count Jainan." The corporal didn't even incline his head. "I would be obliged if you refrained from sudden movements."

"To what do I owe this visit?"

"You are under arrest for the murder of Prince Taam," the corporal said, "and the attempted murder of Prince Kiem."

Jainan breathed in slowly. Everything was suddenly very simple: the smallest of movements, like the wavering mouth of the capper nearest him, had a sharp, almost otherworldly clarity. A direct hit on the skull would be fatal; anywhere else would knock him out. "I see," he said. "If this is legitimate, then you will not mind if I inform my partner."

He slammed his hand down toward his wristband to trigger an emergency command. Before he could finish the sequence, the mouth of the capper blazed with a shimmer of force. It hit Jainan's chest; he fell back, his conscious thoughts ripping like wet tissue. He had failed in so many ways. It was almost a relief to black out.

The line between consciousness and sleep was very thin, and Jainan was still unsure he'd crossed it when he opened his eyes. His vision was hazy. He felt some sort of restraints around his wrists and padding under his back. He was lying down.

What was terrifying was that the dizziness didn't clear any further as he woke. The slightest movement of his head left him drained and sick. He forced himself to try and look around.

At first he thought he was back on one of his student manufacturing placements. The space felt enormous, like a warehouse, though most of it was dark. The gravity was still weak. The only illumination came from a single, jury-rigged floodlight that formed a pool of brightness around a figure perched on the side of a crate, working from a wrist-screen.

Aren.

"Oh hell, already?" Aren said. He idly wiped away the screen. "I'm still waiting for the technician. You've got the constitution of a fucking elephant, anyone ever tell you that?"

Jainan was battling his nausea too hard to answer immediately. The bed he was lying on felt like a hospital bed, with removable guardrails on each side and clips at the foot to hold machinery. He couldn't tell if it was normal to feel this way; he had never been on the wrong end of an incapacitator gun before. He took a deep breath against the rising dizziness and concentrated hard. "We didn't even suspect you," he said. "Why move now?"

Aren pulled his legs up and sat cross-legged on the crate, somehow balancing on the very edge. "Okay, well, here's the thing," he said. "When you send a meeting request to the Emperor's aides and mention the fucking *army,* the first thing they do is get in touch with the supreme commander to find out what's going on.

And the first thing the supreme commander does is *come down on me like a ton of fucking bricks* for not maintaining a minimum level of operational secrecy around Kingfisher. So, thanks for that! Really made my day."

Jainan turned around the phrase *operational secrecy* in his head, where it felt jagged and painful. Kingfisher—not just Taam, but his whole operation—had something to hide, and the supreme commander knew about it. "General Fenrik knew what Taam was doing."

"*Yes*, well done, congratulations on catching up with the rest of us. All those years with Taam really did fry your brain, didn't they? Mind you, I always felt my IQ dropping when I sat down to dinner with him—a boor in the grand tradition of all royal boors." Aren moved again, dangling his legs off the crate. "No wonder Fenrik was so fond of him. Like to like."

Jainan tried to sit up. That was when he realized the cuffs and the guardrails were totally unnecessary; he could barely manage to make his muscles acknowledge him, let alone obey him. There were odd-shaped spikes around the bed, which Jainan would guess projected some sort of field, but they didn't seem to be turned on. He let himself lie back, slowly cataloging his bruises. "Who killed him?"

Aren raised an eyebrow. "Wasn't it you?"

Jainan stayed silent. He finally identified a pinching sensation in his arm as an intravenous patch, which presumably had something to do with the dizziness. If he could roll onto the floor he might yank it out, but with his hands tied, that was a plan with a short shelf life.

Aren broke the silence by laughing abruptly. "No. Our esteemed General Fenrik *still* doesn't know who killed Taam. He gave me the authority to run a confidential investigation, isn't that ironic? I've given him some perfect suspects. It doesn't look like he's going to buy Audel, though, and neither will Internal Security, so you'll have to do instead."

Jainan tasted copper in his mouth. "Why?"

"Why you? Well, you've reached the status of *royal fucking pain*." That wasn't what Jainan had meant, but he didn't interrupt. Aren's heels beat against the crate with a jagged, suppressed energy. "I didn't even realize how much you'd pulled out of those files we released to the College. Taam redacted the shit out of them before he let them go, but apparently not well enough. That got Internal Security sniffing around and Internal Security is hard for even General Fenrik to squash. Then just when I had the perfect plan for you to take the fall for *all* of it, you got in the fucking flybug and ended up in the crash with Prince Kiem. It's like you're out to get me. I don't get how you can be such a miserable bundle of wet atmosphere and still get in my way all the time. Holy *fuck*, it feels good to stop acting," Aren added. "I always envied that in Taam, you know. He could just say what he thought to your face. I have to bite my tongue and smile because I'm not an Imperial bloody Prince and the rules aren't the same."

Aren tapped his heels against the crate he was sitting on, confident and assured, the collar of his dress uniform loosened for comfort. There was something charismatic about him, Jainan thought distantly; that must be how he'd reached his current rank. Jainan hadn't realized how much he was holding back before. Aren in full flow could have talked Kiem to a standstill.

Jainan tried to sort through what he'd said. It sounded like an admission of guilt, but there was something Jainan was missing; some fundamental part of the equation. Aren seemed startlingly sure he could still blame Jainan for Taam's death. Jainan squeezed his eyes shut to try and deal with the headache. "What are you hiding in the refinery?" He suddenly jerked his head around, trying to see farther in the dark. "I suppose that's here, isn't it? We're in the refinery."

"Hah!" Aren said. "So you got that far. What gave that away? I caught your Sefalan comms specialist sniffing around one of our proxies. Was it her?"

Jainan nearly struggled into sitting up through pure adrenaline. "Have you done something to Bel?"

"She's fine," Aren said, smiling faintly. "Just making sure nobody interferes."

Jainan was holding on to his self-control with his fingernails. "Interferes in *what*?"

Aren checked his wristband. "Hey, my technician's here," he said. Something beeped in the distance, swallowed by the dark. The echo made Jainan double his mental estimate of the size of the space. Aren gestured a command sign and a door clanked open in a distant wall. Light started to glow overhead with the whine of industrial floodlights. "Suppose you might as well see."

White light flooded the space. Jainan squinted with suddenly painful eyes. The warehouse could have fit half of Carissi Station's facilities. It was full, despite its vast size. At first Jainan didn't recognize the shapes—metal and crystal and hydraulics—but once he understood one, the others fell into place like terrible dominoes, one after the other.

Jainan stared around Kingfisher's stockpile, his nausea forgotten. His body felt like a drone he could no longer control. He heard himself say, "You want a war."

CHAPTER 24

The staterooms next to the Observation Hall were a wasteland of half-laid white carpet and cleaning supplies in the dim night-cycle lighting. They weren't open to the public until the Unification ceremonies in four days' time, which was why Kiem had ended up there. He couldn't face anyone right now. He sat on a stack of carpet rolls in the dry, musty station air and wished for the clean cold of an Iskat winter night.

Kiem spun through his wristband, his fingers clumsy and slow. He'd been sitting here for too long, and he still hadn't worked out what to do next. He wasn't even supposed to be here. He should go back to the residential modules.

He didn't. He spun compulsively between a short list of names projected from his wristband: Bel, Jainan's sister Ressid, the Thean Ambassador. Bel was in the shuttleport and not answering. It wasn't even fair to try and get hold of her when she was worried herself, but Kiem had been calling her anyway because he was desperate. He hadn't yet brought himself to try the Theans. What could he even say? *We've failed Jainan in every way, but I can't tell you anything more than that?*

He dropped his wristband and let it jar against his leg while it was still scrolling. The display broke up and disappeared. The door of the Observation Hall yawned opposite, waiting to be decorated for the ceremonies, and starlight played across the floor.

His wristband lit up again. Kiem glanced briefly at the caller—not Bel or Jainan—and didn't activate it. This was the first time in his life he'd ignored this many calls in a row.

"Is everything all right there, sir?"

Kiem looked up as a security guard loomed out of the darkness with a flashlight, carefully picking his way through the decorating supplies. "Everything's—fine. Just getting some air."

"In the dark, sir?" The security guard looked like a palace transplant, brought up for the ceremonies. He squinted at Kiem's face. "Oh—Your Highness. Apologies. I'll leave you to it."

A laugh rose up in Kiem's throat that felt like he was choking. He should make an excuse. He didn't.

"Your band, sir," the guard added helpfully as he moved off again.

It wasn't as if Kiem couldn't see it flashing again, shockingly bright against the night-cycle glow. He glanced down, ready to ignore it again—but it wasn't a call, it was a message. From Bel.

He turned away, the security guard already forgotten, and jabbed again to call her. No reply. He groaned and flipped to the message.

Can't talk, it said, *but are you ignoring the Emperor or something? Her Private Office called me four times.*

"Urgh, that's not important! Answer your calls!" Kiem said to the screen. But he had a sudden vision of Bel's face if she'd heard that, and he glanced at the message again, coming to his senses. The *Emperor*?

When he looked properly at the call list, half of them were from someone in the Emperor's Private Office. The last time those people had called him, he'd been summoned to an Imperial receiving room and told he was getting married. Nothing was a good enough excuse for ignoring the Emperor.

He called them back. An aide's face appeared on the display almost immediately. It was the middle of the night in Arlusk, but the office behind them was oddly busy. "Your Highness," said the very proper aide in a voice that was pointedly not impatient. "We have been trying to reach you. The Emperor would like to see you. Please proceed to the remote meeting facilities in your station's secured area."

"What? Why?" Kiem said. The aide's head tilted, deflecting the question. If they were allowed to give out that information, they would have given it already. Kiem amended the question. "When?"

"She expected to see you some time ago," the aide said. Even now that caused a minor echo of panic in Kiem's head. "Now would be a good time."

Four and a half minutes later, Kiem was ushered into the station's armored core. Another guard opened a heavily shielded door to a small suite of comms rooms. Kiem lifted his hand to register his bios at the thinner door behind it, but the door opened before he'd even touched the pad. He pulled back reflexively, screwed up so tense everything came as a shock.

The man who came through was tall and bony with white hair severely clipped in a military cut. The only signs of his rank were the six gold circles of the supreme commander on the breast of his uniform. Kiem stepped back to make room. He hadn't realized Fenrik was on the station; it must have something to do with Kingfisher. His mother had brought him up to be polite to officers, so he gave a belated nod. "General."

General Fenrik turned his head stiffly as he passed. Like the Emperor, he had passed his century mark a while ago. It took him only a split second to place Kiem, and the expression on his face suggested the information he was pulling up on him was not favorable. "Oh hellfire, it's you this is all about?" he said. "Tegnar's boy. I'd forgotten you."

"Um," Kiem said. "Sorry, I'm not up to speed here."

General Fenrik snorted. "Go in." He turned away, his back military-straight. As he turned, Kiem caught sight of his wooden Imperial insignia, and was suddenly reminded of the same insignia on Aren's uniform. Taam had had a circle of young officer friends, part of the backbone of the army. They had *known* Jainan. Why had nobody reported anything? What was wrong with the army this man ran?

"General," Kiem said.

General Fenrik stopped and looked back, impatient and forbidding. "What?"

Kiem stared at him. There was nothing he could say, he realized, unless he was planning to tell Fenrik everything. "No," he said. "Never mind." In the face of Fenrik's renewed frown, he turned and pressed his hand to the entrance panel to start his bios checks.

His eyes took a moment to adjust to the holos covering the comms room. The Emperor had apparently projected her entire inner study. Kiem had never seen her in these surroundings; whenever she talked to him, it was a stiff, formal occasion in her receiving rooms where he sat on an uncomfortable gilded chair to be grilled on his latest unsanctioned interview. But this room was different; this was the Emperor's working room. It was severely plain, no gold at all, with unadorned walls that probably disguised some serious soundproofing back on Iskat. As Kiem crossed the threshold, his wristband went dark. A holo table overlapped awkwardly with the real one on the station, covered with neat squares of projected files. The chairs pulled up to the table weren't even vidchairs, so the whole room must be bristling with sensors. Three projections sat around the table: the Emperor, an aide, and Chief Agent Rakal.

"There you are, Kiem," the Emperor said, cutting across something Rakal was saying. Rakal fell silent immediately. "Where have you been? Sit down."

Kiem bowed, muttered an apology, and pulled out a chair that he hoped was real. That wasn't as bad as it could have been: the Emperor had once kept him standing outside for three hours after he'd been late to an appointment. But it wasn't reassuring either. He sat on the edge of his seat, tense, and looked between them for clues. "May I ask why I was summoned, Your Majesty?"

"I summoned you a good while ago," the Emperor said, her tone crisp. "General Fenrik tells me the army has apprehended your Thean partner on suspicion of doing away with Taam."

Kiem looked at her blankly. The words lined up, but they didn't make any sense. "I don't understand."

"And attempting to do away with you, apparently." The Emperor was always brusque; now there was a note of arch impatience. "Did you notice?"

"Your Majesty," Rakal murmured, in what sounded like a protest.

"Do—*what*? No! Nothing like that happened! Where the hell has this come from?" Shock poured over Kiem in waves. "You've *arrested* Jainan?"

"The armed forces have arrested him," the Emperor said. "How many times do you need it repeated? Compose yourself," she added sharply, as Kiem half rose from his chair.

Kiem dropped back into his seat, realizing he didn't have the information he needed. "Where have you taken Jainan?"

Rakal gave a discreet cough. The table was almost too high for them; they rested their hands on the edge of it as they leaned forward. "*We* have not taken him anywhere, Your Highness," they said. "The military is not the civil authority."

Everything in Kiem's head was protesting, but this rang a faint bell. "That's why General Fenrik was here?" he said. "The military has got him?" He appealed directly to the Emperor. "Ma'am, you're still the Emperor. You can order him to let Jainan go."

It was Rakal who answered again. "Do you recall Count Jainan's behavior around the time of your flyer crash? I believe it was only a few days ago."

It took Kiem a moment to form words out of his shocked and furious bafflement. "Jainan was *in the flybug*!"

Neither the Emperor nor Rakal responded. Kiem had the feeling he wasn't telling them anything they didn't know. There was a moment's silence, and in it Rakal looked at the Emperor. "You see, ma'am," they murmured. "If Count Jainan felt that much animosity toward him, Prince Kiem should have noticed something."

"So noted," the Emperor said, "but not conclusive. I need something for the Resolution, even aside from these wretched remnants."

"Conclusive of what?" Kiem said. "None of this is true! Jainan killing Taam? Trying to kill *me*? This is—this is bullshit!"

"Kiem, if you comport yourself like an adult who has been called in for a briefing, you will receive the briefing I summoned you for," the Emperor said irritably. "If you insist on acting like a child in a tantrum, then you may leave."

Kiem's mouth shaped itself around a response, but he knew she was fully capable of throwing him out. Getting himself cut out here wouldn't help. *Jainan* would have been able to control himself. He shut his mouth and put his hands on his knees. "Of course, ma'am. I would very much like to know what's going on."

The Emperor spared him a fraction of a nod. "This investigation has been dragged out for far too long. I have been given a complete array of half-baked theories, from 'accident' to 'anarchist' to 'insider at the flybug manufacturer.'" Here she gave Rakal a censorious look. They winced. "However, Internal Security *finally* seems to have narrowed it down to either an academic with a grudge—dishonorably discharged, I understand—or your partner Jainan. General Fenrik tells me his investigators have proved it was Jainan from biological traces in the workings of your flybug—"

"Which could have been planted," Kiem said, controlling his voice with a supreme effort. "Ma'am."

"I have seen the case the Kingfisher investigation team put together," the Emperor said. "It is . . . not unconvincing."

"Where is he?" Kiem said. "If Internal Security doesn't have him, then where has Fenrik taken him?"

"A secure site," the Emperor said brusquely. "I fail to see why you need to know more than that. Rakal here has been petitioning me to transfer Jainan and his case to civil authority. General Fenrik is convinced it will come under a military tribunal, as the murder victim was a serving officer."

"I reiterate my opinion, ma'am," Rakal said. "This is not legitimately a military matter."

"Would Internal Security be any better?" Kiem said, roused. "*You* didn't even realize the security clearance flag came from—" He bit his tongue, suddenly realizing that wouldn't help at all.

"Prince Taam," Rakal said, measured. "Yes, my people found out who it originated with. There may have been more bad blood between Prince Taam and Count Jainan than we realized."

Bad blood. Kiem had a crushing view of how much the rest of the story would bolster the case against Jainan if it came out. "Jainan wouldn't kill anyone," he said. Somehow stating it baldly like that didn't seem to have the effect he wanted. "He's *innocent*. He could at least come home, couldn't he?" His mind filled with hiring lawyers, finding evidence, maybe cornering some army officers and shaking them until he found out what was going on.

Rakal's mouth tightened. Kiem saw the shared glance between them and the Emperor, and he knew he wasn't going to like the answer even before Rakal said, "Not if he remains with the military. Her majesty has decided there may be advantages if they conduct an interrogation. If it could be proven that Count Jainan acted alone, the Resolution might accept a replacement treaty representative." The Emperor appeared deep in thought and didn't move to speak. "I am opposed to this," Rakal added.

"*What advantages?*" Kiem said. "The military can't interrogate him!"

"They can," Rakal said quietly. "Effectively."

"And the civilian authorities legally cannot," the Emperor said. Kiem took a breath, but he had no words. The Emperor shook her head slightly as if shedding her vacillation. "No, Rakal, I have made my decision. If Jainan is innocent, they will get nothing usable from an interrogation and you can have the academic instead. If otherwise—that will clear up this part of the mess, and we can work on finding the damned remnants." Her mouth twitched down at the corner. "That lands us with a different mess, of course. But that is politics." She nodded to her aide, who made some sort of note on her special-issue wristband. "I will allow them two days. Kiem, you will cooperate with Rakal and with the military authorities when they require it. You will speak of this to no one: everything is under top level classification. Do you understand?"

"Ma'am," Kiem said, his voice only a thread.

"You will have to attend the run-up ceremonies by yourself," the Emperor said. "The worst of all possible outcomes, but it cannot be helped. I expect you to rise to the challenge. Dismissed."

Kiem's bow was even clumsier in comparison to Rakal's punctilious one, but the Emperor was already dictating orders to her aide and didn't notice. As they both left the room, Rakal's projection faded out at the threshold of the door.

Kiem's wristband woke up and flared into life again as he strode past the guards without speaking. He raised his fingers in a call command, counting in his head the seconds it would take Rakal to walk through the Emperor's outer office where her aides worked, all the way down the tower's elevators, and into the main corridor. Then he called.

He'd calculated accurately. When Rakal opened their screen, the corridor behind them was empty. They stopped, folded their arms, and tilted their chin up aggressively. "Say what you're going to say, Your Highness."

"What can they do to interrogate him?" Kiem said.

Rakal's shoulders were tense. "They have arrested him under military law. There are very few legal limitations, though I'm sure they're aware that if they don't acquire damning evidence, there will be serious consequences if a Thean representative turns out to have been physically harmed. Nevertheless."

"And you're *okay* with this?" Kiem demanded. "Everyone's

okay with this? Jainan *lives* for duty! He's probably never done anything illegal in his life!"

"The Emperor has given a direct order," Rakal said. "The civilian legal process should be followed for civilians, but what is Internal Security against the old guard?" There was a note of bitterness in their voice that threw Kiem off for a moment. The Emperor had called him *General* Fenrik, Kiem remembered, when she barely gave anyone else their title. General Fenrik was the Emperor's generation, back when the military had been vastly more powerful than the civil infrastructure. Rakal was young, could not be more than forty. "Count Jainan may not come to much harm."

"*May* not?"

Rakal glanced around before they answered. "There are drugs."

Kiem took a deep breath. "I'm not going to let this happen."

"I will not be drawn into this line of conversation," Rakal said. "We did not speak about this. However," they added. "If Jainan were to somehow . . . walk out of military custody, I believe that would change matters." They looked Kiem right in the eye. "The treaty situation is changing hour by hour. I believe if Jainan were to somehow leave, I would be able to keep his case under civil authority and stop him from going back in."

"Right," Kiem said. He took another breath, and said again, "Right."

Rakal gave him a hint of a nod.

Kiem canceled the call. Then he raised his wristband and spun up the Thean Ambassador. As he strode back to his and Jainan's guest suite, he wrote out, *Jainan falsely arrested. Petition for release,* and added a précis of everything the Emperor had said. He finished just as the door of his rooms shut behind him.

Then, and only then, he entered the high-urgency code that was only supposed to be used for a life-or-death situation, and called Bel.

He waited so long he started counting the seconds. A minute.

Ninety seconds. Eventually, though, the soft waiting pattern dissolved into Bel's face. She was in what looked like a privacy capsule at the shuttleport, distracted and drawn with worry. "Kiem?" She looked at him and behind him and seemed to reassure herself he wasn't in immediate danger. "I'm literally about to get on the shuttle, they're calling the passengers now. I can't talk."

"Jainan's been arrested," Kiem said. He could hear his voice crack. "They think he killed Taam and tried to kill me. I need to get him out before they interrogate him. I need your help."

Bel's eyes widened, but only for an instant before calculation spread across her face. "Let me guess," she said. "Major Saffer."

"I'm sorry," Kiem said. "You can still go tonight. Just delay by half a day, I'll book you on a new—What?"

"Saffer's somewhere behind this," Bel said. "And if you're worried about interrogation, that means the military have him. Hell fucking damn it."

"*Right*," said Kiem, who had rarely heard Bel swear like that before, but at least someone was having the right reaction. He didn't know where she'd gotten Aren's name from, but that wasn't the most important thing right now. "I need you. Just for half a day. A few hours."

She paused. Kiem realized he was gripping his wristband with his other hand, an old habit from when he was a child and thought you needed to keep holding it to make the other person's image stay there. The edges pressed into his fingers. "Please."

"Kiem," she said at last. "There's not a lot I can do. It's not going to help if you send me to talk to people. They'll need to hear from you. I'm really sorry."

"I'm not going to talk to people," Kiem said. "I'm going to find out where Jainan is and get him out." He lowered his voice, even in the privacy of his own room. "I'll cover you when it comes to the legalities, I swear, but I need you. I know you can get around entrance scanners. You did it for me when I lost my wristband last year. The Emperor's only given them two days, and they can't have gone down to Thea, so he has to be in the station or on one of the cluster modules. I'm going to find where they're holding him, and I'm going to come back with Jainan."

Bel had already covered her face with her hand. "Oh *fucking hell*."

Kiem could feel his momentum crumbling away from under his feet. He barreled on anyway, desperate. "I have to do this before they hurt him. There's stuff you don't know about Taam and—please. I know you need to get to your grandmother soon—"

"Stop," Bel said. Her voice was muffled behind her hand. "Stop, shut up, for the love of everything, *shut up*. There is no sick grandmother!"

Kiem stopped. "What?"

"I've been lying to you!" Bel said. Her voice was lower and faster now, almost a whisper. "I don't know where the hell my grandmother is, she was with the Black Shells last time I spoke to her. She's probably fine. Stop—stop *sympathizing*!"

That put a wrench even in Kiem's current panic. "Black Shells? Is that a monastery?"

"She's a raider!" Bel said. "Do I have to spell this out for you? The Black Shells is a conglom! Like the one I came from!"

"I don't—you—conglom?"

"Raider outfit!"

"Right," Kiem said and bit down on *I knew that*. His limited knowledge of Sefalan affairs wasn't the issue here. He tried not to feel like he was talking to someone else, someone who wasn't Bel at all. "Why did you need to lie to—" No. He found he didn't care. Bel was still the same person she'd been for all the time he'd known her, and she hadn't let him down in anything yet. She would have her reasons. "You know what, if you don't want me to know, I don't need to. But please, can it wait for just a few hours? I'll rebook you on the next shuttle out."

Bel was now staring at him. "You're an idiot. Don't you want to know why I'm going?"

"Did I do something?" Kiem said desperately. "Can I make up for it?"

"No!" Bel leaned in closer. She was still whispering, apparently not trusting the privacy capsule. "Did you hear the part where I said my grandmother split off with the Black Shells? Do you know that kind of trade usually runs in families? I was born on a Red Alpha ship! I was one of our system breakers for ten years! It was my job to break into shuttle communications networks so they couldn't use them when our ship attacked!"

This called for thought. Thought that Kiem couldn't really spare. "I've seen your resume," he said. That hadn't been on it.

"I faked nearly everything I gave you!" Bel said, in a whisper so vicious, it was almost a hiss. "You're not this slow on the uptake!"

"Oh, right, obviously," Kiem said. Every minute he couldn't get Bel to come back was a minute Jainan was still under arrest. "So . . . ? I thought you might have some friends that weren't totally aboveboard. You don't still do that stuff, do you? I know you."

Bel looked utterly taken aback for the first time since Kiem had known her. "*So?* I lied to get this job. I lied to that outfit you use to recommend people—charities are easy to fool. I used to be a raider, do you need this spelled out for you? I used you to get away and go straight!"

Kiem rubbed his hand across his forehead. "Listen, you can break the security protection on any palace system you've accessed," he said. "Or you take it to dodgy back-alley shops and it magically does what I've asked you to make it do. Of *course* you picked it up somewhere, I've always known you had some shortcuts. You're not doing anything bad, so I don't know why I should have cared."

"You will care when Saffer sends it to the media!"

"You're—wait, you're being blackmailed?" Kiem said. "By *Aren Saffer*? That's why you're leaving?"

Bel's mouth pursed shut. Her nod was almost imperceptible.

A wash of relief went over Kiem. "Oh, well, that's *fine* then." He knew he could outmaneuver Aren if it came to the media. "I'll call a journalist. We'll make up a story for you. Come back and help me get Jainan."

Bel looked at him, then something in her seemed to crack, and she covered her eyes with her hand. "You need help," she said. "No, I know Jainan needs help, but so do you, because you're clearly out of your mind. But I'm going to come back, and this is a conversation we're going to have later. Okay?"

"Okay! Yes!" Kiem said. "Come straight back. I'll meet you at our room."

"And you're still going to get me a replacement shuttle ticket even if Internal Security comes after me."

Please don't go, Kiem wanted to say. "No problem." He gave her a thumbs-up. "Anonymous and first class." She nodded and cut the call.

Raiders. Kiem let out a long breath. No wonder she hadn't wanted to give him her real history. He couldn't imagine Bel as part of a hijacker crew, but most of what Kiem knew about raiders came from vid dramas, so what did he know? And what did it *matter*? Since he'd offered Bel the aide post a year ago, she'd been in his corner every time he'd needed her. She was coming back now because he'd asked. He could at least keep her out of trouble afterward, even if it meant she was going to leave.

An emergency ping came from outside the door. Kiem opened it.

Gairad pulled herself from her slump against the corridor wall opposite, scrubbed the back of her hand over her swollen, watery eyes, and glared at him. "Where the hell were you? I couldn't find you! The bastards have taken Jainan!"

Kiem hadn't previously supposed an ally might come in the form of a tearful teenager with anti-Iskat pins on her jacket, but right at this moment he was prepared to consider her Heaven-sent. "You saw them? Who was it?"

Gairad's combative air weakened, as if she'd expected him

to argue. "I was coming here to talk to him, and I saw him get dragged out. He wasn't conscious. What the fuck is going on? They looked military."

"Where did they go?" Kiem said urgently.

"Shuttle docks," Gairad said. She gave the long, ugly sniff of someone determined to be functional. "Unmarked short-range capsule. I tracked the first bit of its flight on the public system."

"You are a vision of staggering brilliance," Kiem said fervently. "Come in. When Bel gets here we're making a battle plan." He passed her a handkerchief and set the door to admit Bel and no one else.

By the time she arrived, Kiem and Gairad had trawled his room in the hope that Jainan had left a message, then had a tense conversation with the Thean Ambassador, and now were obsessively poring over the flight clues Gairad had collected. "I'm back," Bel said from the door, her luggage hovering behind her. She sounded tentative.

Kiem didn't even think before he shoved back his chair and hugged her. She obviously wasn't expecting it, and it only occurred to him he probably shouldn't have done it after he had, but Bel was already patting him cautiously on the back. "You are the only person right now apart from Jainan that could make me feel better," Kiem said. "That wasn't workplace-appropriate, was it. Sorry. I have some ideas about your blackmail thing—"

"Later," Bel said. She let down her capsule, neatened her tunic, and straightened up, gathering her confidence back with the movement. "Sorry I'm late. I stopped to pick some things up. What do you know about Jainan?"

Gairad looked up as well, so Kiem told both of them. He started with the emergency conference with the Emperor and Rakal, adding what Rakal had said about interrogation, but his explanation was jagged and all over the place. He skipped back to Audel's hacking attempts and the folder of blackmail material they'd found on Aren and the other senior officers. Then he stopped. "Sorry,

Gairad, give us a minute," he said, and pulled Bel aside to tell her about the video.

As Bel listened, her expression grew flatter. "Explains a lot" was all she said.

"You *knew*?"

"No," Bel said. "I felt something was wrong, but you can probably guess why I wasn't going to push someone to give up their secrets. We all have something to hide. I think Saffer knew, though."

Saffer. Everything came back to Aren Saffer, Taam's best friend. "And he was blackmailing you?"

Bel glanced at Gairad, who was hunched over the flight plan and scowling as if she could intimidate it into giving her Jainan's exact coordinates. "That shithead was in deep enough with Evn Afkeli and the Blue Star to pick up that I'm a raider. I thought he was just scared I'd figure him out. I should have realized he had a reason to make me leave just now—but I didn't know he was going after Jainan." She eyed Kiem. "Jury's out, but I'm thinking he may have misjudged the blackmail."

"He's going to regret he ever tried it," Kiem said. "If I catch him near Jainan, I'm going to haul him out by his shiny collar tabs and dump him on the Emperor's lap so she can end him. Or on Rakal. No, he'd flatten Rakal. Come and look at this."

He enlarged the screen with a jab and threw Gairad's flight plan up on the wall alongside an image of the cluster. The great bulk of Carissi Station swam among the automated plants and minor habitats like a whale among a gleaming school of fish. The Kingfisher refinery sailed at the edge of the school.

Bel tapped the refinery. "He has to be here," she said. "It's the only military-owned habitat, and we know he's not on the station. Got an up-to-date schematic?" she added, without much hope.

"Yes," Gairad said unexpectedly. She opened up a diagram of the refinery bristling with annotations. "The mass readings are off, but I figured it out. There has to be a section here." One of the annotations glowed red, showing a storage module slotted in at the back of the central cylinder. "Shielded. But it has to be there or the rotation of the whole habitat would be off."

"Nice work," Bel said approvingly. "Shielded clandestine module. That's where I'd put my high-value prisoners."

Hearing *high-value prisoners* felt like someone was scraping a nail down Kiem's spine. He steeled himself not to show that. "If I can get you there, can you break in?"

"Depends," Bel said. She traced some of the antennae that extended from the refinery. "I can brute-force most door models, as long as they're not brand-new. But there'll be monitoring and alarm fields before we even get there—if our shuttle doesn't have the right keys built into it, any alarms will go straight to their control room."

"So we need a military shuttle," Kiem said slowly.

"Yes. Do you have one hanging above your bed?"

"I'll see what I can do," Kiem said. There was an urgent, fizzing feeling under his skin as possibilities unfolded in his mind. "Listen, if anyone asks you afterward: I ordered you into this. You didn't have a choice."

Bel rolled her eyes. "We'll have an uphill job to convince them you're capable of making threats. But keep the kid out of this."

"I'm *eighteen*," Gairad said. "I'm coming too."

Bel opened her mouth, but Kiem got there first. "Yeah, okay," he said. "Just don't get hurt, or you're another diplomatic incident." Bel gave him an exasperated look, and Kiem raised his hands placatingly. "If it were me, I'd never forgive myself if I didn't go and—and something happened."

"Ugh, if we have to," Bel said. "I'm not arming her, though."

"What?" Kiem said. "Arming her?"

Bel leaned down to open her vacuum capsule. She pushed aside clothes and devices until she reached something at the base and gestured a command sequence. The side of the vacuum capsule clicked open in a way Kiem was fairly sure wasn't standard—but he recognized that capsule. He was fairly sure she'd had it when she arrived on Iskat. Inside the false compartment nestled two lumps protected by layers of gray sheeting. Bel unwrapped one. "Seen one of these before? It's an incapacitator gun."

The electric feeling in Kiem's blood grew stronger. This was a bad idea, but he was all out of good ones. He held out his hands and gestured for her to toss it over. "I know what a capper is."

"From vids?"

"My mother." Kiem caught it when Bel threw it. "She sent me to army cadet camp one horrible month when I was sixteen." The capper was oddly light in his hands. He'd forgotten what these things felt like.

Bel eyed him dubiously. "So you can use one?"

"There was a reason they sent me home early," Kiem said. He lined up the sight.

"Don't hold the trigger like that!" Bel said. Gairad leaned away. "Gods, okay, I'm rethinking my position on arming the kid."

Kiem lowered it. "It doesn't matter. We're only going to use them for bluffing, okay? Nobody gets hurt."

"Sure, that will go down well," Bel said. "'Yes, Your Majesty, we *did* steal a shuttle and break into a military base, but nobody got hurt, so that's all right.'"

Kiem forced himself to shrug and reached for a smile. "Here's the way I see it," he said, in a totally reasonable voice that for some reason made both Bel and Gairad look at him warily. "If they didn't want us to break in, they shouldn't have tried holding Jainan there. Let's make them reconsider."

CHAPTER 25

"I wouldn't call it a war," Aren said.

There was a terrible brilliance to him, sitting casually with the warehouse lights casting a halo of white around his hair, in the middle of a weapons stockpile that could take out a small continent. Jainan forced his voice to stay under control. "Then what would you call it?"

"A quick rebalancing of power," Aren said. "A tactical strike, if you like. No offense, but Thea has the military capability of a preschooler with a hangover. We'd barely have to take two cities before you sued for peace. You set yourselves up for this, you know," he added. "If you hadn't kicked up so much fuss about your system resources, Kingfisher might still be a mining operation." He laughed. "No, I take that back, we'd still have the Resolution to deal with."

The remnants. There was a thick lead case beside Aren, the type Jainan had seen protecting radioactive samples. "You stole the missing remnants?"

"*Stole?*" Aren said. "I'm offended. Do you know how much money Taam and Fenrik siphoned from the Kingfisher budgets to secure those? We bought the Sefalan ones off the raiders and had to bribe some civilians for the others. You could say we bought them fair and square." He patted the case. Jainan couldn't feel anything, but didn't know if that meant lead worked as a shielding material or not; he felt so wrung-out that he might not have registered it if a full-size link opened up next to him.

"You don't just want to start a war with Thea," Jainan said flatly. "You want to start a war with the Resolution. You're mad."

"Tell that to General Fenrik," Aren said, grinning. "You can see his point. First we deal with the vassals, then when Iskat isn't distracted by all this compromising, we get independence from the Resolution. We only have one link to defend, after all—a natural chokepoint. What's the use of having an army if you never let them fight?"

"The Galactics will laugh," Jainan said, with a rising sense of dread that nothing he said was cutting through the madness. "This will help you take Thea, but every weapon in the sector will do nothing against a power that has a million ships. We're an *afterthought* to them."

"Oh, forget the conventional weapons. These"—Aren made an expansive, dismissive gesture at the military hardware stacked around them—"are going to be obsolete once we've dealt with the vassals. The remnants let you get into people's *minds*. Give us a few months to develop weapons around them, and imagine what we can do with that. We can defend the link as long as we like."

"These were General Fenrik's orders?" Jainan asked. The drugs made his tongue thick and dry in his mouth. "To annex Thea and sabotage the Resolution treaty?"

"Fenrik's an old-school bully," Aren said reflectively, "but he's right, you know. Why should we hamstring ourselves when other powers get away with it all the time? The Resolution is a collection of hypocrites. They go after the weak sectors and leave the others to do as they like. Other planets have worked out how to weaponize their remnants, you know. An Orshan commander can take over your mind from across the room. The ruling class of the High Chain are near *gods*. The Resolution itself uses remnants to train their scouts—how else could they pilot ships through the link? They only enforce the rules on backwaters like us."

There were footsteps approaching, but Jainan couldn't turn his head far enough to see who it was. He swallowed and tried to make sense of the weapons he could see. He knew very little about military hardware, but he could recognize combat drones and energy weapons when he saw them. This wasn't about him, or Kiem, or even Taam. He could see no way of getting this information out to anyone else. Despair pressed on his chest like a clamp. "You think it's because Iskat is too timid to take what it wants."

"The Resolution never helped Thea," Aren said. "I don't see why you'd want to defend them."

"That doesn't mean I'm happier if all the power sits with you and your commanders," Jainan said hoarsely. "This is a war crime."

"Oh, no, don't get me wrong, I agree," Aren said. "Which makes it *gloriously* hypocritical that when I started skimming my own percentage off the top, Taam found out and threatened to rat me out to Fenrik. Invading Thea without telling the Emperor is fine, apparently, but Heaven forbid someone tries their hand at *personal enrichment.*"

So that was why Aren killed Taam, Jainan thought. He felt numb. In the middle of Taam's grand scheme to bring Thea to heel and start a new, glorious chapter, he'd caught Aren with his hand in the cookie jar and got himself killed for it. Taam had never known when to be subtle.

Aren slid off the crate and to his feet, looking at someone Jainan couldn't see. "You're late."

"Sorry, sir," a gravelly voice said. A woman in a trooper's uniform came into Jainan's field of vision, carefully putting on some antistatic gloves. "Came as soon as I got the order."

Jainan had thought he was beyond fear, but a thread of it sprang up as she approached. Aren wouldn't have told him this if he expected Jainan to remain alive to talk about it. He forced himself to keep his eyes on Aren. "What's the point of this? You can't expect Internal Security and Fenrik to both blame me. Your evidence is too thin, and my death in custody will look suspicious."

"I don't actually want you to die," Aren said briskly. He brushed off his uniform fastidiously, as if bringing the conversation to a close. "I just need someone to take the fall for Taam's death and for the money I borrowed. Then Fenrik can get on with annexing Thea, the Resolution treaty will fall apart, and everything will be back on track."

The trooper was doing something to a machine beside him. Jainan felt a coolness spreading from the patch in his arm and started to breathe faster as he realized it was a sedative. The woman picked up something and turned around; Jainan took a second to recognize it as a medical helmet. It was more complex than the ones he'd seen in hospitals.

He was closer to losing cognitive thought than he'd realized—the new sedative had started to work terrifyingly fast—but he finally put the pieces together with the odd spikes around the bed. "This is the Tau field." No wonder Aren thought he could get Jainan to take the blame. If he had a genuine trained interrogator, a Tau field could make Jainan believe anything. He would implicate *himself*.

"Give the man a medal," Aren said to the world at large, "he's finally caught up." Jainan tried to roll off the bed as the woman approached him with the helmet, but the new sedative on top of the incapacitator shot was too much. The guardrail jammed into his shoulder. *At least they haven't taken Kiem,* he told himself. The last thing he heard was Aren in the distance, clear as a bell, say, "Now, if you'll both excuse me. I have to go and drink champagne with the fucking diplomats."

The noise was like standing underneath a shuttle burner as it ignited. Jainan floated paralyzed in the sea of hammering sound, convinced every scrap of his consciousness was unravelling piece by piece. He tried to scream. He couldn't tell if he'd succeeded or not, so he tried again. His throat was raw before he stopped. He shut his eyes.

When he opened them again, he was upright and standing in front of the palace.

The sky overhead was the bright, clear blue of summer. Of course it was summer, he thought uneasily, why would it be anything else? He rubbed his shoulder for warmth; a nervous tic he'd developed over his first Iskat winter.

A flyer was pulling into the driveway. Jainan's head twitched up for the dozenth time. This time he was rewarded, because when it stopped in front of the palace, the first figure that emerged was Taam's aide, who held the door and saluted as Taam disembarked.

Jainan pulled a smile onto his face as he went over and found to his relief it was genuine. They had argued before Taam left— Jainan could not seem to stop causing arguments—but Taam gave a characteristic half smile and beckoned him to hurry. When Jainan reached him, Taam slung an arm around him and clapped him on the back, then pushed him away, holding him at arm's length. "All right, you don't have to be all over me."

Jainan pulled his hands back, now not sure what to do with them. In the end he let them hang at his sides. "It's good to see you." The minute the words were out of his mouth, they sounded flat.

Taam's eyes narrowed, half in jest. "Rehearse that, did you?"

Jainan shut his mouth. That didn't deserve an answer. But Taam was in a good mood, and Jainan wanted to keep him that way for as long as possible. "Did your trip go well?" The aide was already carrying Taam's suitcase. Jainan tried to ease Taam's personal effects bag off his shoulder.

"Don't grab," Taam said, freeing it and pushing it at Jainan. "It was fine. Bloody Theans obstreperous as usual, but we got around them. The drilling starts next month."

There was a short silence. Jainan settled the bag on his shoulder and turned toward the palace.

"Well?" Taam said from behind him. "That's it? A month away and you can't even pretend interest?"

When I ask questions you tell me not to pry, Jainan thought but bit his tongue. He turned back. "Sorry," he said into the continued silence. Taam hadn't moved, standing by the drive as the flyer left. "I'm sorry. Who did you meet with?"

Taam gave him another stare, this one of disbelief, and burst into sudden movement to walk past him. "Never mind. Nelen!"

"Sir!"

"What appointments do I have tomorrow?"

Taam's aide kept up with them as he carefully consulted his wristband, falling into step with Taam, while Jainan's footsteps echoed out of time on the marble. "Sir, tomorrow you have a debriefing with General Fenrik at ten, physical training at twelve, then you are free until the Thean embassy reception at six."

"More damned Theans?" Taam said. "Why have I got more Theans in my calendar? I've only just got away from them." It was a joke, because he was in a good mood, but that mood seemed to be fraying fast.

"This was put in your calendar by your partner, sir," the aide said, with an expressionless glance at Jainan. He barely ever named him. Taam was unpredictably annoyed if Jainan's Thean title was used in private, but also if his subordinates used Jainan's first name.

Jainan retreated into a statement of fact. "The Ambassador requested our presence, Taam." He could explain further, but it seemed like wasted effort when he knew it was unlikely to help.

"So he could whinge at me about the Imperial soldiers throwing their weight around in Thean space?" Taam's voice went high and nasal on the last part. He sounded nothing like the Ambassador. "Heaven, give me some peace here. I'm not going. Neither are you."

"But—" Jainan said.

"Give it a rest, Jainan." Taam turned the corner to their rooms abruptly. "Anything else?"

"Count Jainan has offered to help with the Kingfisher accounting," the aide said. As he said it there was an odd echo to his voice. The air smelled of copper.

Something in Jainan's head crunched like two gear wheels colliding. He nearly didn't hear Taam laugh and say, "So you finally got tired of lazing around, did you?"

"Did I?" Jainan said blankly. He struggled to remember exactly what he'd said to Taam's aide about it, because his mind suddenly felt slippery. He couldn't let the others see he was having trouble.

Taam waved an impatient hand. "Well, if you're going to nag me about it, we might as well put you to work," he said. "I'll get you permissions to our accounting files."

Jainan stopped in his tracks. He put a hand out to the wall of the corridor: it felt smooth and solid, but for some reason his nerve endings were lying to him. Everything smelled of copper. "This isn't real." He swallowed. "Taam's dead."

The aide's face flickered, and behind it he saw the features of Aren's Tau field technician, overlaid like two projections in the same space. There was a sudden stab of pain in his head and his surroundings dissolved.

"—the Iskat Minister for Thea decided he was coming planetside for Unification Day, which caused a huge hoopla as usual, and now he doesn't like that we're meeting with out-of-system representatives when he's not in the room—oh, you know, the usual mess of my life." Ressid's grin over the screen was tired but wry. "But I've been blathering on. Tell me about your week. Your . . . month? Has it really been a month?"

"It was fine," Jainan said. His head hurt, and he couldn't remember why. It was starting to hurt all the time. "Sorry, Ressid, could you keep your voice down?" He had the bedroom door shut and the volume down, but Taam was due back soon.

"Headache?" Ressid said. She made an effort to modulate her

voice from her forceful alpha-diplomat tones. "Or something else? You're quieter every time I talk to you."

"I haven't been well lately," Jainan said. "I had the flu."

There was a pause that was at least a second too long. "I'm kind of worried about you."

"Don't be," Jainan said. This had to be headed off fast. "I'm much better now."

"It's not that," Ressid said. She leaned closer to the screen. Jainan frowned and glanced to the side, trying to locate the source of a sudden metallic taste in the air. "You seem to have a lot of money recently, and I don't know where it's coming from. I think you're in over your head."

Jainan's head snapped up. Ressid's face was hard and intent, her elbows propped on the table.

"No, you don't," Jainan said, and her image flickered and disappeared.

Hold on to yourself, Jainan thought helplessly as another set of lights and emotion rose up around him. It swallowed his conscious thoughts like the sea.

"Well? What did she say?" Taam demanded.

They were in their rooms. The sky outside the windows was dark. Jainan blinked and remembered what was going on: they had just come back from a commemorative dinner to mark an Iskat anniversary of some victory or other. Jainan had been seated next to High Duke Tallie, who chaired the Advisory Council—a dull name for a group with enormous power over how the Empire was run.

As the conversation came back to Jainan, the muscles in his back coiled up in embarrassment. "I mentioned it."

"Subtly?" Taam said.

"Yes."

"You're no bloody good at subtle," Taam said. "What did she say?"

Taam wanted a committee seat. Jainan had at first had no idea why he wanted Jainan to make the request for him, but he'd found out soon enough: Duke Tallie was a woman of iron-clad opinions, and the ones she held about Taam were scathing. Jainan hated asking favors at the best of times. He could still feel the humiliation of it pricking at his cheekbones. She hadn't even been scathing about Jainan himself, just given him a look as if she couldn't believe he'd had the audacity to make the request. "I don't think she liked the idea."

"Of course she won't like the idea!" Taam said. He threw off his jacket. "Stupid cow can't see past the last time we argued—you were supposed to talk her around!"

Jainan had put a stop to most of his self-destructive behaviors, but not all, and now he felt one of them rising from somewhere deep in him. "How do you expect me to do that?" he asked softly. "It's you she doesn't like, Taam."

There was a moment of silence, as if neither of them could believe he'd said that. Then Taam moved. He grabbed Jainan by the front of his jacket, and Jainan had to fight for balance as the high collar tightened around his neck. "You're a damned liar!"

"I tried," Jainan said, though any apology would be too late now. He had to take breaths carefully, around the grip on his throat. "I'm sorry. I couldn't—I'm not subtle. I'm not good at this."

"That's bloody obvious!" Taam said. He bore forward until Jainan felt the back of his legs hit the desk, only just keeping his balance. "What use are you? If you can't even talk around one old woman, what fucking use are you?" Taam tightened his grip.

Jainan's jacket collar was suddenly his enemy, cutting off his air. "I—" he said, struggling for coherence. "I—I—I'll speak to her next time—"

"You're just looking to undermine me, aren't you?" Taam said.

"You're always in my bloody accounts, you eavesdrop on my conversations—I think you're trying to sabotage my operation."

"What?" Jainan said. Something was wrong, but he couldn't remember what, not with the pressure on his neck.

"Admit it!" Taam said. He gave Jainan a shake, not much, but enough to punctuate the demand. "You'll do anything you can to get at me! You're skimming money from my operation!"

Jainan felt a peculiar rush of anger. *You never needed him,* a voice in his head said. *You hate him. You could get rid of him so easily.*

A wave of abhorrence went through him a split second after the anger. That was wrong; he absolutely needed Taam—he was a treaty representative. Something was wrong. "This isn't real," he found himself saying, but the minute he'd said the words, he couldn't remember why he'd said them. He had thrown up a hand in front of his face. "I can't—Taam, I'm sorry, I can't remember."

Taam gave him one last shove and released him. "What fucking use are you," he said, but it was more of a rhetorical question. He had lost the edge of his rage, as he often did. He backed off a couple of steps and turned away as if he felt the first hints of embarrassment. "Are you all right?"

"Yes." Jainan pulled his jacket straight and didn't rub his throat. It wasn't real, but what *was* real? This room, Taam's fury at Duke Tallie, Jainan's failure at dinner: those were real. Whatever he had been trying to remember slipped away entirely. He felt himself settling into his surroundings like a wheel in a track it had traveled before. It was almost comfortable.

Taam threw himself down on the sofa. Jainan recognized this mood of grudging regret; he would be easier to deal with tomorrow. "I just wanted someone who could pull their weight," Taam said. He stared up at the ceiling. Jainan had been monitoring his drinks and he hadn't even drunk that much, but clearly it had been enough to make him pensive. Jainan felt a stir of pity. He didn't let it show. "I just wanted someone I liked."

"I'm sorry," Jainan said. There was nothing else he could really say. He turned away to make Taam some coffee.

The cup disappeared before he could pick it up. The walls turned gray and started to dissolve, and now the whole room seemed to be fading around him. He felt himself lose a thought that had been very important. He could no longer remember what it was.

CHAPTER 26

"What do you think?" Kiem asked.

Bel craned her neck to survey the shuttle docks. The docks on Carissi Station were a vertical grid of enormous glass tubes, ranging from a few meters across to large enough to hold a freighter. A honeycomb of elevators and stairs ran up and down the space in front of them, filled with people flowing on and off ships from the Transit Module.

A row of docks had been cordoned off for the military behind a semitransparent screen of red light that hid the left-hand row of the grid. There were a couple of obvious routes in, but both went through access gates controlled by troopers.

"You'll need to get us past the guard," Bel said. "I can break the protections on any of the small people-carriers, but I need close access."

"Right," Kiem said. He would bet this was a control gate like the one outside his mother's office, which meant it would need the army's daily passphrase. "Gairad, you've been temporarily promoted to aide. Try to look like you're a huge fan of Iskat." He led the way toward the nearest access gate, firing up his wristband as he went.

"The Imperial Military is a fine institution," Gairad said unconvincingly, trailing behind Kiem and Bel. "I love the Empire."

Kiem's call on his wristband took some time to connect. "Hey," he said brightly when it did. "Sergeant Vignar! It's been a while. Did you catch the race yesterday?" Gairad gave him a sideways incredulous look as they climbed a flight of stairs. Bel was busy watching their surroundings. "No, I was traveling, I'm out in Thean space. You'll laugh at this—General Tegnar finally set me up with a commission. Strategic comms on Operation Kingfisher. Yeah, Major Saffer hasn't filled it since he got his promotion . . . it's nearly a sure thing, with General Tegnar breathing down his neck, but I still have to do the assessment interview. Only thing, this is really embarrassing, I've forgotten the passphrase. My mother's going to space me—"

He wandered toward the access gate while he listened. After a couple more minutes, he wound it up with, "Thanks, Sergeant," loud enough to be heard by the trooper on duty. He put both his hands on the table and gave her his best smile. "Hi. Kiem Tegnar and aides. Passphrase *Tetra Green One*. We have a shuttle booked."

The electricity under his skin peaked as the trooper looked up. Everything seemed to hang in the balance. Kiem was very aware of the weight of the capper hidden at his waist, and even more of Bel's artificial stillness beside him.

It broke as the trooper waved them through. For the first time in several years, Kiem found himself wishing his mother was around so he could say thanks. It was an odd feeling.

"Hey, dozy, pay attention," Gairad muttered. "We're the smoke screen."

Kiem gave a start. Bel had levered open the airlock to the launching tube at the end of the line and was leaning over the shuttle inside, attaching something that looked a bit like a suction cup to its door. Kiem had given up being surprised by what Bel had apparently been sitting on in her luggage this whole time. He angled his body so he and Gairad were covering her completely from view.

Bel hissed as the door slid open. "Got it. Let's go."

Kiem and Gairad squeezed through the airlock into the tiny shuttle behind her, stumbling as they hit the transition to zero gravity. The interior could have sat six people, but only if those people were very good friends. "Do we need to talk someone into giving us clearance?"

"Nothing will be inward-bound while that freighter leaves," Bel said, her eye on a blocky supply freighter. "So we just slip out behind it." She must have noticed Gairad's suddenly pale face, because she grinned and said, "Don't panic, I've done this before."

"Suddenly everything about your speeding fines makes sense," Kiem said. He snapped himself into the zero-grav restraints. The interior had no windows, so he tapped his fingers on his knees and watched the glass walls recede on one of the pokey viewscreens.

Sitting still was agony. It felt like there was a pile of coals lodged under his rib cage, and all he could do was hang against the straps as they accelerated and watch the lighted bustle of the docks give way to black space. The viewscreens flickered and sharpened to brighten the pinpoint scattering of stars. Kiem knew their slow glide was an illusion—the other habitats in the cluster were kilometers away—but he wanted to shake the controls to eke out some speed. Jainan had been taken hours ago. He must be bored and tired, Kiem told himself. He must be sitting there wondering when Kiem and Bel would turn up. Other options were unthinkable.

The silver shells of the other habitats in the cluster rose around them, mainly automated manufacturing plants and storage stations as big as asteroids. The Kingfisher refinery came into view with the excruciating slowness of a planet turning toward the sun.

"Hah!" Gairad said, leaning forward. "Look, I was right about the secret module. They have detection fields," she added sharply. "Bel! You're flying right into them!"

Bel's mouth was, unusually, a straight line. "Kiem, permission to corrupt comms."

"What?"

"I can't completely block their signals," Bel said. "Not without a proper rig. But I can corrupt them, which will give you some time before they reset."

"How long?" Kiem said.

"Maybe twenty minutes. No messages in, no messages out. Not even if the habitat is on fire."

"There'll be safety controls," Gairad said.

"All safety controls have a fail state," Bel said.

Gairad opened and shut her mouth, and then said, "How do you know how to do *that*?"

"Do it," Kiem said, watching the refinery fill their screen.

He couldn't see where the detection fields began, though Gairad went tense a few seconds later, anxiously watching some antennae protruding from the shell of the refinery. Their shuttle slipped away from the well-lit side of the refinery with its docking lights, around the curve of the habitat to the module Gairad had pointed out on her plan. It all looked the same to Kiem, who wasn't an engineer or a pilot. All he knew was he would have drilled into layers of rock to find where they were holding Jainan.

It took them another endless three minutes to close with the hull. "There," Gairad said. Kiem took his eyes off the time display to recognize the cracks in the hull ahead of them as a set of docking ports, unlit and closed. There were a couple of emergency pods, flimsy one-person things with enough fuel for a single hop, so people must use it occasionally.

Bel had brought up a separate screen to communicate with the refinery's systems and was flicking her way through docking commands at high speed. It didn't seem to be going well. "The main dock wants keys we don't have."

"Emergency," Kiem suggested, snapping himself out of his straps. "They must have an emergency port. One of those tiny ones."

"I'm a systems breaker, Kiem, not a combat specialist," Bel said, in a voice that was nearly a snap. "I can't protect both of you if you try and fight your way through a chokepoint!"

"*Bel*," Kiem said. She paused, one hand hovering in the air in front of the screen, and gave him the most hostile look he'd ever seen from her. "Bel," he repeated. "Look at us. If we have to fight, we'll get slaughtered anyway. Our only hope is to get in quietly."

Bel clenched her hand, deleting her docking commands, and breathed out. Her face relaxed back into a more familiar expression. "Okay," she said. "Emergency port. We'll open it quietly. You two had better not get yourselves hurt. Kiem, you do the bridge." Kiem gave her a thumbs-up and floated to the release lever by the shuttle's hatch.

"Wait," Gairad said, "has he ever *done* an emergency bridge?"

"I've seen safety vids," Kiem said, pulling the lever.

The side of the shuttle blew in with a *bang*. Kiem hadn't been expecting it and was blown backward, slamming into the opposite wall of the hull as the emergency docking skin filled a third of the shuttle with a pale, jelly-like mass. He scrambled dizzyingly around until he could get his feet under him.

The door hissed open behind the skin. Kiem recoiled at seeing hard vacuum behind it, but the semitransparent bridge gel did its job, sealing the door and keeping the atmosphere inside. "Help me extend it."

"Oh, God," Gairad said, but she pushed herself across the shuttle and thrust her hands into the pale gel.

A fierce rush of joy went through Kiem at the prospect of finally doing something. He kicked his foot into the gel to stretch it, forcing it to bulge outward from the doorway, and attacked the rest of it with vigor. Gairad did the same, both of them squeezed back-to-back in the cramped door, until the skin had stretched out enough to bridge the last meter to the hull of the refinery. Bel cycled through some more docking prompts.

"Fifteen minutes," Kiem said, pressing the skin to the hull of the refinery. He tried not to think about the vastness of space on the other side of the semitransparent gel. "Is it—"

"Got it," Bel said.

Gairad yelped and slammed her hand on the skin, finishing the seal just as the emergency hatch slid open. The gel was starting to solidify into a hard, waxy shell, forming a narrow, air-filled tunnel between the shuttle and the refinery's hull. Kiem slithered through it first.

He fell out onto a metal floor. As he picked himself up, his eyes had to refocus: the space was enormous, as if this whole module was just an empty shell. The only lights were blinking indicators and dim glows in the distance, highlighting the dark clutter all around them without being enough to see by. It looked like a warehouse.

"We were wrong," Kiem said. It was hard to remember to keep his voice low when his chest felt like something was ripping inside it. He pressed the toe of his boot against one of the nearest pieces of machinery, repressing the urge to kick it. "He can't be here. This isn't a detention block, it's storage for some kind of mining rig."

White light flared. Gairad had clambered through the tunnel, feetfirst and swearing, and now fished a marble-sized flashlight out of her pocket. It lit up their surroundings like a miniature star.

Bel had frozen in the act of picking herself up, staring at the nearest pile of clutter. "Kiem," she said. Her voice sounded very distant. "Why am I looking at a stack of reaper warheads?"

Kiem stopped just before nudging another rack with his foot.

Gairad was already moving over to a nearby rack with the flashlight. "These are military drones. Guess we are in the wrong place." Kiem could hardly bear to listen. Anything could be happening to Jainan while they were in the wrong place. But if not here, then *where*? Gairad was still restlessly moving around. "Why the fuck would you put an armory up here?"

Kiem's scattered thoughts realigned in a new, cold direction and then slowed to a halt. Bel was wearing a grim smile. She was having the same thoughts.

"Usually," Bel said, "you stash your weapons as close as you can to where you plan to use them."

Kiem's skin was numb, like they had plunged into hard vacuum after all. "I would know," he said. "The Emperor would—she wouldn't marry me to Jainan just to turn around and *invade Thea*, that's—" He looked around at the military hardware hiding on the Kingfisher refinery. "That's not . . . possible."

"Coup?" Bel suggested. "Does the Emperor have to know?"

Gairad wasn't looking at either of them. She was moving among the piles, pulling aside coverings to check what was beneath. She looked down at the abstract silver emblem printed on a storage rack. "Prince Kiem," she said, in a preoccupied tone. "What *is* a kingfisher?"

"Oh—they got culled into extinction," Kiem said, his mouth on autopilot as he ran his fingers over the side of what he now recognized was a tank drone. It was the last one of a whole row. "Two-meter wingspan. Venomous. The bioengineers didn't realize their prey instinct would include humans." He looked over and saw Gairad's expression. "There were some weird design fashions around the time Iskat was terraformed."

"What the fuck," Gairad said. "Who names their operation after something like that?"

"The military?" Kiem said. He squinted into the distance, trying to see how far the row of tank drones stretched. "Fairly standard. Something macho."

Gairad turned around to glare at him, but for once Kiem didn't feel it was directed at him personally. "There is something seriously wrong with Iskat."

Kiem took his hand away from the tank as if it were suddenly hot. "Yeah," he said. "I'm starting to think you're right."

Bel emerged from a shadowy aisle between the stockpiled weapons. "Model 46–5 fluid disruptors, various reaper-grade missiles, gas launchers," she said. "And that's just scratching the surface. Can the military invade an allied province with no excuse? At least on Sefala the congloms were already racking up the body count."

Gairad's face turned sallow. "Oh, sweet God. The protest."

"What protest?" Bel said sharply.

"There are protests scheduled for Unification Day," Gairad said. "Our student society was coordinating with some other activist groups. Sit-ins and marches, nothing violent. But I guess"— she swallowed, her face an even more unhealthy color—"I guess an outsider could start something, if they wanted. We wouldn't vet everyone who joined."

Kiem exchanged glances with Bel. He thought about *strategic comms,* and about Aren, who had known so much about fringe newslogs on Thea. He forced himself to reason it through. "You have to tell them," he said. "Call it off. Tell them the Empire's sent saboteurs—they'll believe *that,* right? Tell them you think Kingfisher has been feeding inflammatory news to your press."

"You won't get any comms out from here," Bel said. "Take the shuttle—no, leave the shuttle for me and Kiem. Take an emergency pod."

Gairad pressed a hand to her face, looking between the rest of the warehouse and the door. "We still haven't found Jainan."

"You don't even know if he's here," Bel said brutally, making the tearing feeling in Kiem's chest worse. "I wouldn't keep a prisoner with the weapons. He may be in the uncloaked modules."

Before Gairad could reply, something clanked in the distance. It came from the depths of the warehouse, away from the door, and was followed by the sudden absence of a background hum that Kiem had taken to be part of the warehouse environment. Then, worse: smaller noises that were too intermittent to be mechanical. Someone was moving around farther in the warehouse.

All of them went still. Kiem nearly stopped breathing. They must have been heard; they hadn't been quiet enough for stealth, and they had the flashlight. Gairad reflexively stifled it with her hand and plunged them into darkness.

Bel reached for her capper and started toward the source of the noise, her shoes making no sound at all. Kiem followed, slower, praying he didn't make an incautious movement.

Another loud clank. The hum started up again, quieter this time. Now Kiem was listening for it he could triangulate its direction a bit better. They rounded the last of the tanks while Kiem and Gairad tried to minimize the scuffing of their footsteps, and a gap in the stockpiles showed a pool of light.

Before Kiem could see much in the light, a solitary trooper stepped out from behind a pile of crates, a helmet under her arm. She was peeling white nonconductive gloves away from her hands.

"Don't shoot yet!" Bel shouted, already at a flat run across the space. Kiem belatedly remembered he had a capper.

The trooper stumbled back, dropping the helmet. Her eyes were unfocused as if she'd just come out of a simulation. "Who are—"

Bel grabbed the trooper's arm. Gairad passed Kiem from behind and threw herself into the struggle. Kiem backed off; he found himself raising his wristband, but of course that was useless. The trooper drove her elbow at Bel's stomach; Bel twisted, Gairad yelled, and a few brutal seconds later they had the trooper in a headlock between them. Blood was streaming from Gairad's nose, and her wrist was at the wrong angle.

"Sorry," Kiem said to the trooper. She was in some kind of technician's uniform, but she seemed to have taken off her rank and division badges. "We're just passing through. Do you happen to have seen—"

"Oh, fuck," Bel said softly, looking behind the technician. Something about her tone of voice made Kiem break off. "Kiem. Over there."

Kiem stepped around the crates so he could see the lighted area she'd come from. The technician tried to break away again—

she hadn't shouted for help yet—but he didn't really have time to think about that, because now he could see the makeshift cleared area, and the form lying on a medical bed, strapped into a helmet like the one the trooper had just dropped. Jainan.

It shouldn't have taken Kiem as long as it did to reach him. It felt like gravity had doubled. He leant over Jainan when he reached his side and touched his shoulder to wake him up. But Jainan wasn't asleep. Through the view panel on the medical helmet, his eyes were wide open in a fixed rictus, his face drained and frozen. A wire ran from his skull underneath the helmet to a transmission spike. His shoulder under Kiem's hand was as stiff as a board, and little tremors went through his taut muscles.

"Jainan. Wake up." Kiem hadn't ever felt fear like this, fear that gripped his back and shoulders like a paralyzing current. He loosened the straps that held down the helmet. "We're here." His voice cracked on the last word. Jainan didn't show any sign he'd heard. Kiem grabbed the wire running from his head, but he came to his senses just in time. He was not a medic. He would do damage. *You've done enough damage already,* he thought, and turned to look for the technician.

Bel brought her over, still in a chokehold, her capper pressed under the trooper's chin for a fatal shot. "Let's make this very simple," Bel said. "Get him out of that or I shoot you."

"I can't," the technician said.

"And I'm the Emperor," Bel said. She adjusted the angle of the capper. Gairad was holding on to a crate, looking sick. "One more chance."

Kiem's head was flooding with anger like incendiary fumes. He took a breath of it, let it fill his head, let himself use it as fuel. "Wait, Bel," he said, turning away from Jainan. He smiled at the technician. Bel raised her eyebrows. "I think this is the Tau field machine, isn't it?" he said. He didn't let himself shout. Instead, he forced his voice to an even, conversational tone that sounded like it was coming from someone else entirely. "We all thought it had been abandoned. You know, since the remnant it was built on was supposed to be surrendered to the Resolution. But I get it, you're trained on it, and someone senior told you to use it. But this isn't exactly a normal detention block, and you've taken off your insignia. Call me stupid, but I think you're doing this unofficially, aren't you? For my friend Major Saffer, by any chance?"

The technician didn't reply. Bel's eyes had narrowed as she looked at Kiem.

Kiem's composure was snapping thread by thread like a fraying rope. Every minute Jainan was in the machine counted—Kiem didn't know how long someone could be in a Tau field without brain damage—and he had no idea how to bring him out without persuading this technician. "You could come out of this so badly," he said, forcing his tone to sound coaxing. "Court martial. Execution. The military had permission to interview Jainan, not commit a war crime, so they'll have to come up with some story about an overenthusiastic junior soldier. Saffer will throw you to the wolves without a second thought."

That got a reaction. The technician's eyes widened, only slightly, but it was a crack. Kiem seized on it. "This is way above your pay grade," he said. He couldn't let her see his fear. "When the authorities come in, you don't want Saffer to leave you holding the bag." He jerked his head. Bel picked up the signal and slowly removed her capper.

After a long moment, the technician said, "The field has to run its course. I can't turn it off. I programmed it for eight hours."

Kiem didn't even feel relief at her capitulation. He couldn't feel anything past the furious terror that hovered at the edges of his vision like static. "How long's he been in there?"

"Four." The technician's voice was still flat.

Control yourself. Jainan would be able to control himself. "Four hours. What were you trying to do to him?"

"Alter some memories," the technician said, still reticent. "He's got strong thought patterns. We haven't made much headway."

So that either meant Aren was trying to make Jainan forget the embezzlement and the murders—unlikely, since other people knew as well—or he was trying to frame him. Kiem stopped trying to think. "How do we stop it?"

In a sudden moment of animation, the technician looked at the console. "If we get what we need, we can sometimes go in and get them to cut the simulation short themselves. Bring them out early. They have to believe it's a simulation, though—most people want to get caught up in their memories."

"She could be lying," Gairad said. Her voice was thick with pain, and she'd used the sleeve of her good hand to try and staunch the nosebleed. She looked on the verge of collapse.

Bel jerked her head at Gairad, though her eyes were still on Kiem. "Kid, you're walking wounded. Go and sit down." She jabbed a thumb meaningfully toward the docking hatch. Gairad's eyes went wide, and she turned and disappeared into the dark.

Kiem couldn't make himself care about anyone else. He forced himself to parse the technician's words through the static of his fury. "You're saying if we convince him it's really all fake, he wakes up?"

"He rejects the brain pattern the field overlays," the technician said. "I can try."

"And how do you make sure you don't get caught in it?" Bel said skeptically.

"I can shape it," the technician said, with an edge of almost condescension. "They're not my memories."

Kiem's gaze went to Jainan's shivering, wide-eyed form on the bed. "No," he said roughly.

The technician's eyes narrowed. "You said—"

Kiem didn't have to look at Bel to know she shared his visceral revulsion at letting the technician mess around in Jainan's head any more than she already had. "You're going to send me instead."

He knew it was a bad idea. Invading Jainan's privacy like that would probably be the end of anything between them. Kiem wasn't even sure what they'd *had* between them, but there had been something that had made Jainan smile when Kiem came into the room, something Kiem had been trying desperately not to hold too hard, in case he broke it. He might be breaking it now. But the alternative was letting someone else—a stranger, someone who had already hurt him—into Jainan's mind again. "You're sending me in," Kiem repeated. "And you're going to do it now."

The technician nodded, slowly. She pointed at the helmet that had rolled away in the struggle. "That will make you part of the simulation," she said.

"Great!" Kiem said. He strode over to pick it up and smiled at the technician. For some reason, her face went even stonier. "Bel—"

"Already on it," Bel said. She rested her hip on one of the crates and pointed her capper at the technician. "I'll keep watch. If you take more than ten minutes, though, I'm pulling that helmet off your head and shooting someone."

"Don't do that," Kiem said. "I won't take ten minutes." He put the helmet on.

CHAPTER 27

For a nauseating moment, Kiem could see two images overlapping each other. He blinked hard, suppressing the lurch in his stomach. His muscles ached in a strange way, as if he wasn't fully using them. He stretched out his hand. It looked normal.

When he blinked again, the refinery warehouse had disappeared. In its place was a light, airy space with grand marble arches that he recognized: the lesser banqueting hall back at the palace, in the middle of some sort of formal dinner. He was sitting at a long table with people around him, and at first he looked around wildly, because that seemed impossible. Then he realized they must be hallucinations, laughing and talking like real people.

Now that he was looking properly, he could see the gaps in his surroundings. The arches and tables were clear enough, but the corners of the room were fuzzy and indistinct. When he looked at them straight on, he saw they were actually a gray, unformed fog, as if the projection didn't reach that far, but as he kept watching, detail would start to creep in: a chair appeared, a patch of wall, a side table with ebony inlay. It made his brain itch. More unsettling still was the realization that some of the people farther down his table were also incomplete: they gave the impression of bright uniforms or court fashions from the corner of his eyes, but when he turned to look directly at them, they were only patches of color with a gray oval for a face. Color and features flowed across them as he watched like they were being brushed on. Kiem frowned as he placed the new faces—a friend from prime school, his tutor in university. This looked like a military dinner. The Tau field was putting these people where they had no reason to be.

Wait. Wasn't this place made from Jainan's memories? Jainan couldn't know those people; did that mean the Tau field was grabbing memories from Kiem's own head now? The idea was skin-crawlingly unpleasant. He put up his hand to touch the helmet he knew he'd put on. He couldn't feel it. His fingers seemed to graze his hair instead.

What was this event, anyway? When he looked around, he saw posting insignia from Rtul, Kaan, Thea, all the inner system planets. The officers were mainly Iskaners, though, so it must be an internal military thing. Some significant date, maybe. His mother had attended dinners like this. But this one—

Kiem's head swiveled as if it were drawn to a magnetic point. He homed in on Jainan and Taam sitting at one of the long tables on the dais.

He pushed his chair back and rose to his feet. One of the other diners made an incomprehensible protesting sound, so Kiem said, "'Scuse me," politely, and shoved his way between the tables until he was within earshot of Jainan. He raised his hand to catch Jainan's attention. Jainan wasn't looking at him. Kiem recognized the way he was sitting, taut and tense. He also recognized Taam's manner, but only because he knew what people looked like when they were being drunk and loud at dinner. Taam looked too solid and confident to be a hallucination, and he wasn't alone in enjoying the evening. Everyone at that end of the table was several glasses into the festivities. Except Jainan.

Then Kiem saw Aren sitting a few places down from Taam and froze. But Aren's gaze went right through him as if they were strangers. Kiem recalled he was wearing the only headset. This Aren was just a memory, pulled from Jainan's memory of the dinner.

Suddenly Jainan's spine went rigid, and people were looking

at him. Someone must have made a comment. The person next to him leaned over and clapped him on the shoulder. Jainan flinched.

Kiem couldn't help himself: as he reached them, he grabbed the wrist of the offending officer. "You're drunk," he said. "Have some bloody manners." The officer stared at him with outraged, slightly fuzzy eyes, and Kiem remembered it wasn't real. He dropped their hand and turned. "Jainan . . . ?"

Jainan was real. Kiem knew every tiny line and shadow on his face as Jainan stared up at him in shock, and he knew the way Jainan wiped the shock and rapidly replaced it with a mask of blankness.

"Prince Kiem?" Jainan said. "I didn't realize Your Highness would be at this dinner."

"Who the hell are—Kiem?" Taam said from the other side of Jainan. As he did, Jainan leaned back to allow him space. "What are you doing here? This isn't for civvies."

Kiem opened his mouth to say, *Jainan, you're in a Tau field.* But then something strange happened. As he started to form the words, an invisible current around him took hold, and what came out was, "Yeah, not sure why I got the invitation."

"Makes two of us," Taam said. "Maybe your mother's hoping we'll rub off on you. What do you want?"

Kiem's head felt fuzzy. He seemed to have forgotten his next line. He looked around for inspiration and caught Jainan's frozen expression. Oh, yes. "I just wanted to see if Jainan was all right."

Now Taam's face took on a look of suspicion. "What does that mean? How do you know Jainan?"

Kiem frowned. "We've seen each other . . . around."

"We haven't," Jainan said, quiet and tense. "Taam, I've barely met him."

"Have you?" Taam said.

Kiem looked between the two of them. Something was wrong.

"People are looking," Taam said. "Go and sit down, Kiem, they're bringing out the next course."

Kiem opened his mouth, and once again that strange thing happened where words he hadn't planned came out. "Right," he said. "Sorry to bother you." He nodded—to Taam, not to Jainan—and turned away.

He was nearly back to his seat before his mind slipped out of the grip of the flowing current. He'd let himself be hijacked into being part of the scenario. Was that how Jainan saw him? Someone who'd abandon him at the first sign of trouble? He turned back, horrified, and saw Jainan hunched over his food with Taam pointedly ignoring him. "Jainan!" he shouted, throwing any attempt at subtlety to the winds. "This is the machine they put you in!"

Jainan looked up, bafflement on his face. Taam turned with an oath. "It's called a Tau field!" Kiem said. He tried to stride back across the banqueting hall, but there were chairs in his way, and people getting up, shocked. He was making a scene. Damn right he was making a scene. "Aren put you in it to alter your memories! I think he's trying to frame you! And where the hell does Taam get off, talking to you like that?" As he spoke, he saw Jainan mouth the word *memories*. And then the walls disappeared.

Kiem sat at a table—one of the curved, horseshoe-shaped ones used for duller meetings—in a conference room filled with thin white light. The sky beyond the windows was pale. He must be here for a meeting. He squinted at the others around the table, who all had an attenuated quality, as if the spectrum of the sun's light had shifted slightly while Kiem hadn't been paying attention.

It must be something to do with Thean affairs, because Jainan sat across from him, as did some of the staffers from the Thean embassy. Taam was also there—of course, Taam was heavily involved with Thea—and some other Iskat officials. An elderly man seemed to be presiding, but his head had nodded down to his chest, and every now and then, he gave a gentle snore.

"Next is the proposal for a replacement Thean Ambassador," one of the officials said. "Objections? She looked at the elderly man, realized she would get nothing out of him, and turned to Taam.

"That woman they've put forward is a no," Taam said, his elbow propped on the table and his forehead in his hand, as if it had been a long meeting already. "Tell them to find someone else."

"Taam," Jainan said quietly. "We've done this twice now."

There was a general rustle around the table. "Count Jainan?" the official said, as if this was an unexpected turn of events.

Taam ignored her and spoke directly to Jainan. "And?"

Jainan looked unwell, but said, "The clans are getting impatient, Taam. Please, can we just confirm someone?"

Taam leaned in. "You want this woman," he said, "because she's a friend of your family. I'm losing patience for how everyone on Thea gets appointed because they're someone's brother's aunt."

"That isn't true," Jainan said. "Her clan is neutral toward Feria, but if you want an enemy of Feria's, they can find one. We desperately need someone in the ambassador role. I promise I am not playing clan games—I am not *Thean* anymore, Taam."

"Oh, for fuck's sake," Taam said, with the general air that they'd had this conversation before. "Moving on. Next item."

Kiem had been keeping his mouth shut since his opinion didn't seem wanted, but he wasn't going to let that pass. "Hey," he said. "Taam. Jainan's right, you need someone to be"—he hesitated. The new Thean Ambassador? Didn't Thea already have an ambassador?—"whatever job you're talking about. Don't ignore him."

Taam frowned at him. "Why are you here?"

Kiem had no idea, but wasn't going to let that slow him down. "To stop you from making really boneheaded decisions, apparently."

"*Kiem,*" Jainan said.

"I'm not sitting here to be insulted," Taam said. "Who invited you?"

"I'm the Thean treaty representative." That felt wrong, but Kiem knew it was true. "Aren't I supposed to be here?"

"You're bloody *not* the representative," Taam said, pushing back his chair to stand. "Is this a joke? I'll take this behavior to General Tegnar if you don't get out."

Kiem glanced at Jainan, who was rigid, his hands resting folded on the table in front of him. "I'm fine right here."

Taam propped his hands on the table and leaned forward, scowling. "Meeting over, then. We're done here. Get out, Kiem."

"I'm sorry," Jainan said.

The officials were already packing up, clearly used to rapid changes of direction from Taam. Even the elderly man was prodded awake. "Wait," Kiem said, but the officials only paid him cursory attention. "Wait—you can't just cancel the meeting because you *want* to, Jainan had a point, this is ridiculous—" He tried to stride forward and catch up with Taam as he left, but as he stepped over the threshold, everything around him wavered. Taam turned back, an incredulous eyebrow raised, but he was fading, and the walls around him started to dissolve. Jainan was sitting in the room behind him, alone.

Kiem thought, *That was the wrong person to chase,* at the same time as everything disappeared again.

When Kiem next opened his eyes, he heard voices even before the dark surroundings resolved enough for him to see.

"I don't know what it is you want." That was Jainan's voice. It was low and close to him.

"Will you just shut up?" That was Taam.

Someone took a heavy breath, but Kiem couldn't tell who. The hair on the back of his neck prickled. It felt close and warm in here, but not pleasant. He started to realize that wherever the field was generating, the surroundings weren't going to get much lighter. The murk was resolving into the faint silhouettes of a bedroom. Kiem felt a sick guilt rise. Invading Jainan's memories was bad, but this felt like a part he shouldn't see at all.

"Hell," Taam muttered savagely. "Do you have to just lie there? I could pay for better." There was silence, then rustling in the dark. Taam made a noise of disgust and moved, and now Kiem could see him faintly outlined, rising to kneel over Jainan. "Is that why Thea sent you? Send someone to marry the Iskaner, but let's make sure they're like a damp flannel in bed?" Jainan said something nearly inaudible. Taam cut him off. "You don't have to talk."

It only took Kiem three steps to get over to the bed. In the next moment he had Taam's bare shoulder in his grip and yanked him roughly away.

Taam grunted in shock. He flailed backward with his arms for purchase on the bed, and Kiem shoved him away. The lights came up enough to see by, showing Jainan half sitting up with one hand near the light sensor, frozen in surprise. He was naked, and Kiem didn't want to see; it felt like a profound violation just to be in the same room.

"Kiem?" Jainan said.

"The—the hell!" Taam pushed himself upright, choking with rage. "Who are you? The hell do you think you're doing?" He shoved himself up and grabbed Kiem by the collar of his shirt.

Kiem was done being reasonable. He caught Taam's arm and went to shove him back, but suddenly realized that would put Taam closer to Jainan. In that moment of indecision, he'd forgotten Taam had military training. Taam drove a punch into his gut. Kiem doubled over.

He tried to pull back before the next punch. He might not have combat training like Taam, but he knew he was in a horribly vulnerable position, and a blow to his face now might knock him out. But it didn't come.

When he looked up, he saw Jainan had caught Taam's wrist.

Taam looked as blankly shocked as if the bedspread had come to life and held him back. He tried to break out of Jainan's grip. His muscles flexed, but it didn't have any noticeable effect. "Let go."

"No," Jainan said. "Kiem, you had better leave."

"Let go," Taam said again, low and dangerous.

It felt like the haze around Kiem was starting to clear. "Wait— Jainan," Kiem said. "This is the Tau field."

"I don't know what you're talking about," Jainan said. His eyes were on Taam. "Please leave."

"Jainan!" Kiem said. "The interrogation machine Aren put you in to alter your memories, remember? Bel and I came to get you!"

Jainan looked up in shock. With a roar, Taam broke free of his grip and swung for his face, but even as he did, he was starting to become transparent. So were the bed, the walls, the floor beneath his feet. It all faded into black. Kiem braced himself for the next room.

It didn't come. Instead, as he stared into the darkness around him, he realized it was actually a kind of gray. His feet were on what felt like solid ground, but it was completely featureless. He couldn't see more than a few meters—or maybe he could see for kilometers, and it was just all unbroken gray.

"No," a voice said behind him. Kiem whirled to face it— dizzyingly, because it was hard to keep your balance when it wasn't obvious where the floor was. Jainan was standing there with his hands over his face, now dressed in light-shaded casuals. "Something's wrong."

"Jainan!" Kiem's initial wash of relief drained away when

Jainan took his hands away from his face. His eyes were tightly shut and his skin had a sheen of sweat.

"My name is Jainan nav Adessari of Feria," Jainan said in a barely audible voice. His eyes were still shut. "I am a diplomatic representative to the Empire. I am an engineer. I. I. I am proud to represent my planet. I have always tried to do the right thing for Thea and the treaty. I have nothing to be ashamed of." The litany turned his voice into a bleak, steely thread, like the safety tether that spooled a spacewalker into the void. "I might be easy to manipulate. But I am very difficult to break."

Kiem felt like he had been punched in the stomach. "Yes."

Jainan opened his eyes and fixed them on Kiem. It was like watching shutters open behind a porthole: they were black and glassy and had shut off all ways in. "You are not real."

Kiem didn't realize he'd taken a step toward him until Jainan deliberately backed away. Kiem froze. Right. "Uh. No. I'm real. I thought we'd sorted that just now."

"You are not," Jainan said. "You're the technician. The interrogator."

"I'm not," Kiem said. "Jainan, listen, we found you and followed you in here. We took the interrogator out. Bel's keeping guard over her."

"How long have I been in here now?" Jainan said. "Am I to expect you to go off-shift at some point?"

Kiem stared at him, then scrubbed a hand through his hair in frustration. "No, it's really me. Look." He held out his hand for Jainan to take.

Jainan declined it with a slight gesture. "I am well aware this place can simulate sensation."

Kiem recoiled, horror running down his spine at that on top of the last scenario. He dropped his hand, frantically trying to think of better arguments. "Really. I got Bel back from the shuttleport. She basically broke us in here—she says she used to be a raider? She doesn't do that anymore. I mean, obviously. You were already in the Tau field when we found you. We're probably going to get arrested when we get back out, but arrested is fine as long as we get you out of here. This is classified as an instrument of torture, did you know?"

"I know," Jainan said. His expression was preternaturally calm. "You don't need to make things up about Bel to add color. I am aware Kiem is not coming to get me. Nobody is. Please don't insult us both with this tactic."

Kiem took a deep breath. "I can prove this. Ask me a question only we'd know the answer to."

"Everything I've seen so far has been from my own memories," Jainan said. "The field clearly has access to them. You could let it play back the correct answer to anything I asked."

"Then why do you *think* I'm here?" Kiem said. "Why do you think I was in your last three memories?"

"I don't know," Jainan said. "It could be to get me to trust you so I slip up later. Or you may not be the interrogator; maybe she's on a break. You may be entirely a production of my own mind." His mouth quirked into another non-smile. "That would be depressing. I would rather not be such a sad fantasist that I hallucinate you coming to find me."

Kiem felt a hollow open up in his belly. "That isn't a fantasy," he said. "Listen to yourself! Why wouldn't I be here?"

"Mm," Jainan said. "Now I'm back to thinking you're my interrogator. You should really have let the field handle that response."

"What? Why?"

Jainan sighed. "You may have been briefed, but you're missing a vital piece of information about how I last left Prince Kiem."

"We . . . argued," Kiem said.

Jainan's smile was quick and mirthless. "Yes, my question gave that away, didn't it?"

"What does that have to do with anything? I didn't think about how to bring up that vid with you and I screwed up," Kiem said slowly. He could feel the edges of what Jainan was putting together, and he wished he couldn't see how it looked. "You thought I . . . would just abandon you because we argued? You don't think very much of me."

"It's not you," Jainan said, his controlled voice beginning to fray around the edges. "It's me. I know it's me. I am not worth you risking yourself to get out of trouble, and I wish my mind had not produced this delusion of you turning up anyway!"

"Jainan—" Kiem started, but Jainan deliberately turned away. He walked a little distance, fading into the gray, but seemed to realize at the same time as Kiem did that there was nowhere for him to go. He sat down with his legs crossed, neat and self-contained.

Kiem rubbed a hand across his face, then went and sat a few feet in front of him. Jainan ignored him.

"It wasn't your fault," Kiem said tentatively. "I think it was mine. I mean. I don't know if it was even an argument, really."

"You are not getting anything out of me with that," Jainan said flatly.

"All right, have it your way," Kiem said, exasperated. "Truce. I'm not real."

"I know." There was an expectant pause, as if Jainan was waiting for Kiem to disappear.

"No," Kiem said. "It's not going to work for you to dive back into your memories. I may not be the sharpest knife in the set, but—"

"Stop it," Jainan said.

"What?"

Jainan looked up at the empty gray air above them. "That's the one thing the real you does that very much annoys me," he said to the space above. "You aren't stupid. Stop saying you are."

Kiem stopped, thrown. "You should know. You've tried to explain your work to me."

"That's not a difference in ability, that's a specific skill set," Jainan said. "You're manifestly better at—at life than Taam was. Than I am."

"Not true. You—"

"Don't," Jainan said. He gave something that was half a laugh, half a cough. "It just makes me think of where I am right now."

There was a long silence, while Kiem drummed his fingers on the spongy, featureless ground, and Jainan stared straight ahead. After a while, Kiem said, "Was that . . . something that happened to you? The Taam thing?"

"Which one?" Jainan said colorlessly.

Four hours, Kiem remembered. "The ones I saw."

"They're my memories." Jainan didn't look at him.

All of the words Kiem had were wrong. "I'm sorry," he said. It seemed pathetically inadequate.

"Why?"

"What?" Kiem said. "Because—because I didn't help you? Nobody helped you! Someone should have figured out what was going on and dissolved the marriage! Taam should have been—prosecuted, disgraced, stripped of his rank, all of that. And not just him. Anyone who covered it up!" He realized he was starting to go off and cut himself short. "Sorry. I know you don't want it raked over. But it just makes me so angry that Taam died before it came back to hurt him. You didn't get any justice."

Jainan was finally looking at him, his forehead creased and his lips slightly parted.

"I don't know how you survived it," Kiem said. "Being—alone like that, with all that shit happening. I wouldn't have got through—"

"No," Jainan interrupted. "No, you don't understand. It was *me.*" He got to his feet in agitation, turning away from Kiem. "That wouldn't have happened to anyone else. Taam had good intentions. He had a sense of honor. It was just unfortunate that he ended up with someone he didn't like."

"Screw Taam's good intentions!" Kiem said. He got to his feet as well, moving around to face Jainan. "Nothing was good about what he did to you! Are you trying to tell me this was your fault?"

Jainan didn't move away. "It would have worked," he said. "It would have worked, if I'd been someone else."

Kiem made a chopping motion with his hand. "No," he said. "Rubbish. Bullshit. I may never be right about anything again, but I'm right about this." Jainan hadn't moved away. Kiem reached out and touched his shoulder. "If he couldn't cope with you, then he couldn't have coped with anything except curling up with one of his own rank medals. Nobody could want more than who you are."

For a moment, the gray world seemed to hang in the balance. And then Jainan raised his hand to Kiem's wrist, and Kiem stepped forward, and Jainan let him put his arms around him. Jainan took a ragged breath and dropped his head, resting his forehead on Kiem's shoulder. "You're a hallucination," he said, though he no longer sounded certain of it. "You're telling me what I want to hear."

"I'm not," Kiem said. "Listen, if I'd met you before you got married, I'd have fallen over my own feet trying to get you to look at me. You're out of my league. You're out of most people's league, especially Taam's. I've been trying to tell you this for weeks. I don't know how to say it so you'll believe it."

Jainan was silent for a long time. He was a solid warmth in Kiem's arms, his head a weight on Kiem's shoulder. Kiem shouldn't be happy, but he was.

"I don't know where that comes from," Jainan said. "You can't be one of my own hallucinations. I haven't thought that."

"That's because I'm real?" Kiem said. "I thought we'd sorted that."

Jainan let out half a breath of laughter. "It's not sorted just because you say it's sorted."

"That's all it should take—" Kiem started.

Kiem's eyes slammed open into blackness. He drew a huge, painful gulp of air that felt like his first breath in minutes. There was something on his head; he clawed at it desperately for a moment before realizing it was the Tau field helmet and managed to still the panic for long enough to lift it away. His sight flooded back.

They were in the warehouse again. The technician lay slumped on the floor. There was no sign of Bel. Jainan sat up on his narrow bed a couple of meters away and pulled the medical helmet off. As he moved, the wire attached to his head came with him; he reached up and brushed it off. The end came away in bundles of filaments, like dead plants.

Jainan's eyes went to the technician. "Asleep?"

"I don't know," Kiem said. "And where's Bel? She was supposed to be watching us." It felt like there was a lump lodged between his lungs and his throat. He knelt down to check the body.

"Kiem, I have to tell you what's going on," Jainan said, with a sudden thread of urgency. "Taam and General Fenrik were organizing an unsanctioned invasion of Thea. They used Kingfisher as cover to buy weapons and steal the remnants. They want to break with the Resolution and use the remnants for war. Aren saw the dark money flowing around and diverted some for himself, then killed Taam when he found out."

Kiem had gotten halfway there already. He wished the rest of it came as a surprise. "And then Aren decided to frame you, right?" he said grimly. Aren had known what was going on in Jainan and Taam's marriage. Was that what had made him think Jainan was an easy target? "Fuck Aren. *Fuck* Taam."

"What happened to me is not important right now," Jainan said, his voice thin and determined. He removed the guardrail from the side of his bed and swung his legs out. "People need to know. Someone needs to recover the remnants. We are all in danger."

"We'll blow it wide open the minute we're out," Kiem said. "Sunlight will cure it. Can you walk?" He couldn't feel the technician breathing. He searched compulsively for a pulse; he couldn't leave someone dying here. His fingers had only just touched her pulse point when someone else stepped into the pool of light.

The footsteps were such an ordinary, everyday sound that at first he didn't even look up, preoccupied with trying to find a sign that he didn't have a corpse on his hands. It was Jainan's cut-off, strangled choke that made him raise his head.

A voice Kiem had heard far too recently said, "So Aren wasn't lying. You are here."

The form supporting itself with one hand on a storage rack wasn't the hallucination Kiem had just seen. Taam was almost unrecognizable. He was wearing casual civilian clothes, but he didn't fill them out anymore; his body was wasted and stringy. There were the shiny outlines of burn scars on his neck. His mouth curled in a nasty echo of his previous expressions as he met Kiem's gaze. "You might as well stare, *cousin*. Thought I was dead, didn't you?"

"You are dead." Jainan looked transfixed; his voice was strained. "You can't be—we would have known."

"I was in some trouble," Taam said. "Not that you were a lot of help, were you?" His voice sounded more tired than anything else.

Kiem stepped between him and Jainan. "Keep back."

Taam's manner turned uglier. "Keep back from your partner? Oh, no, wait, from *mine*. I heard about your sham of a wedding. Don't get between me and Jainan." He went to shoulder Kiem aside, but Kiem planted his feet and didn't move. "I'm not going to fucking repeat myself." Taam drew the capper at his hip.

A rustle of cloth was the only warning either of them got. Jainan seized the loose guardrail from the bed, stepped around Kiem, and cracked it down on Taam's arm.

"Fuck!" Taam dropped the capper and grabbed his shoulder, swearing, while his wrist hung limp.

Jainan faced Taam, shifting his focus away from Kiem. He pulled his makeshift staff back. "Don't touch him."

Taam stared. He didn't seem to be able to process what was

happening. "What are you doing? Put that thing—*shit*." He'd tried to move his wrist. The strain of ignoring it wrote lines of pain across his face. "Jainan!"

"Step away," Jainan said. His voice sounded measured, though Jainan was capable of sounding measured well past when normal people would fall apart. "Two steps back will do."

"Jainan," Taam said. It wasn't clear what he expected the word to do. Jainan didn't move. Kiem's fist clenched, but he stayed still. "Jainan. Look at yourself. You're making a scene with that ridiculous . . . thing."

"Very possibly," Jainan said. "Step back from Kiem, Taam. I will not tell you again." His grip tightened on the length of rail.

Taam took a step back. "You need me," he said. The edge of anger hadn't left his voice, but now there was something else there: he sounded lost. "I'm your partner."

Jainan stood disturbingly still. He looked at Taam like he was a stranger. Kiem found he was barely breathing. The air smelled of metal.

It was a long, long moment before Jainan shook his head slightly, as if freeing himself from a cobweb. "No," he said. "I think I was finished some time ago."

He dropped the makeshift quarterstaff on the floor. It clattered, metal against metal, with a ringing sound that was shockingly loud and made even Taam flinch away. The ringing didn't die away. Instead it hung in the air and echoed, unnaturally, growing louder and louder until Kiem had to clap his hands over his ears.

Taam's form was blurry in front of him. Kiem looked down once more at the technician; she had the face of his prime five friend. The room wavered.

CHAPTER 28

And Kiem opened his eyes.

The first thing that hit him was the headache. That and the faint smell of station air circulation; he realized that though the hallucinations had been near-perfect, there had been no smell at all. He lifted the helmet off his head and saw the storage module as they'd left it.

"Welcome back."

Or not quite as they'd left it. Aren Saffer sat on a pile of crates in front of him. He had a military-issue capper in his hand, and it was pointing straight at Kiem's head.

Kiem groaned internally. He was almost sure this wasn't another loop, but of all the things *not* to be a hallucination. "Thanks," he said, to buy time. Jainan was on the bed, but his eyes were closed, and he was slumped and still. The technician was unconscious on the floor. At least both of them were breathing.

Bel stood uncomfortably against the storage rack opposite, her hands behind her head. Her capper was on the floor by Aren's feet. She looked ruefully back at Kiem. "Sorry," she said. "He got the drop on me while I dealt with her. I was never a combat specialist."

"Now," Aren said conversationally, keeping the capper trained on Kiem. "I don't mind admitting that I'm in a bit of a hole, here. No, don't move," he added, "I will absolutely fucking shoot."

"You might have been able to cover up Jainan's death in custody," Kiem said, "but no way are you going to be able to cover up mine."

"I don't need to," Aren said. "If you don't start cooperating, I can get rid of you, and the Tau field will convince Jainan he did it. Don't talk to me about sunk costs. *Don't move.*" He swung the capper back and fired a ray in front of Bel, who had shoved herself off the wall and was halfway to her own weapon. He'd shot too fast: it only hit her outstretched hand, but even that was enough for the shock to run through her. She choked and fell to her hands and knees as she fought for consciousness. Kiem started toward her instinctively but pulled back, raising his hands, as Aren turned the capper on him.

Aren got to his feet, still aiming at Kiem, and kicked the extra weapon under the nearest pile of hardware. "Why is everyone an idiot?" he said. "Your Imperial Highness, do me the favor of getting the fuck away from that machine. I've put a lot of effort into tying up this loose end, and you're ruining my technician's hard work."

"So you can try brainwashing Jainan again?" Kiem said. "No thanks. Wait, have you used the Tau field before? You must have. Actually, I *know* you have—you used it to make Colonel Lunver forget what we told her, didn't you?" That must have been a less drastic adjustment than the one Aren had just tried on Jainan, but Kiem felt a chill about how well that had worked. "Why? Did she find out what you were doing?"

"Listen," Aren said, his patience visibly fraying, "It's the middle of the night. In about six hours, I have to walk into General Fenrik's office and give him proof that Jainan was behind Ta-am's accident or I'm finished. I'd rather keep the number of dead royals to a minimum, but I don't *have* to. Step away and let my technician back in."

A coughing sound from the bed made both Kiem and Aren look over. Jainan had opened his eyes and now raised his head with what looked like painful effort. "Let Kiem leave."

Aren swung the capper toward Jainan, then back at Kiem. "Thought that might have an effect," he said, sounding more cheerful. "It took me a while to understand what was going on with you two, but now I get it. Your romantic mountain trip, this quaint rescue mission—you're *attached*, aren't you?" Kiem didn't hate easily, but he was starting to now. "So this whole thing becomes easy. You're staying here until the Thean invasion has started. And Jainan cooperates with the Tau field, or I shoot you."

Jainan's hands were still cuffed in front of him, but he had managed to push the helmet off his head and was now painstakingly using both hands to try and remove the wire patch from his forehead. A trickle of blood was forming around it. His face was a corpse-like mask.

Aren was part of the plan to invade Thea. Cooperating wasn't an option. Kiem tried to catch Jainan's eye without Aren noticing and somehow communicate that it was all right, he knew Jainan would let both of them die before he helped Aren, but Jainan wouldn't look at him.

"I'll do it," Jainan said hoarsely. "I'll help you. Leave Kiem out of it."

Kiem choked. "Wait—"

"Kiem." Jainan grasped the guardrail and pushed himself up as far as he could with the wire still attached to his head. "I need you to understand." He took a breath, as if it was hard for him to speak. Then he turned his head to meet Kiem's eyes and snapped, "*Five!*"

Kiem felt the word settle into his brain. Jainan yanked the guardrail out of its sockets and threw it awkwardly at Kiem's feet. Kiem's thoughts ran slow as treacle as he watched the rail clatter to the ground, and then it clicked. *Five.* The quarterstaff lesson with Gairad. He grabbed the rail.

Aren started to realize what was going on, but it was already too late. Jainan shoved himself off the bed so violently the wires ripped out of his head and his arm. His falling body crashed straight into Aren's legs, just as Kiem brought the rail whistling around to smack into Aren's wrist. It wasn't a good blow, but Aren wasn't prepared. The capper skittered across the floor. Aren fell heavily and sprawled after it, smashing into one of the metal crates. Jainan's body landed on top of him.

Kiem abandoned the loose rail. He fought down the sick terror and crouched to scoop up Aren's dropped capper. Aren was on the floor halfway between Kiem and the bed. Kiem aimed the capper at his chest. "Don't move."

By this time Aren had managed to sit up. Jainan was no longer conscious, but was still a dead weight on his legs. "That's a lot of blood," Aren said. He touched the dark patches on Jainan's scalp.

Kiem kicked Aren's hand away and stepped back again. "Don't do that," he said. Jainan's eyes were shut. How much bleeding was too much? Kiem aimed the capper very carefully with both hands. He had never shot one of these at a person. He couldn't risk hitting Jainan, but Aren was at an awkward sideways angle to him. Would hitting Aren's arm be enough to knock him out? It had worked on—

Bel. The space where she had been lying was empty.

Aren saw the look. "Where's your raider friend gone?"

"I don't know."

Aren gave him a rueful smile. "So much for loyalty, eh?"

Kiem leveled the capper at him. He wasn't going to shoot lethally; he just needed to put him out. There was no reason for his heart to be hammering this hard. His finger closed on the trigger.

"Careful," Aren said. He wrenched Jainan's body up to cover him. A wave of terror went through Kiem and made his arms spasm up. The capper ray passed over Aren's head.

Aren had Jainan by the shoulders, cradling him in front of him. Jainan's eyes were closed and his head hung down on his chest. Kiem recovered his aim, but his hand was shaking now.

Aren smiled at him. "You wouldn't want to hit someone you don't mean to," he said. "A capper ray would probably be *really* bad for Jainan right now."

"Let go of him," Kiem said.

"Or you'll . . . shoot me?" Aren said. "No. Let's talk."

Kiem took a long, slow breath. The capper felt heavy in his hand. "I'm listening."

"If you're still trying to salvage some kind of treaty from all this, you'll need my cooperation," Aren said. "Let's just say, you need to convince the Auditor that Thea *really* wants to be part of the Iskat Empire. I have some stories on you and Jainan that could tank both your reputations and sink any chance at a treaty. The Thean newslogs always love stories about their representatives."

"You're bluffing," Kiem said.

"Do you want to chance it, though?" Aren said. "I can see why Jainan thinks you're an improvement on Taam, but let's face it, once he's adjusted, the shine's going to wear off. What have you really got to offer? Even *Taam* managed to keep him from getting savaged by the press."

It hurt too much to look at Jainan's face. Kiem turned his capper around in his hand compulsively, fidgeting in the way that had made his instructors at cadet camp turn white. "Okay," he said. "All right. Just . . . just step away from Jainan. Please."

"I'm glad we're on the same page," Aren said, smiling. He lowered Jainan down to lie on the floor and freed his own legs, until he was kneeling beside Jainan. "Better?"

Kiem gripped the capper, flung up his hand, and shot him in the chest.

Aren didn't have time to get out any words. He choked, his eyes wide, then slumped forward over Jainan.

Kiem dropped the capper. He had to press one hand over the other to stop them from shaking. He fell to his knees beside Jainan and shoved Aren off him. Jainan was unconscious, either because of the Tau field or the blood still coming from his scalp, but that was all Kiem could tell. He laid Jainan out on his side so he could breathe properly. When he touched a hand to his hair, a wave of helpless despair went through him.

He couldn't fix this. It hurt more than anything had hurt in his life. He didn't know when Jainan had gone from someone he just wanted to draw a smile from to someone he would rather die than lose, but it was true, and he was desperate.

A whine in the distance started and stopped. It took Kiem a moment to register it was an alarm.

When the soldiers burst in on them, accompanied by station security, Kiem was crouched beside Jainan watching his chest rise and fall. Aren and the technician lay slumped not far away. Kiem glanced up as the handful of guards and soldiers clattered down the aisles and surrounded them, pointing cappers at him and the unconscious forms on the floor, and said, "You could have gotten here faster."

That seemed to stymie the two soldiers who had their cappers trained on Kiem. The one in front of him had sergeant markings. "Hands on your head!"

Kiem lifted them without taking his eyes off the sergeant. "This man needs a medic," he said. "This is Count Jainan of Feria, the Thean treaty representative, and if you don't get him to a medic *right now,* you'll be answering to the Emperor for the diplomatic crisis that is going to ensue at any moment."

"Quiet," the sergeant said, but Kiem could hear a crack of doubt in it. The station security guards—the civilians—seemed to be at least as suspicious of the soldiers as they were of Kiem. "Everyone in this module is under arrest."

"After you've answered to me," Kiem said flatly, "the Emperor will seem like your nursery teacher."

"You can't—"

"Internal Security is already telling the Emperor you used a

Tau field on a diplomat," said a familiar voice. "They made using it a war crime for a reason." At the back of the group, just coming through the door, a man in a station security uniform was guarding Bel. She had her wrists handcuffed in front of her. "Don't think you can cover it up either. I called Chief Agent Rakal before I found you bunch. Even the Emperor wasn't expecting you to go that far." She raised her eyebrows at Kiem. "This is the first and last time I get voluntarily arrested. How's Jainan?"

"Bad," Kiem said. "But this sergeant here is about to get him medical attention. Right?"

The sergeant crouched beside Jainan to check his breathing. "He's still under arrest," he said. "Corporal, fetch the paramedic unit. Move!"

The corporal left at a run. "The other man is Major Saffer," Kiem said. "He tried to kill me. The woman was his accomplice."

The sergeant got to his feet again and had a short, intense argument with one of the station security guards. "Everyone is in custody until we sort this out," the sergeant said. "Secure the other two on the floor. The . . . the diplomat will have all possible assistance. Prince Kiem, will you cooperate?"

"I'm waiting until the medics come," Kiem said. "You can arrest me after that." He took Jainan's hand and didn't move.

CHAPTER 29

Jainan could not establish a strong enough grip on his own mind to understand what was going on. There were wires attached to him again, and sometimes it was light, and sometimes it was dark, and terror was like a sea beneath his feet. Beyond that he knew very little.

People's faces melted into other faces. They asked him about Aren, about Kiem, about himself. Jainan refused to answer. Mostly the words were indistinct, but sometimes he was nearly tricked into saying something and had to bite his tongue to stop himself. Once he bit it so hard he tasted blood, and then there was a commotion and figures leaning over him, and someone pressed something into his mouth to force his teeth apart. He swallowed, over and over again, and felt sick with the taste.

Sometimes he knew it was the skin on his head that hurt, and everything else was his imagination, but other times he forgot that. At one point he realized he'd cried out, and a voice said, "At least he's talking," and another, "Wouldn't call that talking."

Then there was a moment when he opened his eyes and all he saw was the white ceiling of a med room. A screen on the wall played a loop of ripples lapping at a riverbank.

He drew a cautious breath. The air smelled faintly of antiseptic and had a dry, filtered feel he associated with nanocleaners. His head hurt fiercely, but there didn't seem to be anything attached to it. A tube from a drip fed into his wrist. He felt—not like death, but like death had happened some time ago, and against all odds he had recovered.

He tried to pull himself forward, and to his relief found that his body responded enough for him to sit up.

An orderly he hadn't seen in the corner of the room lifted his head from his reading, startled. "Awake?" He propelled himself up from his bench. "Here, let's fix that bed for you." He adjusted it so it rose with Jainan.

"I can sit up," Jainan said.

"Sure you can," the orderly said cheerfully. Jainan leaned back against the upright mattress and chose not to pick a fight.

"Am I on Carissi Station?" he said. His eyes went to the screen. The tiny yellow flowers on the bank looked like the ones that grew in the hills around Bita. Someone must have captured the vid on Thea.

"I'll tell you, you wouldn't have liked being put on a shuttle back to Iskat in the state you were in, Your Grace," the orderly said. "You're in the station's med suite." He was taking some form of reading from the diagnostic unit at the head of Jainan's bed. "How's the pain? Any blurriness of vision?"

"It doesn't hurt," Jainan said. "Does anyone know where I am?"

"Blurriness of vision?" the orderly said, and waited expectantly until Jainan shook his head, causing himself a stab of pain. "Well, I'd say there must be fewer people who *don't* know you're here. You've got two Internal Security guards out in the waiting room, another guarding the suite door, palace agencies harassing my manager, and a visitor list as long as your arm."

"Kiem?" Jainan said. "I mean—Prince Kiem?"

"I couldn't say," the orderly said. "Now, do you think you could drink some water?"

"Am I under arrest?" Jainan said. "Has anything happened on Thea?"

"Under . . . ? Nobody told me anything about that," the orderly said. But Jainan could see him reassessing Jainan and his security arrangements with a sideways glance. Jainan also saw the moment when he resolved that his superiors would have told him if his patient were a dangerous criminal, and the professional upbeat manner returned. "I wouldn't worry, I don't think so. At least you've got all the bits of your brain in working order, how's that for luck? How about that water?"

So he wasn't under arrest, but Internal Security had people outside his door. Fenrik couldn't have succeeded in starting a war; the orderly would surely have heard. "Yes," Jainan said, though his stomach felt like a shriveled, nauseous lump. He needed to be functional. As the orderly got up and fetched a plastic cup from a tray, memories piled into Jainan's head, feeding the sense of urgency pumping through him. "I would like to see Kiem, please."

The orderly handed him the water. "Drink that for me," he said encouragingly.

Something inside Jainan snapped. His fingers curled around the cup. "I have had enough," he said, in a voice that surprised even him, "of being treated as if I am incompetent. Last time I saw my partner, he was tackling a man with an incapacitator gun. Please show me the visitor list so I can ascertain if he is alive."

The orderly seemed taken aback. "If you'll just calm down there, sir," he said, in a quelling voice, but he was already reaching over to gesture the bedside screen awake. "We'll get you that."

Kiem would have found some way to soften what Jainan had just said. Jainan raised the plastic cup to his mouth mechanically. "I appreciate the water," he said. "Thank you."

This seemed to mollify the orderly. "There we are," he said as the names flashed up. "It's visiting hours, so if any of them are still around, your readings are stable enough to see someone."

"Thank you," Jainan said. He scanned the list.

Kiem's name wasn't on it. The omission was like a hand clenching at Jainan's throat. He spun down to the bottom with the screen's clumsy sensor and then read it over again, but unless

Kiem had given an alias, he hadn't requested a visit. Were Jainan's memories of him from the Tau field even real? A beeping noise started up next to the bed. Jainan realized it must be his heart rate monitor.

"Steady there," the orderly said, checking the tube going into his wrist. Jainan swapped hands and spun back up the list.

He told himself it didn't mean anything final. The situation was complicated; Kiem could have been instructed not to visit him. And surely everyone on Carissi Station would have heard if a member of the royal family had died, just as they would have heard if combat drones were dropping on a Thean city. He glanced at the orderly, who was frowning over his readings.

He needed more information. He took a deep breath and looked down the list again. He needed someone who would help him.

Nearly every name was someone he knew. Bel. Gairad. Professor Audel. Bel again—she seemed to have called every hour. The Thean Ambassador, and the Deputy Thean Ambassador, and others from the embassy. He realized, with a light-headed feeling, that he could call on any of them, and they would tell him what they knew and help him find out more. He didn't understand how he suddenly had so many options.

But it was obvious whom he should talk to first. He lifted his head. "Could you see if Bel Siara is still waiting, please?"

The orderly left him in private. After much less time than he expected, a familiar face appeared in the doorway. "Welcome back to the world of the conscious," Bel said.

Jainan's neutral mask fell away in relief. Even Bel wouldn't be using that sardonic tone if Kiem were in danger, but he asked just to make sure. "Kiem's alive? General Fenrik hasn't made a move?"

"Oh, Heaven, of course Kiem's alive," Bel said. Her professional Iskat accent was back, Jainan noticed. She hadn't sounded like that when he'd last seen her. "Alive and operating like there's a time bomb under his feet. No military strike on Thea either, not since we told the Emperor what General Fenrik was planning. She isn't pleased. Are you out of danger? I'm guessing you are, since you're talking, but the medics were making grim faces at me right up until yesterday."

"Yes, I'm fine," Jainan said. "You're not hurt? You took—" He faltered. Some of his memories were still blurry, but he could piece them together. He hadn't been hallucinating when Aren shot Bel.

"He missed anything vital," Bel said. "I'd bet most of the palace officers have never seen real action. I was fine by morning."

Jainan looked at where his wristband should have been, then at the time display on the screen, and had to conceal his shock. It was the day before Ressid was due to land; the Unification Day ceremonies began tomorrow. He had been unconscious for three days. "I was told I'm not under arrest."

"You're not," Bel said. "But Kiem definitely is."

Jainan's hand clenched in the bedsheet. "*Kiem* is? Why have they arrested Kiem?" The tube in his wrist tugged in its bandage, and he realized he was leaning forward. "I was the one they accused! What is Aren going to charge Kiem with? Sabotaging his own flyer? *Aren* was the one who killed Taam! He was the one who tried to kill both of us!"

Bel held up a hand. "Saffer's also under arrest. Sorry. I'm not explaining well. It's been a long few days. Let's take this back to the beginning."

She did have the look of someone operating on too much stress and no sleep. Jainan felt a pang of guilt and looked around for a chair. The bench the orderly had sat on was bolted to the wall, so he drew up his legs, leaving a space on the bed. "You should sit down."

Bel looked down and paused. Jainan realized it was uncharacteristic of him to let anyone who wasn't his partner that close, and felt his throat close up in embarrassment before Bel unceremoniously dropped the folder she was carrying on the end of the bed and made herself comfortable next to it. "Tell me if I'm on your feet. How are you really feeling, by the way?"

"Fine," Jainan said. Bel raised an eyebrow, and he gave ground. "My head hurts. It's not too bad."

"Ye-es." Bel said. "You know prisoners who spend too long in that thing tend to suffer permanent brain damage?"

"That's very reassuring," Jainan said. "I'm glad we all went through this, or I might never have experienced your tactful bedside manner."

"You should hear me when Kiem thinks he has a cold," Bel said. She brought a foot up, resting her shoe on the bed, and slung her arm around her knee as she apparently collected her thoughts. "So. They found where Fenrik had stashed the stolen remnants, but the treaty is still on shaky ground, and the deadline is tonight. Even though the Emperor told the Auditor that Saffer killed Taam, the Auditor still says Thea doesn't have enough indications of population consent. He *might* be talking about the newslogs."

"The newslogs," Jainan said, with some dread.

"Saffer—may he run out of air on a junkship—threatened to leak the story to the press, and he did. All the Thean newslogs are running articles about how you were kidnapped. Some of them even picked up the Tau field angle. The entire planet is up in arms about what happened to you. It was technically a war crime."

Jainan didn't have time to think about that. The Resolution deadline was tonight. "The Auditor has his remnants back," he said, frustrated. "What's the problem? Is the Thean embassy refusing to sign the treaty?"

"No, at this point your embassy says they'll sign anything," Bel said bluntly. "But everyone on Thea is furious and the newslogs are out for blood. If the Auditor needs implied popular consent, Saffer has managed to royally screw us all over. You can't change the opinion of a whole planet in six hours."

Jainan needed allies. He needed *Kiem*. "Why is Kiem under arrest?"

"He broke into a classified facility."

"To get me."

"Yes," Bel said. "Well. That's where it gets a bit murky. They're reading all our communications, so we don't write much. He said to tell you he's sorry."

Jainan's tongue felt dry. Kiem clearly hadn't told anyone about Taam and Jainan's history. "You're free, though?"

"I'm out on Imperial sufferance," Bel said. "And only because Kiem confessed to all the actual crimes and sent the Emperor a clemency plea for the rest of us. The Emperor now has the real version of my career history," she added. "Kiem says, and I quote, 'It probably tickled her.'"

"The real version," Jainan said. He struggled to pull up his tattered memories of the Tau field. "Kiem said something about . . . raiders?"

"Raider," Bel said. "Singular. *Ex*-raider." She was watching him carefully.

Jainan felt a long-ago stir of suspicion rise again and take shape. "That's how you knew the leader of the Blue Star group." Bel nodded, only slightly. "Why are you pretending to be an aide?"

"I'm not pretending," Bel said sharply. "I wanted to go straight. I applied for this job, I got it, and funny thing, being in the center of the Empire's power base means any of my old colleagues who might want to argue find it very hard to get to me."

"So it's for safety?"

"No," Bel said. "Well, a little. But no. I'm good at this job. I enjoy getting respect that doesn't come at gunpoint, and I don't want to make a living out of screwing over merchants and freighters. I don't like shooting people. I was *born* on a Red Alpha ship, you know, I didn't pick it." She added, defensively, "I like it here. At least I get more career options than 'raider captain.'"

"And all those times you solved our technical problems—?"

Bel spread her hands. "I didn't hurt anyone."

Jainan longed to press his knuckles into his eyes but held back.

Kiem apparently knew all this already. And Bel had saved their lives, and there was really no time for this. "Thank you," he said, at last. "I did wonder how Kiem had broken in. It makes much more sense now."

"Don't get arrested again," Bel said. There was an odd undercurrent of relief to her voice. Had she really cared what Jainan thought of her? "I can't get an Imperial pardon twice."

"No, I do see that," Jainan said. "Can't I at least take responsibility for the break-in? This whole mess is"—*my fault*—"not your fault. Either of you."

"Kiem said you might say that," Bel said levelly. "And I would like you to know that if I could travel back five years with a burn gun and put a six-inch hole through Taam's torso, I would also have been able to solve everything. *It's Taam's fault.*"

It took a moment for Jainan to reply. "I know that."

"Apart from the part where you got tortured," Bel said. "That was mainly Saffer. Fenrik's still walking around, by the way. I suppose if you start imprisoning Imperial stalwarts it sets a bad precedent. I haven't heard what the Emperor is going to do with him. *Someone* is very anxious that I don't do anything illegal right now, which includes bugging the Emperor's private message branch."

That roused Jainan from his tangled thoughts about Aren and Taam. "You should *certainly* not do that," he said, then caught the gleam in her eye and realized he had risen to the bait. The side of his mouth quirked involuntarily.

The visitor's light by the door beeped insistently. Jainan automatically reached out to sign it open when he saw Gairad's face on the screen, then hesitated and glanced at Bel. "Do you mind? She's clan."

"You might as well," Bel said. "She's been camping out in the waiting room. She came on the rescue mission, you know."

"Pardon?" Jainan said as the door slid open to admit Gairad. She looked somewhat the worse for wear. There was a healing bruise on her face and an inexplicable gel cast on her arm. She put one hand on the door frame—the other was hampered by the cast—and said, like she was hammering the words out of a punch press, "Will you please stop almost *dying*?"

"What happened to your arm?" Jainan said, alarmed. "Why were you with Bel and Kiem?"

That seemed to take some of the wind out of Gairad's sails. She touched the gel cast with a mixture of embarrassment and pride. "I hit an Iskat soldier."

"Punches badly," Bel said. She sounded darkly amused. "Fractured her wrist. I've shown her how to do it better."

"That was *highly irresponsible*," Jainan said, not sure which one of them he was talking to. His mind was still reeling at how many people had been involved in finding him. Both Kiem and Bel had been strangers two months ago, of course, but he couldn't shake the feeling that Ressid might have something to say about Jainan putting a junior clan member in danger.

"We found the weapons," Gairad said defensively. "Jainan, Iskat is trying to cover up the whole Kingfisher invasion. Even the Ambassador says to keep it quiet. That's not right. And what's going to happen with the Resolution treaty?"

Jainan tried not to show the urgent fear driving the wheels in his mind. "It will be fine," he said. "The palace will release a statement. Nobody saw the abduction. It can be passed off to the newslogs as a misunderstanding."

Gairad stood in the middle of the room, rocking back and forth on her toes and staring at him. There seemed to be something else. "Didn't anyone tell you?"

"Tell me what?" Jainan said.

"Bel says it isn't true," Gairad said. Her expression had clouded. "I don't believe it, if it helps."

Jainan couldn't tell if the spike of nausea was part of the field aftereffects or not. "Bel," he said, "please tell me what is going on."

"Take a deep breath," Bel said. "There's a nasty rumor that's making the whole thing worse. I suppose Aren thought the abduction wasn't enough to screw up public opinion."

"What rumor?"

"That Kiem's the one who was violent to you." Bel said.

She said something after that, but Jainan didn't hear it. He had to stare at her and follow her lips until his brain started to make sense of what he heard again. ". . . after you had that argument at dinner, it's muddied the waters, and a couple of anti-royalist newslogs on Iskat got hold of it somehow . . ."

He ceased to hear her again. He felt as though his skin had been stripped away and every particle sleeting through the universe could now hammer into his exposed flesh, tearing away what he used to defend his core. His fingers were numb; his muscles no longer worked.

"Jainan?"

Jainan realized Bel had spoken to him more than once. With an effort, he cut short the fugue state that wanted to take hold of his mind. "Oh," he said.

"Shut the hell up," Bel said, jabbing something beside his bed. The beeping that had filled the air stopped. "Jainan? Didn't mean to give you a relapse. Kiem's denied it, of course, but nobody knows about you and Taam. It's hard to explain away some of the evidence without—you know."

Without telling the truth about Jainan and Taam's real relationship, which Kiem wouldn't do. Of course. "It's not a relapse," Jainan said. Oddly, his head now felt very clear. "Bel, could I ask a favor of you?"

"Break you out of the med room?" Bel said, only semi-facetiously.

"Not quite," Jainan said. "I would like the contact details for the Emperor's Private Office."

Bel raised her eyebrows. "Going straight to the top? It didn't work so well for Kiem. She'll just tell you to keep everything under wraps."

"I understand," Jainan said. He did, that was the thing. It was a delicate matter. "I don't plan to ask her to do anything. I would also like you to contact a visitor for me."

Ten minutes and a few calls later, Bel and Gairad had gone—Gairad to reassure Professor Audel and Bel to message Kiem. Jainan waited in bed, keyed up to unbearable levels, and jumped as the door chimed.

"Your Grace?"

"Hani Sereson," Jainan said. He held himself as straight as he could, sitting up in bed. "I hoped you were on the press list. Do come in."

The journalist gave him a blinding professional smile and sketched a bow. "I must say, I didn't think I'd ever hear from you like this." Her eyes flicked over his body and the drip in his wrist with a hungry shimmer of silver. "We heard you were ill. All of us were wondering if you were well enough for the ceremonies."

"I'm saving my energy. Forgive me for not rising to greet you," Jainan said. "And thank you for coming on such short notice." He opened his hand to indicate a chair Bel had brought in from the corridor.

"Believe me, no journalist would turn down a message like the one I just received." Hani sat down and crossed one leg over the other. "I do hope you're recovering well from . . . well, it looks like you've been through some kind of ordeal." Her hand hovered over an expensive mic button, which she detached from her collar and left to float in the air between them. "Do you mind if I record this conversation?"

Jainan's smile came from some deep, sharp place within him. "Of course not," he said. "In fact, I would be very pleased if you would."

CHAPTER 30

"I see where you're coming from," Kiem said into the recording. "I want you to know that it's not *true,* but I get that you have to tell reporters you've done something. Fine. You want me to resign as a patron, I'll do that." He swallowed another spike of frustration. "Let me know if I can find you someone else, though. You should have someone from the palace on the board." He paused. "Stay in touch."

He cut the recording to the latest charity and slumped back from the tiny desk. The steel of the chair dug into his shoulder muscles. He stretched his arms out. The room was large enough for him to do that, at least, though his knuckles grazed the frame of the bunk bed.

But his surroundings were luxurious compared to what they might have been. The armored core of the station had a holding room that Internal Security used for who knew what nefarious purposes, and when the military and civilian wrangling had been sorted out, that was where Kiem had ended up. For a holding cell, it didn't lack for frills: there was a tiny bathroom, an exercise machine, and even a flickering screen with hundreds of preprogrammed media in the corner.

Depending on how you looked at it, it might not even be a cell. The door wasn't *locked,* just guarded by agents with instructions to keep him in and no sense of humor. Kiem had played with the idea of seeing if he could bluff his way past them to get to Jainan's med room but had reluctantly abandoned it after the first unsuccessful attempt. It would be a bad idea to make the Emperor any more furious than she already was. He had Bel and Jainan to think about.

He knew what the newslogs were saying. Bel had started sending him copies as soon as they realized Aren, even in detention, had managed to make good on his threat to smear them. Kiem had winced at the abduction articles, but at least they were true. Then the first accusation that Kiem mistreated Jainan had appeared in a small-time gossip log on Thea: it had spread from there to fringe newslogs and anti-royalist streams across both Thea and Iskat, who'd all eaten up the scandal. It wasn't hard to find pictures of Kiem looking drunk and unreliable. One of the newslogs had even decided their wedding photos looked miserable enough to illustrate the article; Kiem had abandoned his reading at that point and gone to bed. Then he'd asked Bel to stop sending cuttings.

His latest message of resignation—this one his third, for an education charity—hung as a small glowing circle above the table. Kiem drummed his fingers on the edge of the table, outside the sensor area, and sent it before he could give in to temptation and add anything else. His messages were getting more like babbling as the hours went on. He should stick to writing, but even talking to an imaginary recipient staved off the awful silence of not having *anyone* to talk to. He had seen only Internal Security agents for the past four days, usually Rakal or one of their interchangeable deputies. He was going to go mad if this carried on too long.

When the message was gone, he put his head down on the desk. What he wanted to do was send a message to Jainan—an honest one—but he knew Rakal's people were reviewing everything that went through his account while he was in here, and he wasn't going to hand them anything else about Jainan or Taam. It had to wait until Jainan woke up. Whenever he did wake up.

He made himself breathe out slowly. What he needed was a fraction of Jainan's calm. When things went wrong for Jainan, he didn't flap around uselessly like Kiem. He just got . . . more focused. For a moment Kiem wasn't even afraid for him, he just missed him. Just not having Jainan there hurt.

A message added itself to the depressingly short list in the corner of the desk. Kiem abandoned his attempt at serenity to see what it was.

It was from Bel. Kiem wasn't expecting much: his messages to and from Bel were short and businesslike, so neither of them accidentally contradicted the details about Taam that Kiem had fudged in his original story. This one was short even by her standards, though, and contained a clipping with a single line above it.

Jainan's awake. Brace yourself before you read this.

Kiem's surge of joy left as fast as it had appeared. He frowned and opened the clip.

It was a press cuttings file; not fringe newslogs, but some of the biggest outlets on Iskat and Thea. The moment Kiem recognized it as news he nearly shut it off before it could spread over the desk. But he'd left it a moment too long to cancel. The pages fanned out and settled in front of him. Kiem's stomach gave a lurch.

Jainan's face stared back at him from every cutting, from every newslog. The same photo: he was propped up in a hospital bed, looking directly, almost defiantly, at the camera. He had made no attempt to hide that the wrist lying across his lap was hooked up to a drip. The most shocking thing was what he was wearing— Jainan, who rarely let himself be photographed, and never in anything less than full formal dress, had let them take his photo in a hospital gown.

The first time Kiem tried to read the headlines, his brain rebelled, and he couldn't take them in. His eyes kept going back to Jainan's diamond-hard gaze. The biggest picture, the one Bel had placed in the center, was under the familiar green-and-black header of the *Consult*. The words next to it read, "TREATY REPRESENTATIVE 'SETS THE RECORD STRAIGHT': ACCUSES PRINCE TAAM OF ABUSE."

Kiem stopped breathing.

The *Consult* was a restrained, respectable outlet. Their headline was the least sensational of the bunch. The rest of the articles started at "FREED FROM HELL" and went downhill from there. At first Kiem wondered wildly who had leaked this—who had done this to Jainan—but then he looked farther down the *Consult* article. A smaller candid shot showed Jainan and Hani Sereson talking in the same hospital room. Jainan had done this on purpose.

Kiem should be able to read the article. He didn't understand why he was so afraid of it. It hadn't happened to *him*.

He took a deep breath and made himself read it.

Jainan was very clear on who was to blame. He took apart Taam's character—and Aren's—like a surgical strike. Every time they quoted him, he was dry and emotionless, but the details themselves were blunt weapons. Taam's monitoring of his calls. His order to revoke Jainan's security clearance. Incidents both in public and in private. Set out in black-and-white with dates and places, it looked surreal, grotesque, and yet whenever it was in Jainan's words he made it sound very ordinary, while Hani's careful arrangement of the article threw his descriptions into stark relief.

Kiem and the rest of Iskat came out better than they deserved. Jainan carved out Taam and Aren like pieces of rot, separating them from the rest of the Empire and creating a story that both the Iskat and Thean press could swallow. He had decided to get the treaty signed and he had used his own past to do it. Kiem was torn between feeling sick to his stomach and being overcome with desperate admiration.

A side article showed a set of messages from Taam, though heavily redacted, since even the *Consult* was wary of the palace and the law. But Hani had done her legwork: there were confirmations of the events Jainan and Taam had attended, a physician's record, a barely diplomatic quote from the Thean embassy.

Why now? Hani asked, in the last column. *Count Jainan seems more intense, as if he's been expecting this. "Because it's over, and justice can now be done," he says. "Prince Kiem has been a hero. The Emperor has pledged a full investigation. She has looked at the Thean treaty and promised further concessions to make up for this. Iskat is trying to bridge the gap." Both the Emperor and Prince Kiem, his current partner, were unavailable for comment at the time of publication.*

Kiem couldn't bring himself to read through to the end. He swept his hand compulsively across the desk. The press clippings spun and winked out, but the burst of uncontrollable energy didn't dissipate, just propelled him pointlessly to his feet. He leaned over the table and had to press on it to stop his arms from shaking—with what emotion, he wasn't sure. He wanted to hit something. He wanted to fix the universe so the last five years had never happened. He wanted to find Jainan and kiss him.

He didn't do any of that. Before he could get any further in his thoughts, the door gave a perfunctory chime and opened to admit Agent Rakal.

"Your Highness." Rakal's stride didn't slow as they threw their wristband projection onto the small screen on the wall. "Her majesty wishes for an audience with you."

Any similarity that had to a request was purely superficial. Kiem only had a couple of seconds to try and tug his crumpled shirt straight before the Emperor's face was on the wall.

He bowed. Rakal, somewhat unexpectedly, went to one knee.

"Oh, get up," the Emperor said. Rakal rose. Their jaw was tightly locked in an expression that, Kiem realized, looked a lot like shame. "Assigning responsibility will come afterward. Clean up this mess first. Kiem!"

Kiem jumped. "Ma'am?" Suddenly Rakal's salutation didn't seem like an overreaction. Rakal had definitely made some mistakes, but from the Emperor's point of view, Kiem was the one standing by the blaze with a gas canister and an innocent expression. He was probably heading up the Least Favorite Relative list right now.

"Did you tell him to do this?" the Emperor said.

Kiem's first instinct was to say, *Do what?* But Jainan had flung this up like a flare in the dark, and the time for cover-ups was over. "No," Kiem said. "But aren't you glad he waited until Taam was dead before he did? *Did* you volunteer to give Thea more concessions in the treaty, by the way? You'll have to draft them fast."

"Your blasted partner has left me little choice," the Emperor said. "We'll find them some baubles. The Thean newslogs are contacting me for quotes. There is a press conference directly before the treaty signing tonight. How you and Jainan conduct yourselves will be crucial for planetary opinion over the next few hours. Jainan has family in the Thean diplomatic contingent."

"Oh, shit, Ressid," Kiem said, dismayed. "Sorry. 'Scuse the language. Is Jainan . . . ?"

"He will be at the opening press conference," the Emperor said. "So will you." She adjusted her old-fashioned glasses, grimacing. "So, of course, will every Thean and Iskat news outlet that can possibly scramble their staff to the station. I have decided you are the most appropriate one to deliver the official apology for his previous treatment."

"Official—apology?" Kiem said, taken aback. It must be bad. Of course Jainan deserved it, but the about-face was so fast, he might get whiplash. "Yes? I mean, I'd be happy to, Your Majesty."

"*Don't* improvise," the Emperor said. "I will send Hren to brief you. Listen to him and to Rakal, and do not even think of going off script. You have less than an hour to prepare—the Theans are arriving by shuttle even now." She peered closer at the screen. "And what in Heaven are you wearing? Burn it immediately. Put on something suitable."

"Yes, ma'am," Kiem said, barely paying attention to the last part. "Can I see Jainan before the press conference? They haven't let me see him yet. I know he's awake." He glanced sideways at that, including Rakal in the request. They were looking even more mortified at the talk of the official apology, though they must have known in advance.

"You will certainly talk to Jainan afterward," the Emperor said. "That boy has gone a great deal too far. You will remind him of his duty."

"I will?" Kiem said. "Saving Your Majesty's presence, it sounds like he's already said what he's going to say. You can't wipe it off the *Consult*'s pages."

Rakal said, in a low, flat voice, "It is ongoing. He leaked a security camera video and pictures of you and him to four organizations after the initial *Consult* interview."

"And how do we know, you ask?" the Emperor said. "Because the dratted man apparently requested that each of them send a copy of their article to my Private Office—why are you wearing that particularly vacuous grin?"

Jainan did not strike out and create a random mess, like Kiem would have done. He caused deliberate, targeted mayhem. "I love him," Kiem said. He shouldn't say it. Jainan's declarations had just been politics, he knew that, but Kiem was unable to stop smiling.

"Of course you do," the Emperor said. "You have never made good choices. Sell this, or the Empire falls."

She cut the connection. Kiem stepped back, his mind whirling with hope and doubt, and let Rakal cut theirs.

Everything in the corridors leading to the Observation Hall had been freshly cleaned and polished. The white walls glittered, a pristine runner had been laid underfoot, and silver light fittings shone like mirrors. As Jainan turned into the curved walkway to the anterooms he was sharply visible against the pale background in the deep green of his clan uniform. Feria used several shades of green with gold patterns boldly climbing over them like vines, and whether it was the un-Iskat patterns or the fact his face was in all the newslogs, he had felt stares on him all the way from the med room. It made him ensure his head was up and put a fraction of extra length in his stride. Let them stare.

He knew Ressid had landed, along with the rest of the Thean contingent. He had kept his messages with her brief because Hani's interview wasn't something he wanted to talk about unless it was in person, but he knew she had seen it. Right now Ressid would be in the pre-treaty press conference—and according to Bel, that was where Kiem was as well. Jainan suspected that the moment he walked into the press conference, he would become the center of attention himself, but it couldn't be helped. He had gone to the press and the world had not ended. He could weather it.

And he had waited long enough. He was well enough to walk, he was looking presentable, and he was going to find Kiem and nail down this treaty if he had to go through half the station to do it.

The hallway and staircase leading up were nearly empty, although a low murmur of voices came from the Observation Hall itself. A couple of glamorously dressed women with newslog equipment had just reached the top of the staircase, awkward in the light gravity, and were being ushered in by an attendant. Jainan was late; it had taken longer for the doctors to do the final checks than he had anticipated.

He slipped into the side of the hall. It had been set up for the conference with a semicircular dais in front of the grand sweep of windows, a wash of stars forming the backdrop to the podium itself. The first thing he saw was the Auditor, seated at the back with his arms folded, the seats deserted for three rows around him and his staff. The second thing Jainan saw was Ressid at the podium in the middle of an answer, her emphatic cadences so familiar it was disorienting. As Jainan silently closed the door behind him, he scanned the handful of Theans and Iskaners sitting behind her on the stage. He barely looked at any of them except Kiem.

Kiem was at the end of the row, sitting uncomfortably on the edge of his seat. His elbows rested on his knees and his foot jiggled restlessly, as if he couldn't bear to be in a space as confined as a chair. His face was lined with anxiousness, but he was solid and real and alive, and for a moment Jainan was an invisible observer in a private bubble of affection.

It only took seconds for one of the reporters in the audience to turn their head and notice the newcomer. Jainan's arrival spread out through the crowd like a ripple. Photographers turned their lenses. At the front, Ressid hadn't yet noticed.

". . . remains committed to the treaty," she said. "Discussions are still underway with the Resolution's Auditor . . ." She faltered and stopped.

Jainan swallowed, ignoring all the press, and returned her gaze. He wasn't twenty-two, newly married and naive anymore. He wasn't twenty-six and trying to hide. He and Ressid would have to talk, and until then, he could at least look her in the eye.

Not everyone in the front row had noticed. One of the reporters took advantage of the gap to jump in. "And Count Jainan's press statements today? Can you comment on that?"

Ressid was not a trained diplomat for nothing. The steel returned to her voice as she turned her attention back to the press. "I must disclose a personal interest. You are all aware Count Jainan is my brother." As she said *my brother,* her eyes went briefly back to Jainan, fierce and uncompromising, and then bored into the reporter again. "After the treaty is signed, we demand that Count Jainan comes to live on Thea."

Jainan stopped in shock.

A murmur rose around him. On the dais behind Ressid, Kiem

looked as if someone had finally landed a blow he'd been dreading. His shoulders slumped.

"Next question," Ressid said. Jainan realized she was trying to protect him from the glare of attention.

"No," someone said sharply. "Stop." Jainan realized it was him.

Kiem looked up. The whole room was paying attention now, but that wasn't important. Jainan saw the moment Kiem realized he was there. He saw the way Kiem straightened from his slump like someone had pulled him up, and he saw Kiem's whole expression light up with hope.

Jainan had never been good at communicating, but he didn't have to be, because now his certainty was a cascading river buoying him along. As he strode up to the front, camera lenses started turning on him. He ignored them. He ignored everything except the way Kiem shot out of his chair, caught his foot on the leg of it, stumbled, reached out.

Jainan caught his hands. He hadn't meant to clutch them as tightly as he did. "Kiem."

"*Jainan,*" Kiem said, as if his name was the first breath of air he'd drawn in minutes. "You—you're—you're—"

"What's this about?" Jainan said.

"Splitting us up?" Kiem said. He didn't seem to be able to string more than a few words together. People had started to call questions from behind Jainan, but neither of them paid attention. "I didn't—"

"I'm clearly not leaving now," Jainan said. "This should be obvious. I love you."

"You *do*? You do. I mean. Yes!" Kiem's face was incredulous and joyful. "I do too! Of course I love you! I have for ages! Ressid thought—"

The dam inside Jainan burst. "*Kiem,*" he said, and grabbed his wrist. "How did they let it get this far?" Kiem came with him, confused but willing, as Jainan turned to the front of the stage.

"Your Grace!" a reporter shouted, cutting across the babble of voices. "Will you make a statement?"

"Yes," Jainan said. He took the microphone from the podium. Elation was running through him like a drug. "I certainly am going to make a statement." That was enough to quiet the room down. A reporter called out another question from the back but cut off in the middle as Jainan tapped the hovering button.

"I think I may have been misleading before," Jainan said. "I am not very good at talking about my feelings. I said in my previous interview that Kiem was a great help. What I meant was: I love Kiem, he is truly extraordinary, and there is nobody I would rather be married to. I hope this is now clear."

A ripple went through the room—half shock, half amusement, but the only sound Jainan focused on was a low, involuntary noise from Kiem beside him and the way he pulled his wrist out of Jainan's grip so he could take Jainan's hand. Jainan clasped it tight, and it buoyed him up like a wave. He leaned over the microphone and gave the crowd of reporters a beatific smile. "Questions?"

Several people shouted over each other. Jainan picked out a woman in the front row, who called, "What about the treaty? Is the Emperor granting concessions?"

"She will be," Jainan said. At the back of the room, the Auditor had sat up. Jainan turned his head to Ressid, who had the same look on her face as she'd had when Jainan blew up his first experimental shuttle drive. Jainan was exhilarated enough to nearly grin, but he suppressed it and then turned his attention on Kiem. "Does Your Highness have a statement?"

"Honestly," Kiem said, the corners of his eyes crinkling, "I think my partner covered it." He was talking to the reporters, but he was only looking at Jainan, and his words were only the edges of what he was saying, like the breaking crests of waves on a tide. Jainan didn't laugh, but only because laughter was no more than a fraction of what he felt. He stepped up and kissed Kiem.

It was easy to ignore the cameras this time. Jainan shut his eyes and didn't break away even in the bustle that surrounded them, encouraged by Kiem's arms wrapped possessively around him. They didn't stop until the coordinating steward announced, "Honored citizens, I believe we should suspend the conference here," and the Ambassador coughed politely behind Jainan and said, "Your Grace?"

Jainan turned, putting his polite face on, which was hard because fireworks kept fizzing in his brain. "Yes, Your Excellency?" he said. But he realized what it was the next moment, as Ressid strode across the dais toward him.

She stopped a bare arm's length away. Jainan searched her face, not knowing what else to do. She was achingly unchanged. All you could ever tell from Ressid was that she was in the grip of strong emotions, not which ones they were.

The press conference was breaking up. Kiem was apparently giving an impromptu interview to a handful of journalists at the edge of the dais, so they had a small pool of quiet away from everyone's attention. "Ressid," Jainan said uncertainly.

"Sweet children of *God*," Ressid said, and flung her arms around him in a way that was not at all commensurate with her image as a senior diplomat. "I am going to murder you," she added, low enough not to be heard by anyone else. "Or possibly myself for being so slow. *Someone* is going to get murdered."

She'd last hugged him like this when he'd left for Iskat. He'd last heard her threaten to murder people when they were teenagers. Jainan suddenly wasn't afraid, only elated and relieved, and he wanted badly to laugh. "I thought they'd made you tone down the death threats," he said. "What if an Iskaner hears you? How was your shuttle trip?"

"*Somewhat tense*," Ressid said, "'Full-blown diplomatic crisis' doesn't seem to cover it. We need to talk."

Jainan realized belatedly that Ressid would be tasked with cleaning up the chaos he had left. "I—yes. Sorry."

"We need to go to the Auditor as well, and we're almost out of time—excuse me? Jainan, don't you dare apologize." It didn't take much for Ressid to default to the extreme condescension that only an older sibling could manage; Jainan probably shouldn't be glad about that. "You're the one who pried a decent negotiating position out of this whole mess. Don't go shy and retiring on me. I'll need you at the table."

"Oh," Jainan said. "Yes." The gathered reporters and dignitaries were slowly dispersing around the plates of refreshment provided at the side of the room, but there was a reporter still hovering hopefully at Ressid's elbow to try and get to Jainan. "Have you met Kiem, by the way?" He could have sworn Kiem's attention was fully on his conversation with a journalist, but the minute Jainan mentioned his name, Kiem stepped up beside him. His hand brushed Jainan's. Jainan deliberately caught it.

Kiem bowed without detaching himself. "I've had the pleasure over vid," he said. "Though I think I've worked out some things about the call you gave me on our wedding day."

Ressid sized him up. "Hm," she said. "Me too. We'll have to catch up." She eyed the crowd around them. "Go and find a room we can talk in, Jainan. I'll hold them off. So sorry to keep you waiting," she added loudly to the reporter edging up to her—that was Dak, the reporter from the wedding, who had apparently managed to avoid being blacklisted. "I'd be delighted to give you a statement on the treaty amendments." She took Dak's arm and bore him off firmly, leaving Kiem and Jainan to escape from the others. In the crowd beside her Hren Halesar was holding court with a group of other journalists, and he caught Jainan's eye and flicked his fingers to his forehead in an ironic salute.

"'Scuse me," Kiem said, engineering a path around the back of a particularly burly reporter. "No more questions, sorry, we have to change for dinner. Call me tomorrow. Have a good day!"

After a few more moments of Kiem's excuses and innocent-seeming shouldering, they found themselves near the exit, where they could make a polite escape. "I am never going to read a newslog again," Jainan murmured as his elbow brushed Kiem's.

"Are you kidding?" Kiem said. He was grinning at Jainan in a way that made it seem like he'd just discovered Jainan's face and was delighted with it, which was unfair and exhilarating at the same time. "I'm going to laser tomorrow's front page posts on our bedroom wall."

"I will *void the treaty*," Jainan threatened. Kiem laughed and bowed him through the door.

CHAPTER 31

Jainan was outwardly sober and controlled again when he left Kiem—who was moving his belongings out of his cell and back into their guest suite—and made his way to the meeting chamber the Theans had secured. It felt like the gravity had been turned down; his feet came farther off the ground when he walked. He no longer even registered the people he passed in the corridors, until one of them blocked his way.

"Your Grace?"

Chief Agent Rakal, in a freshly pressed uniform. They dipped their head in a meticulously proper bow. Jainan stopped with a faint trace of unease. But he recognized that fear as part of an old pattern, one that he didn't have to maintain. He sketched a nod. "Agent Rakal. I'm afraid I have an appointment with the Thean delegation."

"I would take it as a personal favor," Rakal said, "if you could stop your aide from threatening Aren Saffer while he is in my custody."

Jainan could not easily categorize his immediate reaction to hearing Rakal say Aren's name. Aren had always been linked to Taam. Even everything Aren had done felt like something from Taam's world, spinning on after Taam's death. Jainan was almost surprised to find he had his own opinion of Aren, separate from Taam: something like cold aversion, as if he wasn't important enough for Jainan to spend further time on.

Then he said, "*Bel* threatened him?"

"Saffer attempted to get a message out to his raider allies," Rakal said tersely. Jainan noticed that despite their ferociously neat appearance, there were shadows of fatigue under their eyes. "We blocked it; I have no idea how she intercepted a copy. It makes it very difficult for me to overlook your aide's past if she threatens my prisoners with her conglomerate connections."

Jainan took a moment to arrange his face to reflect an appropriate degree of seriousness. "I can see that," he said. "I'll speak to her."

Rakal didn't move. "One more thing. I have drafted my resignation."

"Have you," Jainan said.

"I have not yet formally tendered it. If you wish to make a preference clear to the Emperor, please do so over the next couple of days."

Jainan looked at them. "Why?"

There was an unpleasant struggle going on behind Rakal's attempt at professional neutrality. "My agency failed to handle this as we would ideally have done. In hindsight I should have paid more attention to the . . . personal angle."

Jainan felt a distant stab of discomfort. "The personal angle is often irrelevant."

"You came to the Empire in good faith. Internal Security could have looked more closely, and earlier, at Prince Taam's activities." It would have sounded like equivocation except for the way it clearly caused Rakal some pain to get the words out. They seemed determined to do it anyway. "Matters were handled improperly."

"I don't think you should resign," Jainan said.

"I do not require a polite fiction."

"I think," Jainan said slowly, "that it's very possible to spend all your energy doing the right thing but still miss something obvious. I think that doesn't make your effort meaningless. Does that make sense?"

Rakal's eyes narrowed, as if this was another piece of an investigatory puzzle. "I will consider it." They shook their head as if to clear it and moved aside. "I apologize for taking up your time."

Jainan gave them a fractional nod and quickened his pace down the corridor. He was late.

"Jainan!" Gairad hurried to catch up with him outside the meeting chamber. Her work coveralls were gone, replaced by a semiformal outfit with a jacket in Feria green. "Wait for me. I barely know anyone in there."

Jainan searched her face for signs she was looking at him differently now that she knew about Taam. He found nothing. She seemed to regard him as a handy clan member who would do as an ally in a pinch, the same as she had before the newslog coverage. It was an odd, refreshing feeling.

Gairad misread his scrutiny, and her expression turned defensive. "Ressid invited me because I know about Kingfisher, as long as I gave my word not to tell any of my friends. Don't let me look bad in front of her," she added, with a sudden flash of nerves, leading Jainan to wonder how Ressid overawed younger clan members so easily and how he had completely missed that gene.

Ressid opened the door herself. There were nearly a dozen people around a table in the room behind her; half diplomats who had come up in the same shuttle as her, half embassy staff. Ambassador Suleri was at the head of the table.

When Jainan walked in, Suleri rose. It was a gesture of formality he didn't have to make; he and Jainan were roughly equal in rank. Jainan had no time for his nerves to return before the Ambassador inclined his head, one diplomat to another.

"Thank you for coming, both of you," the Ambassador said gravely. "Please have a seat. Lady Ressid is standing in for the principal for Foreign Affairs until her shuttle arrives.

Ressid waited until Jainan and Gairad had both sat. "Citizens," she said. "The treaty signing is in three hours. Any papers to be drawn up must be drawn up now. The Auditor has let us know he sees the possibility of reconciliation. I have promised the Thean press another story on our treaty with Iskat, and Jainan"—a nod to him—"has bought us an opening. My principal wants your agreement on our course of action."

The Ambassador glanced at Jainan. "Iskat has broken our trust in many ways," he said. "However, I encourage the meeting to consider the consequences of a large-scale conflict."

"The Emperor is willing to give us a small reduction in trade tariffs," the Deputy Ambassador said, indicating a document spread out on the table. Jainan realized this was also aimed at him. They had already been through this among themselves. They were nervous about obtaining *his* support.

"Taam wanted a war," Jainan said. "I have no desire to continue his work. What are the other options?"

Ressid let out a small, satisfied *hah,* as if Jainan had proved her right. She swept aside the documents glowing on the table, spinning them into oblivion. "Citizens, I propose the Emperor has *not* offered us a small tariff reduction," she said. Her smile was that of a shark. "I posit that what she has offered us is, in fact, a blank sheet for our demands."

She glanced at Jainan, as if she felt his gaze on her. When he met her eyes, Jainan felt the solidity of his clan underneath him, of all the clans, as if his feet weren't on the metal shell of a station but on the packed earth of Thea below.

"Yes," Jainan said. "And, if you'll allow me to suggest something, I think I know the person to deliver them."

The Emperor sat in an upholstered chair the color of alabaster, almost exactly matching the heavy white of her full-formal tunic and skirts. Behind her head, filling the wall of the anteroom, was the gold-brushed curve of the Hill Enduring.

Her eyes were fixed on a wall screen. It showed a slow bustle in the vast space of the adjoining Observatory Hall as staff prepared it for the treaty signing with dozens of cameras, both fixed and aerial, and a covered table on the dais at the front. On the table was a row of handscribing quills but no papers. The Auditor stood in front of the table, turning his head slightly from side to side, as if he could hear something nobody else could. Some of the treaty representatives had started to file in, tiny on the screen.

Kiem paused in the doorway to the anteroom, a slim, gold-embossed case in his hand. Vaile broke away from a hushed conversation with a pair of aides and swiftly crossed to him. She was past stressed; instead she had gone distant and steely. "Kiem, what are you doing here?"

"I need to talk to her majesty," Kiem said, tilting his head at the statue-like figure of the Emperor. "What's the status of the treaty?"

"We don't know what she's signing," Vaile said, brutally honest. "Things change every five minutes. The *bloody* Auditor doesn't seem to mind that if we don't sign it, we'll be at war within the year."

"Can I talk to her?" Kiem said. Vaile gave an ironic go-ahead gesture.

As he strode across the room, he studied the Emperor's lined face. She couldn't be any less worried than Vaile, but you couldn't see it; even under a degree of pressure that would crack a ship's hull, she wore the exact expression she used for council meetings and press appearances. Kiem couldn't help a twinge of admiration.

The Emperor tore her gaze away from the screen as he approached and raised her eyebrows a fraction. "So," she said. "Kiem. Have you finished your Thean dramatics?"

Kiem gave a shallow bow. "You did give me the Thean representative post, ma'am."

"I did," the Emperor said. "You have certainly taken it in directions I did not expect. However, I am currently dealing with larger problems."

"About that," Kiem said. "I might have a solution to one of them."

She gave him a look that contained more than a hint of disbelief. "*You,*" she said, "have a solution?"

"Well, I'm more like the messenger," Kiem said. He opened the embossed case, drew out some paper documents—real paper, that crackled under his fingers—and handed them to her. "The Theans drafted this and are willing to sign it. The other vassal planets have seen it. Half the Thean newslogs have positive stories ready to run. The Auditor says he'll accept it if you do."

There was dead silence in the anteroom as the Emperor read the papers. Even the aides had stopped muttering.

She raised her eyes when she had finished reading and examined Kiem in further silence. Kiem had very rarely been the subject of the Emperor's unflinching, undivided attention. It was a little like standing in front of a glowing rock you suspected was going to give you radiation poisoning.

"This," she said, "nullifies our current Resolution treaty."

"And forms a new seven-way agreement," Kiem said. "Yes."

"Do you know what this would do?" the Emperor said.

"It splits up the link trade equally," Kiem said. He ticked things off on his fingers. "Gives all the vassals an ambassador to the Galactics. Requires seven-way consensus before any changes to the next Resolution treaty. Seems pretty straightforward: I think we're a federation now. Did you read the coda to the Thean treaty?"

"I did," the Emperor said. "I am willing to grant them control of Operation Kingfisher. Total withdrawal of our military from Thean space . . . we can speak about later."

"We can't," Kiem said. "In five minutes, the treaty ceremony will start, and you have to sign the whole package or sign nothing. Oh, and one more thing," he added.

"Which is?" the Emperor said, in a tone which reduced the temperature of the air around her.

"General Fenrik retires," Kiem said. "No advisory role. No part in politics. You can't just tinker around the edges and jail some soldiers who worked for him, because none of this works if you keep someone in power who tried to start a *war*. He has to go. Maybe you can find him a monastery."

Both the aides and Vaile started to speak at once, but everyone stopped when the Emperor held out the slim stack of paper and dropped it on the table by her side.

"You've got some nerve," she said.

The radiation-poisoning gaze was back in full force. Kiem swallowed and just about stopped himself from apologizing. Instead he said, "The choice isn't *stasis or war*, ma'am. We can change."

"By undermining the Empire?"

"I'm a loyal subject of the Empire. Ma'am."

The Emperor's mouth cracked open. Kiem had so rarely seen her smile that at first he didn't recognize it. It was terrifying. "I am pleased to hear it," she said slowly. "You may go and tell the Auditor I will sign this."

"What?" Kiem said at the same time as one of aides voiced the start of a protest. "I mean. Thank you?"

The Emperor got to her feet. She ignored both interruptions in favor of picking Kiem apart through the sheer force of her stare. Kiem felt his metaphorical skin start to peel. "Needless to say, this was not what I intended when I chose you for the Thean marriage."

The door to the Observatory Hall opened. A noise filtered through: the low, nervous buzz of a small crowd.

"I only want the best for us," Kiem said. "For Iskat."

"Do you?" the Emperor said. Her thin, unsettling smile hadn't gone. She scrutinized him like a new piece that had turned up unexpectedly in the middle of a long board game. Kiem was suddenly even more nervous, for reasons that had nothing to do with the negotiation. "I suppose I can work with that."

She swept ahead of him through the door. Her aides and Vaile hurried to follow.

The staff had finished preparing the Observation Hall. Nobody except the treaty representatives and their guests was allowed in the room, so the attendees were few; the crowds would be let in for the events and celebrations afterward. The Hill Enduring was blazoned in white light every twenty paces on its walls, interspersed with symbols and drapes from the other six planets. Kiem could now put names to a dozen or so of the Thean clan flags.

The Resolution had no symbol. Instead, the junior staffers stood around the edge of the immense space at intervals, each with a silver rod that projected a white illusion field over the floor. It broke across Kiem's ankles, like the floor had been flooded by a thin layer of shining cloud.

At the front of the hall, the Auditor's face-field had gone pure silver. He raised a hand, and a gong sounded. Kiem hurried over to the Thean delegation, who were about to take their seats. He met Jainan's eyes and apparently didn't need to say anything, because Jainan searched his expression and gave a slow, cool smile.

CHAPTER 32

Kiem was probably the smuggest person at the after-dinner drinks, but he'd decided he was fine with that.

When he and Jainan emerged from dinner into the reception room, it was already crowded; the Theans were bright splashes of clan patterns among the more conventionally dressed Iskaners and the smattering of delegates from other planets. With the treaty safely signed, all the diplomats should be preparing to disperse back to their home planets, but instead most of them were settling in for weeks of talks to hammer out the implications of Thea's last-minute deal. Iskat's stranglehold on trade was broken. The Empire was in flux. The vassal planets had their own slow, cumbersome governing structures with their own internal pressures, so none of them seemed keen to upset things immediately, but there were twenty years to hash things out before the next Resolution treaty. The Emperor was in for a lot of arguments in the near future. Kiem sometimes suspected her of enjoying arguments, so that would at least keep her entertained.

But for now, this reception was really just an excuse for all the relevant people on the seven planets to get dressed up, hobnob with their opposite numbers, and have some very good champagne. The noise level was already high.

Kiem felt bubbly and light, more than he'd expected even from the champagne and the relief of sealing the treaty. Jainan was at his side, his silhouette sharp in the deep green of his clan, and a good part of Kiem's glow came from the certainty that he had the most desirable person in the room right next to him, and everyone was probably jealous. He could be magnanimous in victory. More than that, actually, he felt so bubbly that he had to sit on the impulse to hug nearly everyone he met.

"The toast was probably a bit much," Jainan murmured. "You didn't have to do that."

"I can propose toasts if I want," Kiem said. "Toasting your partner is practically de rigueur. It's what you do at dinners. Totally unexceptional."

"That is an absolute lie," Jainan said. "You are trying to sell me a blatant untruth." His hand tightened on Kiem's arm. "And giving me that smile isn't going to help you get away with it."

"I'm not smiling," Kiem said, but as he said it, he realized he had been, and must have been for a while. "I'm having a good time."

"I can tell," Jainan said. There was a thread of something in his voice, everything proper and controlled except this odd—affection? Kiem decided it was affection and felt warm all over. "You may want to steer away from that colonel up ahead," Jainan added, in a more neutral tone. "She knew Taam. She's probably read the interview."

"She won't say anything," Kiem said cheerfully, escorting Jainan in a slightly different direction. "Not after you eviscerated that politician who mentioned it."

"I was polite."

"You froze him dead," Kiem said. "I felt the temperature drop and I wasn't even the one you were staring at."

"Well, *you* somehow steamrollered him into volunteering for the Municipal By-Laws Subcommittee."

"He clearly doesn't have enough to do, if he's going around reading interviews in newslogs. Someone's got to . . . by-law those municipals. And everyone says it's the committee nobody wants to be on."

Jainan stifled a laugh, trying to disguise it as a cough. "You're incorrigible. You're abusing the system."

"Very badly," Kiem agreed. He recognized Ressid on the other side of the room, but since there were dozens of people between them, Ressid only gave them an acknowledging wave. Kiem and Jainan stopped to greet the Thean Ambassador and a small circle of dignitaries; Prince Vaile was also there, fashionable in a dress made of some floating, mist-gray Galactic fabric. She seemed to be hatching something with the Ambassador.

"Your Grace!" the Ambassador said, with more pleasantness than Kiem had ever seen him display. "Good news. We've secured the Kingfisher operation for you."

"Excuse me?" Jainan said.

"The Emperor has generously transferred all the mining equipment to Thea and offered a team of specialists," Vaile said. "Kingfisher did have some real mining engineers to provide it with the cover Taam needed. I believe you've met some of them."

"Run . . . the regolith mining operation?" Jainan said. "Run *Taam's* operation?"

"On a temporary basis," Vaile said. "You could do a trial period of six months to start."

"I don't—I—"

The Ambassador coughed genteelly. "It would be advantageous to have someone in your position publicly attached to it."

Jainan glanced at Kiem. Kiem almost said something but realized he didn't have to. Jainan was already turning his attention back to the Ambassador. "I. Yes. I'll do it on a trial basis." Kiem squeezed his shoulder, which was all the delight he could politely show in company. "I have some ideas. That catalytic intensifier Audel and I were . . ." Jainan trailed off, apparently in thought, and then focused on Vaile again. "I would like Professor Audel and her students on the operation."

"I believe that's a matter for Thea," Vaile said blandly. "The Emperor would never impose the Iskat way of doing things."

"Excellent," the Ambassador said, while Kiem had a coughing fit and Jainan looked thoughtful. "Count Jainan, I must set up a meeting with the Infrastructure Bureau back home. I look forward to working much more closely with you. Ah. The Emperor."

They all turned to make their bows as an attendant opened the doors, and a wave of polite obeisances rippled out from the Emperor's entrance. The Auditor was next to her. The people in their group gave them a nod and drifted away, part of a general realignment of the room as people flowed into the Imperial orbit.

"Not very anxious to see her unless you are," Kiem said to Jainan under his breath. "She's probably got over the worst of it, but we may not be her favorite people right now. Just a guess."

"I imagine not," Jainan said. "Neither do I have any desire to speak to the Auditor. Is that Bel?"

Kiem followed his gaze. Bel was apparently deep in discussion with one of the Emperor's soberly clothed aides. She looked up, as if she felt their eyes on her, and gave them an unreadable look before going back to the conversation.

"None of our business, apparently," Jainan said dryly.

"Looks like it," Kiem said. He had something of a premonition about what they might be discussing, fueled by the realization that the Emperor as a matter of course employed aides with bodyguard skills. Perhaps Bel demonstrating the ability to break into a military base to help out her employer wasn't so much a problem as he had thought. The Emperor *had* granted that pardon to Bel without too much persuasion, now that he thought about it.

"Dammit," he muttered. "I think we're going to get our aide poached."

"By the *Emperor*?"

"I'd bet money that she's trying," Kiem said. However much alarm he felt at the prospect of losing Bel, it would probably be a good move for her career. The Emperor's ex-aides went on to run committees, palace departments, spy networks. Bel was too clever to stay as an aide for long.

Jainan was hailed by someone else from the Thean contingent, a woman wearing a jacket in the same greens as Jainan's uniform. As they spoke, Vaile stepped away from the Ambassador and touched Kiem's arm discreetly. "I'm glad I caught you," she said. "The palace has been organizing the Thean side when it comes to events like this, but the palace coordinators have a lot on their plates. Taam was supposed to help, but of course, he was *Taam* . . . and the Minister for Thea wasn't really up to it by the time he resigned."

Kiem became wary out of habit whenever Vaile went elliptical. "What are you getting at?"

Vaile fluttered one hand. "The Emperor's shuffling around the Diplomatic Service. She wants you to take the post of special liaison to Thea."

Kiem swallowed what felt like a sudden stone in his throat. "Er." Someone had gone mad. He hesitated to say it was the Emperor, but it was that or Vaile, and Vaile seemed to be in full possession of her faculties. Kiem wasn't fully acquainted with the Diplomatic Service, but a liaison post was *definitely* something that came with more responsibilities attached than just a treaty representative.

On the other hand, that was a command if Kiem had ever heard one. "What happens if I don't?"

Vaile spread her hands. "Nothing."

Kiem paused and looked over at the Emperor. She was greeting various dignitaries, apparently holding five conversations at once while leaving everyone in no doubt that she saw everything happening around her. Her hard, black eyes skimmed over the crowd and caught Kiem's. She carried on as if she hadn't noticed him.

Making him a diplomat was a terrible idea. Kiem found himself starting to grin.

"Sure," he said. "What's the worst that could happen?"

"That is certainly one way of looking at it," Vaile said. "It seems they'll be searching for more ambassadors to the Resolution soon as well. I'm sure you'll have a flourishing career in the Diplomatic Service."

"*Vaile,*" Kiem said. "I'm not going anywhere near the Resolution."

Vaile gave him a small smile. "I'm glad at least someone in my family almost has themself together. Ah," she added, just as Kiem was trying to work out if that was a compliment or not. "Speaking of family." She nodded over to the double doors that led out from the reception room.

The doors had swept open to admit a group of latecomers in military dress, bedecked with medals and rank emblems. The crowd opened like a flower around them. Kiem took one look and groaned. "Oh, great."

"Kiem?" Jainan detached himself from his conversation and discreetly fell in beside him. "What's wrong?"

"My mother," Kiem said, under his breath. "She's not supposed to be here yet. She must have taken an earlier shuttle. Argh." He wondered for a fleeting moment if one of the gilded chairs would give him enough cover if he concealed himself behind it and thought chair-like thoughts.

"Kiem!" A short, stout woman, her uniform bars sagging with the weight of medals on them, emerged from the center of the group.

Kiem raised a hand. "Welcome back, Mother." He gave Jainan a *sorry this is probably going to be awful* look and held out his arm. Jainan took it, and they approached her together.

"General Tegnar," Jainan said, bowing. Kiem bowed as well.

Kiem's mother looked them up and down. "Well, at least you two are in one piece," she said. "No sooner do I hear you're married, Kiem, than I hear you've lost your partner to some sort of kidnapping."

Kiem raised his head from his bow. "Mother!"

"He didn't lose me," Jainan said. Kiem tried to shoot him a sideways apologetic look, but against all odds, Jainan was obviously trying to suppress a smile as he looked down at her. "I conveniently located myself in a classified military facility, which you must admit is hard to misplace."

Kiem's mother snorted. "Could say that." Her face crumpled into something even sterner, like continental collision happening on an accelerated timescale. "Heard about Fenrik. Kingfisher. Bad business all around."

"Have you heard what's going to happen?" Kiem said.

"Word is they're retiring him," his mother said shortly. "Might bring me back to Iskat."

"Ah," Kiem said. He tried and failed to process how he felt about having his mother back on-planet. "Good?"

"Thean," his mother said, examining Jainan. "Hm. I hear on the grapevine you're handy with a quarterstaff."

Jainan inclined his head. "I do my best."

"You'll have to show me." Kiem's mother folded her arms and stared at Kiem. "Hear you hijacked a shuttle."

Kiem felt tongue-tied and lumbering and cowardly, as he usually did when confronted with his mother's judgment. "It was for a good cause."

General Tegnar reached up a hand and unexpectedly clapped him on the shoulder. "Bet it was. Good show. Your Thean must be a good influence. Kiem wouldn't even shoot at a target when we sent him to camp," she added to Jainan. "Hope you can light a fire under him. Needs some backbone. Some ambition." Her tone at the end turned hopeful.

"I don't think he needs to join the army to prove any sort of backbone, ma'am," Jainan said gravely. "And I don't believe you seriously think he's going to."

"Sharp. Oh, well," she said philosophically. "This diplomacy thing isn't bad. Soon have you out in the system representing us. Military attaché." She swept a look up and down him, winced, and appeared to reconsider. "Cultural attaché." Kiem felt slightly like a pebble under the exhaust of a shuttle that had just launched. He managed a cultural-attaché sort of bow, but she wasn't looking at him. "Oh, there's the Fifth Division. Must talk. Jainan, come and find me tomorrow about the quarterstaff."

She gave them both a nod and strode off. Kiem let out an explosive breath, half frustration and half laughter. "Could have gone worse," he said. "Sorry about that."

The smile was still playing around Jainan's mouth as he watched her cross the room. "I see what you meant about her," he said. "She's not very like you."

"I understand her about as much as I understand the *Emperor*," Kiem said. "Did I tell you Vaile's trying to make me a diplomat? I'm hoping I can quietly slide out of it."

There was a flash of something curious in the glance Jainan gave him. "Yes, you wouldn't enjoy that at all," he said. "Imagine you trying to cope with meeting people, talking to people, persuading people to agree on things . . ."

"Wait," Kiem said. "Wait, what? One argument with the Emperor, fine, but I'm not clever enough for—" He broke off. "I'm not used to the other stuff. That's politics."

Jainan didn't reply immediately. Instead, he took two fresh glasses of champagne off an attendant's tray and handed one to Kiem. After taking a sip, Jainan said, "I would like it if we went to Thea for a proper visit."

Diplomatic missions went to Thea. Of course, so did tourists. "We'll definitely go," Kiem said slowly.

"Think about it," Jainan said. "I suspect you would be very good at it." He slid his arm into Kiem's again and politely brushed off another conversation. The reception seemed to be getting into its stride; the younger staffers from Rtul and Kaan had split off into a noisy group around them. "How many more people do you think we're obliged to talk to?"

"None," Kiem said instantly. "Let's find one of the balconies." He steered them toward the balconies at one end of the observation hall: bubbles of glass that bulged vertiginously out of the dome, giving an uninterrupted view of the stars. They might be open to the galaxy, but they were the only shot he was going to get at having some privacy with Jainan.

"Kiem?" Bel had slipped out of the crowd and stood between them and the balconies. Both of them stopped. She looked unsettled, less put-together than she normally did, and her eyes on Kiem were accusatory. "Did you have anything to do with the job I just got offered?"

"What?" Kiem said. "No! Wait. So she did offer you a job." He realized he wasn't helping his case. "I didn't have anything to do with it. Why would you think I had something to do with it?"

"Because it's exactly the kind of thing you'd do," Bel said.

Kiem cast a glance of appeal at Jainan. "It is exactly the kind of thing you would do," Jainan said.

"Hey," Kiem protested. "It wasn't me. That would be shooting myself in the foot." That wasn't the thing at stake, though. He shouldn't influence Bel's choice; he tried to make his voice more neutral. "The Emperor made you a job offer."

"Her Private Office is offering me a pay raise," Bel said. "If I can 'handle the job.'"

"Might be good," Kiem said. "Her aides go on to big things. I heard Rakal used to work for her. I mean, obviously you can handle it. You've been the brains of the outfit for the whole of the last year."

"I could," Bel said. There was a long pause, uncharacteristic for her. "On the other hand, I also heard you might be joining the diplomatic corps."

"How did you know that?" Kiem said. "Okay, wait, first of all, I'm only taking over social duties for the Theans, and second, I can't believe you knew I was joining the diplomatic corps and you didn't tell me." Bel sort of smiled. Kiem knew he was putting off asking the question.

Jainan asked it instead. "What are you going to do?"

"I was thinking," Bel said slowly, "it might be nice to see some more of the galaxy. There isn't much chance of that, with the Emperor."

Kiem found he was smiling again. "We could probably match

the pay raise. Since there's two of us now and all. And you could always go and work for the Emperor later."

"I could," Bel said. "No promises about how long I'll stay. But I do want to see how Jainan's engineering thing works out."

"How did you know about—"

"She asked the Emperor's aide," Jainan said, amusement running through his voice. "Keep up, Kiem."

"And now I need to go and put them off for a bit," Bel said. "I'll leave you to it." She gave them a quick flash of a grin, turned away, and disappeared into the crowd again.

"And *now* can we have some privacy?" Jainan murmured.

"Yes! Right. Of course." Kiem opened the door with a flourish that he turned into a bow halfway through. "Your Grace?"

"Your Highness," Jainan said, with a grave nod. They passed out of the fug of light and noise into the stark, clear darkness outside.

The stars spiraled around them in countless points of light. Thea's dark and glittering bulk rotated below, limned in sunlight at the end of its night as the station rose around it like a moon. But neither of them really noticed, because the corner of the balcony was the ideal place to lean against.

It was a while later that Kiem took a breath and leaned his head back. Jainan was warm and solid in his arms. "You know," Kiem said, "we've had a shared bedroom for weeks, and instead we've decided to go around sneaking kisses on balconies."

"Your mother was wrong," Jainan said. He detached himself from Kiem and took his hand instead, leaning next to him against the glass so their bodies were pressed side by side. "I appear to be a very bad influence."

"I didn't want you to *stop*," Kiem said. Jainan smiled in the starlight, and Kiem leaned over to kiss the corner of his jaw. He was stopped only by the doors bursting open.

"Oh, sweet God," a Thean voice said, dismayed. "I only came out to grab Jainan. I really didn't want to catch you necking."

Kiem groaned theatrically and raised a hand to his forehead.

"Jainan," he said, "tell me Thean law says you're allowed to space members of your clan in moments like this. I can find an airlock."

Jainan laughed. It took a moment for Kiem to realize he hadn't heard that before—Jainan had smiled, joked, suppressed a chuckle, but he'd never given in to it freely like this. Jainan's laugh was joyful and infectious, and Kiem discovered he loved every nuance of it. "No," Jainan said, rubbing a hand across his jaw to bring himself under control. "It unfortunately does not. Gairad, try making your entrances more discreet."

"A bunch of aides from Rtul and Kaan just set up a game of darts in the overflow hall," Gairad said. "I won my round. Go in and fight for Thea."

"Gairad," Jainan said reprovingly, but his heart wasn't in it. Kiem could feel the way he half turned his head—not in a request for permission, or to check what Kiem was doing, but as an invitation.

Kiem grinned. "All right," he said. "Let's go in there, and I'll watch you win."

"I'm not going to *win*," Jainan said. "I have done it on Thea, and I just think I could outperform some of the more inebriated guests—"

Kiem turned to sneak in one last kiss, extraneous clan members be damned. "You'll be the best," he said.

"You don't know that," Jainan said.

His eyes reflected the light from the hall; behind him, beyond the void, the stars burned in enduring points; far beyond them, a telescope could have seen the maelstrom of the link, and a million more stars beyond that; and this tiny station spinning around a tiny jeweled planet like the fulcrum of the universe. "I do," Kiem said. "You'll see."

ACKNOWLEDGMENTS

Some of you have already read a version of this story. To those of you who have encouraged or worked on it: I can't say thank you enough.

But while they've given me a whole page for this, special thanks go to:

Those who read the first drafts, particularly the very kind people who left comments on early snippets or on AO3, or recommended it on Tumblr, Twitter, blogs, or to a friend. You are all part of the reason it got here. Thank you so much.

Emily Tesh, who beta'd the heck out of this over *years* from the first conversation to the final edits, you're the best.

Tamara Kawar, my agent, who was an early champion of Kiem and Jainan's story, and whose endless enthusiasm, kindness, and keen eye for edits has made this book what it is.

Ali Fisher, editor extraordinaire, for immeasurable improvements to the story as a whole and for gentle editorial hints such as "have you considered putting all the many world-building things you've just told me about . . . in the actual book?"

A. K. Larkwood, Sophia Kalman, Ariella Bouskila, Megan, and Maz for continuing encouragement, jokes, and good opinions. I don't know how I managed to join a writers' group made up of these unfailingly smart and funny people but I'm extremely glad it exists. Thank you also to the other authors who kindly took time to read the manuscript and offer advice, and to the Serpents for world-building help and early comments.

My family, who have supported my writing over the years, championed the book, and fed me at Christmas when I was having an editing crisis. Particularly to Mum's heroic efforts in reading it twice!

The team at Tor with especial thanks to those who have put so much work into the book: Kristin Temple, Caro Perny, Renata Sweeney, Becky Yeager, Natassja Haught, Megan Kiddoo, Steven Bucsok, Greg Collins, Eileen Lawrence, Sarah Reidy, Lucille Rettino, Devi Pillai. Also to Magdiel Lopez and Katie Klimowicz, artist and designer of the US cover. And at Orbit UK: Jenni Hill, Nadia Saward, Nazia Khatun, Madeleine Hall, Joanna Kramer, and Anna Jackson.

And finally and most to Eleanor. I love you, and you were right. It *did* need more dinosaurs.